Also by Kim Redford

SMOKIN' HOT COWBOYS

A Cowboy Firefighter for Christmas

Blazing Hot Cowboy

A Very Cowboy Christmas

D0441904

HOT *for a*
COWBOY

KIM REDFORD

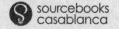
sourcebooks
casablanca

Published by Sourcebooks Casablanca, an imprint of Sourcebooks, Inc.
P.O. Box 4410, Naperville, Illinois 60567-4410
(630) 961-3900
Fax: (630) 961-2168
sourcebooks.com

Printed and bound in the United States of America.
OPM 10 9 8 7 6 5 4 3 2 1

Chapter 1

"AND THAT OLDIE BUT GOODIE FROM THE HIGHWAYMEN, all you cowboys—and the cowgirls who love 'em for whatever wild and crazy reason—is how we celebrate springtime in Wildcat Bluff County. This is Wildcat Jack coming to you from KWCB, the Wildcat Den, serving North Texas and Southern Oklahoma since 1946. Our ranch radio is located on the beauteous Hogtrot Ranch for your listenin' pleasure."

Eden Rafferty stopped mid-stride when she heard the legendary DJ boom loud and clear over the outdoor speakers of the Easy In & Out convenience store, bait shop, and gas station. She chuckled, feeling happiness bubble up. Hogtrot was a local joke. Jack knew good and well that the radio station was on the Rocky T Ranch. He was seventy-nine—and not budging from that number no matter how many years flew by, as he liked to say. Only a disc jockey with Jack's kind of staying power could keep a joke going for more than half a century.

Everybody knew Wildcat Jack was an institution in the county. He could say whatever he wanted, whenever he wanted, however he wanted in that big, deep voice that Texas men grew like muscles, along with their throw-down attitudes. He was also a shoot-from-the-hip kind of guy rooted in the same era as the down-at-the-heels radio station and her held-together-with-baling-wire-and-duct-tape Volkswagen Beetle.

She was grateful for the whole kit and caboodle since they were all she had left in the world.

She stepped off the curb onto the parking lot of the truck stop that was tucked out of sight, on a side street well away from Wildcat Bluff's popular Old Town, so as not to detract from the Wild West 1800s ambience. She'd have almost preferred a horse and buggy to her current ride, but she couldn't afford anything that pricey, and she sure couldn't afford to be picky.

Where had all the huge trucks come from? And why did pickups have to take up more than their fair share of parking spaces? She shook her head. She'd obviously been in the land of sedans and crossovers too long. Maybe living in Hollywood had twisted her view of Texas reality.

She refused to let her past intrude on her beautiful morning, so she adjusted the paper bag on her hip and her purse strap on her shoulder and looked around for Betty. The bug had been named by Uncle Clem for Betty Grable, the number one pinup girl of World War II. At one time, Betty must have been a shiny beauty, but now she'd seen her share of life, sporting four crushed fenders and dull turquoise paint. Beggars couldn't be choosers. Betty still ran, even if she did backfire at random moments like an old dog expelling gas.

"Gotta get 'cause I'm gosh darn hungry. I know it's early, but when your belly feels like it's running on empty, it's time to fill 'er up," Wildcat Jack growled over the airways. "I've got a hankering for some finger-licking ribs at the Chuckwagon Café. What about you? You know it, you love it, so you best get right on down there before I scarf up Slade Steele's latest lip-licking pie."

She exhaled in relief. At least the station still had local advertising to help keep it afloat. For safety and security reasons, Jack was also cautious never to announce on the air that he was leaving the station untended or to imply that he was the only person there. He'd leave Billy Bob or Rae Dell, his faked voices, on the recording he had running while he was gone, or he might pay a flat fee for a "canned special" of country music with another recorded host.

"Now, guys and gals, I won't leave you lonely whilst I step out for a bite of the best barbecue in North Texas at the Chuckwagon Café. Billy Bob is here to take over from me and bring you more of your favorites to keep you company while you ride herd on those ornery critters just waiting to give you what for."

She appreciated Jack's gift of gab. The former cowboy could talk all day and into the next week about roping and riding or about little to nothing, while making it interesting to boot.

A smile edged past Eden's mountain of worries. At least something was going right. Jack knew how to name-drop local businesses without making it sound like he was filling an ad space. He was a pro, no doubt about it.

She hoped, with spring in the air, shoppers were ready to come out of their winter dens, taste the air, and decide now was the time to make good on the offerings of advertisers. The spring equinox, usually about March 20, was coming up in a couple of weeks, and folks around here liked to celebrate longer days, birds and bees, and new life in all its forms. She hoped this year was a prosperous one for everyone, because a steady revenue stream meant life or death to local merchants, as well as to the Wildcat Den.

She pulled a key ring with a silver horsehead fob out of the cranberry-tinted designer handbag bought when she had money to burn and people to impress. She crossed the black asphalt at a swift Los Angeles pace, noticing the clear blue Texas sky held not a single fluffy cloud in the still-dry air. A tricked-out ATV zipped past in a blur of blue jeans and cowboy hat. She hadn't seen that colorful sight in a while, and the sheer novelty lifted her spirits. It was good to be back.

When she reached Betty's back bumper, her smile fell like a rock. Sunlight glinted off the dented chrome. She was sandwiched like a sardine between a six-wheeled dually and a jacked-up pickup. A cowboy had parked his pickup so close to the door that she couldn't open it. She was up a creek without a paddle. Betty's driver's door locked from the outside but not the inside, while the passenger door locked from the inside but not the outside. She could get to the passenger door, but she couldn't open it. She sighed, figuring that, umpteen years ago, some car designer had decided to add a little challenge to locking and unlocking VW doors.

Normally, she'd laugh at the quirkiness, but today she was on a tight schedule. She needed to return to the radio station while Wildcat Jack was at an appointment on his late lunch break. She'd promised him that she'd just run into town, pick up a few things, and be right back.

She paced a few steps to one side of Betty, then back

again, wondering how long she'd have to wait for the pickup driver.

"Got a problem?"

She not only heard but felt the deep male voice roll up her spine like a wave coming to shore on the soft, warm sands of South Padre Island. A voice like that could melt honey on ice and she'd like to market it on the air with a show all its own. But that wasn't her present concern. She didn't need to add another iron to her already-raging fire.

She impatiently tapped her toe as she pointed at the narrow space between her VW and the pickup, hoping the stranger would understand without words. She didn't look at him, keeping her head down because she wanted to limit interaction.

He took a step closer, the leather soles of his cowboy boots scuffing against asphalt.

She had to admit he showed good taste in boots—black snake with crimson thread in a classic wing design. High-end and high style. She'd always liked a man who knew his cowboy boots.

"Do you need to leave?"

She nodded in relief that he understood her problem.

"If you'll step back, I'll have you out of here in no time."

She felt his can-do words run up and down her spine again, causing tingles and chills and a sort of remembrance that went way beyond how she should be reacting to a stranger.

"It won't take me a moment."

She stepped back from Betty's bumper to make room and got a good view of the south side of the cowboy. He was tall, with broad shoulders, narrow hips, and long legs. He wore a black felt hat with a rattlesnake band and a starched red shirt tucked under a black snakeskin belt threaded though the loops of faded blue Wranglers. Not only were his boots prime material, but he was right at the top of that category, too.

She'd like to see him on the back of a horse. He'd sit tall and proud and ready for action. She felt her mouth go dry, imagining a different kind of action that might benefit a lonely cowgirl. Just the thought of what he could do with that strong, lithe body set loose a wildfire that warmed her all over.

She was done with men, of course, but this cowboy was so yummy she might be tempted to make an exception. If so, she knew just how she'd like him to put those muscles and that stamina to good use.

He leaned down, flexed his knees, and presented her with a taut butt that strained his jeans in a ridiculously enticing way. He reached under Betty's bumper with both large hands, lifted the rear end with the heavy engine, and set the bug to one side as if he did it every day, allowing plenty of room for her to reach the driver's side.

Wildfire raced through her again. He was strong as a bull. Who in their right mind simply went about picking up cars and moving them? Really, who even thought about doing it? A tough cowboy, she supposed, with enough get-up-and-go to do whatever crossed his fertile mind. Now that she thought about it, a cowboy with a creative mind joined to a powerful body might come up with all sorts of ways to work out the kinks in a hard-riding cowgirl.

"There you go." He turned around to face her.

Oh my, yes, he looked just as good from the front as he did from the back. She let her gaze wander up his long legs, narrow hips, broad shoulders, until finally coming to rest on his tanned face of strong planes and angles with sharp hazel eyes. Wait, hazel eyes? She looked closer, feeling a lurch in the pit of her stomach. She tried to make his eyes blue or brown or gray or anything but the familiar, distinctive brown and green and gold bands that at one time totally captivated her.

Shane Taggart, no doubt about it. She stepped back in shock, cursing her bad luck. No wonder his voice had resonated with her. She was surprised she hadn't recognized his body, although he'd filled out with even more muscle since she'd last seen him. He'd been Wildcat Bluff County's bad boy, smart boy, hot boy, and her very first boy before she'd left town eleven years ago. She doubted he'd changed much in that time, but she was nowhere near the same needy girl who'd lusted after him. She was a whole lot stronger and wiser now.

Still, she wasn't ready for a discussion with the man who held all the aces in his hand. She hadn't wanted to see him, or vice versa, before she had a chance to get the lay of the land and her feet under her again. Even more, she needed time to come up with a plan to save everything she held dear in life.

"Well, as I live and breathe." Shane tipped the front of his hat back as he gave her a big white grin that appeared more feral than tame. "Eden Rafferty."

She clamped her lips together as she tried to think of some way to back out of this encounter, but he was right up in her face.

"I didn't expect to see you here anytime soon," he said in a deep, growly tone.

She knew voices. Shane's was rich with underlying meaning that didn't bode well for her emotions. Still, she gave him a slight, mollifying smile as she stepped back. She hadn't expected to see him here, either. And she sure hadn't expected to feel the old sparks fly.

He looked her over from head to toe while his hazel eyes spoke for him, so much so that she understood everything that simmered unsaid between them. Yes, he knew her in the most intimate sense of the word. Yes, he hadn't forgotten their fire. Yes, he was stoking old flames.

But it'd only been *once*. That midnight. She'd thought it had been enough for a lifetime, but right here, right now—no matter the big hole in her heart…or maybe because of it—she desperately wanted to make that *once* a blazing-hot *twice*.

Chapter 2

"WERE YOU PLANNING TO CONTACT ME OR LET ME FIND OUT you were back on my lonesome?" Shane Taggart asked, feeling his heart melt a bit at the sight of Eden. She'd always had the ability to turn him into a molten pool of lava, but he'd thought that was well and truly over and done with—apparently not, though, if his jeans suddenly shrinking a size was any indication.

She shrugged, glancing at the VW then back at him as if she wanted nothing more than to escape.

He wasn't about to move out of her way, not when he finally had her face-to-face again. She was as beautiful as ever. He wanted to run his fingers through her dark-blond hair and stroke her heart-shaped face. She was wearing a gray sweatshirt promoting some country band, with designer jeans and scuffed cowgirl boots that had seen better days. A big diamond stud sparkled in each earlobe, but she wore no rings—wedding or otherwise. She was a mix of upscale and downscale overlaid with a wistfulness and sexiness that did bad things to him.

When she didn't answer, he decided to push it. "I remember that time when you came after me up on—"

"Please, no," she whispered, holding up a hand as if to stop him from where he was headed down memory lane.

For now, he let it go because he could see her luminous blue eyes darken with heat as she remembered that midnight up on Lovers Leap. She might not want him now, but she sure as hell had wanted him that night. "When did you get back to town?"

"Late yesterday." She swallowed, stroking her throat. "Jack picked me up. DFW."

"Jack! He never could drive worth a damn, and now—"

"We're fine."

"Why didn't you call me? I'd have picked you up, or if you didn't want me, most anybody around here would've done it."

"I drove back," she whispered, continuing to stroke her throat.

"Not in the bug?"

"Truck."

"Jack's pickup is about as old as the VW. And Dallas traffic is crazy." Shane felt like busting something at the thought of those two putting themselves unnecessarily in harm's way.

"I'm used to LA."

"Good point." He stuffed his hands in his pockets to do something with them other than grab her and hold her and smell her and kiss her. "You got a place to stay?"

"KWCB."

He felt like she'd hit him upside the head again, so he took a deep breath not to growl out what he really thought about the idea of her staying there alone. It was as bad as Jack driving around the DFW airport and probably not even wearing his eyeglasses for sheer vanity's sake. He didn't even want to think about Jack trying to maneuver on and off that crazy double-decked LBJ freeway. "I'm sure Ruby would be glad to have you at Twin Oaks."

She rubbed her throat so much the skin turned red. "I'm fine."

"I'm not sure it's safe." What he really thought was that a high wind just might blow the old building over with her trapped inside. "The Wildcat Den needs some repair." Even better, a bulldozer and trip to the trash dump would suit it to a T, but he had to admit he was prejudiced about the whole place.

She coughed, then swallowed hard. "For now, it'll do," she said in a strained voice.

A lightbulb went off in his head. Memory crashed in on him. Her throat. Her voice. Her fall. *Hell*. He was being an insensitive jerk. He backtracked. "What I'm trying to say is that you're welcome to stay up at the ranch house just to hang out or whatever. Make yourself at home. You'll be safe there and near the radio station."

She turned pink as she dropped her hand from her throat. "Kind of you."

He nodded, feeling like a fool for ragging on her when she had so little in life. Maybe pride was about all she had left, and she didn't need him doing his best to strip it away. "How are you?"

"I'm home." She gave a smile that went clear to her eyes, crinkling around the corners in happiness.

"You deserve better than what you got in LA. You know that, don't you?"

She touched her throat again, happiness leaching from her eyes. "I can talk a bit. I have the Den. And Wildcat Spring."

He felt like a heel, knowing they were going to lock horns over the property, but she didn't need to know his plans yet. First, they'd best air out the LA thing. "Do you want to talk about it?"

She gave a shake of her head.

"I mean, if you'll give me the gist of it from your viewpoint, I'll spread the word and you won't need to repeat your story around here."

"It was all over the news," she whispered, voice breaking.

"Yeah, but that's the news...not reality."

She gave him a tight smile. "Most people think the news is all true."

"I'm not most people."

She cocked her head to one side as if considering his suggestion. "Good idea, telling my story once."

"You know you can trust me to tell only what you want told to folks."

"I don't trust..." She looked him up and down, nodded as if coming to a decision, and stepped closer. "Ever do something really stupid?"

"More times than I care to count." He felt as if life were reeling backward, drawing him into her world again.

"Heard about Graham Tanner?" She gently stroked her throat as if for reassurance.

"Yes. Let me help out. I know you lost your voice due to trauma."

"I'm getting better." She looked off into the distance, then glanced back at him. "He was a good-looking fast-talker. Married me. Wormed his way onto my show." She took a deep breath, then raised her shoulders and dropped them again. "We were a red-carpet power couple."

"I saw photos on the news." Shane didn't want to ask,

but he had to know the truth. "Did you love him, or was it for publicity?"

She looked down at the VW, then leaned over and traced a heart in the dust covering the window before she turned back to him. "My heart's always been in Wildcat Bluff."

He felt his own heart give a lurch and pick up speed. Did she mean what he thought she meant? Had she left her heart up on Lovers Leap? No, he was a fool to think that night had any play here.

"He told me what I wanted to hear. Love. Family. Babies. Working together," she whispered. *"Lies."*

"I'm sorry." Shane suddenly realized they were standing in a parking lot where anybody could overhear their words. He could hardly have picked a worse place to ask her to spill her guts. He glanced around to make sure they were still alone. "Maybe we should go somewhere less public."

"*Cowboys*. Caretakers."

"Lots of folks and critters depend on us."

"Bred in the bone." She gave him a warm smile.

He felt that smile clear to *his* bones, setting a blaze he hadn't felt since she went away.

"Bottom line—he won. I lost."

She was breaking his heart with her story. She'd always been a trusting, innocent girl, but he'd figured she'd wised up in the big city. Now he knew different. He wanted to hold her and comfort her and give her everything she'd been denied in a man.

"You saw?" she asked.

"Big news." He stayed quiet to give her space, knowing what she was remembering as her face went sad.

Famous husband caught in bed with starlet. Wife goes berserk, falls down grand staircase...unable to speak due to emotional trauma.

She took a deep breath as she stroked her throat again. "The fall. I tried to get away. Graham—"

"You don't have to tell me more, not now." Shane couldn't stand to see her standing so strong, but so lonely, a second longer. He placed his hands gently on her shoulders and felt her too-thin frame, as if she'd been wasting away for a long time from lack of nourishment. He knew from caring for cows, horses, dogs, cats, wild critters that they survived and thrived on so much more than something to eat or drink. If he didn't miss his guess, Eden was wasting away from broken dreams, and maybe a broken heart, as much as anything else. He wanted to crush her to his chest and make everything right, but it'd be too much too soon. Instead, he gently tugged her closer, wanting to see if she'd trust his touch like she had when they were younger. She gave a little sigh and laid her head against his chest, and he could've sighed, too, because she needed a shoulder to cry on and maybe that was all she would ever need from him.

She clung to him a moment before she pushed away and stood up straight. "Thanks. The past gets to me."

"No wonder."

"My voice gone, he took over *Sugar Talk*. Persuaded the studio to drop me. Said I was unstable."

Shane clenched his fists in frustration. He'd known what he'd heard on the news hadn't been the whole story. Now he wanted to take Graham Tanner out behind the woodshed and teach him right from wrong.

"So you divorced him, and he took everything except the Wildcat Den?"

"Yes," she said in a hoarse tone. "Came home."

"About the station—"

She jingled her key ring. "Later," she whispered in a voice almost gone.

"If it helps, everybody around here thinks Tanner is lower than a snake's belly for doing you dirty."

She put a hand on Shane's chest, then rose up on tiptoes and placed a soft kiss on his cheek. "Helps."

He felt that single word and her simple kiss like a match touched to dry kindling as his heart sped up in response. He wanted a whole lot more from her than a sisterly kiss. He watched as she got into her car and drove out of sight. He worried about her driving the old VW and staying in an even older building, but he couldn't do much about it—at least not yet. Anyway, his own priorities had to come first. She'd gotten a raw deal, but she was strong and resilient, so she was moving forward with life. He felt proud of her.

He thought back to Lovers Leap. He'd been standing near the edge of the bluff considering his future as he'd watched the Red River roll its way toward the Gulf of Mexico. He'd wanted to follow the river to explore unknown territory, and he'd done that later on the rodeo circuit. That night, Eden had ditched her prom date for him. He'd never known why. She'd come to him on the bluff all dolled up like a princess, smelling like heaven and tasting like lemon chiffon pie. She'd had her long hair curled and up on top of her head with some sort of crystals sparkling in the moonlight. She'd worn makeup that made her look older, and she was five feet five inches of long legs and hourglass curves, with high heels that put her closer to his six-foot-one. *Hot* hadn't begun to describe her.

He'd lusted after the good girl, the popular girl, the on-her-way-to-stardom girl for as long as he could remember. She'd said she'd wanted him to be her first. How could he not give her what they'd both wanted in the back of his old pickup under the bright stars of the heavens? Midnight still had the power to bring back that scorching memory.

He shook away the thought, turned on his heel, pulled out his keys, and headed for his pickup. Facts were facts. Eden was back. Not only back, but living on the Rocky T. He wouldn't rest easy till he knew she'd safely made it to the ranch. Hell, he wouldn't be able to sleep nights with her so close, teasing and tormenting his dreams until they turned white-hot. She might as well gig him with her spurs, leave him raw, and be done with it.

Chapter 3

EDEN SWALLOWED HARD, THEN TOOK A SIP OF THE BOT-
tled water she carried everywhere to help her voice
return to normal. She tried to relax, since it was supposed to be good for her throat, as she drove along
Wildcat Road with the wing windows ajar to catch a
fresh breeze.

She hadn't expected her first encounter with Shane
to be so soon or so intense. She wasn't even sure why
she'd opened up to him except that he'd been there,
made a good point, and he'd always been sympathetic
when they were young.

For now, she needed reassurance that she'd done
the right thing in opening up to him, particularly since
she'd become so self-protective. He'd never given her
cause to doubt or mistrust him in the past, although he
might've changed over the years. Truth of the matter,
more than anyone right now, she didn't entirely trust
herself, whether it was evaluating people, using her
voice, or getting back into broadcasting. She took
a deep breath, straightening her spine. She hadn't
returned to Wildcat Bluff to cower in a corner, licking her wounds. She'd come back to save KWCB and
herself in the process. If that required a high level of
confidence, she'd just have to fake it till she made it.

For now, all she wanted to do was ditch her doubts,
so she could enjoy the beauty of Wildcat Bluff County.

She felt safe in a way she hadn't in a long time as she looked out across the countryside of her youth.

She passed acres of pasture that stretched on either side of the road behind barbwire fence, coughing when dry dust swept inside and sipping more water to soothe her throat. She wondered how long it'd been since they'd had rain. She hadn't thought much about the effects of weather after she'd moved away except as it applied to needing an umbrella or reading reports on the radio. Here and now, she was reminded that lack of water could be a major problem for ranchers and farmers. Maybe the clear sky would suddenly fill with clouds and drench the entire county. She hoped so.

As she drove, free for a moment between worlds, she felt her shoulders relax and stress leak out of her. She'd almost forgotten how much she loved this unique part of Texas. Wildcat Bluff had started out as a ferry point on the Red River between Texas and Indian Territory. It had grown over the years, from transient cattle drives to settled farms and ranches, and it eventually became the small town that was now a popular tourist attraction.

Nowadays, most folks didn't know much about the Cross Timbers that made up Wildcat Bluff County, but the unusual landscape had once been part of the Comancheria, the Comanche empire that had stretched from central Kansas to Mexico. The prairie was bordered by interwoven trees, shrubs, and vines consisting of post oak, cedar elm, bois d'arc, dogwood, Virginia creeper, and blackberry vines that could be as narrow as three miles in some places or spread out to thirty miles in others. In the old days, there'd been a brush fire every year, and the border would grow back too thick and thorny to penetrate. Comanche warriors had used the prairie between the two vegetative lines as a secret passage, so enemies couldn't see or attack them.

Unfortunately, most of the Cross Timbers old growth was long gone. It had once extended from Kansas deep into the Hill Country and separated East Texas from West Texas. But folks in Wildcat Bluff County had saved their section for posterity. She figured that was because many of the residents were descended from the Comanche and still protected their original homeland, where rich grasslands and rolling hills provided grazing for cattle, buffalo, horses, and wild critters such as rabbit and deer.

It felt good to be home in Texas. Los Angeles was in her rearview mirror. She was looking at her future out Betty's cracked front window, and at this moment, the Wildcat Den was a familiar gift from her past. She wished the radio worked, so she could listen to the Den, but the original car radio been unrepairable for many a long year.

As if her thoughts conjured KWCB, she saw the black, metal Rocky T Ranch sign arching over the entry into the ranch. She slowed, turned off the road, crossed the cattle guard, and drove up the asphalt lane between bright-white three-slat horse fences. Shane lived on this ranch, too. He owned the Rocky T, while she owned the radio station and adjacent buildings after inheriting it all from her uncle. Maybe partly why she'd trusted Shane earlier was because she had a deep connection to him way beyond that midnight up on Lovers Leap.

Shane's grandfather had met Eden's grandfather in the South Pacific, where they'd fought back-to-back in

World War II for the U.S. Army. They'd continued their friendship once the war was over.

Eden's grandfather had worked as a gofer, learning everything he could about radio at KVOO in Tulsa, Oklahoma. He'd wanted to start a ranch radio station, and he'd saved most of his money from the war years to do it. Shane's grandfather had plenty of available land on his ranch for the transmitter tower and equipment building, and he'd thought North Texas could support a new radio station. An even bigger draw to the Rocky T was the fact that it had a natural spring. Transmitters were frequently built near water sources because boggy ground boosted the power to transmit greater distances. They'd signed a long-term lease for ten acres, giving birth to the Wildcat Den. Local folks were eager for music and entertainment, so it had been a success from the get-go.

Now time had passed—year after year, generation after generation. The radio station's lease was coming up for renewal soon. But KWCB had fallen on hard times and was now at the make-or-break point. She didn't know what would work and what wouldn't, but she hoped to try new technology to reach out to the world from Wildcat Bluff County. She envisioned a media center, maybe adding acreage to a new lease for more building space. Unfortunately, she was short of everything to make her dream come true except that there had always been a lot of heart in the Wildcat Den.

When she thought about it, everything came down to a matter of heart—who had it, who didn't, who shared it, who didn't. She wished she'd taken better care of her own heart. She realized now that Graham had a heart of stone. She'd finally put her own heart under lock and key, even as she'd returned to the one place where she'd known big, open hearts awaited her.

"Deep in the Heart of Texas" meant more to her now. It wasn't just a song made popular by Gene Autry in 1942 and played on all the radio stations. It was a state of mind. If that song wasn't on Wildcat Jack's playlist, she was going to make it her lead-in when she got that far with her own voice again.

Thinking about heart, she drove up the road with a rising sense of expectation and turned in at the crooked KWCB sign that had been pockmarked and knocked askew by hail and high winds. Several chestnut horses grazed on the ranch's side of the fence near the base of the tall metal transmitter that rose like an oil derrick high into the sky.

Home sweet home. Maybe some folks wouldn't call it much, but for her, the ten acres comprised everything good in life. She turned off Betty's engine, but it sputtered a few beats before it got the message and stopped on a hiccup—at least it wasn't a backfire. She opened the door, caught the scent of dry, dusty grass, and picked up her sack and purse. Gravel crunched under her feet as she walked to the radio station that had led to her career in broadcasting.

The building was a long, narrow shotgun, meaning a single front door led straight through the building to a single back door. When both doors were open, somebody could shoot through the house and the bullet would exit outside—if it didn't encounter an obstacle along the way. At least, that's what she'd been told. She'd never seen it demonstrated, but she suspected Jack would be an authority on the subject. She could only figure that shotgun houses had earned their name for a reason.

The wooden structure had stood the test of time with faded white paint and a silver metal roof that matched the nearby silver transmitter. The building had been moved from another location. Set on cement blocks, it had an open crawl space underneath with wooden stairs for entry. In a twist of mixed eras, Old West with a tall false-front made of vertical wood slats met the vibrant fifties with a flat overhang, which had rounded corners edged in silver metal reminiscent of old movie theaters, attached to the front wall by four long silver wires. *KWCB*, fashioned in tall, silver sans serif letters, rode on top of the overhang that protected folks from inclement weather.

She glanced to each side of the building, where a corrugated steel Quonset hut crouched as if to protect the heart of the Wildcat Den. The huts were long semi-circle buildings with flat ends, designed for the military in World War II. They'd been used for barracks, chow halls, medical facilities, and whatever needed housing. At the end of the war, the military had sold its surplus huts to the public. Her grandfather had snapped up two of the 960-square-foot units so he could turn one into storage and the other into his home. Eventually, her uncle had moved into a hut to be on-site with the radio station.

She walked up to the front door of the radio station and twisted the porcelain knob. Not locked, of course, since it never had been in all these years. In fact, there wasn't even a lock on the door. She simply shook her head at the contrast to big-city security. If she was safe anywhere, she was safe here, even if she wasn't much used to that feeling anymore.

She started to step inside but stopped in her tracks. She needed a moment, maybe a long moment, before she returned to a business that would run on its own till Jack got back. She looked around outside. She'd only gone to the store, but somehow everything felt different. Yet nothing had changed except she'd run into Shane Taggart, and she had to admit he'd unsettled her.

She opened the door, then leaned down and set her purse and bag to one side on the scarred oak floor before she closed the door again. When she questioned her direction in life, there was one place that always soothed, comforted, and inspired her.

Turning around, she quickly stepped down and hurried around the side of the building to the back. She stopped at the sight of Wildcat Spring, a round rock structure that enclosed a constant flow of mineral water. She couldn't hear a gurgle from here, so she walked down the stone path that wound past overgrown flower beds, herb gardens, and a long bench created out of a single slab of red stone with stacks of flat rocks under each end to give it height.

A trickle of orange-tinted water ran out of the springhouse, down an incline, and disappeared under the low-hanging tendrils of a weeping willow just beginning to turn green and create a deep shady oasis.

Wildcat Spring's flat-roofed building had three archway entries. She walked up and stroked the smooth rock surface, marveling once more at the clever construction by folks employed by the Works Progress Administration. Almost every community had received a new park, bridge, or school. Wildcat Bluff County was lucky to get this gazebo. She'd also discovered several interesting books written by WPA authors in her school library. She'd learned that the spring had long ago provided water for the Rocky T in addition to the ranch's natural ponds.

She looked above the main entrance, where an elaborate sundial dated 1929 had been created using Roman numerals to show the time of day. Right now, she could see that it was well past noon.

She stepped through the archway and onto the stone slab floor, feeling the instant drop in temperature. It was always cooler here because the walls were two feet of solid stone plastered and painted white inside. A bench made of a long stone slab on top of stacked rocks like the one outside hugged the wall between each arch. On one side, a round cement basin constantly filled with water from a tall vertical metal pipe. A long red cushion with silver piping covered each bench, inviting visitors to sit down and rest a spell.

She did just that, taking a deep breath of the mineral-scented air as she relaxed her back against the cool stone structure. Home. Hearth. Heart. How had she ever left it? And yet, she well knew why—because two generations had trained her to take her broadcast ability out into the wide world of radio and make them proud. She'd done just that, knowing she couldn't have done anything else, even if she'd had the inclination.

She'd been here many times after the sudden death of her parents in a car accident when she was in the tenth grade. The spring had soothed her broken heart, so it was the natural place for her to come again. She'd worked in the Wildcat Den with her uncle once he'd inherited the station. After school and on weekends, she'd always done her homework here as she relived memories of the happy moments she'd spent with her mom and dad.

She'd left Jack in charge of KWCB after her uncle's death, while she'd continued her old life and then disassembled it. Jack had needed help for some time running the Wildcat Den, and in the aftermath of her divorce, she'd found she needed him and the station. So, she'd come home. From here on out, she needed a plan that merged the past with the future, but she wanted one that relied on mind, not emotion, because she'd endured enough drama from her ex and the media to last a lifetime.

As she sat there, letting the peace and quiet and security sink deep into her, she heard the growly engine of a pickup as its tires crunched over the gravel entry. She wondered why Jack was already back, but she shrugged, not letting his return disturb her peace of mind. He'd see her car, purse, sack, and he'd understand she needed a moment out here alone. He'd get on with the work at hand till she joined him.

When the truck's engine cut off, quiet descended on the spring again. She leaned her head back against the stone wall and listened to the soothing trickle of water. She'd thought she'd miss the fast pace of Los Angeles, with all the important lunches, dinners, interviews, meetings. Instead, she realized the frantic pace and her power marriage had masked the heart that was missing in her life. And yet, she was now so used to protecting her own heart and no longer trusting her own instincts that she didn't know how she could ever allow her heart to be vulnerable again.

When she heard footsteps on the walkway leading to the spring, she sat up, surprised Jack would come out here…but then again, the footfalls didn't sound like his carefully measured step. These were long determined strides.

She tensed, feeling vulnerable for the first time at the spring. She'd always been perfectly safe here, but she could no longer take safety for granted after her LA experience. She jumped up, all of her self-defense classes flooding her mind as she braced for trouble.

A tall man's silhouette—midnight against sunlight— filled the west-facing archway with the shape of a cowboy, from his tall-crowned hat to his pointy-toed boots.

She felt her heart ratchet up a notch, not from fear but from excitement. She'd know that breadth of shoulder and narrow-hipped stance even in the dark, if not by his strong body, then by the power emanating from him.

"Shane."

Chapter 4

"HOPE I DIDN'T STARTLE YOU." SHANE RAISED HIS RIGHT arm and planted his palm flat against the rock surface of the archway entry, as if waiting for Eden's invitation to enter.

"I wasn't expecting anybody out here." She realized her words had come out warm and strong. She hadn't spoken this easily in months. She'd been so right to come home to heal.

"Barbecue?" He held up a sack in his left hand and shook it. "I figured you might be hungry and not want to go back to town."

"Thanks." She'd thought about food when Jack mentioned lunch on the air, but she'd only brought apples, peanut butter, and crackers in her bag from the Easy In & Out. Now, the delicious smell made her stomach growl.

"Peace offering. I probably came on too strong earlier. I'll be the first to admit I'm sometimes too pushy." He shook the sack again. "Do you want me to stay or go? If go, I'll just leave the food for you and Jack."

She felt cold—she wanted him to go. She felt hot— she wanted him to stay. Bottom line, she felt as if all her wires were crossed in his presence. A thick wall of self-preservation had been right in LA, but could it be wrong here?

"No hard feelings?" He set the sack down on the rock floor, then stepped back.

"Wait," she whispered, conserving her voice while sifting through her surging emotions.

He hesitated, still a dark silhouette bathed in bright sunlight—as if he were a sun king offering her a precious gift.

"Are you hungry?" she asked.

"Starving."

"Me, too." She smiled as a shared memory warmed her. He'd always eaten like a ranch hand and turned every calorie into muscle.

"Am I forgiven?" He leaned down but hesitated before he reclaimed the sack of barbecue.

"First, I'll have to see what you brought me." She teased, falling into their long-standing pattern. She motioned him to come inside the gazebo before she sat back down. "Take a load off."

"Looks like you're going to drive a hard bargain." He picked up the sack, walked across the stone floor, and sat down on the bench facing her. He set the food between his feet.

"Chuckwagon?"

"Where else can you get the best barbecue in Texas?"

"That's a point in your favor."

"How many points do I have to earn before I dig out of my hole?"

"I'll let you know when you get there."

"Now that's flat-out cruel," he said with mischief sparkling in his hazel eyes. "You could have me brush-hogging, fixing fence, rounding up cattle till May Day, and I'd never know how close I was coming to earning my full points."

She couldn't keep from laughing at the image he'd conjured for her.

"It's good to hear you laugh again."

She nodded in agreement. She hadn't felt like laughing or teasing in a long time. Maybe she needed to make up for lost time. "How hard did you say you were willing to work?"

"I'm willing to work as hard as you like." He gave her a hot look.

"That hard?"

"So long as I get a reward—or several."

"How about if I send you on Chuckwagon Café runs? I'm beginning to think I may need a lot of comfort food."

"You let me, Eden, and I'll get you as much lip-smacking"—he paused, allowing his double meaning to sink in—"comfort as you desire."

"Oh, Shane." She felt his words go straight to her heart. His teasing ways had always revealed just how much he cared about her.

He grinned, flashing white teeth, picked up the sack, and glanced around. "No table, so—"

She stood up, breaking the intimacy that threatened to make her vulnerable, and grabbed the cushion off her bench, picked up another, and set them across from each other on the stone floor.

"Suits me." He tucked the barbecue between the two cushions, set his hat on a bench, and then gave a wide sweep of his arm to indicate her place to sit. "So glad you could join me for this fine dining experience."

She chuckled as she gave him a slight curtsy. He'd always had the power to ease her sorrows, and he obviously hadn't lost his touch. "My pleasure, kind sir." She sat down with only a slight creak of her knees. "I'm sadly out of shape."

"I doubt it." He sat across from her. "But if you are, you won't stay that way long on the ranch. A little horseback riding will do the trick."

"I haven't ridden in ages," she said softly, still not trusting her voice even though it was so much better here.

"It's like riding a bike. It'll come back to you, just like all manner of Texas things."

She leaned forward, took a deep whiff of tantalizing barbecue, and ripped open the sack. She quickly divvied up two bottles of water, two wrapped sets of plasticware with napkins, and two flat, white containers.

"Nothing fancy."

She opened her box to find a beef brisket sandwich, potato salad, and coleslaw. She grabbed a fork and took a big bite of potato salad, moaning in delight. "Oh yes, lots of mustard. Best food I've had in ages."

"Mostly salads?"

"I haven't been hungry in a while."

He gave her a sympathetic look. "Maybe being back in Wildcat Bluff will whet your appetite—for a lot of things."

"Hope so." She smiled, realizing that just the sight of him was whetting her appetite in a way that hadn't happened with a man in a long time. She grabbed her sandwich and bit into spicy beef as a distraction.

"Good sandwich?"

"Great. At this rate, I won't have any clothes."

"Is that a promise?"

She couldn't keep from chuckling as he teased her.

It felt good and overdue. Wildcat Bluff was having an amazingly positive effect on her, from her voice to her emotions, or maybe she was simply experiencing the healing power of a cowboy.

"Whatever you want, I'll get you, but clothes are always optional with me," he said mischievously as he gave her a once-over again.

She sighed dramatically for his benefit, then looked him up and down with a teasing glint in her eyes. "Ever go skinny-dipping?"

"What do you think? Hot summer day?" he said with a big grin. "Did you?"

"What do you think?" She returned his grin, feeling more lighthearted than she had in a long time.

"I think we should've gone together."

"Oh!" she squeaked, suddenly struggling with her voice again. "Can you imagine our parents' reactions if they'd found out?"

"It's a big ranch." He gave her a considering look as he finished his sandwich and took a drink of water.

"True, but—"

"If it weren't for the drought and the pond being so low, I'd take you there right now."

"It's still a little chilly. And aren't we too old?"

He laughed, shaking his head. "If Wildcat Jack still skinny-dips, then we'd be in good company."

"He doesn't."

"Sure he does...and with a ladylove."

Eden felt her mouth drop open. She closed it with a snap.

"Guess I let the cat out of the bag, didn't I?"

"Yeah." She quickly pushed their empty containers

back into the torn sack as she tried not to think about Jack naked in the pond. He could do whatever he wanted to do. Shane was a different matter. She imagined sunlight glinting off his bronze skin while water drops sparkled in his auburn hair.

Shane leaned forward, tucked a finger under her chin, and raised her face toward him. "I've only ever wanted to skinny-dip with you."

She sighed at his touch. She hadn't felt such strong desire since that midnight up on Lovers Leap. Once more, she needed him, wanted him, craved him to fill all the aching places that had lain empty for so long.

And yet, when he bent to kiss her, she couldn't do it. Even physically gone from her life, Graham lingered, ready to reach out and taint anything good. She thrust all the bricks in her wall firmly back into place, leaning away from Shane and placing her palms against his broad chest. She felt his heart beat hard and fast, mirroring the pace of her own heart.

"Are you going to make me wait?"

Still, she could tease him and stay on solid ground. "At least till summer and a big rainfall."

"I've got a hot tub up at the house that'll work right away."

"No doubt." She chuckled to take the sting out of her rejection.

"We could go there now."

She started to respond but heard a sound outside. She held up a hand to stop any more words, then pointed in the direction of footfalls coming closer.

"Do I smell barbecue?" Wildcat Jack burst through one of the open archways, all long limbs and kinetic energy thrust into faded Wranglers and a dark-brown pearl-snap shirt. Two long plaits of thick, silver hair wrapped with multicolored, beaded leather cords dangled over his shoulders.

"You're a day late and a dollar short," Shane said, gesturing toward the empty containers.

"Fine friends you are." Jack turned his sharp, chocolate-colored gaze from one to the other. "You'll have to make it up to me."

"Will do," Shane said.

"So, did you tell her?" Jack gave Shane a look that spoke of closely held secrets.

"Tell me what?" Eden suddenly felt uneasy, as if Wildcat Bluff was no longer quite such friendly territory.

"Long and short of it," Jack said, rubbing the silver stubble on his strong square jaw, "he needs your water."

"Do you mean Wildcat Spring?" she asked in shock, her voice ending on a squeak.

"Yeah," Jack agreed.

"Is that true?" She glanced at Shane, hoping against hope that he'd disagree. If he didn't, she'd suspect the food, the words, the intimacy were all for an ulterior motive, just like Graham's self-serving ways.

"Bottom line, we're in the middle of a drought. Cattle need water," Shane said in an uneasy voice. "Wildcat Spring never runs dry."

"But you know the transmitter needs boggy ground to reach KWCB's complete audience."

"I'm sorry, but we need to change with the times."

She felt completely betrayed by Shane's words. She couldn't be near him a moment longer, so she stood up, turned her back on both men, and walked over to the basin. As if to lay claim, she thrust her fingers under the spout and let cool water wash over her hand for a long moment. Finally, she swiveled around to face them, feeling ready for battle as she carefully positioned her body protectively in front of the spring.

Why had she ever thought all the big hearts were in Texas?

Chapter 5

SHANE REALIZED TOO LATE THAT HE WAS WAY OUT ON A limb regarding Eden and Wildcat Spring. He honestly hadn't thought she'd care that much one way or another if he closed the whole place down. He'd even thought she'd probably want to get out of the business altogether after that sorry affair in LA. He'd also thought that if she came back to Wildcat Bluff to settle accounts, it'd just be another pit stop on her way to something bigger and better. She'd always been a star. He was hard-pressed to imagine her any other way.

Now he realized he'd bet on the wrong horse. She wasn't going to make it easy for him. And he couldn't back down—no matter how much he might like to give her whatever she wanted in life. He cleared his throat, not sure where to go next. He glanced at Jack but only got a shrug in response. He felt the barbecue in his stomach turn over as if agreeing with Eden and disagreeing with him. How the hell had he read the situation so wrong? He rubbed his belly, realizing he'd thought what he'd wanted to think, and it'd been easy to do without input from her. Now that she was here with him in person, obviously hurting from life, everything looked different. And yet, he had the survival of the Rocky T depending on his decision.

"Show's waiting for me." Jack's deep voice broke

through the impasse like a whirlwind dusting up a dry pasture. "I've got a dog in this hunt, but he's not gonna bark up the wrong tree."

"What's the right tree?" Shane asked, hoping Jack would take his side of the matter.

Jack gave him a look with his dark brown eyes that said plainly he'd been there, done that, and he wasn't going there again. "I'm short. You two are looking at the long haul—higher stakes."

"Eighty is the new sixty." Shane didn't like to hear Jack allude to age because he couldn't imagine life without the Voice of Wildcat Bluff County.

"Tell that to my bones." Jack shook his head as if life were creeping up on him with the intent to bludgeon.

"Hah!" Eden flicked a hand in Jack's direction. "You've been complaining about your bones as long as I can remember, and nobody is as spry as you."

Jack puffed out his chest a little bit, then winked at her. "Nothing a lady likes more than to lift the spirits of an ailing man."

Shane chuckled, not putting anything past Jack. Everybody knew he had a way with the ladies. He always had and he always would.

"Like I said, I've got to get back on the air. As long as there's a KWCB, Wildcat Jack won't let down his listeners." He gave a smart salute that he'd obviously learned in the military, did an about-face, and exited the spring.

Quiet descended again, broken only by the sound of trickling water. A slight breeze kicked up, causing the few remaining leaves of winter to rustle against the stonework as a reminder that while the warmth of spring was coming on strong, the cold of winter was still waiting in the wings to grab it back.

Shane couldn't help but wonder if Eden had brought spring with her or if she was wrapped in the last of winter. From where he stood, he was definitely getting a blast of winter's chill from her when he wanted summer's heat.

"If you think I'm going to change my mind, you're mistaken," Eden said, breaking the silence in a breathy voice. "Against all odds, our grandfathers built the Wildcat Den. How can you even think of destroying it?"

"Things change. Time moves on." He felt like the worst sort of insensitive lout when he said those words, but they were basically true. Even if she didn't want to hear it, she needed a reality check. Those heady high school days when responsibility was on somebody else's shoulders were long gone.

She gave a loud, frustrated sigh as she gestured toward the station. "I know KWCB needs help, but I'm willing to work hard to update and upgrade."

"It'll take time and money. You got it?"

She bit her lower lip, just a small gesture, white teeth indenting soft, pink flesh, but it sent him spiraling back in time. He'd almost forgotten how she used to do that when she was stymied by life. He wanted to ease her tension in the best way possible by replacing bad memories with good ones. He'd done just that when they were young. Why couldn't he do it now? Why couldn't they take up where they'd left off—not only from after the prom, but from when Jack had interrupted them? He took a step toward her.

Eden held up a hand to deter him. "KWCB's lease

doesn't run out for a bit. I can use that time to rebuild the station."

He hated to see her rejection of him, hated for them to be at an impasse. Still, he stopped and stood steady as he tried to think of some way to persuade her to understand his position. He wasn't against her. He was against his situation. "I'm worried about my herds. We ought to be getting rain by now, but we're not."

"I'm sure the Rocky T has weathered lots of droughts. What is the difference this time?"

He glanced past her at the golden stubble of his dry pasture. He hadn't meant to get into the details so soon, but maybe it'd help if she knew the lay of the land, at least from his viewpoint. "When I said things change, I really meant it."

"If anybody knows how fast things can change, it's me." She followed his gaze outside, as if distancing herself from her own words or desperately wanting separation from her past or maybe just trying to see what he was looking at out there.

"Look, I don't want change any more than you do. I want life the way it was, particularly now that you're back."

"What do you mean?"

"Lazy Q Ranch. You remember it, don't you?"

She nodded, glancing in the direction of that land. "Mr. and Mrs. Simpson owned the ranch next door. She made the best chocolate chip cookies."

Shane nodded in agreement, fondly remembering they'd once shared that special treat.

"How are they doing?"

"They're gone."

"What? Where?"

"They decided to sell the ranch while they were still young enough to kick up their heels and visit places they'd only seen in travelogues."

"I can't imagine they'd want to leave the county."

"They didn't—not entirely. They bought into a new town house development south of Wildcat Bluff that offers easy maintenance and security while they're out seeing the world."

"But what about the Lazy Q?" She turned her back completely on the spring and focused on him.

"That's the big change."

"Did you buy their ranch?"

"I wish, but I couldn't afford it."

"Did another local rancher?"

"Nope."

She put a hand over her heart. "Please tell me a Dallas or Houston developer didn't buy the Lazy Q with plans to divide it into five-acre ranchettes?"

He chuckled without much mirth as he shook his head. "So far, they seem to be focused on the Hill Country, but with the way folks are pouring into Texas, that could change any moment."

"When I flew in, Dallas looked a lot like LA, spreading out in all directions."

"Folks need to live somewhere once they get here."

"True. But what about the ranch?"

"You ever hear about the Tarleton outfit in East Texas?"

She cocked her head to one side. "Oil, gas, and cattle?"

"Right."

"What about them?"

"You know Old Man Tarleton struck it rich with black gold in the thirties. Frank Lloyd Wright designed and built them a fancy mansion. They haven't let any grass grow under their feet since then. A daughter branched out into western wear—Lulabelle & You."

"Great line of western clothes. I remember promoting it on my show. Impressive family."

"Yeah. But not so much when the outfit moves in next door." He rubbed his chin, already feeling the beginnings of stubble. The prickly feeling reminded him of the Tarleton business expanding into Wildcat Bluff County.

"Are you telling me Lulabelle & You bought the Lazy Q?"

"Might as well have done it."

"What do you mean?"

"Guess what I'm trying to say in a roundabout way is that the Tarleton family bought it."

"Well, that's interesting. It could be good for the area."

"Maybe. But not for us." He knew he was drawing out telling her what was going on, but he hated to tell her and hated to say it.

"Okay. Spill. Are they all hat and no cattle, or—"

"I haven't met a single one of them. So far, I'm not too fond of Kemp Lander, their ranch foreman."

"I suppose they've got a lot of irons in the fire."

"The Lazy Q may be small potatoes to them. My trouble is that I'd been leasing a big, deep pond that never runs dry from the Simpsons, after they didn't need it." He felt the irritation well up in him like it had for months, but he did his best to control a feeling that did him no good.

"And?" She took a step away from the spring toward him, as if physically mirroring his agitation.

"Lander had a fence put up that cut my cattle off from the water source."

"What about your water lease?"

"I never signed one with the Simpsons. Didn't need it."

"Oh, Shane." She ran a hand through her hair as she covered the distance to him. "No warning, so you could make other plans?"

"No nothing. Just the fence."

"I guess you talked to him about it."

"Stone cold nothing."

"I see your problem. And why you're looking at Wildcat Spring." She reached out to him, then quickly dropped her hand to her side as if reconsidering her reaction.

"No choice. I'm between a rock and hard place." He wanted to touch her, wrap her in his arms as much for her comfort as for his own, but he doubted she'd take kindly to it. Women tended to deal with issues by talking them out, while men needed physical action.

"That's not all of it, is it?"

"You still know me, don't you?"

She simply smiled in response—a little sadly—and placed her palm on his chest, over his heart.

He captured her hand with his own, basking in the warmth and softness of her touch. He took a long breath to still the gnawing need to crush her to him—and hang on forever.

"We shared our troubles when we were young."

"I've sustained a few grass fires. Drought makes

them worse. So far, I've caught the blazes in time, but there's always the chance I won't be there next time."

"Brush fires are normal around here, aren't they?"

"Right. But not too often. And nobody else is getting them."

She rubbed her fingertips against his shirt, digging in a little as she gazed thoughtfully at him. "What are you saying?"

"I'm beginning to think Lander, representing the Tarleton family or on his own, is trying to cripple my ranch."

She shivered, shaking her head in horror. "Surely not."

"It'd make sense if they wanted to buy the Rocky T at a fire-sale price."

"They'd have the biggest spread in the county then, wouldn't they?"

"Right. And lots of power to go with it."

"I hate even the idea of this news." She reached up and twined her hands around his neck.

He didn't care if he was getting a sympathy hug instead of a romantic hug. He simply put his arms around her and drew her close, closing the gap between them till they were pressed body to body, heat to heat, need to need. He caught her scent—somewhere between sweet and tangy—and it transported him right back to that special night.

And then she broke the spell she'd woven around him by pushing away, stepping back, and giving him a considering look. "I wish things were different. I wish I hadn't just had a man manipulate me for all kinds of needy sympathy. I wish I hadn't fallen for all his clever words."

"I'm not asking for your sympathy." He felt his heart sink. She was protective of herself, and he couldn't blame her. She'd been through a lot of heartache. Now, she wanted the security, familiarity, and continuity of the Wildcat Den. He wished he could give it to her, but he couldn't.

"Maybe not," she said in a low, raw tone. "But you're asking for Wildcat Spring. And I need it."

"I need it, too." Now was the time to lay his ace on the table, even though it'd seal his fate with her. "And I own the land."

Chapter 6

EDEN FELT AS IF SHANE HAD TOSSED HER INTO A CATTLE trough full of ice water. She shivered as she stepped farther back, wanting to put distance between them so she could think clearly. Okay, he had a problem. Okay, she had a problem. Okay, they both had a problem—the same problem. *Water*. Or more exactly, the lack of it. Unfortunately, they were standing on either side of a situation that should have brought them together, instead of tearing them apart. Maybe they could yet come up with a solution that would benefit them both.

She slowly retreated until she felt the spring basin behind her. She reached back and stroked the rough cement with one hand, drawing strength and determination from it. She couldn't let another man take away something she held dear.

She looked at him standing there—so tall, so strong, so much the boy that she'd once thought she'd loved with all her heart turned into a man. Maybe she didn't know him anymore or maybe she'd never really known him, but she felt the loss of her dream-Shane in a way she'd never felt the loss of Graham. Surprised at her own reaction, she thrust down her fantasy feeling for the reality of her situation.

"I'd like you to leave now." She'd wanted her words to come out strong, but they didn't. She sounded weak to her own ears, when, a short time ago, she'd gloried in the fact that her voice was stronger again. Maybe he had influenced her more than she'd realized, not only about the spring but about her voice as well. Not a happy realization. She'd let Graham influence her far too much. She wouldn't make that mistake again.

"Eden, it doesn't have to be this way." Shane reached out to her. "I'll help you any way I can. We can move the station, if that's what you want, or—"

"I understand," she whispered, protecting her voice now just like she was protecting her emotions. "But I'd like to be alone to consider my options."

"Like I said, you can stay at my place. I'm not sure you're safe here."

"I've always been safe here." She heard her voice grow stronger as she emphasized her point. "It's my home."

He rubbed his neck, as if developing a crick from her words. "I'm just up the hill in case you need me."

"I won't need you."

"Please don't let this water situation come between us. Nothing changes till the lease runs out. Unless—"

"Unless what?"

"I could buy out the lease, then you wouldn't have the expense or trouble. And you'd have funds to start over."

She felt her determination harden. "I just got back. I'm not ready to make any type of decision."

"Just ideas to help us both out." He held up his hands as if in surrender or to placate her.

"Please go."

"When will I see you again?" He stepped under an archway, becoming a dark shape silhouetted by sunlight again. "I could bring barbecue or one of Slade's pies."

"Don't you get it?" she said in a ragged voice. "I want to be alone."

He braced the flat of his hand against smooth stone as he leaned toward her. "You can't blame me for the water shortage. I'm doing the best I can for my herds."

"Will you just go?"

"Blame the Tarleton family. Not me."

"I don't blame you. I truly don't." She desperately needed to be alone because she didn't know how much longer she could keep holding up her wall.

"Thanks. I guess we both need time to figure out how we go forward." He hesitated, thinking through the situation. "I'll make a run to the Chuckwagon tomorrow and bring you something. After Jack goes home, put a chair under the front doorknob and the back doorknob. Fact of the matter is, I'd better put locks on all the doors, so I'll know you're safe."

"We've never needed locks. I don't want to start now."

He just shook his head. "At least you'll bar your doors, right?"

She saw his concern, felt his concern, understood his concern, but she'd been so long without someone caring about her safety that she had to find her way to the realization he needed reassurance. "Okay. But I'm safe here."

"If you need me—anytime—I'm nearby." And then he was gone with long strides down the stone path toward his pickup.

She took a deep breath of mineral-scented air, drawing peace and security and happiness from the past into the present. Shane was as steadfast as ever, not only to her but to his ranch. She was the one who had changed in the years they'd been apart, and yet nothing had dimmed her love of home.

She stepped out of the gazebo, moving from concealing shadow into illuminating light, as if she were leaving the darkness of LA for the brightness of Wildcat Bluff County.

She glanced at the beauty around her as the sun lowered in the west. A slight breeze sent a row of yellow daffodils gently nodding in her direction. The pretty flowers were always a happy portent of spring, particularly since these had struggled out of an overgrown flower bed that had once been her mother's pride and joy. She felt her heart lift at the sight. Somehow, someway, she couldn't let the radio station that was a tribute to her family fritter away to nothing. And that meant fighting Shane—or helping him. *Maybe both*.

For now, it was time to check in at the Den. Radio was her thing, even if her voice wasn't back to normal. She heard a flutter of wings in the weeping willow and glanced upward. A blue-and-gray mockingbird clutched a limb while cocking his head to look at her with one eye, then turned his head to study her with the other eye. Seemingly satisfied with his audience, he opened his beak and filled the air with a wide repertoire of sounds picked up from here and there.

Eden smiled. She was so attuned to sound that she caught the nuances of the bird's wonderful song. Oh yes, she was an appreciative audience, and the mockingbird encouraged her to get back in the saddle and create a bigger audience for the Wildcat Den.

Soon, he completed his song and flew away to serenade other listeners. She clapped her thanks, then

followed the stone path to the front door of the radio
station. *Now or never.*

She opened the door and stepped into the building
that had been gutted and divided into two sections long
ago. First, she noticed the smell of stale coffee, ciga-
rettes, and old paper. Next, she saw the hazy, golden
light of two nicotine-coated milk-glass light fixtures.

Reception housed a battered wood schoolteacher's
desk, an office chair on squeaky rollers, four dented metal
file cabinets, a lumpy sofa, and two visitors' chairs with
faded red vinyl seats patched with silver duct tape. On
the dusty, yellowed acoustic-tiled walls hung out-of-date
Loretta Lynn and Hank Williams posters and a curly-
edged bank calendar/football schedule from the eighties.
Near the desk, a big black typewriter with a black-and-
red ribbon stood on a rusty metal stand as if sentinel to a
bygone era. It was manual, not electric. She didn't know
where Jack kept finding ribbons to keep the typewriter
going, but maybe he had a cache from the sixties. At least
she had her laptop that could be put to immediate use.

Jack had placed her purse and grocery sack squarely
in the middle of the desk on top of a pile of paper
that looked to be everything from contracts to mail to
Chuckwagon takeout sacks. Dust coated every available
surface. Light tried to break through a grime-encrusted
window but gave up about halfway into the room. She
knew there had once been drapes on the window, but
now everything appeared to be stripped to bare bones.
She hadn't checked the bathroom with the closed door
on one end of the room, but she really didn't want to go
in there yet.

They could use a clean-up crew and a decorator, but

that'd still just touch the surface of the situation. She wasn't sure how structurally sound the building was anymore because the wood floor creaked, groaned, and undulated underfoot as she walked across it. Maybe Shane knew what he was talking about. The Den might actually be on its last legs. But no, she couldn't think that way. Where there was a will, there had to be a way.

She could see Jack through the window on the wall that separated the two rooms. He was talking, gesturing, and throwing out a lot of energy as he talked into the mic to his many listeners. She couldn't help but smile at the sight, knowing she'd do about anything to keep him on the air. A door near the window led into the soundproof studio, but she'd wait till he took a break before she ventured in there. She knew how much she disliked being disturbed when she was on a roll.

She walked up to the glass, peeked inside, and was transported back to the days when typewriters were queen. Jack sat at a horseshoe-shaped console with an outdated reel-to-reel tape deck on his left side, a worn-but-top-quality turntable on his right for vinyl, and a technological dinosaur of a control board with toggles and dials in front of him. A boxy cheese-grater-like microphone on a retracting arm was nestled in his left hand as he glanced at notes typed on pages lying on the board in front of him. Not a CD in sight.

Warmth filled her at the familiar view. She'd sat right in his sagging, coffee-stained office chair many a time over her youth, so she knew just how the turntable would jump if you stepped on the wrong floorboard and how to calm a reverb and tickle better sound out of the system. But it all looked hopelessly old and out-of-date,

particularly after she'd been using the best of current elec-
tronics. Fortunately, it all appeared to work fine, and that
said something for well-made products and DJ ingenuity.

The large room had space for visiting musicians to
play live over the airwaves. At least, that'd happened in
the past. She doubted anybody on tour had stopped by
Wildcat Bluff in many a year. But she could remember
the larger-than-life country singers filling the studio with
rich sound in her youth. One time, a rancher even brought
his pony into the studio, although she couldn't remember
why now. It'd probably been a promotional stunt.

She basked in the memories a moment, then noticed
the vast tangle of wires that linked all of the equipment
together. It was a firefighter's nightmare. She needed to
get the mess sorted soon.

First up, she must make a list of what was possible,
what wasn't possible, and prioritize. It was a big under-
taking, but who better to do it than someone who loved
the Wildcat Den?

Jack glanced up, saw her, and winked, motioning that
he'd be on the air for a while longer.

She waved. She needed Jack's input. She needed to
get her voice back so she could help him. And she needed
to figure out what she could do on a nothing budget.

If she thought about all that had to be done, she'd just
go to bed and curl up under a warm quilt. There'd be no
confrontation with Shane or worry about her voice or
struggle to save the station. But that wasn't the person
she'd been raised to be or the one she'd worked hard to
become all her life.

With that in mind, she picked up her purse and sack of
groceries, then quietly shut the front door behind her. She

hadn't had much of a chance to unpack her few things in Uncle Clem's Quonset hut, so now was a good time.

She turned left and headed down the path to her new home. As she neared the front porch, she saw someone sitting in the outdoor swing. She'd know the shape of that big cowboy anywhere.

Shane was already back.

Chapter 7

EDEN STOPPED IN HER TRACKS, FEELING AS IF TIME HAD unwound to those long-ago, heady days when Shane would wait for her to get off the air and come outside. He'd sit in the swing just like he was doing now, as if he had all the time in the world as long as she came to him at the end of it.

Uncle Clem had attached a deep front porch made of cedar planks across the width of his Quonset hut. He'd added a flat, corrugated-tin roof to protect him from the sun, and changed out the single-entry military door for fancy double French doors painted bright turquoise. He'd hung a turquoise swing on one end of the porch and placed two big cedar rocking chairs on the other end. For more color and comfort, he'd added red cushions to the chairs and the swing. High above it all, he'd attached a large crimson star to the front of the hut, just under the curving roofline, to represent his beloved Lone Star State.

She smiled fondly at the memory of her uncle sitting on his front porch and watching the world go by from his beautiful view of Wildcat Bluff County. She'd sat with him, as well as with Shane, many an evening to watch birds, fireflies, squirrels, or cattle and buffalo. Home sweet home.

She and Shane had started out as kids playing together, riding horses, feeding cattle, or simply running across fields for the sheer joy of being alive. As they'd grown older, they'd gotten caught up in that awkward phase when neither of them knew quite what to do with their surging hormones and changing bodies. Still and all, they'd remained friends, even though they'd strayed in different directions, particularly after the death of her parents.

She didn't blame Shane for the change in their relationship. She'd been the one who'd pushed it over the edge that midnight when she'd sought him out before she'd left Wildcat Bluff for Hollywood after graduating. Not that he'd resisted her—not for a single moment. Yet that time loomed between them now, as well as Wildcat Spring. She didn't want to face him on either account, but here he was, big as life and twice as determined, by the look on his face.

"I see you still like Uncle Clem's swing." She used the words as a defense to keep the conversation away from their personal agendas. Even so, she felt her voice catch in her throat, reminding her that she had more healing to do.

"Come here." He patted the cushion beside him. "Sit with me like you used to do."

She hesitated, not wanting to let renewed friendship sway her upcoming decisions. "That was then. We were friends."

"And we aren't now?" He leaned forward, putting his elbows on his knees as if to make his body appear smaller and less of a threat.

"Now? Maybe friendly enemies."

"Never!" He abruptly stood up, letting the swing gyrate behind him. He strode over to her and didn't stop till he invaded her personal space. "We've been friends all our lives. Are you going to let a little water come between us now that you're finally back?"

She had to tilt her head to look into his hazel eyes. What she saw made her uncomfortable. *Frustration. Concern. And lust.* Just like her, he was obviously still harboring thoughts about that midnight.

"Friends, right?" He leaned forward, catching her in the dark cocoon of his shadow. "I'll carry these in for you later." He plucked the sack of groceries out of her hands and set them on the nearby table.

She stifled her protest at his take-charge attitude. They had to live not only in the same county but on the same ranch. Still, she wanted him to back up because she couldn't give ground, not with so much on the line. When he didn't move or even glance aside, she placed the flat of her palms on his broad chest and pushed. He didn't budge. He didn't even look as if he felt her resistance to his nearness. He simply leaned in closer.

"You've got me playing with fire," he said, drawing out the words in a raw hiss of a whisper.

She'd heard strong emotion before, but nothing with this sort of intensity that made her want to follow wherever he might lead her. Flashes of Lovers Leap, them sprawled together on top of a quilt in the bed of his pickup, played across her mind like snapshots cascading one atop another until she felt almost overwhelmed by a passion so pure, so deep that it refused to stay in the past. She dug her fingertips deeper into the soft fabric of his cotton shirt even as she knew she should uncurl her fingers and step away.

"*Our fire.*" As if those two words explained it all, he

gently grasped her hands and slid them from his chest to his neck with an economy of movement that he might have used to gentle a horse. He clasped the small of her back with one large hand while he caught the curve of her neck with the other. And then he lowered his face toward her.

She felt caught in a pivotal moment as he looked from her eyes to her mouth, then back to her eyes, then her lips again, where he finally lingered, giving her all the time in the world to protest, to resist, to push him away. Still, she couldn't, not when she was caught in the snare of his hazel gaze, the leather-and-sage scent of his body, and the white-hot heat of his hands cradling her as if she were spun silk.

When he finally pressed a soft kiss to her lips, he ignited a blazing spark between them and drew her body against his long frame. She thrust her hands into his thick hair, glorying in the softness even as she pulled him closer. *Our fire.* Oh yes, she felt the sizzle between them as he teased and tormented, licking, sucking, nibbling across her lips until she opened for his deep thrust into her mouth. She returned his kiss with a passion she'd thought long put to rest, buried in the ashes of her marriage, but here and now, every single burning sensation came back as if neither of them had ever left Lovers Leap.

He groaned deep in his throat as he stroked over her back, then lower, to cup her round butt with his large hands, tugging her tight against him as he pressed his hardness against her.

She tingled all over, feeling heat give way to chills, then back again, responding to his raging need as he kissed her, pouring more fuel on their escalating flames.

Suddenly, he tore his mouth away, breathing hard, and looked deep into her eyes. "Let's take this inside."

He might as well have doused her with cold water. She shook her head, abruptly waking up at his words. What was she thinking? Had she forgotten Graham's perfidy? Shane threatened everything she held dear—perhaps even her own heart. She shouldn't get anywhere near him.

He clasped her hand, threading their fingers together as he turned toward the doors to go inside.

She jerked her hand free and stepped back, shaking her head. "Not a good idea."

"Why not?"

"It's because of that midnight, isn't it? You think we can just pick up where we left off."

"No, it's not that. Well, yeah, I guess it is. Partly." He ran a palm over his square jaw as if in frustration. "Don't you get it yet?"

"I guess not because I seem to lose every sense in my head when I'm near you."

"I've never known you to lose your head."

"If we stay away from each other, we should be okay."

"Can't do it."

"Of course you can. I'll stay here. You've got the whole ranch to roam free."

He stepped off the porch, so they were face-to-face again. "I'm only going to say this once."

She wasn't sure she wanted to hear what he had to say, because she feared once she did, she'd never be able to forget his words. And every little word that fell from his lips had the possibility of changing her life when she was already dealing with so many changes. She wanted the security of the past, not the uncertainty of the present. She'd built her wall to keep out change. Now he threatened every single brick in it.

"Eden, we're meant to be together," he rasped in a voice that conveyed much deeper emotion than mere words. "It's always been that way. You ran long and hard, but you came back when the time was right."

"Yes, the time was right to come home, but—"

He gently stroked the side of her face, roaming her features with a tender gaze. "You're so beautiful, so smart, so strong. You can't even begin to imagine how dear you are to me."

She felt her eyes burn with unshed tears because she hadn't felt dear to anyone in such a long time. And she hadn't felt tenderness, either. He made her feel needy and greedy for what he was offering her. How could she resist? And yet, she'd come home to save the station, not reconnect with an old love.

"It's just a matter of time." He rubbed his thumb across her high cheekbone, then lowered his hand to his side, as if giving her space now that he'd said his piece. "You can't resist me any more than I can resist you."

She sighed. "Lovers Leap was just that one time."

"We can go now, whenever you want."

"That's not what I meant."

"I know," he said gently, tenderly, quietly. "But I want to go up there with you again."

She smiled, basking in the warm feelings that had lain dormant until now. But Shane had always brought out the best in her.

He returned her smile, reflecting her warmth in his hazel eyes. "Let's don't wait too long since—" he started, but he was interrupted when a pickup horn blasted out "The Eyes of Texas Are upon You," instead of a regular honk.

"Who is that?" She whirled around to see who was barreling up the lane toward the Wildcat Den.

"Morning Glory," he said. "She had that horn specially installed in her truck down in Dallas."

"She's one of my favorite people. It suits her." Eden watched as the bright-red pickup came to a quick stop in front of the radio station.

"Eden!" Morning Glory hollered as she slammed her pickup door behind her. "I heard you were back in town."

Shane leaned down. "Midnight on Lovers Leap. Soon." He grinned, a mischievous gleam in his eyes. "Just the two of us."

Chapter 8

SHANE WATCHED AS MORNING GLORY HURRIED TOWARD them in a flurry of bright color—long, full, rustling skirts and long, dangling, clanging necklaces. Somehow, she never looked a moment past her glory days as a flower child of the sixties. And she kept that time alive at Morning's Glory, her store in Old Town, where she made and sold perfumes, creams, bath powder, and anything else that struck her fancy. Tourists particularly loved her wares.

Eden and MG hugged each other in that special way women of long friendship and deep respect do.

"Still wearing patchouli, are you?" Eden said, laughing at their old joke.

"Still got a sensitive nose, do you?" Morning Glory joined her laughter.

"That's a strong scent."

"Got hooked on it at Woodstock. Well, that and the music and, well, maybe a good-looking guy or two."

Eden chuckled harder, shaking her head. "I didn't know you were at Woodstock."

"Oh, I've been a few places in my lifetime." Morning Glory gave a big grin as she motioned toward her vintage pickup with big, colorful flower decals that looked as if they were left over from the sixties.

A towheaded boy of about twelve stepped down from the passenger side and slowly, reluctantly, trudged over, dragging one ratty-sneakered foot after the other as he made his way toward them. He wore faded blue jeans and a red T-shirt with "KWCB, the Wildcat Den" emblazoned on the front.

"Eden, Shane, I'd like you to meet Ken Kendrick, my great-nephew."

Ken stopped just back of Morning Glory with his head hanging low and gave a loud sigh.

"Good to meet you." Shane tossed MG a questioning look. He'd heard her great-nephew was staying with her, but he was surprised she'd brought him to the ranch.

"Hey, Ken," Eden said in a soft, friendly voice. "I'm glad to meet you, too."

Ken nodded in response but said nothing.

"Ken's living with me while his mother goes back to work after a difficult time. Let's call it a challenging divorce."

Ken glanced at Morning Glory, rolled his eyes, and looked back at the ground.

"He's in school," Morning Glory continued, "but it's—"

"Lame," Ken finished for her.

"So he says," Morning Glory said. "Our school system is good, but he had more options in Dallas."

"Guess it's a big change for you," Shane said, trying to encourage Ken to be more comfortable with them.

Ken glanced up at Shane, then down again. "Yeah."

"Anyway," Morning Glory continued, "I thought it'd be good for him to get outdoors and work with animals."

Ken groaned out loud and scuffed the toe of his sneaker in the dirt.

"Ken, we discussed this, and you agreed," Morning Glory said with an impatient lilt in her voice.

Ken shrugged and continued to dig his toe in the ground.

"He spends all his time on his cell phone or his laptop when he's home." Morning Glory shuddered, as if horrified at the thought. "Outdoors is good, particularly for energetic boys."

"Are you saying you want him roping and riding?" Shane asked, trying not to sound as skeptical as he felt about the idea.

"Yes." Morning Glory nodded. "If it's not too much trouble, I'm hoping he could come out to the ranch on Saturdays and after school some days. He could help out and learn a few cowboy ways."

"Ken, what do you think about that suggestion?" Shane didn't want to commit his time and energy to a lost cause. But if the boy was keen on learning about ranch life, then he'd be more than happy to help.

Ken glanced up, then back down. "I got kicked out of my house in Dallas, so I guess I've got to do whatever it takes to stay here."

"Your parents didn't kick you out," Morning Glory said. "They're in a transition period in their lives. We all agreed you'd do better with stability at home."

"Whatever." Ken shrugged his shoulders.

Shane exchanged a glance with Eden. She looked about as convinced as he was that Ken could be made into a cowboy. As he was trying to come up with a diplomatic way out of the situation, he heard the front door of the radio station open and footsteps pound down the steps.

"Morning Glory, you gorgeous darlin'," Wildcat Jack called in his deep, melodious voice as he walked quickly toward the group. "Did you come all the way out here to see me and then get waylaid by these insensitive hooligans?"

"Oh, Jack, of course I came to see you," Morning Glory trilled in an excited voice. "I just happened to run into these two on my way."

"I knew it!" When Jack reached them, he caught Morning Glory in a big hug, raised her off her feet, and swung her around, grinning all the while. "How's my best girl doing? And who's the young'un you got in tow? You didn't go and get married behind my back, now, did you?"

"You know I'd always give you first chance." Morning Glory slapped Jack on the arm, chuckling and blushing and smiling at his teasing ways.

Ken appeared fascinated as he tracked the back-and-forth between Morning Glory and Jack.

Shane had seen Wildcat Jack in action before. There didn't seem to be a woman alive who could resist Jack's good-old-boy Texas charm. Every man should be so lucky with the ladies.

"You honor me. You really do." Jack nodded toward Ken. "So, who's your assistant here?"

"This is my great-nephew, Ken Kendrick. I don't know if you've heard, but he's staying with me for a while."

"Well, aren't you the luckiest of boys?" Jack checked Ken over from head to toe. "You appear to be a might undernourished. What's she feeding you?"

"Veggies."

"Hogwash!" Jack gave Morning Glory a stern look. "A growing boy like that needs steak and potatoes. It'll put meat on his bones."

"Yeah, I could use some real food," Ken quickly said, sidling toward Jack with a reverent look on his face. "You wouldn't be…well, the famous Wildcat Jack, would you?"

"I better be, or I've been living a lie for seventy-nine years."

"Wow." Ken rubbed the front of his T-shirt to call attention to the fact that he was promoting Jack's brand. "Not much to do here. I get you on the radio."

Jack nodded, shrugging his broad shoulders. "Most folks do."

"Not lame."

"Thanks," Jack said. "I do my best."

Ken tugged the neck of his T-shirt, scuffed his sneaker again, and gestured with his chin toward the station. "That where you do it?"

"Yep," Jack said.

"Don't look like much."

"It's not much. But it works. I play reel-to-reel tapes and vinyl on the turntable."

"Tape? Vinyl?" Ken gave a big grin with a sparkle in his eyes. "You've got the real deal? I mean vintage stuff?"

"Guess I do." Jack chuckled, rolling his dark eyes. "Keep in mind, vintage to you is new to me."

"Right." Ken gave a serious nod of agreement. "No CDs?"

"Nary a one."

Ken glanced at Morning Glory, then back at Jack. "Seeing as you're friends with MG and all, think I could see your lair in the Den sometime?"

"Now I don't let just any Tom, Dick, or Harry into the Wildcat Den."

"Course not!" Ken looked offended at the very idea. "I'd be real careful. I wouldn't touch anything. I mean, it'd mean a lot if I could see the tech and stuff."

"Might could do it." Jack glanced at Morning Glory and raised an eyebrow in question.

"If it wouldn't be too much trouble," Morning Glory said with a smile of relief, "I'd appreciate Ken getting a chance to see how a radio station works."

"Nothing's too much trouble for you, my dear Morning Glory." Jack clasped her fingers and pressed a kiss to the back of her hand in a courtly gesture.

Morning Glory smiled as she pressed her kissed hand to her heart. "Wildcat Jack, you're just too much."

"Thank you, MG. Truth of the matter, I haven't felt a day over Woodstock lo these many years."

"That makes two of us," Morning Glory said with a twinkle in her eyes.

"Maybe it was something in the water," Jack added with a sly grin.

"You were at Woodstock, too?" Eden glanced at him in surprise.

"Now that's a story for another day—or not." Jack tossed a long silver braid over his shoulder. "Today we're discussing the possibility of Ken's tour."

"Seeing as how you're *really* good friends," Ken said, "maybe I could help out at the Den. I'd do anything. I'd even sweep floors or run errands." He pointed toward the ranch. "I've got to be out here anyway."

"Are you going to get that boy roping and riding?" Jack gave a big whoop and holler. "I was a cowboy before I was a DJ. There's nothing like a singing cowboy to bring home the bacon—and attract the ladies."

"I thought DJs were the top of the line." Ken gave Jack a wide grin as if catching him in a fib.

"You got me there." Jack laughed. "Let's say it's always best to keep all your options open."

"Ken, I don't know if I should let you spend time around Jack," Morning Glory said with a chuckle. "He'll fill your head so full of tall tales that we'll never get it shrunk back to regular size again."

Shane smiled as everybody laughed at her joke, cementing Ken's new place as part of their extended group.

Ken straightened his shoulders, appearing taller and prouder.

"I'd really appreciate any help y'all are willing to give," Morning Glory said. "We tried Ken in my shop, but that didn't go very well."

Ken rolled his eyes. "Girl stuff."

"We've got plenty of stuff for guys to do here on the ranch." Shane made a quick decision. "And you're welcome to join us as long as you're willing to pull your own weight."

"I'll do it." Ken gave Jack a hopeful glance. "And the Den?"

"Best look to Eden," Jack said. "She's the boss."

"I'm not sure what needs doing," Eden said. "I just got back to town."

"Whatever you want, I'm your guy." Ken pointed at his T-shirt with the Wildcat Den logo. "I'm already a fan."

"Okay then," Eden said with a smile, "but no complaints if you're washing windows and sweeping floors."

Ken pantomimed zipping his lips shut.

"Thanks." Morning Glory gave a loud sigh. "This is a big load off my mind. Ken is a quick study and he won't be any trouble."

"Hah!" Jack said. "We boys got to stick together because *trouble* is our middle name."

"You know it." Ken gave everybody a self-satisfied grin.

"Come on." Jack nodded toward the station. "I'll give you and MG a quick tour, then you best let me get back to my listeners."

"See you later." Eden called to them as they walked away, then she turned toward Shane. "I hope this all works out great."

"At the least, you'll get some help."

"So will you."

Shane gestured toward the swing. "Maybe we should sit down and discuss how we're going to handle Ken." He couldn't help but think that if she hadn't left town they might have a boy of their own about Ken's age. He liked that idea a lot.

"You're bound and determined to get me on that swing, aren't you?"

"Yeah. And a whole lot more."

Chapter 9

EDEN FELT AS IF SHE'D STEPPED BACK IN TIME, HANGING OUT with Shane, seeing Morning Glory in her flower-child finery, watching Jack's shenanigans, and now discovering a wild card in Ken. LA was unpredictable, but Wildcat Bluff held its own in that regard. Texas wasn't just about heart but about living on the edge. Maybe that's why so many folks in the 1800s had written "GTT"—"Gone to Texas"—on their front doors as they took off ahead of debt collectors, love gone bad, or the law, to disappear forever. Still, she suspected plenty of folks with a strong independent streak had answered the call of the wild, willing to bet it all on a chance to start over and build a powerful legacy.

Was she willing to bet everything on the here and now? Maybe she was already all in, but she just hadn't put it together till this moment. She'd thought the station and the spring were all she had left, so she'd come home, but maybe they were what she needed at exactly this time in her life. She looked at Shane, feeling an unaccustomed emotion well up. Maybe she needed more in life than all work and no play.

"Glad to be back?" He cocked his head to one side as he gave her a concerned look with his hazel eyes.

"Am I that transparent?" She felt her voice catch in her throat, as if stuck on a lump that mirrored the sudden ache in her chest. Had she been homesick and never realized it as she galloped forward to meet whatever life tossed at her?

"Remember, I know you."

"For better or worse, I've changed. LA changed me. Life changed me."

"Life changes us all—on the outside. But we're still the same on the inside. That means you're without a doubt the Eden I know from way back."

"I thought I'd left her behind, but now I'm not so sure." She sounded wistful and knew it.

"Trust me. You're my Eden come home."

As she watched, he looked her up and down with a tenderness that echoed what she was feeling inside. "I think I'd like to be that Eden again."

"If I promise to be good, will you sit in the swing with me like we did when we were kids?"

She couldn't help but chuckle at his hopeful tone. "When have you ever been good?"

He joined her laughter. "I remember a time when you thought I was pretty good."

"You don't give up, do you?"

"Never. Not when it's something I want."

And she did remember that about him. They were alike in this particular way. Maybe it was the fact that they'd both been raised in Texas, or they'd just had this quality naturally. In either case, she understood him, so maybe he was right. Maybe neither of them had changed down deep in their souls, where seeds waited to be nourished at just the right moment, with sun and wind and water, so they'd ripen and unfurl into colorful fragrant blossoms.

He clasped her hand—gently, tenderly, carefully—and

threaded their fingers together as if she were that delicate flower, just on the edge of bursting into rich, vibrant color and tantalizing scent.

She felt drawn back to a simpler, happier time of life, when they were so much more innocent and carefree.

He drew her up to the porch and across the deck to the swing without letting go of her hand.

She squeezed his fingers, then released them before sitting down. When he sat beside her, she felt content in a way she hadn't for such a long time.

He cleared his throat, as if reluctant to bring up something, while he fiddled with the chain that tethered the swing on his side to the wood rafter above them.

"Go ahead. Whatever it is, I can take it."

"It's not that." He looked out into the distance. "It's Graham Tanner."

"Graham." She gripped the edges of the swing, tensing all over at just the mention of her former husband's name. "What about him?"

"I want to make sure you're over him." Shane slanted a glance at her. "Are you?"

"How can you even ask?"

"Some women and men never give up even when—"

"That sidewinder!" She abruptly stood up, unable to sit still as furious energy poured through her. "Trust me, if I never see him again, it'll be too soon." She walked over to the edge of the deck, feeling chilled to the bone. She rubbed her upper arms with her palms as she tried to get warm.

"Are you mad at all guys now?" He got up and walked to her side.

She glanced up at him, so impossibly tall, dark, and

handsome. She shook her head and looked away again. "I'm not thinking about guys at all."

"What about now?" He clasped her hands, tethering her gently but firmly to him.

"We're old friends. It's not the same."

"We're a lot more than old friends."

She knew he was right, but she was still a bit reluctant to let down her guard.

"You're cold." He drew her closer ever so slowly, then gently placed her hands around his neck before wrapping his arms around her and completely enclosing her. "You're used to LA weather."

She shivered, not from cold now but from body memory of when they'd come together so many years ago in a driving force of passion, as they'd thrust away everything except their burning need for each other. She clutched the soft fabric of his cotton shirt, her emotions in turmoil.

"Let me warm you." He tightened his embrace, pressing soft kisses into her hair.

Despite everything, she still wanted him. She wanted every little thing about him. She pushed long fingers into his thick hair, inhaling the scent of him as if she were drawing him deep inside, while the sound of his breath grew more ragged with every feathery kiss.

Something broke in her, like water gushing over an earthen dam or a wall collapsing from its own weight. He was a powerful temptation. It was as if every one of the years they'd been apart had twined into a tight ball in the hours since they'd come face-to-face again, so there was no distance at all between then and now.

He sighed, a deep, husky sound of desire, and pushed

back tendrils of soft hair to expose her ear. He gently nibbled, then kissed the delicate whorls before blazing a hot trail to the high plane of her cheekbone, stroking up her back with one strong hand while he held her as if he'd never let her go.

When he pressed a gentle kiss to her lips, all that had been dark and gloomy and oppressive in her life turned light and bright and expansive. He nibbled her lower lip from one corner to the other, teasing, tormenting, exploring. When she felt the tip of his moist tongue, she opened to him, wanting to taste him, feel him, know him—and luxuriate in his power.

She greedily drank him in, teasing him back with her tongue till he groaned under her onslaught and kissed her with enough pent-up passion to make her gasp and press her body against him, unable to get close enough fast enough. She felt his broad hands caress her back and move downward till he grasped her bottom and pulled her against him.

At the knowledge of how much he wanted her, needed her, desired her, she felt her own inner heat spike and spread out from her center, making her ache all over. She rubbed against him, inciting them both to higher and higher flames. She knew she was pushing them toward a point of no return, but she didn't care. She wanted what she wanted and that was Shane Taggart in all his cowboy glory. The past ceased to matter. Only the present held any allure.

He tore his mouth from her, breathing hard, looking at her face with eyes that were dark with hunger and something she couldn't identify. Now, she simply gloried in feeling like a beautiful, beloved, wanted woman again.

Until this very moment, she hadn't realized how badly Graham had damaged her self-esteem and how he'd made her run from the pleasure a man could give her. She didn't need or want love. That emotion might lead to the danger of someone like Graham. No, she realized now that she needed simple passion. All she wanted was unemotional, no-strings-attached sex with a strong cowboy who could meet her needs with no questions asked or given. Was that so much to ask?

"Perhaps we could make an arrangement," she whispered, feeling driven to have him but not hold him.

"Is this some sort of bet?" he asked in a rough tone, as if having trouble speaking at all. "If it is, I'm not at my best right now."

She smiled slyly, knowing she looked pleased and all too much like a cat in the cream. "I think you're at your very best."

He groaned and hugged her harder, plowing long fingers into her hair to hold her still against him.

"I doubt we're ever going to agree on the spring."

He sighed, squeezing her tighter. "Not now anyway."

"Let's agree to disagree on that matter."

"I'll give you anything within my power to give you."

She licked the little indentation between his collarbones at the base of his throat, tasting salty tartness. He made her feel bold. "Will you give me your body?"

He shuddered down his entire length, then set her back so he could look into her eyes. "If you're toying with me, it's not funny. I'm hurting, and your words aren't helping."

"Would joining me in my bed help?"

He rubbed a hand over his square jaw, abruptly

turned away, then glanced back. "If this is a dream, I don't want to wake up. If it's real, you can have me any which way you want me."

She smiled, feeling her body come even more alive. "No strings attached."

"If this is the way you want it, I guess you have changed." He shook his head, as if not liking the situation but not willing to back out, either. "Come up to my place. There's no way we're getting into Clem's bed. His ghost might haunt us forever."

She chuckled at the thought, feeling relieved that Shane was making light of the situation, but she knew he was right, too.

"Besides, I've got a king-size bed."

"Think we might need it?" she asked teasingly, feeling lighthearted and a little dizzy with her proposition. That he'd agreed so readily was slightly scary in that leap-off-a-cliff-without-knowing-how-far-down-to-the-bottom kind of way.

"Oh yeah, we just might." He gave her a smile that was part lascivious and part challenge.

"Okay." She held out her hand for him to shake. "We agree to fulfill our physical needs with no emotional involvement."

He clasped her hand between his two strong ones. "LA must have been something. In Wildcat Bluff, men keep their women happy, no matter what it takes."

"But I'm not your woman."

He raised her hand to his lips and placed a warm and tender kiss on her palm before he looked up again. "Not yet."

Chapter 10

ONE STEP AT A TIME, SHANE CAUTIONED HIMSELF. EDEN HAD been badly wounded by a man, her work world, and a city that cared only so long as she was on top. He hadn't helped matters by getting off on the wrong foot about Wildcat Spring. Still, the Eden he'd known would never have suggested such a bargain, much less followed up on it.

He might be setting himself up for a world of hurt. What she couldn't take out on her ex-husband she might very well take out on the next man who came along, namely him. Was it worth the chance? Sure it was. He was a big guy. He'd had ups and downs, so he knew he could take it. That wasn't the issue. He wanted to heal her wounded heart. He wanted to be there for her like he had been when she'd lost her parents. He wanted them to be a team again, like they were before hormones and careers had gotten in the way of friendship.

As much as he hated to admit it, he wasn't convinced sex was the right way to get Eden back on her feet and into his life. Maybe some guys would be satisfied with simple carnal pleasure, but he wasn't one of them—at least, not where Eden was concerned. Sure, he'd had relationships after she'd left town, but the cowgirls had all complained that his heart wasn't really there for them before they'd left him in their dust. Only now did he have an inkling of how they must have felt. He wished he could change those days, but now he realized his heart had always belonged to Eden—the others hadn't had a chance.

Would he tell Eden that fact? Hell no. A man could only show his soft underbelly so often before he started crawling on it all the time. She needed a strong man, not a weak one. Even so, he feared losing her before he had a chance to win her, particularly with Wildcat Spring standing like a boulder between them.

Maybe more than anything, she needed to be held, touched, valued for herself, instead of what she could bring to a bottom line or inspire in others. Maybe he needed the same thing. He'd been a rock for so many for so long that sometimes he lost sight of what he might need in his own life. He'd been there for his parents when they'd both lost their battles with cancer, while his brother had taken off, disappearing into the rodeo circuit with only infrequent calls. He'd managed the ranch, medical issues, and funerals all on his lonesome except for local friends.

He knew what it was like to carry the weight of the world on his shoulders. He didn't want Eden to have to do the same thing, not when he was here to help her—if she'd only let him.

As he held her hand, realization hit him, like a bolt of lightning out of the sky, that he was just as alone as she was right now. He'd covered up his longing for someone who meshed with him by working hard, volunteering at the fire station, visiting with friends, but underneath it all, he was alone. And he didn't want to grow old alone. He wanted love and family to sustain him. Not just anybody would do.

Spring was in the air. Maybe it was time for a little touch of the birds and the bees.

"I could throw a couple of buffalo steaks on the grill tonight and—"

A blaring horn interrupted Shane, so he glanced down the road and saw a dark-blue pickup with bright chrome trim barreling toward them before stopping in a swirl of dust. A tall, lean cowboy dressed in scuffed boots, blue jeans, blue plaid shirt, and tan hat leaped out and jogged over to them.

"What's going on?" Shane asked as he nestled Eden into the crook of his arm.

"Yeah, yeah, you don't have to say it." The cowboy gave Eden a big white grin meant to charm her as he doffed his hat, revealing thick chestnut hair worn a trifle long. "You're right. I'm Mr. September."

"What?" she asked, looking puzzled but charmed.

"Yeah, yeah, I know. It's hard to recognize us with all our clothes on," Mr. September joked, then stopped and gazed at her with blue-gray eyes emphasized by long lashes. "Don't tell me you haven't seen the Wildcat Bluff Cowboy Firefighters Calendar? If so, you're the only one."

"I haven't had the pleasure," Eden said before glancing up at Shane with a mischievous smile. "Are you in it?"

He gave a loud sigh, wishing Craig—the county heartbreaker—hadn't let the cat out of the bag. "It was a charity benefit. Sydney Steele roped us all in to it last Christmas. And I sincerely doubt we'll ever hear the last of it."

"Yeah, just wait till your month comes up, then you'll really hear about it." Mr. September gave a big, deep laugh of amusement. "By the way, if you don't know it, that's Mr. June you're letting cuddle up to you. You might want to keep him at arm's length due to the fact that local cowgirls could get a bit testy over a stranger cozying up to their Mr. June. Now I'd be happy to squire you about town, seeing as how my month is still far away."

"You're squiring her nowhere," Shane said in irritation. His friend had a well-deserved reputation with the ladies, particularly since he was a singing cowboy who wowed cowgirls onstage and offstage. "Eden Rafferty, meet Craig Thorne, better known as Mr. September from a horse ranch out Sure-Shot way."

Craig cocked his head as he looked closer at Eden. "You wouldn't by any chance be Clem Rafferty's niece, would you?"

"That'd be me."

"Well, I'll be." He stuck out his large hand for a shake. "Glad to meet you. Ole Clem had nothing but good words to say about you."

"Thanks. He was wonderful."

"In town on a visit?"

"She's here to deal with the station," Shane said, hoping that'd put an end to Craig's interest, although it'd probably just up it, because he'd been known to sing a song or two live on KWCB.

"Good." Craig put his hat back on his head and adjusted it to suit him. "Anything you need to get the place shipshape, count on me. Here about, we'd be lost without the Wildcat Den."

"Thank you." Eden shook his hand, smiling. "I may just need your help."

"Anytime." Craig focused on Shane. "Almost forgot my errand, what with a pretty lady on my mind."

Shane could've punted Craig over the fence. His friend well knew the station was on its last legs and the spring was needed for his cattle. He resisted rolling his eyes, knowing Craig flirted like he took a breath, one just as natural as the other. "What brings you out here?"

Craig pointed toward a smear of dust on the horizon in the direction of the Lazy Q. "Looks like that new neighbor of yours is burning pasture. Not smart in a drought and late in the season to boot, but maybe the new owners are just catching up."

"Did Lander alert the fire station?"

"Nope. I saw the smoke when I drove by, so figured I ought to let you know just in case. And I called Hedy down at the station."

"Thanks." Shane shaded his eyes as he looked closer at what had been just a smudge on the horizon. "Smoke's coming this way."

"Didn't appear too bad when I first stopped by, but the wind's kicked up," Craig replied. "Maybe Lander's got cowboys out ahead of the blaze, but I wouldn't count on it."

"I've got cattle in a nearby pasture."

"Is the radio station in danger?" Eden sounded alarmed as she touched her throat.

Shane exchanged a knowing look with Craig. He didn't want to upset Eden, but he didn't want to endanger anybody, either. "Just in case, we ought to get MG and Ken out of here. Jack and Eden, too."

"I'll stay," Eden said. "KWCB may need to be on the air to alert the county and field updates. If this fire gets out of control, we'll be seeing something similar to Southern California fires driven by the Santa Ana Winds."

"Our wind isn't as bad as the Santa Anas, but a prairie fire moves fast." Shane kept his eyes on the growing line of smoke now being driven by a gusting wind toward the Rocky T. "Eden, you're not prepared to fight a fire. I want you out of here."

"I'm staying," she insisted. "If the fire gets too close, I'll go to the spring."

"Not good enough," Shane said.

"That's as good as it gets." Eden stepped off the porch and headed for the station. "Come on. Let's get those three to safety."

Shane watched her take long strides. He'd forgotten how stubborn she could be once she set her mind on something. He turned to Craig. "Best check in again with Hedy. Let her know the wind's come up, so it's not looking good. We'd better have the dozers and boosters. See who's available."

"Okay. I'll meet them at the fire station and get back here with the rigs."

"If I can, I'll get hold of Lander and ask him to stop setting fires."

"Ought to have stopped by now."

"He's from East Texas. They've got wetter land over there. He may have just bitten off more than he can chew."

"He'll learn." Craig hit speed dial on his cell phone, then started to talk as he jogged back to his truck.

Shane jerked his phone out of his pocket as he hurried to the radio station, thinking about his foreman being nearby at the barn. "Max, the Lazy Q is doing a late burn, so—"

"Saw it and on it. Cowboys are already moving the herds away from the blaze, but it's coming at us fast now."

"Firefighters are on their way. I'll be at the barn in a minute." Shane tucked his cell back in his pocket as he wrenched open the station's door, stepped inside, and almost ran into MG and Ken.

"We're on our way," Morning Glory said. "I'll head to the fire station as soon as I get Ken safely home."

"No." Ken dug in his heels. "I'm not a kid. Let's go straight there. I'll help Hedy."

"He's right," Shane said. "We were already helping out and learning stuff at his age."

Ken gave Shane a thumbs-up, then bounded out the front door.

"Okay. Rigs will be here in no time." Morning Glory gave him a quick hug before she followed Ken outside.

He strode over to the sound studio and jerked open the door, even though the red light outside was on to indicate it was in use. He wanted Eden and Jack gone right now.

With mic in hand, Wildcat Jack glanced up, shaking his head to let Shane know he wasn't going anywhere. Eden stood right beside him.

"That's right, cowboys and cowgirls. This is Wildcat Jack bringing you the latest news flash out of Wildcat Bluff County. Listen up. We've got us a prairie fire on the Lazy Q Ranch that's now called Tarleton something or other. You know where it's at. Firefighters are on their way, so stay out of their way unless you're on call to help. Best start moving herds and wetting down buildings just in case things get out of hand. Current wind speed is gustin' too fast. Humidity is next to nothin'.

And barometric pressure is risin'. No chance of rain. Hate to say it, but Mother Nature is not our friend today.

"But never you worry. Wildcat Jack is on the job. I'll keep you posted every step of the way. If you've got news about this fire, give me a call. Otherwise, stay off the lines so folks who need help can get help. Once more, Wildcat Bluff County residents, there's a fast-moving prairie fire on the old Lazy Q, so be on the lookout and stay out of danger.

"We'll be back after this outlaw country hit from The Highwaymen with the latest report from Wildcat Bluff Fire-Rescue. Hold tight, folks. We're in for a bit of a rocky ride today, but we'll be okay, like we're always okay in Wildcat Bluff County."

"Thanks, Jack," Eden said as she handed him a piece of paper. "Here's the latest report from the national weather station." She sounded stronger than she had all day as she turned toward Shane. "Jack and I are staying. We'll be in touch with Hedy at the fire station. Jack will stay on the air to keep up spirits and let the county know what's going on. I'll stay on top of the weather reports."

"But—" Shane started to protest.

"It's our job." She gave a brisk nod of her head. "We don't just entertain listeners. We're here to serve our community with all the critical news."

He suddenly saw her as the professional she'd come to be—efficient and dedicated in an emergency. She wasn't a woman to be protected, although that was his instinct. She was a woman to be supported in her life's work. He was grateful to have her here, along with Jack, to be the voice of calm, reason, and reassurance during a difficult time.

He and Jack shared a brief look acknowledging the fact that Eden Rafferty had, indeed, grown up and taken the bull by the horns.

"Looks like you two have this well under control," Shane said. "As soon as the rigs roll in, we'll start getting that fire under control. If you need me, I'll be up at the barn."

As he strode toward the door, Eden caught up with him. She gave him a quick hug and a fierce kiss. "Stay safe."

Chapter 11

SHANE STEPPED OUTSIDE, RAISING HIS HEAD AS HE CAUGHT a stronger scent and saw a larger area of white smoke billowing his way. He hit speed dial as he jogged toward his truck, checking in with Hedy Murray, who was the backbone of Wildcat Bluff Fire-Rescue. Nothing in the county got past her, so he knew she'd be on top of the brush fire and whatever else was going on.

"Shane, how does the fire look from your position?" Hedy answered in a crisp, no-nonsense voice.

"I'm at the Den and headed up to the cattle barn to get a better view on higher ground. We've got wind gusts that are sending flames and smoke my direction."

"Rigs are on their way. Kemp Lander on the Lazy Q is opening his gates, so—"

"Even if he wanted to cause trouble and keep fire-fighters out, he couldn't because you know good and well the station has keys to all the ranches in case of fire."

"He doesn't want trouble," Hedy said. "I doubt he'll ever admit it, but he sounded embarrassed and worried about starting a fire that got out of control."

"Lander ought to be ashamed and a whole lot more."

"He's got his guys moving his herds away from the blaze. For now, let's go ahead and figure out the LCES."

"Right." LCES—Lookouts, Communications, Escape routes, Safety zones. He hoped this fire was small enough not to need much LCES, but safety always came first for firefighters.

"You're on-site," Hedy said, "so you take lead, as fire captain, when they get there."

"Okay. I figure you're sending the rigs to the Rocky T?"

"Right. You've got the high point at your barn and double gate, so I assume you'll want that area to be your lookout, escape route, and safety zone."

Shane couldn't keep from smiling at her words. "Sounds like you've already worked out the LCES."

She sighed into the phone. "You caught me. I was just trying to let you think you were more than a pretty face."

"That's what smart cowgirls like you always say. We'd be lost without you and you know it."

"Oh, go on, you silver-tongued devil, and get up there. This fire's waiting for nobody."

"I'm on it." As he reached his pickup, he called Kemp Lander.

"What?" Lander growled in a deep voice. "I've got my hands full here."

"Shane Taggart at the Rocky T."

"Guess you called to rag on me."

"Wildcat Bluff firefighters are on their way."

"Good. It's not my fault the grass here wasn't cut last season."

"You could've brush-hogged."

"And been at it till June—no thanks."

"Have you at least stopped setting fires?"

"Yep." Lander sucked at his teeth. "If the wind hadn't come up and if there was any moisture in the ground around here, then—"

"No ifs, ands, or buts will help my cattle one damn bit." Shane wrenched open the door to his truck. "If I lose one piece of equipment, one line of fence, one head of cattle, you'll be hearing from my lawyer."

"We're doing all we can here. We'll work with the firefighters. Let's save any bickering for later."

"I don't bicker. I make promises." Shane stepped into his truck and slammed the door. Right now, all he could do was hope for a bit of luck with the weather and the sharpest firefighters around.

As he backed up, he cast a long look at the station, wishing above all else that Eden and Jack were safely in town, but they needed to support the community on the radio. He had to put others ahead of his own desires, even if it went against every instinct he had to get Eden out of harm's way.

He forced his mind away from her and back to the matter at hand as he drove fast onto the single lane bordered on each side by the bright-white fence line that marked the entry into the Rocky T Ranch. He needed to stop this brush fire before it damaged his ranch or anybody else's in the county. He particularly didn't want to see wild critters, like rabbits or birds or even ornery armadillos, lose their lives due to one man's incompetence.

He headed up the hill toward his house, horse barn, indoor arena, cattle barn, and outbuildings. The thought of losing a single one of the structures, much less all of them, made his hair stand on end. No way was he going to let that happen, not on his watch.

Besides that lurking disaster, he knew that compartmentalizing was easier said than done. Eden still tugged at his thoughts. He could be strong and he could make fine decisions, but he feared every good intention in the world would fly right out the window if she well and truly set her mind on taking him to bed.

The fire chased her out of his thoughts as he reached the top of the hill. He had a better view of what was happening on the Lazy Q. The wind was gusting, pushing the fire east, then twisting it south, then back east, leaving behind black pasture with white smoke above it. The only good thing about the situation was that the blaze hadn't reached the Rocky T yet. They couldn't stop the fire or extinguish it. They'd have to contain it, cut it off from its source, and let it burn out. Once the rigs got here, they'd put a line around the blaze or at least on his side of the fire and start a backfire, so the line would get wider.

Shane gave the area a cursory glance to make sure all looked safe. His ranch house was built of multicolored native rock on two levels, with the main living quarters on the rise of a hill that extended across to a rec room with a balcony above a three-car garage. A white porch ran the length of the first level, which opened into a living room with a vaulted ceiling. So far, he saw no evidence of fire damage, like blistered paint or black soot. Perfect. This home had been his mom's pride and joy, and he couldn't imagine letting anything happen to it.

He drove past the house, the horse barn, and indoor arena, then stopped in front of the double open doors of the big red cattle barn. Its aluminum roof glinted in the sunlight. Cowboy trucks in all colors and sizes and repair were parked around it, meaning Max must have called in every one of their workers—even the off-duty ones—to move horses, cattle, and buffalo to pastures away from the spreading fire. Good thing, too. He'd be able to focus on the blaze, instead of worrying about the stock.

He pulled out his cell and checked for texts. Max had left several that confirmed the ranch's cowboys were out on horseback and four-wheelers, moving herds to far pastures. Max's confirmation relieved Shane's mind, because once firefighters were out in the pastures, they'd get scant reception on their cell phones, although they'd stay in touch with each other via radios.

For now, he needed to compartmentalize again. He leaped from his truck, opened the back door, and started hauling out firefighting gear. He didn't want to slow down the rigs once they got to the ranch, so he quickly changed clothes. He turned from cowboy to firefighter when he put on a thick, yellow fire jacket, stout, green fire pants, special black leather work boots, and a cherry-red helmet that served as a hard hat. He checked to make sure he had fire-resistant, thick leather gloves in a jacket pocket. He shrugged into a backpack that contained a fire-resistant tent along with a fire rake and other gear. In case he got caught in a conflagration, the tent was supposed to save him, but he doubted it'd actually work. Still, it was something if there was nothing else. He tossed his cowboy gear—shirt, jeans, boots, and hat—onto the back seat of his truck and slammed shut the door.

While he waited for the rigs and teams, he walked to higher ground to assess the fire. No matter Hedy's evaluation, he'd go ahead and get the LCES in mind, so there was no question later.

He walked over and opened the double gates into the pasture, setting them so they couldn't accidentally swing shut after the rigs drove through. He looked across the prairie, evaluating the rate of speed and width of the red-orange blaze cutting an erratic path with swirling, white smoke obscuring the leading edge. Fortunately, the large rolls of hay were up near the barn and not presently in the path of the blaze or his ranch structures would be in even bigger trouble with that type of superheated conflagration.

In his mind, he ran through the fire size-up. Access route: good. No fire barriers: good. No water sources: bad. Land ownership access: good. Area fire history: bad. Responding resources capabilities: good. All in all, the fire scene was doable.

He heard sirens and whipped around. Wildcat Bluff Fire-Rescue rigs barreled up the Rocky T's single lane. Hedy had sent the two red boosters that each had a three-hundred-GPM pump capacity and a two-hundred-gallon water tank. They were basically pickups with flat beds that carried water with a pump and coiled hose that could be automatically extended and retracted. She'd also sent their two dozers, towed behind pickups. Each bulldozer had an eight-foot blade that would push, or plow, a line, leaving behind bare dirt. If that apparatus didn't do the trick, she could still send out the big engine that had a two-thousand-GPM pump capacity and one thousand gallons of water, but it'd have more trouble getting up the lane and into the pasture. He didn't think they'd need the pumper, but he liked knowing it was available for backup.

As the rigs pulled into the yard, he directed them

to park near the fence line till they made their plans to engage the fire. They'd been trained never to rush into a dangerous situation without adequate preparation.

He watched as Slade Steele stepped out of a pickup, limped to the back, and released the dozer. Slade was over six feet of solid muscle, with a thick crop of ginger hair and bright eyes. He'd been a bull rider before an injury put him out of commission. Now he was famous for his award-winning pies and muscadine wine. Nobody doubted that, between his flirting and his cooking, he topped most cowgirl lists in the county as prime male material, but he mostly rode solo in his pickup these days. Shane could only wonder when some lucky gal was going to pierce Slade's tough hide and reach his soft heart.

"I'm Slade's dozer backup." Jim Bob Williams—all sharp-eyed, hard-muscled go-getter—stepped down from the other side of the truck.

"Glad to see you're all already in gear." Shane watched as the other firefighters left their rigs and assembled around him.

"Dune and I are on this booster. We'll pump and roll." Sydney Steele clasped hands with Dune Barrett, her fiancé, as she glanced over at her twin, Slade, giving a final check of his equipment.

"I've got the other booster with Kent," Trey Duval said, gesturing toward his cousin Kent Duval.

"I'll run the other dozer," Craig said, nodding toward the crouching machine, "but you'll need to follow me."

"Okay," Shane replied, "that'll do. Stay in close contact by radio." He made a visual check to make sure all radios were on their shoulders, at head height for optimal use. "If necessary, you've got picks and shovels ready to dig ditches for containment, don't you?"

"Hah!" Sydney said. "That's the dozer's job."

"But we've got them just in case," Slade said.

"Good." Shane glanced back at the fire. "So far, we're looking at a class A fire, and if the wind dies down, we'll be on easy street."

"And if it doesn't?" Trey asked, shaking his head.

"We'll work a little harder and a little faster," Shane said, knowing they all understood exactly what he meant.

"Suits me," Kent said.

"Did Hedy tell you that we're using this area near the barn as our LCES?"

"Yep," Slade said, putting his hands on his narrow hips as he glanced around the area. "Looks good."

"Let's make a direct attack, wetting, smothering, and separating burning fuel from unburned fuel." Shane checked from one to another of the expectant faces, well aware that he was repeating what they already knew, but reminders didn't hurt anybody and might help. He heard Hedy's voice in the background, coming over the apparatus radios as she kept updates flowing to all parties involved in the fire. "And we'll radio Hedy if we need more help."

"Okay." Slade gestured toward the blaze. "Let's get this fire before it gets us."

"Right," Shane said. "Visual, radio, or vocal communications. Sydney and Dune, Kent and Trey, take your boosters to the far side of the fire and make a running attack. The wind's whipping the fire this direction, so we'll use the dozers on our side to cut a line that the blaze hopefully won't cross. Okay, firefighters, initial attack. Let's engage."

"Dune," Sydney said, heading for a booster, "let's pump and roll."

Kent and Trey quickly followed in her wake to the other booster.

After they drove away, Shane turned to Slade and Jim Bob. "You take one end. We'll take the other. Let's meet in the middle."

"Hah!" Slade laughed, shrugging his muscular shoulders. "When did I ever meet anybody in the middle?"

Shane just shook his head, knowing how competitive the former bull rider could be. "Bet?"

"Winner buys a round of pie at the Chuckwagon Café." Slade opened the bulldozer door to the enclosed cabin with a single seat.

Shane chuckled, knowing the pie would be great and taste mighty good after fighting a fire. His friend had become the county's blue-ribbon pie baker since leaving the rodeo circuit.

"Beers all around at Wildcat Hall or nothing doing." Craig jerked open the door to the other dozer, reached inside, and pulled out a backfire torch.

Slade burst out laughing as he pointed at Craig. "Is it beer you're looking for or a mighty fine gal named Fern who's running the Hall now?"

Craig glanced to the side, as if visualizing the woman in question, before he looked back up with a big grin and heightened color on his handsome face. "Just keep to your pies and I'll keep to my beer."

"Way it's looking, pretty quick, I may be the only single guy left standing in the county," Slade said, teasing his partner as he sat down inside the dozer.

"Your time's coming," Craig called while turning to Shane and holding out the red torch.

He grasped it, not about to say a word on the subject because he understood only too well just how vulnerable a man could be when he was falling hard for a woman. "Firefighters, let's roll!"

Chapter 12

So much for easy street, as if that term had ever come into play with a fire. Shane felt sweat trickle down under his hard hat to hit his cheekbones, sliding down the sides of his face and dripping onto his jacket. He was hot and sooty and grumpy, but he kept going. No choice. He was on foot and more vulnerable than Craig, who was inside the bulldozer.

They'd been at it for hours, and he was flagging behind the dozer. Craig was removing flammable material, like dry leaves and dead grass, to leave a line of bare soil. Shane's job was to create a firebreak, widening the line as he followed the bright-yellow dozer that left a continuous line of track plates similar to those of a caterpillar or military tank.

They'd flanked the fire and gotten in front of it, but that meant the gusting wind was blowing smoke and flames directly toward them. He knew only too well that it was critical to make the line as wide as possible between the fire and his ranch structures, so he kept moving forward, no matter how tired or hot he got with the flames beating ever closer.

He figured most ground critters and birds had left the area, but he still kept an eye out for any that might be injured or unable to get away. Unfortunately, that was getting harder to do all the time, as the smoke was growing denser and the fire roaring closer. He coughed, feeling his lungs clog up with smoke. He leaned down to get a better breath, knowing only too well that smoke rose, so the air was always clearer near the ground. At least Craig had plenty of oxygen, since he was inside the enclosed cab of the dozer.

Shane couldn't tell how close they were getting to Slade and Jim Bob, mainly because Slade kept upping the ante over the radio with jokes about pies and beers for the winners. Slade had always used humor to lift flagging spirits or motivate tired bodies. He appreciated his longtime friend for that ability, even if it could get annoying in the long haul, when he was so exhausted he could hardly put one foot in front of the other. Still, he was glad for the jokes.

Craig had plowed a long enough line again for Shane to widen it. He held his canister filled with two-thirds diesel and one-third gasoline in his gloved right hand. The backfire torch had a ten-inch-long spout, with the igniter extending beyond the nozzle. He walked across Craig's bare line toward the blaze, lit the wick, held down the nozzle, and set the dry grass on fire. Yellow-orange flames leaped upward as he kept moving down the far side of the line, setting a firebreak.

As he lit the fire, he kept an ear out for the backup beep of Craig's dozer, along with news over the radio. If he heard Craig start to back up, he knew to turn and run because Craig would never give ground unless the fire had turned fast, furious, and out of control. If that happened, he'd be more vulnerable than ever, not only to the fire but also to being run over by the dozer.

For now, he made steady progress behind Craig, widening the line as the sun slowly sank in the west. He didn't want to be out after dark because it'd make his job harder, but he'd be there—like all firefighters—till the job was done. He was having more and more trouble breathing as smoke from his backfires met the original blaze coming toward them. He coughed, leaned down, tried to breath, but it wasn't enough. He couldn't afford to take a chance on blacking out from smoke inhalation, so he got down on his knees, where the air was better.

He didn't like to crawl on the ground beside a raging brush fire while backfiring with a flammable torch. But he did it anyway, continuing to fire the dry grass as he gasped for breath. He couldn't stop yet, particularly not now, when so much was at stake.

He felt completely alone in a world of red flames, black ground, and white smoke. He was getting just enough oxygen to keep going, crawling on his hands and knees, dragging the canister, raising it, lowering it, then struggling forward as he followed the dozer again. In that woozy state, he saw Eden starring in her own video from gangly kid to prom star to radio host to back at the Den. Somehow, she looked right at him out of her video, eyes wide in alarm as she pointed toward red-orange flames.

For some reason, her action galvanized him. He snapped out of his dream state, realizing that he was prone on the ground with flames arching over the bare line toward him. He took a deep breath, or as deep as he could get, and realized he was hearing the *beep-beep-beep* of the dozer backing up. If he didn't move, he'd get run over. Beyond that, he heard Slade calling his name over the radio, demanding he answer or give up all thoughts of pie and beer. They must have been trying to reach him for some time. He coughed and choked as he realized he was oxygen deprived. He couldn't get on the radio to reassure them until he could breathe properly again.

Had they met in the middle, or had the fire overtaken the dozers, sending them all scrambling to safety at the barn? He wasn't thinking straight. He didn't know and couldn't tell from Slade's shouting over the radio and Craig's dozer's *beep-beep-beep*.

He struggled to his feet, shaking his head to try and clear it. He could hear the roaring of the fire and smell the scorched earth. He started one last backfire, then, clutching the heavy canister against his heaving chest, he took off running and stumbling on leaden feet back toward the barn, hearing the dozer right behind him, gaining ground as it came faster and faster. He doubted Craig could see him for the smoke, and he didn't have enough breath to answer Slade or Hedy, who'd now taken up calling his name. He didn't want to worry them, but he had just about enough breath and stamina to try and get out of Craig's way.

He cut across pasture, heading uphill as he struggled through tall grass, stumbled over blackberry vines, and gasped for oxygen in the hot, smoky air. He could hear the beeping of the dozer and the snap, crackle, and pop of the brush fire that seemed to follow him every step he took toward safety. When he saw the fences of his ranch were still white up ahead, he took a deep breath of fresh air and grinned in triumph. He'd made it. He felt relieved, tried, hungry, and thirsty, but those were all fixable as soon as he got home. Sweet home.

He turned to look behind him and saw two dozers

covered in soot trundling up the line. Jim Bob trudged along behind them, carrying his fire torch in one hand and his fire rake in the other. Best of all, the fire line they'd worked so hard to create held back the blaze. They'd won.

Shane keyed his radio for dispatch. "Hedy, the fire's under control."

"That's what I hear," she responded in her no-nonsense voice. "Did you decide to take a nap or something?"

"Yeah, something."

"Full debrief later."

"Right."

"By the by, Slade says you lost the bet. He says you owe pie all around. Craig says beer."

Shane chuckled as he walked toward the fence. "How does Slade know they won? Maybe I was checking the halfway mark."

"Is there a mark?"

"Doubtful. But I'm ready to argue the point."

"No doubt." She cleared her throat. "Want my personal opinion?"

"Sure."

"I'd call the Chuckwagon and say you're buying pie for all the firefighters. And then—"

"Do you want me to admit defeat?"

"Hear me out."

"Okay."

"Call Wildcat Hall and say you're buying all the firefighters beer."

"Sure, I can do that, and sure, I can pay later. But why?"

Hedy gave a deep, rich chuckle. "If you go straight

back to the Den, I bet there's a gal just waiting for you there."

Shane couldn't keep the smile off his face. "Not get cleaned up?"

"You got my point. Jack and Eden have been worried sick…and not just about the fire. But they didn't let it stop them doing their jobs. She's been getting reports from me, and he's been staying on the air to keep the county in the loop. I'm proud of them both."

"Thanks, Hedy." He watched the others go through the gate near his barn. He hurried to catch up with them. "I'll send the firefighters back to the station, then I'll go to the Den. It's only right I give them details about the fire in person."

"Good idea. Glad you thought of it."

"I'm just full of good ideas."

Hedy chuckled again. "I bet you are. And don't think this lets you off the hook. You still have a report to file come tomorrow."

"You got it."

"For now, I'm sending out fresh firefighters with the two old boosters to keep watch till the fire is completely out with no chance of reigniting."

"Sounds great. We could use a break." He clicked off, then grinned as he walked up to his friends clustered near the barn. "Hedy's sending the other boosters with fresh teams, so we're off duty pretty quick."

"Just what I wanted to hear." Slade pulled off his helmet, giving Shane a sideways glance. "You just had to go and create some drama out there, didn't you?"

"I didn't want you to be disappointed since you lost the bet."

"Lost?" Jim Bob hollered. "How do you figure that? We couldn't even find you."

"I was marking the middle to make sure there was no doubt about who won," Shane said with a straight face as he teased them.

"It's possible," Craig said, backing up his partner.

"Did you fall and bump your head?" Slade pushed his point, glancing mischievously all around.

Shane shucked off his gloves, tucked them in a pocket, then walked over to his truck, opened the door, and pulled out his cell. "I'm not agreeing or disagreeing about who won our bet, but I'm a magnanimous kind of guy." He hit speed dial. "Maybelline, Shane Taggart here. I'm sending you a bunch of sorry-looking firefighters for pie. Give them as much as they can eat. I'll cover the check tomorrow. Right. Slade, too." He clicked off as he gave the others a challenging look to agree or disagree with him.

"I'm suspicious of your motives," Slade said, pulling off his helmet.

"I've only got the best firefighter's interests at heart." Shane hit speed dial again. "Shane Taggart here. Hardworking firefighters will be coming to your place for beer and pretzels. I'll pay their bill tomorrow. Right. Let them drink their fill." Shane set his phone back in his truck, wondering how his generosity would be taken by the others.

"Now I'm really waiting for the other shoe to drop." Slade nodded at Jim Bob. "You believe what you're hearing?"

"Sure," Jim Bob said. "We ought to have him mark the middle every time. I don't care why he's covering our tabs, but let's get going before he changes his mind."

"Okay." Slade motioned toward Shane. "We'll take the gear and rigs back to Hedy, then meet you at the Chuckwagon."

"You go on," Shane said. "I've got something else to do."

"What?" Slade looked around the group in astonishment. "When's he ever got anything better to do?" He stopped, gave Shane a suspicious look, then glanced down the hill toward the Wildcat Den. Finally, he gave an all-knowing grin. "Guess you wouldn't have any reason to stop by the radio station to give them an update, would you?"

Shane shrugged, wondering how Slade had guessed his intentions so fast—namely that he wanted to get rid of the other firefighters so he could cut a straight line to Eden.

"Eden Rafferty's back in town and suddenly Shane don't have time for his old firefighting buddies." Slade gave everyone a sad look while obviously trying to contain a big grin. "That just takes the cake—or pie in this case."

"Go on." Shane pointed toward the other side of the double gate, then down the ranch's main lane. "Here come the boosters. Y'all need to get back to Hedy and give her a report."

"Wait till she hears how you stood us up for a lady-love," Slade said in his deep voice.

"I never said that's what I was going to do." Shane quickly shrugged out of his jacket. "I just said—"

"You're leaving more for the rest of us. I'm headed

for the Hall." Craig tipped his helmet to Shane, then tucked it under his arm. "We'll catch you tomorrow."

"Right," Shane said, hardly hearing Craig's words because he was already thinking about Eden and how maybe he'd gotten a burn or abrasion or something on his face that she could tend to—up at his house.

As the firefighters piled into their vehicles and headed down the road, he got into his pickup and followed behind them. When he reached the turnoff to KWCB, he hesitated as he watched the others continued on to Wildcat Road.

He noticed a small sedan in a nondescript color, probably almost invisible anywhere except pickup country, parked on the side of the road just beyond the entry to his ranch, which was odd.

He glanced up at the Den, then back at the car. He didn't want to take the time, but he'd better check in case the stranger needed help. He took off down the lane, figuring that, if necessary, he could call for a tow into Wildcat Bluff.

Even odder, when he reached the cattle guard to exit his ranch, the vehicle tore off, sending gravel flying as the driver gunned his engine and zigzagged down Wildcat Road, as if not wanting to be seen. Shane caught a glimpse of a person wearing sunglasses and a hood pulled up around the face. A man, he figured, but he couldn't be sure.

All in all, it was definitely one for the books, but with the fire in the local news, lookie-loos weren't out of the question. He'd also been trained to keep an eye out for someone watching a fire because frequently arsonists stayed around to see their handiwork. In this case, he knew fires had been set on the Lazy Q, but it was within the realm of possibility that somebody could have taken advantage of the situation to start an extra fire closer to the radio station and his ranch house. Maybe his mind was working overtime, but he still didn't like a stranger watching the ranch, not with Eden living there again.

For now, there wasn't much he could do, but he'd definitely keep a lookout for that vehicle or somebody else lurking nearby. He rubbed his face on the back of his sleeve and turned his truck around, heading for the radio station. And Eden.

Chapter 13

EDEN PACED BACK AND FORTH ACROSS THE SCARRED OAK floor of the Wildcat Den, checking from one window to the other for any sign of Shane or the other firefighters. She could smell smoke inside, and she could see smoke outside billowing up out of the pastures into the sky overhead. Neither was a good sign. Still, Hedy kept reassuring her by phone that their firefighters were on the job. Yes, but were they winning the battle of the blaze? And even more important, were they safe? She couldn't help but worry.

She paced faster, glancing through the window of the studio, where Jack continued talking to the county's listeners, making chitchat, spinning vinyl, and giving weather reports—unfortunately, dry and gusty. She'd never felt so tense in a radio station before because she was trained to be calm, like a firefighter, no matter how horrific the circumstances. The public needed her voice to be steady and confident when she shared updates and news. Right now, she didn't feel calm or steady, and she knew she'd be hard-pressed to speak with her throat so tight. Fortunately, Wildcat Jack was as smooth and reliable as ever while he relayed information and gave reassurance.

She glanced at the ancient square rotary phone on one corner of the station's beat-up wooden desk. She'd placed her cell beside it, old technology versus new technology, black versus color, heavy versus light. Both were excellent communication devices. She didn't care which rang first, just as long as Hedy or Shane called with good news.

She waited, pacing even faster as if every footstep would bring Shane, and all the other firefighters, safely home. She felt drawn back into the center of Wildcat Bluff's community, and with that feeling, she wondered how she could have been so bold as to suggest to Shane that they have no-strings-attached sex. Maybe that'd be okay in LA, Phoenix, or Dallas. But in Wildcat Bluff? She felt like a child caught with her hand in the cookie jar. What would people think if they knew what she wanted from him? Or maybe nobody would be surprised at all... He was definitely a hunk of a cowboy. Still, she wondered about the small-town versus big-city viewpoint. Could she really fit back into this world?

As she pondered her future in Wildcat Bluff and the future of the Den, she heard footsteps on the stairs outside. She whirled, her heart in her throat. Paramedics due to injuries in the field? Firefighters with evacuation orders? Sheriff and deputies here to close down Wildcat Road?

As the front door squeaked open on unoiled hinges, she felt her breath catch in anticipation. She'd be calm and helpful and supportive no matter what the news or situation. If she couldn't speak past the lump in her throat, she had pen and paper nearby on the desk. One way or another, she'd communicate. She'd do anything to help Shane and the other firefighters.

When Shane stepped inside, she felt as if she'd been granted a reprieve. His gear was covered in soot and dust and his work boots were caked with dirt. A broken twig had somehow lodged under a corner of the Wildcat Bluff Fire-Rescue shield on the front of his red helmet. He smelled of the great outdoors. Wild, free, dangerous. And burnt. He looked okay—more than okay. He looked gloriously alive. And he was smiling, so all the firefighters must be okay, and the station and the ranch as well. He looked good enough to hold to her heart.

He pulled off his helmet and tucked it under one arm. He rubbed a hand across his face, smearing soot and dirt and sweat in dark patches, then he pushed back his damp hair. Despite it all, he gave a big grin of triumph.

She returned his smile even as she froze, feeling rooted to the floor because she was suddenly overcome with one thought and one thought only—*he was her hero*.

With this sudden rush of clarity, she realized he'd always been her hero because he'd been there for her through thick and thin when they were young. How had she ever thought she could feel no emotion for him? How had she ever thought sex could be enough between them? How had she ever thought he was just a passing fancy?

Yes, he was her hero. But he was so much more than that. He was a star in Wildcat Bluff. And in her world. He'd always said she was the big star from hometown to Tinseltown, but he was wrong. He was the bigger star because he put his life on the line to save worlds from going up in flames, while she simply reported on them while staying safely at a distance. Suddenly, she felt shy in his presence.

"Wanted to let you know we're all safe." He coughed

several times. "Ranch is safe. Fire is controlled. Wildcat Spring isn't in danger."

He obviously expected her to say something. She wanted to reply, but her throat was too tight with all the emotions swirling within her.

"Smoke steal your voice? It almost did mine." He coughed harder, trying to clear his lungs.

Still, she didn't speak. How did you talk to a superstar? And then she was struck by another revelation. Had he seen her as a superstar when they were younger and felt shy in her presence just as she now did with him? If so, they stood on either side of a wide river with only a narrow hanging bridge dangling between them. One wrong step onto the bridge could set it swaying, swinging, tossing either of them into the rapids far below.

They weren't just on opposing sides of Wildcat Spring and everything they both held dear—they saw each other as bigger than life, with all the baggage that entailed when trying to close the gap between them. She didn't see how they could overcome either monumental obstacle.

And then she realized she was overthinking the situation, just as she'd been doing with everything in her life since Graham had destroyed her world. She didn't trust her own instincts anymore. She tended to second guess every little thing. Somehow, someway, she needed to learn to trust again. She needed to get her life back together—not just for herself but because Shane deserved it, too.

"Are you okay?" Concern darkened his hazel eyes.

"Yes," she finally managed to whisper, feeling more frustrated than ever that her voice wasn't at full strength. "I was just so worried about you and the other firefighters."

"We're all okay now," he reassured in a husky voice.

She reached out to him because he appeared as rooted to his spot on the floor as she was to her spot. Maybe they'd moved too fast with each other. Maybe they needed time and space to develop their relationship. Maybe she shouldn't have said anything about sex earlier. And there she went again, analyzing pros and cons when she simply wanted to throw her arms around him.

He stepped toward her, moving to bridge the distance between them with his body as well as the longing in his eyes. "I just stopped by to give you and Jack the good news."

"Thanks." She felt as if their words were superfluous, repetitive. Their bodies were speaking for them, drawing them together like two magnets that couldn't stay apart.

Just as they touched fingertips, the studio door burst open, causing them to jerk apart.

Wildcat Jack poked his head out, looked around, and gave Shane a thumbs-up. "Saw you out there and figured you wouldn't be here if you didn't have good news. Besides, Hedy called to tell me the fire was contained. Congratulations!"

"Thank you," Shane said. "Wildcat Bluff Fire-Rescue deserves all the credit. We're a team."

"After saving lives and property, what's on the agenda now?" Jack cocked his head to one side and grinned as he gave Shane a once-over. "Are you planning to leave soot all over the county?"

"Yep," Shane said, teasing right back. "I'm wearing enough to coat the entire area."

"Nobody'll care," Eden said. "You're our hero."

Jack chuckled as he looked from her to Shane. "That right? You're our new Wildcat Bluff hero? I thought you were Mr. June."

Shane gave a big sigh as he looked down, tried to dust off some of the debris covering the front of his jacket, and stopped the effort as soot drifted to the floor. "If I never hear another word about that calendar, it'll be too soon."

"Never mind me," Jack said. "I'm just jealous Sydney didn't think to put out an old geezers calendar. Now that'd have really brought in the bucks. Get to be my age, and we guys are as scarce as hen's teeth. I'm here to tell you that gives us an exalted status all our own. If I didn't want to cook another meal for the rest of my life, there'd be plenty of ladies willing to do me proud."

"Maybe they'd even pack a picnic basket for a bit of skinny-dipping this summer." Shane teased Jack back with a big grin.

Jack laughed harder, giving Eden a just-shy-of-embarrassed look. "I wish, but I'm not sure my heart's up to it anymore."

"You've always been a heartthrob," Eden said, smiling. "I'm sure you always will be."

"If you're looking for a PR job, you've got it." Jack gave her a wink, then turned back to Shane. "What are you doing hanging around here now that all the excitement's over?"

Shane backed up a step and put his hand on the doorknob. "Yeah, I guess I'd better go and get cleaned up and all."

"Where's the crew?" Jack demanded, trying to see behind Shane.

"Pretty quick, they'll be down at the Chuckwagon eating pie or over at the Hall drinking beer or sarsaparilla."

"And they left you behind to…?"

"I'm buying," Shane said, shrugging his wide shoulders.

"Okay by me. I'm eating and drinking." Jack quickly turned toward the sound studio. "I've worked as hard as you firefighters this afternoon, so I deserve a reward, too."

"Right," Shane said.

"Give me a chance to spool up Rae Dell, so she keeps the county company while I stuff my gullet." Jack opened the door, then looked back. "Eden, are you coming with me?"

"I, well, no. I'd better close up here."

Jack glanced quickly from Eden to Shane, then back again. "Don't bother. I'll return and tidy up. Seems to me you better get this firefighter up to his house, get him cleaned up, and get him fed before he collapses from smoke inhalation or whatnot."

Eden quickly focused on Shane. "I didn't think. Smoke. Are you hurt?"

"That's right," Jack said. "Hedy told me Shane got too much smoke in his lungs but is too proud to admit it or go to the clinic."

"Shane!" Eden felt horrified that she hadn't realized he'd been injured and that's why he wasn't out celebrating with the other firefighters. "I'll drive you to the clinic right now."

"No." Shane held out a hand to stop her.

"Hedy said best thing for him was to give him a lot of liquids and maybe a sojourn in his hot tub to flush out all the impurities."

"I never heard that remedy before." Eden sounded skeptical. "Hedy said that?"

"Or something close to it." Jack backed into the studio. "Best get on your way. Shane's looking pretty unsteady on his feet."

"Hot tub?" Shane asked, giving Jack a puzzled look.

"Don't look a gift horse in the mouth." Jack glared before he slammed the door behind him.

"Hot tub?" Eden echoed. "Aren't you already too hot?"

"Steam, I guess." Shane nodded with a confident smile. "I think they're trying to explain I need to breathe steam to clean out my lungs."

"That makes a little more sense."

"Now that Jack mentioned it, I am feeling a little woozy on my feet." He coughed into his hand.

"I knew it!" Eden jerked open a drawer of the desk, pulled out her purse, and stuffed her cell into it. "It's just like you to be hurt and not want to admit it."

"I'm not that bad off. I just need to get home."

"If you're sure about the clinic, I'll drive you up to your house."

"Not in that VW, you won't."

"I don't know what you've got against poor little Betty."

"Don't get me started." He felt around in his pocket, pulled out his keys, and tossed them to her. "Let's take my truck for safety's sake. You can drive."

She caught his keys in midair and curled her fingers around them, feeling the heat from his body start delicious warmth that spread throughout her.

"I don't want to put you out." He leaned wearily back against the doorjamb. "You could just run me home before you join the others for pie or beer or—"

"Stop right there. You're not going to distract me with goodies." She opened the door, then urged him outside where the stench of fire still hung in the air. "I remember that time you fell off Ole Blaze, conking your head and splitting it right open. I'd never seen so much blood."

"Who knew that old bag of bones had a run left in him?" He peeled off his jacket and helmet as they walked to the truck.

"And who knew you'd do practically anything to keep from getting stitches."

Shane reached up and rubbed his forehead just at the hairline. "Yeah, I've had you on my mind every morning when I see that scar."

"Me? I didn't do anything to cause it."

"You snitched to my mom, or she'd never have known."

"What about all that blood?"

"I'd have thrown away the shirt."

"Right. I'm sure she'd never have noticed a missing shirt." Eden rolled her eyes, trying not to laugh at their old argument. He'd always been falling out of a tree or roping without gloves or skinning some part of his body for another reason. She'd always been the one to patch him up or see that he was doctored. Maybe times hadn't changed that much after all.

"Well, if she had noticed, I could've blamed something or somebody." He opened the passenger door, eased down inside, and picked up a bottle of water.

She joined him, flipped on the headlights, started the engine, and headed out. "As usual, I'll just have to make sure you live to see another day."

"Thanks." And he gave her a sly smile.

Chapter 14

EDEN DROVE UP THE CIRCULAR DRIVE TO THE FRONT OF Shane's ranch house, forgoing the three-car garage since it'd take more time and be more effort for him to get inside from there. She parked the pickup and then glanced over at him. He looked bone weary.

"Is this okay?" she asked. "Do you need help getting inside?"

"I'm fine. I just need to get cleaned up, eat, and rest a bit." He finished the bottle of water and tossed the empty on the floorboard.

"What about the hot tub?"

"That's on my to-do list." He opened the truck door. "Why don't you change into your swimsuit while I get a shower?"

"I don't have a swimsuit. I don't think I even brought one from LA."

He gave her a sidelong glance. "I bet you'll find one of your old ones in the guest room."

"My stuff is still there?"

"Guess so. I haven't changed much of anything since Mom and Dad passed, and Mom would never have thrown out anything of yours."

"Really? That's so touching." She put a hand over her heart, feeling the love she'd felt for her second mom almost overwhelm her.

"Either that, or she was a pack rat." He chuckled as

he stepped out of the truck, leaving his helmet and jacket behind.

Eden smiled, glad he'd made light of the moment, so she could get her own emotions under control. She quickly got out and hurried up to the double hand-carved oak doors. She felt as if life had rolled backward. How many times had she thrown open these doors and rushed inside on some errand or another? Now she was here with Shane again, as if no time had passed at all.

"I've got your keys, so let me open the doors," she said, trying to be practical now that she was here.

"No need." He quickly thrust wide both doors and gestured for her to precede him inside.

"I see you're still not locking your doors any more than Jack is locking the station." She handed him back his car keys, almost regretting the loss of their connection to him.

"No need to around here—or there wasn't any need. Now you're back, I think you ought to start locking the Den and Clem's place."

"Maybe so." She'd think about that later, after she'd had time to settle in and take stock of everything.

Right now, she needed to stay focused on Shane. He liked to think he was invincible, but he was probably suffering more than he wanted to admit. She suspected he'd inhaled way too much smoke. There was a hitch in his breathing and soot around his nostrils.

She stepped into his home that appeared warm and cozy from the ebbing sunset's pink-and-gold glow coming in through four windows at the top of the front wall. Dark oak beams ran the length of the vaulted ceiling straight to matching windows on the far side of the house.

She felt her breath catch in her throat at the unchanged beauty of the open floor plan that had always greeted her. A huge rock fireplace took up most of one wall with natural leather couches and armchairs arranged around it. The grand piano stood in its usual place, just waiting for Shane's mom to return and play those classical pieces by Mozart and Schubert that she'd loved so much.

"What is it?" Shane walked up behind her and put a hand on her shoulder. "Is the house smaller than you remember? It's like that sometimes when you see something familiar after going from child to adult."

"I expect your mom to walk out of the kitchen smelling of cookies or some other treat she's baked for us."

He squeezed, letting his fingers trail down her upper arm before he dropped his hand to his side. "I know. Hits me that way sometimes, too, but I haven't the heart to make a lot of changes. I'd hardly know where to start anyway."

"No need." As she glanced around, she realized the house had become frozen sometime in the late eighties, when the redecoration had been the pride and joy of Shane's mom. It was an unusual sight after all the update and upscale she'd seen in LA.

"I redid the old rec room over the garage into my bedroom with an attached bath, so I'm there now. I'll get a shower and meet you by the pool. If you need anything, just holler or find it yourself." He tweaked the tip of her nose like the old days, tossed his keys on the entry table, then headed toward a hall. "Remember, my house is your house."

Suddenly alone in the echoing main room, Eden felt a chill run up her spine. How often had she stood just like this in the past? But there was a big difference now—quiet and stillness, instead of noise and activity. Shane's home felt almost forlorn, as if it were waiting for his family life to begin again. She shook her head, tossing off her maudlin thoughts. She was here to get Shane on his feet, nothing more and nothing less.

Yet, as she moved deeper into the house, she felt old feelings and memories come alive. She'd always felt welcome here, and she still did. When she opened the door to the guest bedroom that had been next door to Shane's room, tears stung her eyes. Nothing had changed—*absolutely nothing*. It was like coming home. How could that be? And yet, Shane had told her. Still, it was hard to believe.

She carefully stepped onto the oak floor, feeling like if she disturbed the scene, it might all disappear. She took another step, and nothing changed, so she eased cautiously to the center of the room. She slowly turned in a circle, cataloging everything in sight.

Cowgirl, oh yes, here was the feminine cowgirl room that had yellow wallpaper with pink and blue flowers accented with a narrow oak chair railing around the entire room, a blue-wood-pattern wallpaper under it. The double bed had four thick pine posters with scalloped wood in between for head- and footboards. There was also a matching dresser, cabinet, and bench. A soft-blue bedspread with pink pillows that Shane's mom had hand stitched with a horse-and-cow design still beckoned her to snuggle. An oil painting of a cowgirl riding hard across a prairie graced one wall, while the sheer, blue drapes that covered a large three-paned window had been pulled back to let in sunshine.

She walked slowly across the floor, running her fingers lightly over the bedspread, and ended up at the window. As always, she could see the swimming pool below. Within the protective iron fence, Shane had added a glossy, new hot tub, a fancy barbecue grill, and several comfy-looking chaises. The original table that seated eight was still in its place in the shade of the house.

She abruptly felt weak, as if she couldn't stand a moment longer. She sat down on the bench, simply shaking her head. How had she ever let this go? Let Shane go? Let her Wildcat Bluff life go? And yet she knew, had always known, that she was the one who was supposed to carry their dual family legacy out into the world and make it big-time. Well, she had done it. She'd given all she had to give to fulfill their dream and make them proud.

But now she didn't owe anybody anything. She didn't even have to restore the radio station or keep the spring. She could finally let them go. It'd make Shane happy. And maybe it'd make her happy, too. Nobody needed her for anything anymore. She was free in a way she'd never been in her life. She could still live in her uncle's quaint Quonset hut, healing her wounds, getting back on her feet, choosing a new path.

And yet, was that truly what she wanted in life? She shrugged, not knowing anymore, so she got to her feet and looked out the window again. This time, she didn't see the pool, the hot tub, the table, or anything except Shane. In contrast to his firefighter gear, he wasn't wearing much—just faded denim cutoffs that left way too much bronze flesh stretched across broad shoulders and washboard abs. He could be instantly booked for a swimwear photo shoot, but she didn't want to share him with other women, not even a photo of him.

Suddenly, she realized that she did want something after all, something very special, and that something had a name and one name only: *Shane Taggart*. And she had him all to herself this very moment.

She tossed the past into the dustbin of history as she whirled and crossed the room in one fluid motion. She jerked open the first drawer of the dresser, but she saw only rows of neatly stacked underwear in many colors. When had she left so much here? She doubted it'd fit anymore. She tried the next drawer. Cotton socks. Another drawer yielded old T-shirts from country bands. And jean cutoffs. Finally, she found the bathing suits. Two of them. She chuckled at the sight. They were both one-piece, typical of what she'd worn in Wildcat Bluff. She hoped at least one would fit, or at least near enough to get by.

She tossed her purse on the bed and stripped off her clothing, glad the last bikini wax she'd endured in LA was still good. She couldn't fit into the green-and-pink-striped suit, so she tried the basic black. She'd recently lost weight, so she was able to shimmy into it, although she was revealing deeper cleavage than when she had been a skinny teenager.

She checked the bathroom for a towel, smiling at the sight of the blue porcelain sink, tub, and tile with pink and blue towels just waiting to be used again. She grabbed two fluffy towels off a rack, wrapped one around her middle, and carried the other as she hurried out of the room, shutting the door behind her.

After she rounded the corner in the back of the living area that overlooked the pool, she stopped and caught her breath. She shouldn't push Shane. He needed to recover from fighting a fire. She ought to be gentle with him—food, water, rest. Yes, that's what he needed instead of a hotheaded cowgirl bent on seeing to her own desires.

She retraced her steps to the kitchen. Nothing had changed here, either, not from the warm wood cabinets to the white tile counter tops to the oversized refrigerator fronted by a matching wood cabinet. She opened a cabinet door and pulled out a wooden tray with a barbwire motif, set two aqua glasses on it, then snagged four bottles of cold water out of the fridge, along with cheese and apples. She found crackers in the pantry and added them to the tray, along with paper plates and napkins.

By the time she headed back outside, she was feeling hungry, so she figured Shane must be starving by now. And yet when she stepped out of the sliding glass door to join him by the hot tub, all squeaky clean now, with wet hair slicked back, she lost all appetite for the food in her hands. She felt hungrier than ever, but now she wanted only him.

She could hardly remember that when she'd landed in Wildcat Bluff, she'd been sporting a protective wall several inches thick. Shane had chipped away at the bricks or she'd thrown them away, until she now stood before him with nothing more between them than her skimpy bathing suit.

He looked over at her, light dancing in his hazel eyes. He glanced at the tray, then at her lips. "What have you got for me? Anything good?"

"Anything you want." She knew her words came out husky, sultry, by invitation only, but she still wasn't in complete control of her voice. At least she could use that as an excuse for the effect she seemed to cause in him, going by the way his eyes suddenly darkened and how he looked from her lips to her breasts straining against the too-small swimsuit.

"Anything?" He sounded husky, too, as if his voice was no longer his to control or maybe still rough from smoke inhalation.

She quickly set the tray down on the table, determinedly reminding herself that he'd just risked life and limb in a fire. He was probably hoarse from breathing so much smoke. He was probably sore from lugging a canister. He was probably exhausted from running all over pastures. But he looked like none of those things when she turned and saw him walking to her.

He appeared much more like a wildcat stalking his prey. And she was supper.

She felt a delicious chill run up her spine as she reached up and stroked her palm over the hard contour of his chest so very slowly, until she covered the hard nub of his nipple.

"Did I get everything?" She tried to remind them both that she was there to help him recover, but the idea seemed far, far away, as if it belonged to a different time and different people in a different country.

"You've got it all." He covered her hand with his own large, strong one and pressed her fingers tightly over his heart. "You've always had everything I could ever need or want."

And with those words, he leaned down, slipped the towel from her waist so he could wrap her tightly to him, and kissed her lips.

Chapter 15

SHANE FELT EDEN SHIVER AND WONDERED IF SHE WAS COLD but hoped she was responding to his touch. He raised his head and looked into her blue eyes turned dark with desire. Not cold. Response. This was midnight on Lovers Leap all over again.

But what had it gotten them? *Nothing*. Where had it gotten them? *Nowhere*. Was it worth taking a chance again? *Yes*.

"Oh," she said, gazing deep into his eyes, "I forgot. You made me forget. I'm supposed to make sure you drink, eat, and lounge in the hot tub."

"When you're dressed like that?"

She glanced down, jerked up her towel, and tied the corners together above her breasts as she backed away from him. "Don't say another word. Just get in the hot tub. I'll take the tray over there."

"It's not like I'm going to forget what I saw."

"Not another word. Just get in the water."

He nodded in reluctant agreement and trudged over to the hot tub. Hedy's brilliant plan was disintegrating before his very eyes. He'd have to tell her later that she was nowhere near a master strategist. For now, he simply got in the water and sat down, letting the water bubble around his chest. Maybe the hot tub wasn't such a bad idea after all. It did feel pretty good after such a challenge of a day.

But it didn't feel nearly as good as Eden looked when she sashayed over to him, set the tray down, tossed off her towel, and slid into the water beside him. He'd have to be comatose not to respond to her every single allure—all of which were now emblazoned on his mind like delicate curls and whorls etched into stained glass. He took a deep breath, wondering how he was going to keep his hands off her while she helped him or if he should even try.

"I brought sparkling water and spring water. Which would you like to drink?"

"Either one." He began to suspect she wasn't going to give him a choice about hands-on or hands-off.

"Let's go with plain first, since I don't want to irritate your throat."

"Fine." How the hell had he managed to get Eden into a swimsuit, into his hot tub, and still get treated like an invalid? He'd mismanaged a major part of the strategy at some point, but he was clueless about how, where, and why. He might as well blame Hedy and be done with it or acknowledge that he could fight a fire but not woo a woman. It was a sad testimony to his life.

"Here you go." She held out a blue glass in a hand with pale-pink nails.

"Where'd you get that?"

"What?"

"The glass."

"In the upper right cabinet where your mom always kept these glasses."

"I haven't seen them in ages."

"What've you been using?"

He realized too late that he'd taken another wrong

turn, so he just grabbed the glass and tossed half the water down his throat.

"Really, Shane, what have you drinking out of?"

"Let's see." He just shook his head, knowing where this was going and unable to back out. "If it comes in a bottle, I drink out of it. If it comes in a can, I drink out of it. Any other questions about how I drink liquids?"

"No." She appeared to shrink in on herself. "I just wondered and wanted—never mind. I guess that was rude of me."

"No." He downed the rest of the water and handed the glass back to her. "Maybe you know the house better than I do. I could tell you what's where in the cattle barn or the horse barn, but household stuff is not at the top of my need-to-know list."

"Right," she said briskly. "That's as it should be, with all you have to do around the ranch."

He hoped she meant those words, since they were true, but also true was the fact that the place had needed a cowgirl's touch for a long time. He missed those homey splashes of warm cookies served on pretty plates at the family table, inside or outside. But he wasn't about to do it for one lone cowboy or even firefighters when he invited them over for a cookout. Paper and plastic ruled the day when he served up beans and beef. Paper towels were better than napkins any day. Still, Eden reminded him of what life had once been like on the Rocky T Ranch. Only now did he realize how much he'd missed it.

"Here. Enjoy." She held out a red-bandana-design paper plate and matching napkin toward him.

"Thanks. I will."

He looked at the fun plate with its pretty arrangement of food, but he'd lost his appetite for anything except her. He could blame her for making him lose every last bit of sense he ever had when he was with her, but he wouldn't place all the blame on her, even if he did feel like he'd been kicked upside the head by a horse when he was with her.

He abruptly stood up, water cascading down his body back into the hot tub. He looked down at her. It was a bad angle because he could see the full shape of her breasts and her taut nipples. He had to get away, or he was going to grab her and meet the expectation in her blue eyes. Yeah, he'd agreed to sex earlier, but now that they were this close to fulfilling that agreement, he suddenly felt protective of her. How many men in LA had bird-dogged her, wanting simply to be with her or take what was quick and easy? How many ways had her ex connived to con her? How many times had her innocence been used against her? She deserved better—from him, at least.

"You stay. Enjoy the hot tub. I'm going to my room," he said with his last bit of self-control.

She rose out of the water, all sleek wet skin and tantalizing curves. "But your food… Do you feel sick?"

"I'm going to lie down." He stepped out of the water. "If you need the truck, the keys are where I tossed them."

He was through the sliding doors so fast it almost made his head spin, dripping water all the way to his suite above the garages. He stalked in through the open door and went straight to the bathroom done up just the way he wanted it with big tub, big shower, double sink, and deep cabinets in shades of gray with black accents.

He jerked off his cutoffs and threw them in the tub, then walked into his bedroom, tossed back the black cover on his king-size bed, and slid in between gray sheets. He gazed blankly up at the huge media screen on the wall just waiting to be turned on for distraction, then over at the telescope that allowed him to check out his pastures all the way to Wildcat Road through his triple windows that overlooked the front of the house.

But nothing could distract him from the tent he was making under his sheet nor make the ultrafine fabric feel any less rough.

He was starved, but not for food or drink. He hungered after only one thing in life—*Eden Rafferty*. He crossed his arms behind his head. He knew damn good and well that nothing could ease the ache, the passion, the need that was going to ride him so long as she was back in Wildcat Bluff.

When a shadow appeared in his open doorway, he couldn't believe his eyes. He blinked, tried to focus, and blinked again. Eden stepped into his room wearing nothing but an old, ratty, green plaid cowboy shirt of his from days long gone. He vaguely remembered loaning it to her one time. It fit her better than it would him now, hugging her in all the right places with the shirt tails riding about the center of her thighs, showing off her long legs.

He pulled the black spread over the sheet to conceal his condition, made even more painful by her presence. "Eden, what are you doing here?"

"Did you really think you could get rid of me so easily?"

"I don't want food or water."

"I didn't bring any."

"Then why are you here?"

"Aren't you still hungry?" She padded softly into his bedroom on bare feet.

"I'm not playing games."

"I'm hungry."

"Then go down to the kitchen." If she came any closer, he was going to spontaneously combust. She'd have to call the firefighters—unless she put out the fire all on her own.

"What I want isn't in the kitchen." She walked into the center of the room, undid the top buttons of his shirt, and let it drop slowly down her body to pool on the floor.

She took his breath away, so that he had no more words, no more excuses, no more anything except desperate desire. She was beautiful, from the tawny hair of her head to her peach-painted toenails. And he lusted after everything in between from her pink-tipped breasts to her indented navel to the triangle between her thighs to her shapely legs. He wanted it all. And he wanted it now. Any good intentions he'd had went right out the window.

He drew his covers down to his waist and scooted over in bed, so he was in the center, with plenty of room for her to join him. "Is this what you want?"

"I want what I've always wanted since that midnight up on Lovers Leap." She stalked toward him, then stopped and put a hand on her hip.

"Why did you leave me?" he asked.

"I couldn't stay."

"When you get what you want, will you leave me again?"

"I don't want to talk about tomorrow or the next day

or the day after that. Let's talk about now—right this very moment."

"I don't want to talk at all." And he tossed back the covers to reveal what she did to him.

She smiled as she looked him over, returning again and again to the long, hard, hot center of him. "Would you care to share?"

"I'd care a whole lot more if I couldn't share."

She placed a knee on the edge of the bed, leaned over, and kissed him gently—almost serenely—on his lips. As she did so, her breasts swung forward, teasing his chest, making his belly clench, winding him up. He groaned deep in his throat as he lost the last of his control and pulled her down on top of him, positioning her body so he could feel her weight pressed tightly against him.

"You know I love you," he said against all his better instincts, making himself vulnerable to her.

"I know." She stretched down the length of him and pushed her fingertips deep into his hair as she pressed light kisses against his forehead, his closed eyelids, his cheekbones, and back to his mouth. "You've always loved me."

"Always," he said, agreeing as he nibbled on her plump lower lip, then licked upward, tasting her sweet tartness. "And you?"

"I love that you love me."

"Oh hell!" And he twisted out from under her, shaking his head to try and clear it. "That's not what you're supposed to say. Couldn't you at least lie and say you love me?"

"Why would I have to lie?" She opened her big blue eyes as she looked at him in wonder.

"I don't know why I fool myself." He ran a hand in

agitation through his hair, well aware that no matter what she said or how she acted, he still had a raging hard-on for her. "You've never loved me."

"Why would you say that?"

"You left." He jerked the cover over them both, wanting to get away from her and yet unable to leave her. "You fell in love and married that good-for-nothing guy." He hesitated, then went with it. "*Not me.*"

She put a hand over her mouth as tears filled her eyes. "You wanted to marry me?"

"Of course!"

"You never said 'love' or 'marriage' or anything." She wiped away tears with the back of her hand, suddenly looking furious.

"How could I when your plans were already made to leave Wildcat Bluff?"

"If you'd said… That's why I went to you on Lovers Leap. If nothing else, I wanted at least that little bit to take with me."

Now he felt angry, trying to figure how the hell, every time they came close, they got into an argument. "Well, you got it. I guess it wasn't enough for you."

"How could it be?"

He quickly slipped the covers off and tossed them to the floor. Nothing stood between them now except the past. And their hunger. "Enough?" He heard his hiss, almost a growl as he got up on his knees and leaned over her. "If you want, I can give you deep enough, hard enough, long enough that you might even think you love me."

She reached up and twined her arms around his neck, pulling him down toward her. "But don't you understand—"

He kissed her, thrusting deep into her mouth. Whatever she had to say, he didn't want to hear it. He only wanted to feel her, taste her, revel in her—at least one more time. And she returned his kiss, revealing a hunger of her own for him as she met him thrust for thrust.

Finally, he lifted her gently, so her head was cushioned on his pillow, and then he smiled at the sight he'd so longed dreamed of seeing in his own bed but never really thought possible. "I love you," he said under his breath as he reached into his nightstand, pulled out a condom, and slipped it on.

He kissed each of her taut nipples, then sucked, drawing out the pleasure for them both, escalating the sensitivity for them both, merging the passion for them both. And then he moved lower, kissing, licking, teasing, till she grasped his shoulders and dug in her nails.

"Enough?" he asked, realizing there might never be enough for either of them.

"Show me." She tossed her head back and forth on his pillow, clutching harder at his shoulders.

When he entered her with one swift thrust, she was ready for him, hot and wet and tight. In the supercharged moment, he was transported back to that night up on Lovers Leap, as if no time at all had elapsed since their first time together and this just-as-magical second time.

She reached up and bit his earlobe, purring, catlike, with pleasure as he drove them higher and higher. And when they spiraled into ecstasy together, he thought he heard her whisper, "I love you."

Yet he couldn't be sure of her words because they were lost in the loud beat of his heart.

Chapter 16

TWO WEEKS LATER, EDEN DECIDED ONCE MORE THAT springtime in North Texas was vastly different than springtime in Southern California. In LA, plants looked a little perkier after their winter tiredness. In Wildcat Bluff, despite the ongoing drought, trees were budding out in vibrant green, wildflowers were springing up in pastures, and daffodils were nodding pretty, yellow heads in a soft, warm breeze from the south.

She felt a satisfied smile transform her face. Perhaps she was particularly attuned to the frolicking birds and bees of spring this year because she was back in Wildcat Bluff—and frequently in Shane Taggart's big, luxurious bed. She knew he had a great deal to do with the smile on her face, but she was also happy to be back at the Wildcat Den with Jack and Ken. Morning Glory's great-nephew was looking happier every day as he did more radio work, sharing new tech with Jack while learning all he could about old tech. He especially loved their collection of vinyl. As far as she knew, Shane hadn't been able to get Ken on the back of a horse yet, but he was handy with a four-wheeler.

All in all, she was speaking more easily and feeling more confident. She didn't need to protect herself so much anymore. She felt safe in the county and on the ranch, where she was no longer harassed by paparazzi or her ex and his minions. She'd taken a chance and recorded a few advertisements for the Chuckwagon Café, and that experience had turned out well. Even if her voice wasn't back to full strength, she was getting there.

Life was good. Unexpectedly so. It'd have been even better if KWCB and Wildcat Spring didn't loom between her and Shane. They'd set their conflicting issue aside for the time being, but she knew they'd have to confront it at some point.

She didn't want to think about losing Shane. She particularly didn't want to now that she was beginning to understand how shallow her feelings must have been for Graham—even when she'd thought she'd loved him—in comparison to how she had always felt about Shane. *Love.* Graham's professed love for her had been a big fat lie. Shane's love she could believe, but he also loved the Rocky T, just as she loved the Wildcat Den. How much stress could love withstand? She didn't know, and she didn't want to learn, but she had an uneasy feeling that, sooner or later, she would find out.

She parked Betty on Old Town's Main Street in front of a long row of one- and two-story buildings built of stone and brick and nestled behind a white portico that covered a long boardwalk. Sunlight glinted off store windows. She felt as if she'd stepped back in time into a Western town like the ones she'd seen in old tintype photographs. Yet everything appeared as fresh as if it'd been constructed yesterday. She knew that happened only because the buildings were lovingly maintained by townsfolk.

The Wildcat Bluff Hotel anchored one end of the street, an impressive two-story structure of red brick with a grand entrance of cream keystones and a second-floor balcony enclosed with a stone balustrade supported by five columns. Next door, an antique, painted-wood cigar store Indian stood to one side of the old batwing-style doors of the Lone Star Saloon, still serving the same function as it had during the 1880s, with food, drink, and music.

On the other end of Main Street, the Chuckwagon Café held the place of honor, with Morning's Glory, Adelia's Delights, Gene's Boot Hospital, Thingamajigs, and other popular shops in between.

Eden stepped out of Betty and caught the scent of lavender, rose, and frankincense, obviously vented out of Morning's Glory to entice shoppers. Inside, they could peruse MG's handmade bath products and other items produced by local artisans.

Eden had come to town at the request of Morning Glory, who'd been surprisingly reticent. MG probably wanted to discuss how Ken was fitting in at the radio station, so that was just fine.

As she stepped up onto the boardwalk, she felt that tingling sensation between her shoulder blades that told her she was being watched. She hadn't experienced it since leaving LA and felt her stomach clench in a knot, making her feel queasy. She whirled around, looked past the businesses, down the row of parked vehicles, but saw nothing that looked out of place. Maybe she was simply anxious about feeling happy, so she was conjuring old worries out of thin air. Still, the feeling persisted, so she quickly headed toward Morning's Glory to try and get away from it.

When she opened the shop's door and heard a bell

jingle to announce her presence, she glanced over her shoulder. A small gray sedan showing red brake lights was parked on the street in front of the Chuckwagon Café. As if the driver saw her noticing the illegally parked car, he, or maybe she—impossible to tell due to a hoodie—sped up and disappeared down the street.

She knew there was no need to be concerned at the sight of a small car. She was most likely simply over-reacting. She'd just continue on with her wonderful day and forget old memories and bad drivers. As she let the door close behind her, she felt that sense of being watched slide away.

"Eden!" Morning Glory hurried forward, wearing her trademark ankle-length, colorful skirt and long-sleeved blouse in rich turquoise with matching cowgirl boots. She opened her arms wide in welcome. "I'm so happy you could make it."

"Me, too." Eden gave MG a hug, then stepped back with a smile on her face. "You smell wonderful."

Morning Glory raised an eyebrow, looking mischievous. "Glad you like my new scent. I believe men will find it irresistible."

"What are you calling it?"

"I haven't decided yet. What do you think?"

"I'm clueless."

"Tell you what. I'll give you a sample, and you let me know if a name comes to you."

"Okay. I'm happy to try it." Eden could only think of where and when she might use the scent with Shane.

"Great! Please take a look around. I'm pretty proud of my shop and all our local artists." She raised an arm and gestured in a wide circle.

Eden couldn't help but appreciate the tie-dyed fabric wallpaper, old oak floors buffed to a waxy sheen, and decorative pressed-tin ceiling. MG had filled the store with wood shelves holding colorful glass jars in all shapes and sizes that contained perfumes, bath salts, lotions, and all manner of beauty supplies. Several sections were devoted to individual artisans. Eden admired hand-carved wooden animals such as wildcats, buffalo, horses, and cattle, as well as beautiful, colorful, original quilts. One wall displayed delicate watercolor paintings in rich frames depicting local scenes of the Cross Timbers.

Finally, she whirled back to Morning Glory. "It's gorgeous. This has to be a shopper's delight."

"I hope so." Morning Glory clasped her hands together over her heart, bracelets jingling on her wrists, long necklaces swaying around her neck. "Now, let me get you that sample before we go next door."

"Next door?"

"Didn't I say?" Morning Glory walked over to a counter, picked up a small glass vial with a stopper, and held it out. "We're having tea with Hedy in Adelia's Delights."

"Really?" Eden accepted the perfume and tucked it carefully in her purse. "That sounds like fun."

"Much more than fun. We have a proposition."

"Now I'm intrigued."

"We hope you'll be more than intrigued, but come along. I imagine Hedy has everything ready and waiting in her tearoom."

Eden followed Morning Glory through the open archway that connected the two stores. She smiled, remembering how much she'd always loved Adelia's Delights. As usual, she felt as if she'd been transported back in time. The sign on the wall read "Established 1883." Knickknacks in all shapes, sizes, and colors filled deep shelves and glass cabinets. One section contained country pickles, jams, and other edible items in canning jars. Tall glass containers of old-fashioned hard candy stood on the checkout counter near the ancient black-and-gold cash register in the back of the store. A prominent display of the Bluebird of Happiness, sky-blue glass birds in all sizes made in Arkansas, gleamed in the front window.

A long-haired, tortoiseshell cat dozed on a glass shelf among the bluebirds, basking in sunlight coming in the display window.

"I see Rosie's on the job," Eden said, enjoying the sight of the beautiful polydactyl's extra dewclaws.

"Always," Morning Glory said. "With those huge paws, she could be quite the mouser."

"Wildcat Bluff has always appreciated cats, hasn't it?" Eden said.

"Back in the day, kitties were worth their weight in gold, since they were all anybody had to keep the rodent population under control. Cat stealing was a serious crime back then." Morning Glory chuckled, shaking her head. "Nowadays, I'd say Rosie's claim to fame is her great beauty."

As if hearing the discussion, Rosie raised her head, gave a sleepy blink of her amber eyes, and went back to her nap.

Eden agreed. "She's definitely a beauty."

"And she knows it, too." Hedy zoomed toward them from a back room in her power wheelchair. She wore her steel-gray hair in a single plait down her back, and her sharp brown eyes took in everything. She'd donned her usual Wranglers, pearl-snap shirt, and cowgirl boots.

"All cats are beautiful," Morning Glory added, "and they know it."

"Goes without saying." Hedy motioned toward the tearoom with small ice cream tables and matching chairs tucked into a quiet corner near a front window. "Eden, I'm glad you could join us."

"Thanks for inviting me."

"We're so happy to have you back in town." Hedy reached up, squeezed her hand, and then gestured toward a table already set with a tea service.

"I'm glad to be home." Eden walked over and sat down at the table with Morning Glory joining her.

Hedy rolled up to the other side of the table. "I picked Mom's favorite china just for you."

"Thank you. This is a beautiful sight." Eden appreciated the delicate rose pattern of the teapot, with its matching cups, saucers, and platter, which held gingersnap cookies. Hedy had added pink-and-green napkins to finish off the pretty display.

Hedy poured three cups of tea, then leaned back in her wheelchair, considering Eden with a glint in her dark eyes.

"Uh-oh, looks like you're up to something." Eden took a sip of fragrant tea and glanced at MG. "I hope I'm going to like this news."

"If you're the gal we think you are, you'll be fine with it." Morning Glory sipped tea, then allowed a mischievous smile to cross her face.

"Okay, let's shell down the corn." Hedy set her cup in

its saucer. "Our cowboy firefighter calendar benefit was successful enough to fund some much-needed equipment at the fire station."

"Still, finances are an ongoing issue for Wildcat Bluff Fire-Rescue, seeing as how we're all volunteers and respond to the entire county," Morning Glory added.

"I hope you're getting plenty of appreciation," Eden said. "I know I'm mighty grateful y'all were there for that brush fire on the Rocky T. If I had any extra money, I'd donate."

"We don't expect you to contribute hard-earned cash," Hedy explained, "but we can definitely use it."

"That's the truth." Morning Glory gestured toward her store. "Our local artisans plan to donate items for a big raffle, but that's all I'd ask them to do. You know, they don't get paid if their work doesn't sell, so most split their time with other jobs."

"I'm glad they have such a wonderful place to showcase their creativity," Eden said.

"I do my best." Morning Glory tapped her fingertips on the tabletop. "Fortunately, Wildcat Bluff is picking up speed as a tourist spot, so we get out-of-towners who want special items to take back home."

"Terrific." Eden looked from one to the other, feeling puzzled about their conversation. "But I don't know how I can help you."

"Right," Morning Glory said. "That's just background."

"We help organize Wildcat Bluff Fire-Rescue benefits several times a year," Hedy explained. "We don't just need rigs and gear, but there's maintenance, gasoline, and plenty else to pay for, too. And we need to train more firefighters."

Eden nodded as she sipped tea, wondering what any of this had to do with her. She had a little training as a firefighter from high school, but she hadn't used that knowledge in years.

"May Day is coming up on us fast," Morning Glory said.

"Yes." Eden nodded. "It's in a few weeks."

"I hope you've heard about our county's upcoming May Day Rodeo. It's a fund-raiser for our fire station." Hedy leaned forward as if anxious to hear Eden's response.

"Yes, I think I heard about it, but I've only been back in town two weeks."

Hedy threw up her hands. "See, I told you so, MG. Nobody knows, so nobody'll be there."

"Me not knowing doesn't mean much," Eden said, trying to ease the sudden tension.

"Proof in the pudding is the lack of rodeo entries." Hedy shook her head as she looked around the group.

"If nobody's roping or riding, you won't have much of a rodeo," Eden reluctantly agreed.

"My point exactly!" Hedy clasped the arms of her wheelchair.

"If the event doesn't make it this year, we'll have to drop it," Morning Glory added. "I'd hate to see that happen, but not too many folks in our county are taking time out of their busy lives to support us. Maybe they're just too harried in springtime."

"They'd snap to if there was no Wildcat Bluff Fire-Rescue for them at the drop of a hat." Hedy sounded frustrated with the situation.

"Are you telling me you're not getting the help and

support you need from local folks?" Eden asked, hardly able to believe her ears.

"That's the long and short of it," Morning Glory said.

"It's a good thing Sydney Steele came up with the calendar benefit that was such a huge hit, or the fire station would be in trouble right now," Hedy said.

"I sympathize." Eden set down her cup, toying with the handle. "But if you think I can come up with a solution, I'm fresh out of ideas. I don't even know how long I'll be able to keep KWCB afloat."

"Oh, I meant to thank you," Morning Glory said. "You've made a world of difference in Ken. He's crazy about the Den. He talks about it all the time, coming up with ideas, doing research online, liking school and everything better."

"I'm so glad." Eden gave her friend a warm smile. "He and Jack are becoming fast friends, and they're talking about transforming the radio station. Bless their hearts. I haven't the will to tell them I can't fund their bigger and better ideas."

"Join the club," Hedy said. "We've all got larger ideas than we've got budgets."

"And that's where you come in." Morning Glory turned to Eden. "You've got the biggest megaphone in the county, if you'll use it."

"Megaphone?" Eden looked from one to the other in confusion.

"KWCB—the Wildcat Den!" Hedy threw wide her arms. "Everybody knows and loves Wildcat Jack, but you're no small potatoes, either."

Eden abruptly felt sick to her stomach and set down

her cup of tea. "I'm a has-been. If you haven't heard my tragic story, you don't want to hear it."

"We've heard it," Hedy said.

"We've hashed it," Morning Glory added.

"And nobody in Wildcat Bluff County cares." Hedy pointed out the front windows.

"That's right. They don't care about that pack of lies," Morning Glory said. "They're mad as wet setting hens because their hometown hero—that's you, Eden—got done dirty."

"Oh." Eden didn't know what else to say because she felt such an upwelling of warmth that she had so much support here.

"That said." Hedy leaned forward again. "It'd give our May Day event a big boost if we could announce that you, personally, will be broadcasting live on KWCB from the rodeo arena."

"And if you'd also volunteer to start heavily promoting our event on the Den right away," Morning Glory added, "it'd be a huge boon."

Eden sat rigid in her chair, feeling almost stunned by their requests. "I appreciate your vote of confidence, but I can't think I'd make that much difference in attendance."

Morning Glory squeezed Eden's hand. "You're our local star. Of course folks will come out to see and hear you, as well as Wildcat Jack, broadcast live from our very own Wildcat Bluff Rodeo Arena."

Eden felt tears sting her eyes, then quickly blinked them away. It'd been a long time since anybody had wanted to see her or hear her for her talent. "I'd be glad to help. I really would be proud to." She swallowed past the lump in her throat. "But I doubt I can do it."

"What do you mean?" Hedy demanded, cocking her head in confusion.

"My voice." Eden hated to admit her weakness, particularly since her current weakness had once been her major strength. "You know about—"

"Fiddle-faddle!" Morning Glory said. "We heard that story, too, but we also heard your recent ads for the Chuckwagon Café."

"Right," Hedy said. "You're still good."

"That's in a sound studio. No pressure. And I had plenty of time to rerecord." Eden took a deep breath. "You're talking about a live broadcast with everyone focused on my voice. I honestly don't know if I can do it."

"I'll make you a concoction of honey, lemon, and my own special ingredients," Morning Glory said. "You drink that off and on while you're covering the event, and you'll be just fine."

Eden broke out in a sweat, not wanting to go anywhere near this May Day Rodeo. She truly didn't trust her voice, or even her body, to hold up to such close inspection. She was barely back on her feet, barely back to speaking, barely back in Wildcat Bluff. And they wanted her to go out there as a star as if nothing had happened to send her running out of LA with her tail between her legs?

Hedy reached over and squeezed her hand. "We know we're asking a lot of you."

"But you're all we've got," Morning Glory added. "Otherwise, we'd never try to get you back in the saddle so soon after a fall."

"On the other hand, we just might at that." Hedy grinned as she tapped the tabletop with the tip of her finger. "You took a tumble. That's life. We all do one time or another, or maybe even more than once. Look at me. I took a major tumble, but my niece Lauren got me on horseback again when I was looking at a slow and steady decline."

"Bert Holloway might've provided just a little incentive, too." Morning Glory chuckled as she gave her friend a knowing look.

"I'll be the first to admit Bert can be a right inspiring man." Hedy winked at Eden. "How about Shane? Do you think he might be able to help you get back in the saddle?"

Eden felt a blush warm her cheeks, but she didn't say a word—she knew she'd give herself away if she did.

"Yep," Hedy said, chuckling, "cowboys do have a way of inspiring us."

"I bet Shane would help, along with Jack and Ken." Morning Glory set down her cup as if all were in agreement.

"You might as well agree," Hedy said.

"Because you know we're not going to take no for an answer," Morning Glory added.

Eden looked from one determined face to the other. They were right. Nobody she'd ever known had been able to deny them. They were a major force in Wildcat Bluff and always for the good of the community. She gave a long sigh. "Okay. You've persuaded me, but I'd better have plenty of backup. Shane. Jack. Ken. And lots of firefighters."

"You've got it," Hedy said, "except for cowboy firefighters that are competing for buckle, bridle, and saddle."

"Thanks," Morning Glory said with a smile. "You won't regret coming to our rescue."

Eden simply nodded, already regretting every little bit of it.

Chapter 17

WHEN EDEN RETURNED TO THE WILDCAT DEN, SHE PARKED next to Shane's pickup and felt a little uptick in her heartbeat at the thought of seeing him again so soon. She grabbed her purse, slung it over a shoulder, picked up a bag of Chuckwagon takeout, and stepped outside into unremitting sunshine. She glanced up at the sky, hoping to see at least one or two fluffy clouds but no such luck. *Water*. Was it all going to come down to lack of water? How could she lose Shane over such a simple thing?

And yet, maybe the word *water* was actually a symbolic flashing neon sign high in the sky cautioning her that a man's love came easy—like Graham's supposed love—when all was right in his world. Add a little salt or turbulence to the water, and love might instantly evaporate just as it had with her ex-husband. Surely she couldn't equate all love with Graham's perfidy. And yet, she couldn't ignore experience, either.

She'd always found comfort at Wildcat Spring, so she walked past the station's front door to the beautiful WPA stone gazebo. She stepped inside, felt the instantly cooler air due to the thick walls, and went to the wide basin. She cupped the stream of water with one hand, feeling the cool wetness, smelling the metallic scent, and noticing the tension ease out of her. It was so peaceful here, so reminiscent of former good times, so filled with nurturing energy.

How could she give it up, along with the Den? They were all she had left of the former happy days with her family and all she had left of her broadcasting career. And yet, Shane was in her life again. How could she give him up? She felt pushed and pulled in both directions.

Shaking her head, she let water run out of her palm and turned away. She couldn't make any permanent decisions yet. And she didn't need to, particularly not when she had to come up with the energy and confidence to help make May Day a success for Wildcat Bluff Fire-Rescue.

She retraced her path to the Den and stepped inside. She stopped in surprise at the sight. Shane, Jack, and Ken sat in a circle on the floor with printouts in their hands and more paper spread out in front of them. They glanced up at the same time, looking a little guilty.

"What are y'all doing?" she asked, shutting the door behind her.

"Goldfish," Ken said, pointing toward a piece of paper.

"You want pet goldfish?" She felt rooted to the spot in confusion. They were having a confab about goldfish instead of figuring out how to save KWCB? Nothing made sense anymore. First, Hedy and Morning Glory had surprised her with their May Day plans. Now, these three wanted to fill an aquarium with goldfish, something that took extra water when they were in the middle of a drought.

"Not pets!" Ken pointed toward a printout. "It says here they work fine in water troughs."

"Are you saying you want to fill an entire stock tank

with goldfish?" She set her purse and takeout on the desk, then turned back to face the group. "Somehow I don't think Morning Glory will care for the idea, although Rosie would probably enjoy watching them swim round and round, if she didn't decide they'd make a tasty snack."

"Ugh," Ken groaned, giving her a dismissive look. "They're not cat food."

"I'm glad we're in agreement on that score." Eden leaned back against the desk, wondering why Shane and Jack had grins splitting their faces.

"Ought to be recording this." Jack laughed out loud. "On air, folks would eat it up."

"News about goldfish? I doubt it." She'd had about enough cryptic talk for the day. She picked up the takeout and dropped the sack on top of the pile of paper in the middle of their circle. "Eat up. I'm going home to try and make sense out of life."

"Good luck," Jack said, chuckling. "I gave up decades ago."

Shane got to his feet. "You two keep up the good work. I'll walk Eden back to her place."

Jack laughed harder. "Don't do anything I wouldn't do."

Eden picked up her purse and headed for the door.

"Guys, grab your grub and give me what's left," Shane said.

"Better fill Eden in pretty quick before she goes out buying goldfish." Jack held up a half-empty sack.

Shane took it. "The best laid plans of—"

"Mice and men," Ken completed before he bit into his hamburger.

"Robert Burns quote," Jack said around a mouthful of burger. "Sounds like they're still teaching kids something in school."

"Some days." Ken reached for fries.

"Do try to remember to broadcast something now and again." Eden chuckled as she pointed toward the studio, feeling happy she was back with good friends who were coming up with new ideas every day.

"Rae Dell's on the job," Jack said.

"Perfect. I'll be back later." She stepped outside and took a deep breath of wildflower-scented air.

Shane fell into step beside her, swinging the sack back and forth as if they were headed to a picnic.

She tossed him a mock annoyed look as she took long strides toward her uncle's hut. "Those two! Separate, they're something. Together, they're a force to be reckoned with."

Shane laughed as he caught her hand and threaded their fingers together. "Can't disagree on that one."

"Wait till you hear about my day."

"What's going on?"

"Come inside. I'll tell all."

"And I've got news for you."

"Good?"

"I think you'll like it."

As they walked up to the front double doors, she felt happy. Home sweet home. She started to open the doors, but noticed one was already ajar. "That's odd."

"What?"

"I always make sure these doors are tightly shut when I leave, so stray animals or bugs or something doesn't get inside."

"Are you sure?" Shane quickly stepped in front of her, checked the doors, and pushed the right one open.

"I guess I could've left a door open, but it'd be an accident."

"Stay here. Let me check the house. I want to make sure it's safe inside."

She felt a chill of apprehension run up her spine. "It's always been safe here. Not like LA."

"I knew we should've put locks on the doors to this house, and the station, too."

"We've never locked doors on the ranch. You don't lock yours, either."

"Times change. Maybe we'd better change with them."

"But still—"

"Please stay here and let me check the place." He slipped inside, shutting the door quietly behind him.

She stepped back, not wanting to feel like she couldn't cope with whatever life threw at her, but she'd begun to shiver as if the past had crept up on her and was ready to pounce again. She quickly sat down on the swing and clasped her hands together in her lap. Only now she was worried about Shane. What if he interrupted an intruder or a dangerous animal or who knew what?

He opened the door and stuck his head out. "It's okay."

She got up on unsteady legs, walked over, and stepped across the threshold of what had once felt like the safest place in the world. Now she glanced around, searching for anything that was out of place and that didn't feel right. Everything looked normal, although she didn't feel as safe anymore, so something had changed and she didn't know what, because most likely the latch had simply not caught when she'd closed the door.

"Okay?" Shane shut the front door, then put an arm around her shoulders and pulled her against his chest.

She leaned into the strength and heat of him. "Maybe we'd better get some locks."

"I'll run into town in the morning and get solid ones. You'll get locks first, then I'll install them on my place, too."

She felt the tension ease out of her at his words, and she looked around her uncle's little nest of a home. Comfy and compact, he'd updated and upgraded a few years before he'd passed away, and she admired what he'd done with it.

He'd kept the Quonset hut an open floor plan that at one end had a bathroom with a closet, stacked washer-dryer, and refrigerator across from it. On the opposite end of the house was a queen bed with a matching dresser separated from the living, dining, and kitchen areas by low bookshelves. The kitchen was all-white cabinets with white quartz countertops in a U shape with a sink on one side and a wide bar on the other. Across from it, he'd nestled a natural wood dining table that seated four near a tall bookcase full of a wide variety of books. He'd set two dark-green recliners with a small table between them across from a matching love seat in the living room section.

All in all, Uncle Clem's home had been perfect for him, and it was just right for her as well. She'd simply moved in with a single suitcase and set up house, feeling all the love and support that he'd always given her.

"Everything look okay?" Shane asked.

"Yes. As far as I can tell, nothing's been messed with, so I must have left the door ajar accidently."

"It can happen." He kissed the top of her head. "Let's eat. Life always looks better on a full stomach."

"You're right." She gave him a quick hug, then walked over to set her purse on top of the bedroom bookcase divider.

"Do you want food on the bar or the table?" he called from the kitchen.

"Bar suits me."

"You got it."

When she looked up, she felt her breath catch in her throat. Shane looked so natural standing in the kitchen, rummaging around in the cabinets for paper plates and napkins. He carried them over to the bar and set them beside the Chuckwagon sack. From there, he walked straight to the refrigerator and pulled out two bottles of water, looking as if he'd done the same thing many times before this moment. And she'd have bet he'd shared companionable moments like this one with her uncle while she was in LA. Now, she wished very much that she'd been with them. She felt a little misty, even sad, as she contemplated the loss in her life that she'd never get back.

Shane set the bottles on the bar, glanced over at her, and cocked his head to one side. "What is it?"

"It's just that you look so much at home in Uncle Clem's kitchen."

"I am. We had a regular poker game once a week with Jack and any unsuspecting cowboys or firefighters that got lured into Clem's web. He was sharp as a tack and cagey as a cougar."

"That was definitely Uncle Clem. I really wish I'd been here to sit at the table with all of you."

"I understand, I really do, but there's no point in fretting about the past. It's done and gone. We're moving forward. *You and me*."

She nodded, knowing he was right and still reluctant to leave this moment, when she felt so close to her uncle again.

Shane pulled out the barstools and motioned for her to join him. She took a deep breath, straightened her shoulders, let go of the past, and joined him at the bar. He set a hamburger and fries on one plate, then placed the same things on another. "Looks good."

"Yes, it does." She eased onto the barstool, but she didn't feel all that hungry anymore. She glanced around, feeling something amiss but not able to put her finger on it. Maybe all the changes in her life were putting her on edge.

"Correct me if I'm wrong, but doesn't the Chuckwagon make the best hamburgers in Texas?" He sat down, grabbed his burger, and took a big bite.

"Oh yes. And that doesn't even mention Slade's fabulous pies." She felt her hunger pick up again as she caught the delicious scent. As she bit into her burger, she realized that, in LA, she wouldn't have dreamed of eating anything so fattening, but at the moment, she just didn't care. She enjoyed the taste and let the calories go hang.

Shane looked in the sack, then back at her. "No pie?"

"Greedy?" she joked, feeling better and stronger with food.

"You bet."

"Another time."

"Okay. I'll hold you to it."

"About those goldfish..."

He groaned as he finished off his hamburger and fries. "I'll tell you, but first I want to hear your news."

She set down her unfinished burger and drank water to moisten her throat. "I had tea with Morning Glory and Hedy."

"That's great. You're really getting back into the community."

"Not so great."

He glanced over at her in concern. "What do you mean?"

"They want me to broadcast live at the arena for the May Day Rodeo benefit."

"And that's a problem for you?"

"Yes!" She shredded her napkin into long strips, trying to contain her agitation. "I'm not sure I can do it."

"Are you kidding?"

"No!" She tossed down what was left of her napkin and jumped to her feet. She paced toward the living area, then turned back to look at him. "I'm just barely getting back on my feet. My confidence is shot."

"May Day's not right away. You've got over six weeks to regain your confidence and energy."

"That's just it. I don't have any time at all. I need to start broadcasting immediately, playing up the event to get cowboys and cowgirls to enter the rodeo and everyone else to attend it."

"But you wouldn't be broadcasting live, would you? You could record in the studio. Wouldn't that help?"

"Yes, it makes a big difference." She slowly walked back, thinking as she went. "But still, I now feel as if the Wildcat Bluff Fire-Rescue benefit rests on my shoulders."

"Jack will be with you all the way. Ken, too." Shane held out his hands to her. "And you know I'll support you any way I can."

"That helps." She clasped his hands, feeling his heat warm her coldness.

"Did you agree?"

"Of course. Do you know anybody who ever said no to those powerhouses?"

"No. Nary a one." He smiled as he gently tugged her against his chest. "I've got absolute faith and confidence in you."

She looked up, searching his face for that belief in her and found it. She smiled, feeling his strength ignite her strength. "I'll need big-time help from you and the other firefighters."

"You got it."

"Thanks." She leaned into him for a long moment, knowing she'd have to pull up her own energy to make this benefit work. Maybe being cast straight back into the fire again would help rebuild her confidence. If so, it'd be well worth overcoming her reluctance.

"Okay now?"

"Yes. Thanks." She stepped back, putting her own worries aside, and smiled at him. "Now tell me about goldfish. This must be some whale of a tale."

He chuckled, clasping her hand and leading her to the love seat. "Kids. With a few strokes on a keyboard, they've got the whole world at their fingertips."

"Guess we all do." She sat down beside him, snuggling into his warmth. "And Ken wants goldfish?"

"It's just an idea that came out of researching ways to get water to my herds."

She suddenly stiffened against him. Here it came at last—all the reasons she should give up the station and the spring.

"I've always had a few stock tanks on the ranch, but I've mostly relied on dependable ponds, even if they do get low in a drought. Now I'm a pond short, and you're not anxious to give up Wildcat Spring. I don't blame you. But that leaves me caught between a rock and a hard place."

"I understand." She stroked her throat, trying to relieve the sudden tightness.

"I'm trying to come up with viable intermediate alternatives." He swiveled to face her. "Your mind's whirling a mile a minute. Please hear me out."

"Okay. I'm all ears about alternate water plans."

"I can get more stock tanks, but I need a way to get water to them."

"What are your options?"

"We can haul water in portable water bladders in the backs of pickups to fill the water troughs, if I get enough bladders. But that's a lot of extra time and work for the cowboys, not to mention expense, because of the size of the herds."

"Maybe too much time and effort?"

"Probably."

She sighed, nodding in agreement. "How do the goldfish fit in?"

Shane chuckled, shaking his head. "Ken discovered that keeping goldfish in stock tanks will keep the tanks clean."

"Won't the fish get eaten or slurped down big gullets?"

He laughed harder. "No idea. I'll ask around and see if anybody else is using goldfish in their water troughs."

She joined his laughter. "It's an interesting idea."

He grew serious again. "It's a lot of water to load and unload over and over again."

She hated to admit it, but she agreed with him. She thought a moment, then leaned toward him in excitement. "You know, we just fought that fire in the pasture."

"Yeah. It got a whole lot closer than I'd like to our houses."

"I'm not getting at that. I mean the rigs drove right into the pasture and sprayed water. Didn't they?"

"Right." He cocked his head at her as if in question.

"Don't those rigs hold a lot of water?"

"The boosters hold two hundred gallons each. The pumper holds a thousand gallons."

"It seems to me that water in those rigs could be driven across your pastures to fill stock tanks, couldn't it?"

A light went on in his hazel eyes and a big grin spread across his face. "Yeah. Wildcat Bluff Fire-Rescue could save my ranch."

She returned his grin, feeling a great weight lift off her chest. "Will Hedy think it's an appropriate use of resources?"

"She'll be happy to help us. So will the other fire-fighters. And I'll pay for the water and gasoline, so the fire station isn't out those expenses."

"Do you really think it'll work?" She leaned into him, feeling a sizzle of heat from the contact and sudden hope in her heart.

"It's not a permanent fix, but it ought to do the trick for now." He pressed a quick, hard, hot kiss to her lips. "You're brilliant, you know."

"You inspire me." And she kissed him for more inspiration.

Chapter 18

SHANE SAT IN THE SADDLE ON THE BACK OF HIS FAVORITE buckskin with Hedy, Morning Glory, and Eden nearby on their own mounts. He hadn't let any grass grow under his feet once Hedy had agreed to his using the boosters and pumper to ferry water to his stock tanks. He'd put it all together in three days, even though he'd had to make special runs to farm and ranch stores in Sherman, Denison, and Bonham to get everything.

He was well aware this was a stopgap measure, but he was researching a more permanent watering arrangement. In the meantime, he'd bought good steel round end stock tanks with crush-proof rims. They were zinc plated and guaranteed for five years. He'd decided on a good size that held about three hundred gallons and was eight feet in length. The Rocky T cowboys already had the tanks in place and ready for water.

Now, he watched with satisfaction as the Wildcat Bluff Fire-Rescue rigs full of precious water drove through the double gates into the northeast pasture of the ranch.

He rubbed his chin, feeling slight stubble where he'd missed a spot when he was in a hurry that morning. He'd wanted to be with the cowboys early, when they left to herd cows out of the way till the troughs were full. Once cattle smelled all that water, they'd be thirstier than ever, and ornery to boot, till they'd filled their big bellies. If at all possible, he was determined to avoid shenanigans like pushing, shoving, or stampeding.

"You'll make a cowboy out of Ken yet," Morning Glory said with a chuckle as she pointed toward her great-nephew.

"He's already an ATV cowboy." Shane smiled at the sight of Ken driving a four-wheeler towing a drinking trailer. He hadn't planned to buy that particular equipment, but Ken had been so excited to get and use it after finding it online that he'd relented and located a rancher in Dodd City selling a used one.

As if he'd heard them, Ken turned back, gave a thumbs-up with a big grin, and headed toward a horse pasture. He'd let horses drink from the low, shallow container connected to the big square tank with a spigot, then return, fill up, and go out again the next day.

"I wish we could get Ken on the back of a horse," Hedy said. "He doesn't know what he's missing."

Shane gave her a quick nod, knowing she was thinking about all those years after her injury when she didn't ride. She'd been introduced to equine assisted therapy by her niece Lauren and happily found out she could ride again. Now she sat tall and proud in her special stabilizing saddle.

"One of these days, we'll get him on horseback," Shane assured her, knowing it was just a matter of time till the city boy became a country boy. He was already well on his way.

"He's worked wonders at the Den, ferreting out details I'd forgotten and making suggestions Jack likes to use," Eden said. "And he's itching to get into the other Quonset hut, but nobody has found the key to its lock yet."

"What's in it?" Shane asked.

"Storage, I guess," Eden said. "Jack says they stuck stuff in there over the years just to make room in the station."

"It'd be interesting to find out." Hedy leaned forward and stroked the mane of her sorrel horse.

"Ken loves figuring out stuff," Morning Glory said, "so I'm not surprised he'd like to get in there."

"He's got plenty on his plate right now." Eden pointed to where Ken had just disappeared over a hill. "We all do."

"I can't thank y'all enough for filling his life with so many new learning experiences," Morning Glory said. "I was at my wit's end."

"You've helped everybody in this county often enough." Shane smiled at her. "You know anybody'd do anything they could for you. Ken's a fine boy who'll grow up into a fine man. I'm happy to help him."

"And Ken's brought a lot of vim and vigor to KWCB," Eden added.

"I'm glad," Morning Glory said. "And proud."

"You should be." Shane lifted his reins. "Now let's take that ride I promised y'all to see how well our ideas are working in the pasture."

"Beautiful day for a ride." Hedy headed for the open gates.

Shane brought up the rear, deciding to enjoy a few hours away from work and worry. He just wished he had a permanent solution for water, a solution that didn't involve losing the woman he'd loved for so long. Not that he'd mention love to her again, at least not for a good long while, since she seemed to shy away from the subject. Maybe her reaction had more to do with her ex than him, but he didn't want to do anything that would crowd her and make her want to run away. He could let it rest easy for now, but he knew they were coming to a time when matters had to be settled between them. He'd do his best so they both came out winners.

But more than anything else, he wanted to keep Eden safe. He'd installed locks on all their doors, but he figured that was only the first step in a good security system. He hadn't suggested more just yet. Jack had already complained enough about having to use a key to get into the Den. Maybe he was being overly cautious by installing locks, but he'd seen the open door at Clem's place and he'd seen the gray sedan parked out on Wildcat Road a couple more times. All in all, he didn't like it, but he didn't want Eden to feel threatened, so he hadn't mentioned his concern to her. He was simply keeping a closer watch for now.

As they followed in the wake of the rigs, he caught up to Eden. They rode side by side behind Hedy and Morning Glory. It felt like the old days when they were kids together, riding across the pastures, laughing, and playing. When she glanced over at him, grinning, he knew she was thinking the same thing.

"Just like old times, isn't it?" he said.

"Except I'll be stiff and sore tomorrow."

"That out of shape?" he asked, wanting to get a rise out of her.

She just shook her head at him. "Don't laugh. It's a

different kind of workout and you know it. I bet I could put you through an LA workout that'd leave you—"

"Begging for more?" he said, letting her know what was on his mind as he gave her an appreciative once-over, starting with her cowgirl hat and moving to jean jacket, T-shirt, tight jeans, and boots.

She laughed, pointing at him. "Don't you have anything better to think about?"

"Not with you around."

She laughed harder, giving him a once-over, too. "Are you trying to fuel my cowboy fantasies?"

"Is it working?"

"Overtime."

"Want to try the hot tub again?"

"After our ride?"

"That'd suit me fine."

She looked him over again as her gaze turned dark with intent. "Maybe we won't need our suits this time."

"Now you're starring in my cowgirl fantasy."

She grinned, mischief twinkling in her blue eyes. "Think you can wait for the real thing?"

"Much more of this and I'll be heading back to the barn with you in tow."

She smiled as she rubbed the palm of one hand suggestively up and down her thigh as she watched him watch her.

He was having serious doubts about the importance of observing cattle with their heads stuck in stock tanks when he saw Ken racing back toward them as fast as the ATV pulling the drinking trailer could safely go.

"Hold up!" Shane called to the group. "Something's going on with Ken."

"Is he hurt?" Morning Glory asked in alarm.

"Don't know." Shane turned toward Ken. "Y'all wait here. Let me find out what's happening with him."

He loped across the prairie, cutting the distance in half so he could reach Ken as quickly as possible.

Ken came to a stop beside him, then stood up on the ATV, pointing back toward the horse pasture. "Gone!"

"What do you mean?" Shane felt his heart speed up as he tried to see what had alarmed the youngster.

"Horses aren't where they're supposed to be."

"What?"

Shane glanced all around, taking in as much as he could in a split second. The three women were bunched together. The rigs were near the cattle troughs. Ken and the ATV were with him. All was as it should be except for news about the horses. It didn't make sense. His string was worth plenty, but nobody worried too much about thieves anymore. It wouldn't be easy to get on his ranch with a big trailer, load up the horses, and get out, much less do it all without being seen by cowboys. He discounted theft, so next up would be downed fence, but he knew good and well that his fences were in order.

And then he was struck by a new thought, remembering the open door, the gray sedan, the sense of unease. Was somebody playing games on the ranch to cause worry and trouble? If so, a single person on foot could easily enough get in and out at night or another time if he watched the ranch pattern of activity. On the other hand, he could be imagining trouble where there was none. It could be as simple as fence slats kicked down and horses changing pastures. He wasn't keen on his horses getting anywhere near the cattle, but it was understandable if they were after water or sport. He had a particularly rambunctious stallion that could be after greener pastures.

"Shane?" Ken asked, looking anxiously around the area, too. "Am I missing something?"

Shane made a quick decision. "I'll check on the horses." He wanted everyone safe till he could figure out what was going on. He didn't want to interrupt the cowboys or firefighters because they had to get water to the herds. He'd handle this on his lonesome. If necessary, he'd contact the sheriff.

"I can unhook the trailer and go with you," Ken said.

"Thanks." Shane looked straight at Ken. "I don't know what's going on, but I don't like it."

"Me either."

"I'd like you to tell the cowgirls that I've called off the ride while I go locate horses that have strayed out of their pasture."

"Won't they want to help?"

"Most likely." Shane didn't like to fool anybody, unless they were teasing and having fun, but he didn't want anybody else drawn into danger, even if it was only a possibility. "I hate to ask it, but would you pretend a stomachache or something so Morning Glory will have to take you and Hedy, since she rode with MG, back home? If possible, get Eden to help Jack in the Den."

"It's not just a downed fence, is it?" Ken suddenly looked much older than his years.

"I don't know, but I'm not taking any chances."

Ken sat down in the ATV, squared his shoulders, and gave a crisp nod. "You can count on me."

Shane watched as Ken took off toward the other

riders, then he turned his attention to the missing horses. He started forward, taking his time, watching the ground for sign that'd reveal unusual tracks, watching the sky for buzzards that'd announce dead animals, watching in between for any type of movement.

After he'd gone a distance, he heard the thundering of hooves behind him. He looked back. Eden had her chestnut running full out. He should've known she wouldn't be put off for any reason. He stopped, waiting.

"What's really going on?" she asked, pulling up beside him. "And don't give me any malarkey."

"Did Ken get the others gone?"

"They're heading out."

"Good." He reached over and squeezed her hand on the saddle horn. "I wish you'd gone back to the Den with Jack."

"You're spooking me."

"I don't mean to be. Truth is I just want to check the fence line. Maybe some slats are down, so the horses got out."

"We could've all done it together."

"Yeah." He cocked his head to one side, considering. She was strong. She'd had to be to make it. He needed to see her that way. Neither one of them was a kid anymore. They were grown-up, with grown-up problems.

"Shane?"

"Come on. Let's see what we can see."

Chapter 19

EDEN RODE BESIDE SHANE, NOTICING THE WAY HE SCANNED the ground and the sky as he looked for anything that moved or appeared out of place. She couldn't help him because she didn't know the land well enough anymore. There'd been a time when she had known where to locate the best blackberry bushes, where to sit on her favorite rock outcroppings, where to find a few Comanche arrowheads. She might still be able to locate some of her favorite things, but many would've been eroded or camouflaged or swept away by wind and rain, cattle and horses, rabbits and birds. Time definitely marched onward.

And yet, here she was beside Shane on the Rocky T again, as if no time had passed at all. And for them, maybe it hadn't. Maybe they were meant to be together. Maybe time had finally changed its beat to one totally in sync with the beat of their hearts. She smiled at the idea.

"Nothing looks out of place yet," Shane said, breaking their silence.

"Maybe not, but you're concerned about something. What's up?"

"I don't want to worry you."

"I've been worried since you sent Ken back."

"Okay. I've got an uneasy feeling."

"About what?"

"My fences are solid. Those horses shouldn't have gotten out."

"Slats can be kicked loose or knocked down or—"

"I know. And that's probably what happened." He hesitated, glancing at her. "Still, there's that open door at your place. And a gray sedan keeps turning up parked on the shoulder of Wildcat Road in front of the ranch. The driver can see up to the station and your home from there."

Eden felt a chill run up her spine, freezing her in the saddle, tightening her throat. "A gray car? Driver wearing a hoodie?"

Shane stopped and turned toward her. "Yeah, a hoodie. You've seen that car, too?"

"When I was in Old Town, I noticed a vehicle like that stopped on Main Street near where I stood on the boardwalk. Still, that doesn't mean anything. It's not an unusual car."

"It is around here."

"Out-of-towners, surely." She noticed her vision change like it had in LA when she'd been on alert—everything came into pristine clarity. "Might mean nothing."

"Might mean something."

She stroked her throat, trying to ease her tension. "Did you get a license plate number?"

"No. Too far away. Did you?"

"It didn't enter my mind. Not then."

"Might be a good idea to alert Sheriff Calhoun," he said.

She clenched the reins in her fist. "Why would anybody be watching me?"

"We can't factor out my new less-than-neighborly

neighbors. Lander cut off my water supply lickety-split. He started a brush fire that almost took out a pasture. I still have to wonder if he's trying to cripple the Rocky T so the Tarleton family can buy it cheap."

"That's a bad thought."

"I never heard they were underhanded, but I never had them next door before, either."

"They're located nearby, so why would they need to be so obvious as to watch you from the road?"

"Good question."

"Graham took everything I had, so he has no reason to come after me for more. Tarleton cowboys can look over the fence at the Rocky T anytime they want." She felt a little more empowered getting their thoughts out in the open, but the situation still didn't make sense.

"I'd like nothing better than an easy answer, but we have to play it smart, too." He clicked to his mount and started forward. "Let's see what we find up ahead, then get the horses back in their pasture. After that, we'll know whether to call the sheriff or not."

"Okay. I'm in no rush to escalate a few observations into full-fledged drama. I've had more than my share of that nonsense."

He reached over and squeezed her hand. "My goal is to keep us safe no matter what happens."

"Thanks." She leaned toward him and pressed a quick kiss to his lips. "Now let's find those horses."

She matched his pace as she had so many times before in their lives, and it felt absolutely right. For now, she could keep moving forward and get as many answers as possible.

"There they are." He pointed to a far corner, where

about a dozen horses were nipping at new growth beginning to sprout in the pasture.

"That's a relief." She followed his line of sight, trying to notice anything that appeared amiss. "They look okay to me. No cattle?"

He pushed back his hat as he glanced around, then set it back in place. "None here. It's a perfect pasture for the horses. I was going to relocate them over there today anyway. It's a fairly small area with a pond well suited to them."

"But how did they get into that pasture?"

"It's got to be the fence. Let's check." He cantered over to the three-slat white fence. "If you'll go that direction, I'll take this one. It'll cut our time in half."

"Okay." She turned her mount and started along the fence line, sighting down the long row as she looked for any sign of trouble. All the posts looked straight and sturdy with the slats in place. No way had the horses come through this section.

"Hey, Eden, over here!" Shane called in an excited voice.

"I'm coming." She turned toward him and followed the fence line. She hoped his discovery would solve their mystery and put everything in its proper place, so she could relax again.

When she arrived at his side, he was already off his horse and kneeling on the ground beside the fence. She didn't have to look far to see that three slats between two posts were not only on the ground but shoved to one side to make an easy exit for horses.

"Wait! Don't get down yet." He glanced up at her as he pointed to the ground. "Shoe prints here.

They're intermingled with hoofprints but still partially visible." He pulled his cell phone out of his pocket, took several shots of the prints before stepping back and taking more photographs of the downed slats and surrounding fence.

"I'd like a closer look."

"Come on now. I want your opinion about what happened here."

She quickly leaped down, ground-tied her mount, and joined him. She was careful not to step on prints, but she inspected the brackets with screw holes that held the slats in place. Next, she looked at the screws in the slats that matched the holes in the fence. She shook her head, feeling a sinking feeling in the pit of her stomach.

"Yeah," he said without her saying a word. "I'll never get those slats to stay in place if there's any pressure on them at all, because those holes are stripped, so they won't hold a screw."

"Took some force to knock those slats out." She knelt down, looked at the shoe prints, easily visible in the dry dirt, and studied the downed slats. "You'd better get closer photographs of these slats. Maybe I'm wrong, but it looks to me like the same shoe transferred dirt from the ground to the slats."

"Kicked, you mean?"

"What do you think?"

"That's exactly what I think." He knelt beside her and shot several more photographs.

"I wish we weren't seeing what we're seeing." She gestured around the fence line before she looked down its length in both directions. "Sheriff Calhoun?"

He nodded as he checked the images on his phone.

"Not officially, but I'll let him know. This is small potatoes and an official report won't get him or us anywhere right now."

"Guess we have to be on alert now." She said those words with a heavy heart as she stroked her throat to help relieve her building tension. "It feels like all that anguish Graham put me through is starting up again."

"But it doesn't make sense."

"No, it doesn't."

"It must make sense to somebody."

"I guess, but—" She felt her words freeze in her throat as she looked at the footprints on the ground, then to the smudges on the fence, then back again. "That's not tread made by a cowboy boot or roper or even an athletic shoe."

He leaned forward as he got a closer look. "No. That looks like—"

"A man's expensive dress shoe. Probably Italian."

"In Wildcat Bluff?"

"How about originally in LA?"

He grasped her shoulders and turned her to face him. "Now you've got me worried. What are you saying?"

"Graham likes a particular type of shoe."

Shane stroked her shoulders as if to comfort her. "And you can tell by the sole?"

She clasped his hands with her own, needing his strength as well as his comfort. "Not for certain, but…"

"Let's get the hell out of here. I want you safe."

"Not till we put those slats back in place. They'll hold till you get cowboys out here to do a better job with nuts and bolts."

He stood up, lifting her with him. "Your ex could be

anywhere. If he thinks he didn't cut a big enough swath out of your back and he's come for more, then he could be sighting down a rifle on us right now."

"I don't think he's handy with a gun."

"You don't need to be too handy to pull a trigger."

She shivered and wrapped her arms around Shane's waist, hugging him hard.

"But that's the worst-case scenario. I sincerely doubt he's got us in his sights because my ranch hands are on the lookout for trouble."

"Good."

"Still, let's play it cautious and get out of here."

"Fence first." She wasn't going to let Graham intimidate or scare her. He'd already run her out of LA. She'd never let him run her out of Wildcat Bluff. She pushed back from Shane, taking deep breaths to slow her pounding heart. "If Graham's watching, I don't want him to think he's spooked us or even that we're onto him."

Shane gently kissed her forehead, smiling down at her. "You've got guts. You always did. Let's get those slats back in place real quick."

She lifted the end of one solid wood slat while he picked up the other. They fitted one end into a post, and then the other end, until the slat was solidly in place. By the time they'd completed installing all three slats, the fence looked almost as good as new.

"I really regret bringing trouble to the Rocky T." Eden picked up her reins. "You know it's the last thing I'd want for either of us."

"Don't apologize. We don't know anything for sure. Till we see the whites of Graham Tanner's eyes, we won't know it's him."

"That's true." She clasped the reins in both hands, wanting connection to the calm assurance of the chestnut watching her with big brown eyes.

"For now, let's get back to the barn. The firefighters ought to be done and gone. I'll check in with the cowboys and alert them to look out more than usual for trouble."

"What about fence repair? I ought to pay you for the trouble."

"Don't go there. Like I said, we don't know what we're dealing with right now. Anyway, it's the cost of doing business."

"I can at least cook you dinner or something."

He grinned, reaching up and cupping her chin with long fingers. "There's plenty you can do for me, but let's do it up at the ranch house."

"Oh, Shane." She pressed a soft kiss against his calloused palm. "I don't know what I'd do without you."

"By the time I'm done, you *won't* be able to do without me."

"If it involves a hot tub, you may very well be right."

"I'm absolutely sure I'm right." He kissed her, nibbling across her plump lower lip, before he stepped back. "Come on. You whet my appetite for much more."

Chapter 20

AFTER ALL WAS SAID AND DONE, EDEN HADN'T RETURNED to the ranch house and Shane until evening. She'd given Jack a break at the Den, recorded several advertisements, and written promo pieces for the May Day Rodeo to run by Hedy and Morning Glory. She wanted to get the station's finances updated to a computer, but that'd have to wait for later. While she'd taken care of her business, Shane had brought the ranch hands up-to-date, seen to their horses, and stowed Ken's ATV with its trailer in the barn.

Now he was talking to Sheriff Calhoun, pacing back and forth across dining room floor outside the kitchen. She listened closely in case she needed to remind him of something important.

"Sheriff, we could be misreading the entire situation," Shane said, "but I have photos I want to send you and see what you think." He paused, listening. "No, we didn't get a license plate." He paused again. "We don't have any better description." He took a deep breath. "Okay. We'll alert you if we see the car again and you'll be on the lookout, too. Thanks."

"What did Sheriff Calhoun think?" She picked up a dish towel and dried her hands.

"Just a minute. Let me forward the photos." After a bit, Shane put his phone in his pocket as he looked at her. "He thinks we might be making a mountain out of a molehill because of what you recently went through."

"I agree."

"But he also wants you, and everybody else in the county, to be as safe as possible. You know how serious he takes his responsibility to us."

"And that means?"

"He's been notified of our concerns. He'll take a look at the photos. And we're to keep him updated on the situation."

"That's good, isn't it?"

"It's exactly what we need at this point. Anything else is too much. Anything less is not enough."

"It's a relief knowing we aren't in this completely alone."

"Did you feel that way in LA?"

"Too many times to count."

He walked over, took the dish towel out of her hands, tossed it on a countertop, and enfolded her in his arms. "You'll never be alone in Wildcat Bluff County. We're all family here."

"And you?" She leaned back and looked up at him, wanting him to talk about the two of them as family.

He gave a little twist of his lips, almost a smile. "There's a lot I'd like to say, but I don't think you're ready to get back on that horse again."

"I was on a horse today."

He kissed the tip of her nose. "Not that type of horse and you know it." He glanced around the kitchen. "I'm starved. Did you find anything worth eating in the fridge?"

She patted his chest, grinning as she let him get away

with changing the subject. There'd be plenty of time later to pursue…well, whatever they wanted to pursue. "I found a lot of questionable produce and tossed it in that garbage bag over there."

"Takeout containers?"

"If they had mold on them, they're in the trash, too."

"Thanks. I get around to sorting through the fridge about once in a blue moon."

"I can tell." She pointed toward a countertop. "Still, we're in luck. I found sliced beef brisket from the Chuckwagon and bread, too. I'll make sandwiches. Best of all, I found a whole pie that looks and smells fresh. How did it get in your refrigerator?"

"Slade Steele." Shane rubbed his jaw. "He treats me like a guinea pig. He found his great-granny's cookbook. You'd think he won his last bull ride. He's trying out the recipes. That's a buttermilk pie. I haven't bothered to try it yet. If it'd been pecan or cherry or lemon or something like that, it'd be gone."

She clapped her hands together in delight. "Aren't we lucky?"

"Speak for yourself. Buttermilk?"

"It's bound to be delicious."

"Is there any ice cream in the freezer to give it flavor?"

"Not on your life. This pie will fix a difficult day."

"It wasn't all bad today. The stock tanks work. I called and thanked Hedy again, particularly since we'll need to use the rigs on an ongoing basis till I come up with a permanent solution."

"Glad the tanks turned out okay."

"Yeah." He cocked his head to one side as he looked

at her slowly, so very slowly, from the tips of her toes to the top of her head. "After Slade's pie, I want dessert."

She smiled at the implication that she would be his dessert while she returned his gaze with a lingering one of her own. As the heat built between them, she cast her mind to pleasure and let go of the worry and tension and confusion that had been mounting all day. She needed relief. They both needed it. "If that's the way you want it, food first, then—"

"I get to choose what I want first."

"Why you?"

"Why not me?" He gave her a sly smile full of unspoken promises.

She sidled up to him, ran her palms up his broad chest, and stroked lightly over his shoulders, feeling his muscles contract in response. He groaned as if he'd been waiting for her touch forever. "That's why."

"You're not an easy woman."

"When did you ever want easy?"

"Right about now."

"In that case," she said as she twirled away and into the kitchen, "I'll make sandwiches and slice pie." She smiled in satisfaction when she heard him moan in reply, knowing the wait would simply up their pleasure later.

"Okay. While you set out the food, I'll grab a quick shower."

"Great." She expected to hear him move away. When he didn't, she glanced up. All the banter in his eyes was gone. He appeared serious as a slight smile teased his lips.

"Eden, did I tell you how glad I am you're back?"

She felt warm all over at his words, but she wasn't

going to let them get bogged down in seriousness. They needed lighthearted fun for a change. She was determined they'd have it this night. "If you didn't, you can show me in the hot tub later."

"That's a deal." He grinned, appearing mischievous again. "Be right back."

After he'd gone, she sighed in satisfaction, feeling more at home than she had in years. They were carrying on a long-held tradition in their families of eating together at the dining table. She opened a cabinet and selected the white plates with black barbwire motif around the edges that brought back fond memories. She set them on the table along with silverware and napkins.

Fortunately, she'd already had her shower and put on a red T-shirt, cutoffs, and flip-flops. All she needed to do now was make a meal for them.

As she set to work, she noticed she was happily humming a tune. She stopped in mid-pie-slice. She didn't remember being happy like this when she was married to Graham. They were always running here and there, trying to find time for each other or maybe not trying hard enough.

She glanced around the kitchen—cabinet to countertop, refrigerator to stove, cookie jar to toaster. Who knew such a small thing as putting together a meal in a beloved home could make her feel so happy? Suddenly she realized that it didn't require being a star, talking to a large audience, or taking home a big-paycheck to feel sublimely happy. It just took being with the right man in the right place at the right time.

And in that moment of clarity, she felt every single last brick—*thud, thud, thud*—drop out of her protective

wall. With that sudden change came a feeling of vulnerability but also a feeling of freedom and new beginnings.
Home sweet home.

She picked up the platter of sandwiches and carried it to the table, where she set it in a place of honor.
She walked back into the kitchen and picked up the
aqua-tinted glass pitcher of sweet tea. As she poured
the amber liquid over ice in matching aqua glasses, she
hummed to the sound of crackling ice.

After she added the glasses to the table setting, she
cut two big wedges of pie, set them on dessert plates,
and carried them to the table. She stepped back, proudly
looking over her creation with pleasure. She'd never
been a happy homemaker with Graham. They'd been too
busy, too distracted, too often gone from home. Now she
wanted the happiness she remembered from childhood
when warm cookies, cold tea, and simple sandwiches
eaten with loved ones made life special and worthwhile.

When she heard Shane's footsteps in the hall, she felt
her heart pick up speed. Just the idea of eating a meal
with him completed her happiness.

When he wrapped his arms around her waist, tugging
her back against his broad chest, she felt tears fill her
eyes. How long had she wanted to be loved and treasured like this?

"Table looks pretty," he whispered as the heat of his
breath fanned the delicate whorls of her ear. "But you're
a whole lot prettier."

"Flattery will get you everywhere." She placed her
hands over his arms and held him tight, feeling the
fabric—gone soft and pliant from so many washings of
his cutoffs and T-shirt—rub against her.

"I'm about to choose you over food."

"Don't you dare! I worked long and hard on those sandwiches." She tried to twist out of his embrace, but he simply spread his hands across her stomach and held her tighter.

"You're going nowhere till I let you."

She knew that was true because of his superior strength but also because she wanted to stay nestled in his arms. And yet, she wanted them to sit down at the table and eat together like a family, as they had done so many times when they were young. "Sooner we eat, the sooner we get to the hot tub."

He groaned, as if in great pain, nipped her earlobe, let her go, and quickly sat down in front of a plate.

She joined him at the table, savoring the moment as she looked across at him and picked up her glass of tea.

He grabbed his sandwich, took a big bite, chewed, and swallowed. "Real good, but I know something better." He gave her a steamy look with hazel eyes gone dark.

She gave as good as she got as she bit into her sandwich, wishing she'd made them smaller, anything to get to the hot tub as quickly as possible.

By the time they got to the pie, she almost giggled because they were wolfing down the food as if they were at an Olympic event.

"Pie's better than I expected," he said as he quartered the piece and made it disappear.

"It's good." She took smaller bites, but she was in no less hurry to be done and gone. She'd had enough family time at the table. She wanted her hands on him and his on her.

He drained his glass of tea, picked up his plate, and stood up. "I'll set this in the kitchen and go get a bottle of wine. Meet you at the hot tub."

She stood, too, watching as he whirled around and disappeared from sight. She couldn't keep from chuckling as she cleared the table and cleaned up in the kitchen. Maybe next time they could keep their minds off each other and on the food. But she sincerely doubted it.

When she was done, she slid open the patio door and stepped outside into a cool evening. A string of hanging bulbs cast a multicolored glow over the long metal table and eight chairs painted bright white and nestled on the flagstone patio. She glanced at the pool, behind its white wrought-iron fence, and saw the expanse of warm-blue glow from its underwater lights. Shane had already set the hot tub to bubbling and tossed gray towels on the aqua-and-white-striped cushions of a chaise longue.

She kicked off her flip-flops and walked down the flagstone path to the hot tub. She'd enjoy the night while she waited for him to bring the wine. She just hoped he wouldn't be long.

She smiled in delight at the hot tub nestled inside a cedar frame with two-foot-wide seating around the square area, with a cedar deck at the base on three sides. She quickly sat down, swung her feet over the edge, and let warm bubbles ply her flesh. She felt much of the tension of the day ease out of her muscles. She took a deep breath of fresh night air, slightly moist with the sweet scent of wildflowers.

When she heard the sliding door open and close, she glanced up to see Shane carrying a bottle in one hand and two crystal, long-stemmed glasses in the other.

"How are you doing?" He asked as he stalked toward her with easy, long-limbed grace.

She licked her lower lip, wanting to taste him much more than the wine he held in his hand.

He stopped beside her, looking down. "Aren't you overdressed?"

"You said no suits—or was that me?" she asked, teasing him as she caught a hint of orange and cinnamon that must have been a Morning Glory original soap scent. He smelled as delicious as he looked.

"I guess neither of us got the right memo." He set the bottle and two glasses on the ledge, sat down beside her, and put both feet in the water.

"What memo was that?"

He grinned as he picked up the bottle. "The one that reads 'birthday suits only.'"

She laughed at his joke, enjoying his light banter. "If I'd gotten that memo, I'd have remembered it."

"If not, I'd have reminded you." He held out the bottle. "Wine?"

"Please. I'm not picky, but what is it?"

"I hate to mention Slade Steele's name again, or you'll think I'm promoting his products all the time."

"No concern. I just recorded several ads for the Chuckwagon Café and his pies in particular."

Shane chuckled as he selected a glass. "Guess he's on our minds. Anyway, you probably don't know that he started a small vineyard on his family's ranch. He's making muscadine wine."

"Wine, too? No more riding bulls?"

"Past tense. Injury."

She nodded thoughtfully, being reminded of how life

could throw a curveball and it was left to every person
to get back up, dust off the seat of their pants, and find
their way back into the game. At least, that's the way
the old adage went, and she was doing her best to get
her hands firmly on a ball again, so she could make a
strong play.

"For now, he's giving wine to friends and relatives."

"And you're his guinea pig again?"

"Yep. And I'm happy to be one."

"If his wine is as good as his pies, I'm all in."

Shane poured the ruby-red liquid into one glass,
handed it to her, poured another, and set the bottle back
on the cedar ledge.

She clinked glasses with him, then took a small sip.
She was pleasantly surprised by the rich, fruity taste
with just a hint of woodsy flavor.

"Not bad." He held up the glass to the light as he
examined its contents.

"I'm no expert, but this tastes wonderful." She
cradled the glass in both hands, sliding deeper into the
passion they were building with every word, every sip,
every look.

"Yeah."

She felt happy and content and relaxed as silence
settled between them while they sipped wine and kicked
their feet in the bubbling water. After a while, he refilled
both glasses, then set the empty bottle on the cedar deck.
And still they said nothing, letting the moment build at
its own pace in its own way. She tilted back her head,
simply enjoying the stars in the night sky that was so
impossible in LA.

"I don't know about you," he said, finally breaking

their silence, "but I could spend a lifetime doing this very thing."

"What 'thing' is that?" she asked, making sure she pronounced it "thang" in their Texas way, instead of her radio way.

He chuckled, putting an around her shoulders and cuddling her against his side. "Feeling smart, are you?"

"Feeling happy, relaxed, content, and—"

"That *thing*, huh?" He downed the last of his wine and set the empty glass down.

"Yeah, that very *thing*." She finished off her glass, too, and handed it back to him.

He smiled when their fingers touched, as if he held back some special secret. He set her glass beside his own, then turned to her. "Want to explore that *thing*?"

"I thought you'd never ask." She reached up and tenderly cupped his cheek, watching his eyes turn dark, hearing his breath quicken, seeing him lean toward her. She tilted her face up for a kiss…and then he abruptly pushed her down into the hot tub.

She surfaced in a fury, splashing water over the sides, pushing wet hair out of her face, glaring at him in outrage. "How dare—"

"Eden, stay down," he rasped, staring out toward Wildcat Bluff Road.

"What is it?" She suddenly felt chilled, even in the hot water.

"I'm a damn fool." He lay down flat but kept his head up so he could see across the pasture. "We're sitting ducks up here."

"What do you mean?" She reached out and clasped

his bare arm, wanting comfort and to be comforted by the simple touch of him.

"There's a car parked near the cattle guard."

And she shivered all over.

Chapter 21

"I'VE HAD ENOUGH OF THIS CAT-AND-MOUSE GAME." SHANE sat up but kept the hot tub between him and the road so he couldn't be seen. He was mad as hell that his night with Eden was over before it hardly started and even madder that somebody was probably stalking her. It had to stop. And he was going to stop it. Right now.

"Let's call the sheriff." She clung to the edge of the hot tub, but kept her head down, watching him over the rim.

"Not only no, but hell no. What can he do? A patrol car shows up and that guy's out of here."

"Good. Scare him off." She gestured toward the road with her chin. "Besides, it might be somebody with a flat tire or some other car trouble."

"Yeah, it might be, or it might be a guy sighting down a nightscope with us as target practice."

She sank deeper into the water, looking at him as if she could hardly believe her ears. "But I'm back in Wildcat Bluff. I'm supposed to be safe here."

"You *are* safe." He glanced at the house, checking lights, shadows, perimeters. They were way too vulnerable, sitting here big as day. He could call Sheriff Calhoun. He could call neighbors. He could call cowboys. Bottom line, by the time anybody arrived, it'd be way too late if a stranger was looking to do them harm. He needed a plan, a good one.

"I don't feel safe."

"I'll confront the guy and take care of it."

"You'll what?" She looked at him with blue eyes gone wide. "What about his rifle?"

"I'll take a pistol." He realized that hadn't reassured her. It'd alarmed her even more. "He probably isn't armed in the first place."

"But what if he is?"

"Here's what we're going to do." He couldn't waste any more time with talk. Either the guy was down in his car with binoculars, or he was on foot sneaking up, or worst-case scenario, he really did have them in his sights. One way or another, Shane had to stop it. "We're going to stay in the shadows as much as possible while we move up to the house. I'll turn off the lights and get you inside, where you'll lock all the doors."

"Where will you be?"

"My truck's parked outside the garage. I'll run to it and drive down to the road without my headlights. If he's in his vehicle, I've got him. If not, he's in the wind and there's nothing else I can do tonight."

"I hate that plan. It puts you in danger." She glared at him with chin jutting forward. "Here's my plan. We're going inside the house, locking all the doors, and calling the sheriff."

"No. I want a look at this guy if possible. And I want his license plate number. After that, I'll call Sheriff Calhoun."

"No way am I letting you go down there alone." She gripped the edge of the hot tub, frowning at him in determination.

He rubbed his forehead, frustrated as all get-out. She

wasn't going to make this easy for him. "Arguing about this is giving that guy the edge."

"You're right."

"I am?"

"You're exactly right." She bit her lower lip and narrowed her eyes. "I've been running way too long. We don't know anything right now, but we have a chance to find out something. Let's go."

He grasped her hand and eased her out of the water. They knelt beside the hot tub, fingers clasped as they held hands.

"I'm of two minds." He looked about, gauging distances and objects for concealment. "We walk back up to the house as if everything is normal, or we make a dash and kill the lights."

"Let's don't alert him that we know the car is there."

"We take a chance either way, so I'm okay with a normal but quick walk."

He stood up, raised her to her feet, kissed her lips, and wrapped an arm around her waist. As they moved toward the house at a fast clip, he felt like they had a target on their backs the whole way, so he positioned her slightly in front of him to give her a little protection with his body.

When she slid open the patio door, he doused the lights and followed her. He quickly locked the doors and pulled the drapes. Only then did he notice he'd been holding his breath. He gulped in air as he focused on his surroundings. So far, all appeared as usual.

"What a relief." She glanced around as if expecting to see intruders jump out of hiding everywhere.

"If we had time, I'd check all the rooms in the house,"

he said, easing her forward. "As it is, let's get to the truck."

She clasped his hand. "I'm ready."

"Are you sure you won't stay inside?"

"Don't even go there."

So he didn't. Instead, he grabbed his car keys off the entry table, threaded their fingers together, and led her through the house. Once outside, he opened his truck's passenger door, wincing when the inside light came on, but it only lasted a millisecond before she was in the seat and he shut the door. He rounded the hood, slipped inside, and started the engine. It sounded way too loud in the stillness of the night.

"I don't need headlights," he said. "I can find my way anywhere on this ranch."

She nodded in reply, reaching over to squeeze his hand on the steering wheel before she grasped the edges of her seat.

He headed down the drive fast, hoping no unwary nighttime critter picked that moment to venture onto the lane. Moonlight glinted off white fence slats as he barreled past them going as fast as was safe. He hit the cattle guard and winced at the loud *click-clack* as the truck rattled over the metal pipes. He made a sharp left onto Wildcat Road and hit his bright lights.

Nothing. He looked in every direction. Still nothing. Maybe he could yet find something. He parked across the road from where he'd seen the vehicle, grabbed his Maglite from the console, and jumped out of his pickup. He jogged across the road and still came up empty.

Eden joined him, wrapping an arm around his waist as she shivered against him.

"You're still wet," he said as he continued looking around them. "It's too cold for you to be out here."

"I'm okay." She leaned harder into him. "See anything?"

"Nothing except what you'd expect to see on the side of the road. You?"

"Not a thing."

He cast the bright light back and forth, hunting for something—anything—that would give them a clue to the stranger. "It's as if he's phantom."

"No. We both saw that car parked here."

He walked along the road in one direction, shining the light on the ground ahead of him, then started back the other way. Eden stayed right with him. There had to be some sign the guy had been here a few minutes earlier. He needed that something.

"Wait!" She walked ahead a few feet and pointed downward. "Shine the light here."

He joined her, focused the light beam past the gravel shoulder, and saw a partial shoe imprint in a bare patch of dirt.

"Yes!" She knelt beside the print, pointing with a fingertip. "Look. It's the same type of shoe sole we saw at the fence. Isn't it?"

"Looks like it." He handed her the flashlight while he pulled out his phone and snapped several shots of the print and the surrounding area.

She stood up, putting a hand on one hip. "But we still don't know much more than we did, do we?"

"We know he's upping his game." Shane felt his sense of elation quickly overwhelmed by apprehension as he looked up the hill at his ranch house. If the stalker was willing to sabotage a fence and endanger horses, what was he willing to do to someone's home? Or to the people who lived there?

"Do you think he's building up to something?"

"I'd guess so or trying to spook you."

"Make me feel vulnerable?"

"Don't go there. If he's trying to get at you, he doesn't know a thing about Wildcat Bluff County. We take care of our own."

She hugged her stomach with both arms, visibly shivering. "Maybe I ought to leave the county. I won't take a chance on endangering you, Jack, Ken, or anybody else that might get caught in the crossfire of Graham's games—if it is my ex."

Shane clasped her hand, tugging her closer. "Come on. There's not any more we can do here tonight. You need to get out of those wet clothes and get warmed up."

"You're wet, too."

"Yeah, but I run hot."

"So true." She grinned up at him, changing the dynamics of the night.

"Let's get back to the house." As much as he wanted to forget their problem and focus on her, he couldn't do it. He had to make sure she was safe and his home was safe.

Once she was in his truck, he drove between the white fences, taking his time with his headlights on. No need to rush now. Whatever was done was done. He just had to make sure there were no surprises waiting for them.

"When we get home," he said in a calm voice so as not to alarm her, "I want you to stay in the truck while I check out the house."

"You think he's been up there?"

"It's possible. We were outside a while."

"I won't let you go into danger alone," she said quietly but firmly. "We'll check out the house together. I'll carry the Maglite. You get your pistol. We're not going into a situation vulnerable again."

He wanted to argue with her, but truth be told, he wanted her with him at all times. Only then would he know for a fact that she was safe. One good thing, he knew this property like the back of his hand. If anything had been disturbed, he figured he'd notice it.

He parked outside the garage again, then unlocked the glove compartment and slipped out his pistol. Eden wielded the heavy Maglite. Together, they each stepped out of their side of the truck. He hurried up to the building and flipped on the outside lights, illuminating the area. Everything looked normal, so they went into the garage. Everything checked out okay there, too, so they moved into the house. Room by room, closet by closet, cabinet by cabinet, under beds, inside bathtubs, behind drapes, they left no area untouched that could hide an intruder or his handiwork. Everything appeared normal, but he locked up behind them to make sure the house was secure.

Finally, they had only his suite over the garages left to search. She was visibly shivering by now, and he was cold, too. He squeezed her fingers. "You okay? Only my space left to go."

"Let's do it." She threw open the door so hard it hit the wall and bounced back.

"Hey, I've got to live here." He joked to relieve the tension because he didn't expect to find any danger in the house now.

"Then tell me there's going to be a long, hot shower at the end of this search," she replied.

He just gave her a quick nod as he eased into the large room, glad he didn't have to flip on lights to see that it was completely empty, since two lamps still burned beside his bed. He checked the closets, then the bathroom tub, cabinets, and under the double sinks. He walked out, locked his pistol in a special cabinet, and flipped the lock on the door to his suite.

"All clear." He turned to her, flashing a big grin that echoed the relief rushing through him.

"Good."

"Give me a moment to text Sheriff Calhoun and send him the photos." He quickly started the process.

"Take your time." She tossed the flashlight onto the seat of a chair. She walked into the bathroom, dropping her cutoffs to the floor with a wet plop, followed by her T-shirt. She glanced back at him with a sly smile before she turned on the shower and stepped inside the glass enclosure.

Chapter 22

EDEN STOOD IN SHANE'S SHOWER, RUBBING AT THE GOOSE bumps on her arms to try and warm up as she gazed at the chrome shower panel. When he'd redesigned his bathroom, he'd obviously gone upscale with travertine shower walls and floor, as well as a super-gizmo waterfall shower, massage jets, handheld showerhead, and maybe more stuff in a high-tech design. Another panel held liquid soap, shampoo, and conditioner in several fragrances with Morning's Glory labels on them. A teak stool with a stack of gray and black washcloths nestled in one corner of the extra-large shower.

After a few stabs and twists with her fingers, she had a gentle, warm rainfall that cascaded over her body. She raised her face to feel the soft massage on her skin, luxuriating in the sensual delight.

"See you figured out how to get that contraption to work," Shane said as he opened the clear glass door, appearing somewhere between naughty imp and hot cowboy with no clothes to cover up his assets.

No sneaking a peek for her. She was way beyond that subterfuge. She looked him over head to toe, appreciating every bit of him from his muscular broad shoulders to his high-arch feet.

"Like what you see?" He closed the door behind him, keeping the steam inside the enclosed area.

"Uh-huh." She felt words escape her as she traced

her lower lip with the tip of her tongue, imagining tasting him.

He didn't move toward her. He simply returned the compliment, looking her over as she'd looked at him, only his appreciation was much more physically obvious.

"I might need more instruction," she said with a teasing lilt in her voice.

"In what?" Still he didn't move, as if now that he had her cornered, he could toy with her as long as he wanted before he decided to slake his desire—along with her passion.

"Looks like you've got a pretty complicated arrangement." She put a hand on the shower panel but kept her gaze on him.

"Not as complicated as you'd think, once you get the hang of it."

"And you've got the hang of it?"

"If I don't, I'm sure you'll show me."

"What if I forget something?"

"You'll remind me." And still he didn't move, now appearing to savor the moment or commit it to memory. Maybe both.

"I'm still feeling a little chilly."

"Bet I can warm you up." He smiled, a quick twist of his lips before he went serious again.

She returned his smile, hers also brief and taut. "I can heat up the water." She glanced at the shower panel.

"Not on your life." Finally, he moved, stepping forward, clasping her wrists, raising her arms to either side of her face, and securing them against the wall with his strong hands. He smiled again, this time with a satisfied, possessive look in his eyes.

"Is this how you take a shower?" she asked, teasing and taunting him as she wiggled in his grasp. She didn't want to get away, but she did want to get her hands on his hot body.

"No. This is how I make love to you."

And he lowered his face and kissed her, slowly at first, then with mounting urgency as his need and her need escalated with each touch of lips to lips, tongue to tongue until she pushed away from the wall, wanting, needing, craving body-to-body contact. Still he didn't release her. Instead, he trailed kisses down her long neck to the hollow of her throat, where he paused to continue his torment, until he stroked upward with his tongue to her earlobe and lightly bit then licked her delicate skin.

She moaned, trying to pull her hands free, but he was too strong as he continued downward, tracing her sensitive flesh with his lips until he reached her breasts, where he caught a nipple in his mouth. She gasped when he sucked and kissed and tongued until she was writhing in his grasp, so hot and achy that the warm water from the shower felt cool against her skin.

Finally, he pressed them body to body, slipping in between her thighs, and looked at her with dark eyes. "Did I forget anything?"

She leaned forward as much as his hands on her wrists would allow and pressed her lips softly to his mouth. She felt gentle toward him—a blossoming of her own feelings even as she recognized that he was giving her a great gift. Love. Vulnerability. Respect. They were all priceless and only to be given, perhaps, once in a lifetime. She wanted to tell him all of those feelings, but she had no voice, no words, no ability to convey the depth of what she felt at this moment in time. Instead, she smiled up at him, letting him know with the look in her eyes that she belonged to him just as he belonged to her.

He placed her hands around the back of his neck as he returned her kiss. She pushed her fingers into his hair as she finally got her wish to explore him as he'd explored her. She traced the hard muscles of his broad shoulders with her fingertips, tracing around to the line of russet hair in the middle of his chest, teasing his nipples into hard tips with both hands as she felt her core grow hotter and damper against the hardness between her thighs.

"Yes," she finally whispered, "you forgot to put out my fire."

He groaned, jerked her hard against him, but then stepped back. "What kind of a firefighter does that make me?"

"One who needs to try a little harder?"

"Let me get some equipment and I'll get to work."

She leaned back against the wall, legs suddenly weak as she watched him in a long mirror over the counter. He opened a drawer, took out a foil packet, ripped it open, and put on the condom. When he turned back, he was obviously as ready as he was ever going to be. She beckoned him back into the shower, feeling shakier with escalating emotion.

He shut the glass door behind him before he picked up the handheld shower with one hand and a bottle of soap with the other.

"That's not the equipment I had in mind." She

sounded a little testy, knew it, and didn't care. She wanted him and she wanted him now.

"You've got a choice." He gave her a mischievous look as he tossed the bottle up and down.

"I suggest you put out the fire, then clean up afterward." She snatched the bottle of soap out of his hand and put it back on the shelf.

"Sure?" He replaced the handheld showerhead. "I can do more than one thing at a time."

She couldn't keep from chuckling as she realized he was being intentionally incorrigible. "Later. Right now, all I want is you." She reached up, clasped his shoulders, and raised one leg around his hips.

He said not another teasing word as he grasped her butt, lifted her up, and impaled her in one smooth motion.

She said not another word either as she rode him, feeling him thrust harder, faster, deeper as the gentle rain of the shower cascaded over them, enveloping their bodies in heat and steam and moisture. She dug her nails into his back, unable to get close enough as she bit his shoulder, neck, earlobe, moaning, clinging, gyrating against him.

He pushed her back against the wall, and she held on tight, her legs wrapped around his waist as he plunged into her with greater force. Soon, she no longer knew where he ended and she began as they propelled each other toward fulfillment. She kissed him, delving deep into his mouth as she fanned their flames to new heights, higher and higher, until their bodies fused in one final moment of utter ecstasy.

And then she was gasping, clinging, crying as she clung to him because he'd taken her to a place she'd never been before and a place she feared she would never be again. Had he always had this ability to complete her? Was that why she'd risked everything for that one midnight with him? Had she always known he was the one and yet he couldn't be because she was leaving and he was staying? Despite it all, here she was, back in his arms again. And she wanted nothing so much as to stay here forever.

"Stay here," he said, echoing her thought. He eased her down his body with shaking arms, obviously as much affected as she had been.

She leaned against the wall, narrowing her eyes against the future as she tried to regain her balance and strength. She watched him leave the shower, get rid of the condom, and turn back. Somehow, he seemed different, as if she were seeing him for the very first time. Bigger, yes. Stronger, yes. But vulnerable, too. Maybe they were both vulnerable now in a way they hadn't been before she'd returned to Wildcat Bluff. Would they be able to handle it?

He stepped back inside and pulled the door shut behind him, a slight smile playing about his lips.

She picked up the bottle of soap—something, anything to get past this too-fragile moment when she knew they both felt vulnerable. She held the soap up to him.

He smiled broader, taking it from her hands. "If you think I'm going to use a washcloth, think again."

She chuckled, grabbing the bottle from him and squeezing a large dollop into her palms. She was instantly enveloped with the scent of lavender and sage. She gloried in the smell as she rubbed her hands together until she had plenty of suds. "Me first."

He followed her actions, coating his hands in slippery soap and smiling at her with a twinkle in his hazel eyes.

Soon, they were running their hands over each other, lathering up every bit of skin but paying particular attention to their most sensitive areas. They added shampoo to the mix, soaping their hair, until they were completely covered in fragrant suds. Finally, they looked at each other and laughed as they let water cascade over them, sending bubbles as well as emotions down into the drain, so that they were both completely clean, inside and out.

She turned off the water and stepped out first, grabbing a big gray towel and tossing him a black one. Again, no words were needed as one look said it all. She started to dry him while he did the same to her. After too much lingering over favorite areas of each other's bodies, she was breathing quicker just as he was.

"There's wine in the fridge in the bedroom." He grabbed her towel and tossed both towels in the bathtub. "And the bed's comfortable."

"Slade's wine?"

"No! And don't mention him again. I don't want him in the bedroom. It's us alone."

"Okay." She smiled as she walked past him. "But it better be good wine or—"

"It'll be as good as we make it." He cupped her bottom as he caught up to her, propelling her toward the bed.

As she started to sit down, she glanced at the bank of windows that now looked like big, open eyes with the drapes drawn back. She pointed at the windows, letting him know she felt uneasy.

"I'll close the drapes." He headed over there, then

abruptly stopped in his tracks. "Would you get into bed and cover up or pull on one of my T-shirts?"

"What do you mean?" She suddenly felt exposed, standing nude in the middle of his room.

"I'm going to take a look through my telescope."

"Do you mean you think he might be back and watching us up here from the road?" She crossed her hands over her body as if she could shield herself from Graham's prying eyes, but she realized that wasn't a bit of help. She hurried over to Shane's dresser and pulled out a bright-yellow Wildcat Bluff Fire-Rescue T-shirt and slipped it on. It hung down to her knees, soft and warm and protective.

"Unless he's got high-powered binoculars, he can't see in here—at least, not in any detail. Anyway, I doubt if he's back out there." Shane drew the drapes on all the windows except in front of his telescope.

She sat down on the edge of the bed and pulled the covers up over her thighs, feeling chilled once more. She watched him bend over the telescope, position it, and spend time looking out over the pastures. She felt more and more tense the longer he watched out the window.

Finally, he stood up, came over, and sat down beside her, cradling her hands in his lap. "He's there."

"What!" She leaped to her feet, hand to her throat. "Did he see us?"

"Doubt it." Shane clasped her hands again. "Look, I'm going to call Sheriff Calhoun. There's probably not much he can do. It's a public road, but there ought to be some ordinance or other that allows him or one of his deputies to have a conversation with the guy. But that means first getting a name and license plate."

She felt her throat tighten again, but she wasn't going to let her ex scare her or run her out of her home. "I agree. Nothing can really be done until Graham—if it is him, and it looks likely—breaks a law. We won't be intimidated."

Shane enfolded her in his arms, pressing a kiss to her forehead. "I know you like living in your uncle's house, but will you please move in with me at least till this is all settled and you're completely safe?"

"I don't want Graham to win." She wrapped her arms around his waist and hugged him hard. "If I let him run me out of my home, I fear he'll win."

"Tanner can't win, not in Wildcat Bluff."

She glanced up at Shane's face and saw the absolute certainty in his eyes. She wished she could be as certain. "I'll stay the night with you. As far as tomorrow, we'll see."

"Maybe I can lure you into living here with pie and wine."

"As far as lures, I do believe you have a better one than those." She smiled as she stroked a single fingertip down his bare chest.

Chapter 23

A FEW DAYS LATER, EDEN SAT IN THE SOUND STUDIO WITH headphones on and mic at the ready. She felt safe enough to leave the front door to KWCB unlocked, since the station was a business, but she locked it during late hours. She'd been staying nights with Shane and enjoying every moment, from skinny-dipping in the hot tub to Chuckwagon takeout. They'd settled into an easy routine that had her spending days in Uncle Clem's home or at the Wildcat Den while he ran his ranch. Neither of them was bringing up the looming end of their lease, but it still nestled in the weeds like an angry rattler just waiting to strike. But the lease wasn't her concern today. She had bigger fish to fry.

Jack had the afternoon off. Ken was driving the ATV with its trailer to water the horses. Shane was tending to ranch business. She figured he wasn't too far away, since they'd been on watch since the gray-vehicle incidents. Maybe they'd alerted the driver that they'd caught onto him, so he'd left the county. In any case, they hadn't seen the car since Shane had spotted him through his telescope. Sheriff Calhoun hadn't seen the sedan either, but he and his deputies were on alert.

For some reason, the car's absence didn't reassure her. She felt something was building to a head, and whatever it was, she wasn't going to like it. But she couldn't understand why Graham would come after her again. He only exerted himself for a payoff. And she had nothing left he could take from her.

She pushed her ex from her mind. He was nothing but past trouble. She was about to go on the air live for the first time since returning to Wildcat Bluff County. She felt tense about it but hoped, once her program started, she'd get in character and be fine. But she still wasn't sure of the strength and staying power of her voice. Just in case, she had Wildcat Jack's Rae Dell as backup.

She wiped her damp palms on her jeans, revving up her energy. She'd found some of her old clothes in a closet at her uncle's place. She'd lost enough weight to fit into them again. As far as western went, she was right in style with a bright-red pearl-snap shirt, jeans, and red cowgirl boots. She'd even applied a little makeup for the event. Nobody would see her, but she still wanted to feel professional, like the old days.

She checked the big analog clock on the wall. Time was ticking down to her lead-in song. Pretty quick, she'd hear the rich, smooth voice of Gene Autry croon "Deep in the Heart of Texas." She glanced to the right of the clock at the faded, yellowed, ripped poster of the Highwaymen with Willie Nelson, Johnny Cash, Waylon Jennings, and Kris Kristofferson looking tough but friendly. The poster had seen better days, but so had all of them. They'd gone through a lot in their lives, and so had she.

As she stared at their famous faces—drumming her fingertips on the board, thinking how strong she needed to be—a top corner of the poster popped free. It was quickly followed by the other corner, causing the entire poster to slip to the floor in a heap. That gave her a start.

Maybe she shouldn't look at any of the other posters that'd been tacked, taped, or glued to the walls over the years, just in case the first one started a downward trend that went all the way into her first show. She needed better mojo.

She looked away from the posters and through the window that revealed the Den's shabby reception room. Maybe in time, with enough money and the right situation, she could bring KWCB back to its former glory. Still, there was nothing to do but set aside that pipe dream for the moment.

She picked up the glass bottle that held Morning Glory's voice concoction. She unscrewed the lid, took a sip, and felt it slide down her throat, warming and soothing as it went. As far as taste, it wasn't too good and it wasn't too bad. It was drinkable—and hopefully helpful. All in all, she was as ready as she'd ever be to strut her maybe-not-too-tattered stuff. She poised her fingertip over a control, took a deep breath, and saw the front door open.

A tall, thin man with silver hair, in a pricey, gray suit and carrying a leather briefcase stepped inside. He was LA chic and carried personal power like a weapon. Z. C. Fontaine, as she lived and breathed. He was Graham Tanner's personal junkyard dog, better known as his upscale attorney. The ax had fallen on Wildcat Bluff. And her very own neck. Again.

She didn't hesitate. No point. Today was obviously not going to be her day. Bad mojo was bad mojo. She gave the country supergroup on the floor an understanding nod, then cued up Rae Dell, took off her earphones, and set them on top of the board. She felt shaky as she got to her feet. She was glad she had on makeup for defense and boots for height because she needed every little edge she could get in Graham's new power play.

She watched as Fontaine gave the reception area a cursory and dismissive glance before he focused on the door to the studio. She wasn't about to let him into the inner sanctum. For one reason, she didn't want his nasty slime anywhere near what was the best part of her life, and for another, she didn't want him to figure out how little or how much the contents might be worth. He had dollar signs for eyeballs, and he wouldn't have come all the way to North Texas for a lark. He saw money, prestige, honor, or something else here that'd benefit him.

She picked up her cell and sent a quick text to Shane, alerting him to trouble, but he might not be nearby at the moment. She had to handle this alone. She quickly stepped into reception, shutting the studio door behind her.

Fontaine gave her a white-porcelain smile. "I'd heard you'd gone back to your hillbilly roots, but I hadn't expected to see you fall so far so fast." He swept his hand around the area and ended up pointing at her clothes.

"Why don't you go back to the rock you crawled out from under?"

He shook his head, making an exaggerated sigh. "No need for insults. Let's backtrack."

"Fine." She pointed at the entry. "There's the door."

"Not quite so fast." He shoved papers off her desk, sending them scattering in a white snowstorm to the floor. He set down his briefcase in their place with a snap, clicked open the locks, and stopped mid-motion as he noticed the black phone. "Does that rotary actually work?"

"Yes."

"Vintage." He cast another smile her way. "I like the looks of it. Who knows what it might bring at auction?"

She returned his shark smile with one of her own. "Good point. Back in the day, all the major and minor country music stars probably used it at one time or another." She had no idea if that was true, but it could be. Mainly, she just wanted to torment him that he'd never get his hands on the Wildcat Den's phone.

"Excellent. I'll keep that in mind." He extracted an official-looking document from his briefcase.

She'd seen way too many of those in his hands.

"To let you know how much I've always admired your talent, if not your personal choices, I'm here to hand deliver this property deed."

"Deed?" She didn't reach for it. She wasn't about to touch anything offered by him. Instead, she was furiously thinking about what she needed to do. She wanted Shane here. She wanted Sheriff Calhoun here. She wanted Jack here. But there was no time to get any of them to the station in time to support her. She'd simply have to draw upon her reserve of strength and handle this moment all on her lonesome.

He snapped his briefcase shut and picked it up. "Graham Tanner and I have concluded that you misrepresented the full scope of your properties during the divorce settlement."

"What?" She stared at him, feeling rocked to the bottom of her cowgirl boots at the blatant lie.

"To make matters right, I would like you to sign this

deed to all property of KWCB, also known as the Wildcat Den, which includes the radio station, two Quonset huts, transmitter, and all contents of said property, transferring ownership to Graham Tanner, my client."

She simply stood there staring at him, speechless at his audacity.

"If you don't sign the deed, we will be well within our rights to demand a reopening of the matter in court. And the media, of course, will no doubt be delighted to pick up the story again." He cocked his head, giving her another fake white smile. "You have my deepest sympathy that the public can't seem to get enough of your bad behavior."

"Not mine! Graham's bad behavior is what drives media stories. I'm an innocent bystander."

"I doubt I need to remind you that it is all about the narrative. Graham worked that angle like a pro. *You?* Well, as I said, you do have my sympathy. For now, I'm given to understand that you are in the process of rewriting your narrative into a more positive outcome."

She felt sick to her stomach at everything he was implying, if not actually saying outright. Graham wasn't the only pro. Fontaine was all-star, too. They were trying to outplay her again, and she couldn't let them.

"With that in mind, I'm sure you would prefer to leave the past in the past. Now, if you would be so good as to sign this deed to my client, I'm sure we can see our way clear to not reopening the proceedings."

She took a deep breath to try and stay calm and strong. "I'm not signing one more thing over to Graham."

"He thought that might be your attitude."

"He thought right."

Fontaine set the deed on her desk and tapped it with the tip of his forefinger. "Please give your answer more consideration."

"Please leave."

"My contact information is with the document. I'm sure you will see fit to change your mind, so I look forward to hearing from you at your earliest convenience that you are in total agreement with my client regarding this property."

"Out!" She jerked open the front door and felt color drain from her face as she stood face-to-face with her smug ex-husband. He looked like a clone of his attorney except he wore no tie, for a more casual, artistic appearance. He'd had his thick, dark hair recently styled, his classic features were sculpted with filler, and his gray eyes emphasized with a touch of eyeliner. He looked ready for a photo shoot instead of an appearance at KWCB.

"Eden, how lovely to see you again." Graham gave her a brilliant-white cap-toothed smile.

"Ms. Rafferty prefers to take more time to think about the matter at hand," Fontaine said, moving to stand behind Eden. "I'm sure she will eventually decide she prefers to make a misrepresentation adjustment out of court."

Graham nodded in agreement as he gave a sad and regretful look. "She may also need a little more encouragement. I suggest we go on to plan B."

"I suggest you leave." Eden couldn't move, even though she was trapped between two vultures, or she'd signal weakness. That'd be like waving red meat in front of their greedy beaks. They stood so close she could smell their expensive aftershave—they wore the same brand—probably necessary to cover up their rancid scent. She clenched her fists, holding on to her anger by sheer force of will.

"Just a few more moments of your time," Graham said with a smile as he turned and motioned toward someone.

Surprised, she glanced up and her breath caught in shock. She'd thought things were bad, but now they were infinitely worse. A videographer wearing a gray T-shirt and faded jeans repositioned his handheld camcorder away from the Quonset huts to focus on her. As he walked forward, he recorded all the way. She'd been suckered and set up—again.

Graham turned so his perfect profile was to the camcorder. "Eden, are you willing to admit that you misrepresented the full scope of your properties during our divorce settlement and to sign over the KWCB property to me?" He gestured toward the two Quonset huts, the radio station, and the broadcast tower with a grand, sweeping gesture, his hand open to indicate trustworthiness.

"You're the one, aren't you?" She realized everything too late as Graham's obvious plan B fell into place. "You've been stalking me."

"Oh no. I simply scouted here to make sure Mr. Fontaine had a good reason to come to the wilds of Texas."

"Leave my property right now." She ended her words on a whisper as her throat tightened and her voice almost failed her.

"You have my deepest regrets that you still have vocal issues." Graham pretended to swipe a tear from one eye. "I'm sure in time, when you are under less duress, you will be in fine voice."

"You're not getting KWCB." She finally had to step down to get in his face over the matter, and she leaned in close.

"As much as I hate to say it, you cheated me in our divorce." Graham made a sad look as he turned toward the camera.

"No. You took everything." She rubbed her throat, trying to slow her stampeding heart rate as well as ease her voice. She had to appear as strong as possible to counter this frontal attack.

"If you sign the deed now, we will go without another word and you may return to your life here, such as it is." Fontaine stepped down onto the top step on the other side of her.

She was sandwiched between the two men with the videographer in front of her. But she refused to give ground. Not ever again.

"Eden, be smart," Graham hissed, leaning close to her. "If you don't sign over this property, I'll trash what little reputation you have left. And believe me, I can come up some pretty convincing photos and stories about you to share with the world."

"Photoshop? Lies?" she whispered, hardly able to believe he'd stoop so low, although she should have easily believed it after past experience with him.

"What is the truth in our world? Its value cratered long ago. Control the narrative and you win. It's that simple. And you well know it."

"Our particular information is on a need-to-know basis," Fontaine said in a reasonable voice. "We need to know. No one else does."

"Eden's smart." Graham leaned in even closer to her.

"You won't give us any reason to have a little fun with the truth, now will you?"

She took a deep breath—nothing left to lose—and willed her voice to support her. "You do realize you're in Texas, don't you?"

Fontaine appeared surprised by her words. "So? Texas is large, sure, but that only means it has more than your average good-for-nothing counties."

She glanced at Graham, feeling stronger as the need to protect her beloved land arose from deep inside her. "Did I ever tell you that we live by the cowboy code of honor here in Wildcat Bluff County?"

"What the hell does that mean?" Graham pointed dramatically toward a pasture with a dozen chestnut horses. "Horses. Cattle. Buffalo. And plenty of dung to heat your houses?"

"We take care of our own." She didn't figure that'd make any sense to them, but she said it anyway, in fair warning as to what they were taking on.

"Got it," Fontaine said, nodding as if he really did get it. "I take care of my own, too, and right now that is Graham Tanner."

"I thought you were going to say something about truth, justice, and liberty belonging to any Tom, Dick, or Harry." Graham scoffed. "Not true. It all belongs to strong arms—and right now my strong arm is Mr. Fontaine."

"If you want to keep your cynical view of life intact," she said, trying not to feel sorry for the pitiful life Graham had chosen to live, "you'd better leave Wildcat Bluff County before you come up against real truth and real justice."

"Believe me, I'll be out of here as soon as you see what's best for you. And if I never see another horse or cow, it'll be way too soon." Graham gestured toward the nearby grazing horses.

"Time for you to go." She raked them all with a sharp, jagged glance from her narrowed eyes. "And don't come back."

"Fine. For now." Graham stepped down to the ground with Fontaine right behind him. "But it's only a matter of time until KWCB is mine."

She looked out at their big black SUV parked haphazardly in front of the storage hut. She wanted them gone before they did any more snooping around the station, so she hurried down the stairs. As they neared the vehicle, she heard the thunder of hooves.

She glanced up to see Shane pounding up the lane between white fences, leaning over his buckskin with his Stetson pulled low on his head. He looked like an invincible combination of power and determination and cowboy justice.

She grinned, feeling her heart swell with pride and happiness. She'd never seen a more beautiful sight. For that matter, the videographer probably hadn't, either. She doubted he'd expected to shoot such a visually stimulating scene and noticed he was getting every bit of it.

As Shane neared the SUV, he pulled his mount to a stop, jumped down, and strode over to the group. He put an arm protectively around Eden's waist, tugged her close, and glared at the intruders.

"What's going on here?" he growled, giving the men a hard-eyed stare from the shadow of his hat.

"Cowboy to the rescue." Graham glanced at her, shaking his head. "I thought you had better taste."

"No matter," Fontaine said. "It makes a good visual."

"True." Graham shrugged.

"I won't ask you again. Get out and stay out," Shane ordered in a deep voice.

Eden felt Shane's arm muscles bunch as if preparing to throw the men off his ranch, so she put a restraining hand on his arm.

"Fine," Graham said. "We're going, but we'll be back to get what belongs to me."

"Don't count on it." Shane followed them to their vehicle. "You set foot again on the Rocky T Ranch, and Sheriff Calhoun will haul you in for trespassing on my property."

"And that'll be the least of your worries," she added for good measure, stopping beside Shane.

"Big talk from the little people. No worries at all." Fontaine opened an SUV door while the videographer slipped in behind the steering wheel.

"Eden, it's always a pleasure doing business with you, although I remember fond times when it was more pleasure than work." Graham gave Shane a knowing smile, hinting at hot nights with Eden, before he entered the vehicle.

She held her body rigid as she watched them drive away, feeling so angry, so sick, so frustrated that she could hardly think straight.

"Are you okay?" Shane tugged her tighter against his body.

"He wants it all."

"What do you mean?"

"KWCB. Every little thing." She wrapped her arms around Shane, hugging him with all the strength she had left.

"He can't get it, can he?"

"Graham believes he can make it so rough on me that I'll give him whatever he wants." She glanced up at the radio tower. "And he's never lost."

Chapter 24

"I'VE GOT NEWS FOR GRAHAM TANNER." SHANE WATCHED the big black SUV turn onto Wildcat Road, leaving a trail of dust in its wake. "If he keeps this up, he'll find out he's messing with the wrong folks. We don't cotton to bullyboys in Wildcat Bluff County."

"I'm so glad you're here." She stepped away to get a better view of the now-empty road. "They're really gone, aren't they?"

"You sent 'em packing." He clasped her hand and threaded their fingers together.

"I did, didn't I?" She grinned up at him. "With a little help from my friend the cowboy firefighter."

He chuckled. "You already had them buffaloed by the time I got here. Sorry I couldn't get to you sooner."

"You did just fine. I'm mighty grateful." She rubbed her thumb across his knuckles. "What do you think Graham will do with the video?"

"Don't know. Don't care."

"I wish I didn't care. He can hurt me and knows it, since I'm trying to put my professional life back together."

Shane dropped her hand and squeezed her shoulders as he looked deeply into her blue eyes. "Do you really think I'd ever let anybody hurt you again?"

"No. But still..."

"Tell you what." He grinned, knowing exactly what he needed to do to get their lives back on track. "Let's throw a welcome-home party up at the house. Mom and Dad hosted the last ranch party. It's time we continue the tradition."

"A party?" She gazed at him in amazement. "But I've got to do something to save the Wildcat Den."

"That's exactly what this party is about."

"I don't understand."

"We'll invite every horse trainer, every cattle rancher, every business owner, every resident in the county. Most won't be able to come, but plenty will be here to support you and the Den."

"Support me? How?"

"Hedy and Morning Glory will get the word out. Everybody will be mad as a wet setting hen when they hear about these sidewinders trying to hurt you and trash-talking our county."

"But you're planning to close KWCB, if you can."

"I'm rethinking my position."

She threw her arms around his waist and hugged him hard again. "That's almost funny. I'm rethinking my position, too."

He set her back, so he could look into her eyes. "Are you telling me that about the time I'm considering renewing the lease you're considering *not* renewing it?"

"I don't want your animals to go thirsty."

"I don't want the county to lose its radio station."

She chuckled, shaking her head. "We're something, aren't we? I don't think we're ever going to agree on a solution."

"Let's set it aside for now. We've got a party to plan."

"Are you sure a party is wise?"

"Hedy and Morning Glory will get their social

network humming, so we'll get more food brought to us than we can shake a stick at."

"That's good."

"Even better, they'll let everybody know we're in a radio station war. If we want KWCB to survive, we're going to have to fight for it."

"I think the battle may be more legal than anything, and I can't afford attorney fees. If Graham gets his hands on the Den, he'll break up the assets and sell them to the highest bidder. The tower would probably go for scrap metal. I can hardly stand the thought."

"Isn't KWCB your inheritance?"

"Yes. Still, I'm concerned he'll wear me down again or come at me from some new angle, like the video."

"We'll fight on several fronts." The more Shane thought about outsiders coming into the county and trying to make trouble, the madder he got. "We'll ask Nathan Halford from Thingamajigs to bring his camcorder to the party. We'll have our own Wildcat Bluff County video to counter Tanner's nastiness. Ken can help us get it up and running."

"He's good with tech stuff, that's for sure. Still, I don't know how any of this really helps me." She sighed, looking up at the KWCB sign.

"Trust me." He clasped her hands again to transmit strength and courage and commitment. "Graham Tanner and his bullyboys just kicked a hornet's nest named Wildcat Bluff County. And he's going to regret the day he ever set foot here."

"I'd like to see that."

"You will." He turned toward the station. "Come on, we've got some calls to make."

"Let's use the black phone."

He glanced over at her. "Now why would you want to do that? You know it'll take a lot longer to reach folks because that behind-the-times phone has no pre-programmed numbers."

She gave him a mischievous sidelong glance. "I have a very good reason. Smarmy Fontaine thinks he's going to get my family's phone and sell it for a mint, or maybe use it as a talking piece in his office."

"Even if it's vintage it can't be worth much."

"I told him all the major and minor country stars in the past had probably used it while in the studio."

"How could you ever prove the provenance?"

"Fingerprints?" She gave him a big grin with fake, wide-eyed innocence.

He couldn't help but laugh, since it sounded so ludicrous. Still, there might be something in it if she could prove that Waylon, Willie, Johnny, Loretta, and others had made calls while at KWCB. Fat chance of that happening, but it was a funny thought. Still, he'd take particular pleasure in making sure Fontaine never got his sticky fingers on the Den's rotary phone.

"You know," she said thoughtfully, "for such intelligent guys, I'm not sure how much country smarts they've got between them."

"Push comes to shove, I'll take smarts." He walked over to his horse and picked up the ground-tied reins.

She looked at the buckskin then back at him. "I called you out in the middle of something, didn't I? I'm okay now. You'd better get back to work."

"I was fixing a fence, but I can pass that along to another cowboy." He pushed up the brim of his hat, thinking about what needed to be done next. "Come on, let's get in the station and start plotting our next move. Max is up at the barn. I'll alert him to our trouble and ask him to come and get my horse."

As he walked beside Eden, he jerked his phone out of a pocket and sent Max a quick text and got an immediate reply. "Max is on his way. Cowboys will keep an extra eye on all the entrances to the ranch."

"Good. I'm feeling better about my situation, but still…"

"Don't go there. We won't let you down."

As she walked up the steps to the Den, he looped the reins around an old hitching post on one side of the building. He gave the buckskin a pat before he followed her inside, where she was picking up papers off the floor.

"Let me do that." He took the load from her, then knelt and grabbed a paper here and an envelope there until he held a whole stack in his hands. "Where do you want these?"

She gave him a mischievous grin, picked up the corner of an official-looking document with one hand, held her nose with the other, and dropped the offending paper in the trash.

"Fontaine's gift to the Wildcat Den?" he asked.

"Some gift! Stinks to high heaven."

"Bet it's some pretty creative writing."

"No doubt."

"I'll get the Rocky T's attorney to take a look."

"I can't afford it."

"I'll cover the expense. KWCB is on my ranchland, so I'm involved one way or another."

She nodded, looking down at the trash. "I'll pay you back."

"We'll talk about it when the time comes." He dropped her stack of paper, which looked like a lot of bills, on top of the desk. "For now, let's get this show on the road. Who knows what mischief they're up to while we're losing time?"

"You're right." She picked up the black phone receiver, stuck her finger in a number's hole, and started rotating the dial. "I'm calling Morning Glory first. We'll need Ken's help, too."

"Don't forget Hedy. We need firefighters for extra patrols."

"I'm on it."

He pulled his cell out of his pocket and hit speed dial for Sheriff Calhoun, hoping he wasn't at some far end of the county and out of reach.

"Sheriff Calhoun here."

"Shane at the Rocky T."

"You got news?"

"Yep. Graham Tanner, Eden's ex, a lawyer named Fontaine, and a videographer paid her a visit a while ago."

"Videographer?"

"I hate to say, but looks like it might get nasty in a trashy tabloid kind of way."

"Not on my watch. And not in my county," Sheriff Calhoun huffed into the phone. "What's the attorney want?"

"KWCB. They figure to get what she's got left."

"No grounds, far as I know."

"Jones'll know what to do, legal wise."

"Best attorney in town."

Shane chuckled at the old joke. "Only lawyer in town."

"That's why the best."

"Listen, I've got the guys here on alert. We can count on our firefighters, too."

"Do you expect trouble?"

"Yes. I just don't know what or where or when." He saw Max outside, so he walked over to the front door and gave a thumbs-up as his foreman settled into the buckskin's saddle and headed toward the barn.

"They're not staying anywhere in Wildcat Bluff, and that's a fact," Sheriff Calhoun said. "I figure they're driving in from another town. Maybe even Dallas. Now we have names, I'll check up on them. And I'll have my deputies on extra alert, too."

"Thanks. No gray sedan today. Big black SUV."

"Got it."

"We're throwing a welcome-home party for Eden tonight at the Rocky T. Hedy and Morning Glory should be inviting the whole county."

"Now that's in your face," Sheriff Calhoun said, chuckling. "Guess you wouldn't mind a little support from my department."

"Hope y'all will come."

"You might be stirring up a hornet's nest."

"Hope so."

Sheriff Calhoun laughed harder. "Keep me posted."

Shane clicked off, slipped his phone back into his pocket, and felt his body kick into gear for battle.

Eden dropped her receiver into its cradle as she looked at him. "Hedy and Morning Glory are on it. Jack is coming in later."

"Ken will be done and up here after a bit."

She put her hand over her heart. "We're doing the right thing, aren't we?"

"What'd I do the other day out in the pasture when that fire was bearing down on us?"

"Fought fire with fire."

"It works."

She suddenly stood up with blue eyes blazing. "You're right. Fire with fire." She walked briskly over to the sound studio's door, stopped, and looked back. "Rae Dell's had enough airtime."

"What do you mean?"

"I started this day about to climb back in the saddle." She squared her shoulders. "Graham knocked me off my feet again, but that's the last time."

Shane grinned, feeling proud of her grit.

"I'm going into the studio. I'll pick up that poster of The Highwaymen and tack it back on the wall."

"Poster? I thought—"

"It fell. Bad mojo. It'll be good mojo to put those singers back in their rightful place."

"Just like you belong in your rightful place."

She jerked open the door, glanced at him again, and gave a small smile. "KWCB is about to welcome back Eden Rafferty."

He grinned. "You can't keep a good cowgirl down."

She mirrored his grin, then stepped into the sound studio and shut the door behind her.

He took a deep breath as he watched her sit behind the board, put on earphones, pull the mic close, and open her mouth.

"Good afternoon, cowgirls...and the cowboys that

make their lives worth roping and riding for. This is Eden Rafferty coming to you from KWCB, the Wildcat Den, serving North Texas and Southern Oklahoma since 1946. Our famous ranch radio is located on the beauteous…Hogtrot Ranch for your listenin' pleasure."

Shane couldn't keep from chuckling as she winked at him, knowing he was listening to her rib him. For many a year now, the Raffertys and the Taggarts had kept that special joke alive.

Nothing could have suited him better than knowing it wasn't going away anytime soon.

Chapter 25

ONE THING EDEN COULDN'T DENY—FOLKS HAD COME OUT in force to welcome her return to KWCB and Wildcat Bluff County. They'd also decided to show just how they liked to party outside on a big ranch in cowboy country. She felt as if she'd stepped onto the set of Southfork Ranch in a rerun of the legendary *Dallas* television series. Any moment, one of the Ewing clan might turn up to charm, threaten, or even ask her to dance.

The Rocky T Ranch might never be the same after this doozy of a party. Hedy and Morning Glory had made it happen with a few well-placed phone calls to galvanize the county. She glanced over tables covered with traditional red-and-white-check cloths that groaned under the weight of platters, dishes, and bowls of good eats from the Bluebonnet Café, Chuckwagon Café, Twin Oaks B&B, and favorite local cooks with drinks from Wildcat Hall.

Folks sat in chairs, clustered in groups, or line danced to a local western swing band comprised of cowboys playing fiddle, mandolin, banjo, guitar, drums, and accordion, with Craig Thorne singing his heart out. Wildcat Jack was in his element as the official DJ and announcer, with Ken by his side as his more-than-willing assistant and tech guru. Nathan was zipping here and there through the crowd with his camcorder at the ready, as if he were a hot paparazzo on the trail of superstars.

She felt a little overwhelmed by the day but completely happy. She'd stood up to Graham and sent him packing, made her debut on the Wildcat Den without losing her voice, and still managed to be on her feet tonight.

She glanced down at her clothes, feeling thankful that Morning Glory had realized she actually had nothing to wear to the party. MG had brought her a vintage western swing dress with fitted waist in a rich turquoise color accented by three bands of white lace on the bodice and three matching bands around the long skirt. MG had even brought matching cowgirl boots that fit. Serena Simmons of the Sure-Shot Beauty Station had arrived with product and talent to fix Eden's hair and makeup. If she hadn't known better, she'd have thought they were preparing her for a photo shoot. As it was, she simply appreciated all they'd done for her.

She looked around for Shane and saw him talking to a group of folks clustered around him. She recognized old friends and new ones she'd just met that evening. Couples getting engaged seemed to be taking over the county—Trey and Misty. Kent and Lauren. Dune and Sydney. They'd been teasing cowboy firefighter calendar guys like Slade Steele and Craig Thorne about when they were going to be roped by a cowgirl from among their throng of adoring fans.

Shane glanced over at her and cocked his head. She held aloft the bottle of water she'd just picked up in answer as to why she wasn't with him. She started to walk back to him, then hesitated on the periphery of the party.

Everything seemed a sudden blur and whirl of too many bright colors, loud sounds, and strong scents. She felt a little dizzy, as if the day had finally caught up with her. She just couldn't take any more input or give out any more energy. She gave Shane a quick smile to reassure him before she quickly walked away from the throng of people and up the steps to the double front doors that had been left wide open. Folks had congregated inside, too.

She kept smiling and nodding, but she also kept moving until she reached Shane's blessedly empty suite. She shut the door behind her and sank down on his big bed. She breathed a sigh of relief, feeling all the happy hours she'd spent here strengthening her.

She slipped her phone out of her pocket and set it on the nightstand. She sipped water, noting it soothed her irritated throat, if not her ragged emotions. After all her bravado today, she still didn't know how this wonderful party could help save her world other than lifting everyone's spirits. And she did feel buoyed by such great generosity.

Still, she'd thought once she got back to Wildcat Bluff, she'd be safe and secure and happy. But Graham had followed her, invading her world again to strip away her assets as well as her confidence. But why? Yes, Fontaine had made his lofty legal excuses, but still, KWCB was peanuts to them. Maybe her ex just couldn't stand to see her happy or successful again.

She didn't have any good answers, and she didn't figure she was going to get any from Graham. She simply needed to defend her world with the help of good friends. As she listened to the muted music and voices coming through the windows, her phone trilled a familiar tune. *Cynthia*. She wondered why her LA friend was calling this time of night. They'd stayed in touch by text since she'd been back, but they didn't have so much in common anymore.

"Hey there," she answered, putting her friend on speakerphone. "What's up?"

"Eden!" Cynthia exclaimed, breathing fast. "What are you doing? Who is that cowboy hunk? Did you really stick it to Graham? I thought he took you for all you were worth!"

Eden felt a sinking sensation in the pit of her stomach, and her throat tightened again. "What?"

"And you can talk! That's wonderful. But really, is that KWCB a real radio station? It looks like it's about to collapse. But you look absolutely fabulous! That shirt. Those jeans. Those boots are to die for. And red, red, red!"

Eden grabbed the bottle of water to moisten her throat before launching her own volley of words.

"The wilds of Texas must really agree with you. Is it the cowboy? I bet a guy like that could turn my complexion all rosy, too."

"Will you please—"

"Well, there is the downside." Cynthia gave a loud sigh. "You are definitely portrayed as a conniving, coldhearted, hot-blooded bitch working her way through the cowboy firefighters of Wildcat Bluff County. And there's the calendar! Did you start with January? Odd or even months? Maybe you began with December and you're working your way backward. Don't leave me hanging. Spill!"

Eden couldn't keep from laughing at the whole fantasy image Graham had created from a bit of video and calendar photos. "I take it Graham put our little confrontation online."

"And how!" Cynthia lowered her voice. "You're getting mega hits—or he is anyway."

"I suppose he's portrayed as the long-suffering ex-husband who just wants to help his sadly out-of-control ex-wife."

"Oh my!" Cynthia hissed like a cat. "You haven't heard, have you?"

"I'm in Texas, not California."

"Don't you get the news?"

"I've been busy."

"Oh yeah, don't we all know it. I could use that kind of R & R. Got a guest bedroom? I'd even take a chance on bedding down in that radio station if there are a dozen hot cowboys on the horizon."

Eden laughed again, finding her spirits lifting even with the news that Graham had kept his word on going with plan B. "KWCB is ranch radio. That means the station and tower are located on a working ranch called the Rocky T. Cowboys are coming and going all the time."

"Be still my heart." Cynthia panted into the phone. "Tell me you're not making this up just to torment my lonely life."

"Several of the cowboy firefighters from the calendar were out here recently to put out a brush fire."

"Did they look as good as they do in their photos?"

"Even better in real life."

"I've always wanted to visit Texas—at least since I saw your hunk online."

"You know you're always welcome here."

"Thanks!"

"But what about that news?"

"Oh, yes." Cynthia chuckled under her breath. "You're going to love this about that loser Graham. You know, I never did think he was worthy of you—even if I did look my best for your wedding."

"You looked gorgeous, as always. Now about Graham—"

"*Sugar Talk* was canceled after your ex made a mess of it."

"Oh no!" Eden felt her heart pound hard in fury and loss. "But that was my baby. I built it from the ground up and took it to the top."

"I know. But he couldn't keep it there. He's a no-talent has-been. He rode you till you dropped like a rock under his weight."

"What's he doing here? Why isn't he looking for work in LA? He's got money. He's got connections."

"Not so much anymore."

"What do you mean?"

"He treated you like dirt. He put you through tabloid hell. People in power don't want that type of backstabbing ego on their teams, particularly when he can't bring in their target audiences."

"I guess I could say he's getting what he deserves, but I don't like to see anybody hurt."

"Hah! And he ran through the divorce money. Now how do you feel about him?"

"All of it?" She took a quick drink of water, hardly able to fathom how he could have spent so much in so short a time.

"It's not cheap being a lonely man."

"I guess that explains why he's come after what little I have left."

"No doubt that's part of it, but online? I'd say he's desperate to get back in the limelight so he can pick up another show."

"Maybe, but—"

"Think about it. From his viewpoint, he reached the top once on your merits, so why wouldn't it work again?"

"Trash me to elevate him?"

"Works for me."

"Talk about a coldhearted…"

"That he is."

Eden stood up and walked over to the bank of windows with the drapes pulled back to watch the party below. There seemed to be some type of agitation in the crowd. They were passing cell phones around, looking angrier all the time. She could hear hollering until Wildcat Jack took control.

"Cynthia," she said. "Wildcat Bluff threw a welcome-home party for me tonight at the Rocky T Ranch. I think folks may be watching my appearance online. They aren't happy about it."

"Are they armed and dangerous?"

"They're definitely dangerous. I suspect Graham may have finally met his match."

"I'd love to see it."

"I'll text you. For now, I'd better go see if I can help Jack quiet the crowd."

"Okay. But remember—don't do anything I wouldn't do."

Eden just chuckled, clicked off, and pocketed her

phone. She didn't know how she was going to face her guests. She knew if she saw the video, she'd be embarrassed at Graham's portrayal of her. She'd be in hot water with their cowboy firefighters, too. They tried to keep a low profile with their photographs in that calendar, and now it'd gone viral. They had nobody to blame but her for dragging Graham into their world.

Still, she might as well face the music now, rather than later. If Graham didn't run her out of town after taking KWCB, the county would do it for him. Maybe she just ought to pack up Betty with a few mementos of her uncle and get out while the getting was good.

She finished off the bottle of water, shut the door behind her, and trudged back into the living room. Everybody had vacated the house, so she kept going, dragging her feet slower and slower as she stepped outside.

Everyone was congregated around the bandstand where Jack was holding court, saying something about losing something. She really wasn't listening too closely, but she might as well go over there and say her goodbyes. At least she could go out with style and dignity.

"There's our hero!" Wildcat Jack hollered, pointing in her direction. "Let's give a hero's welcome!"

Eden turned around and looked behind her, but no one was there. She looked to both sides, but nobody stood there, either. Finally, she turned back around, and she realized everyone was staring at her. *Hero?*

"Ms. Rafferty, will you tell Wildcat Bluff County how it feels to be their hero?" Nathan adjusted his black-rimmed eyeglasses as if for better vision as he focused his handheld camcorder on her.

She looked at the camera lens, at his face, at the

crowd, then just shook her head and smiled at the irony of the situation. Graham had done his best to destroy her, but he hadn't counted on the wild hearts of Texas.

"Eden. Eden. Eden," the crowd chanted her name. "Speech. Speech. Speech."

Nathan held his camcorder closer to her face. "You stood up for all of us in Wildcat Bluff County when you gave those sidewinders what for. Nobody comes here and insults us. If those city slickers want to play online games, we're all in." He patted his camcorder and gave her a wink.

She leaned forward and kissed his cheek. "To answer your question, it feels real good to be back in Texas—where I belong."

Chapter 26

EDEN SLOWLY WALKED TOWARD THE BANDSTAND AS IF IN A dream, not the nightmare she had anticipated at the house. As she put one turquoise cowgirl boot in front of the other, she felt her mid-calf skirt swirl around her legs in a decidedly feminine way while Nathan recorded every step she took, every smile she made, every wave she gave.

How had the Rocky T suddenly become Wildcat Bluff County's version of a Hollywood red carpet event? And even more astonishing, how had she—in borrowed clothes, no less, with a chancy voice—become a local hero, or a "celebrity" in LA parlance? If she was going to give appreciation, she guessed the trophy would have to go to Graham Tanner. And wouldn't that just shrivel his little pea-sized heart?

Shane waited for her at the base of the bandstand, looking as if he'd stepped out of a cowgirl's fantasy in black snakeskin boots, pressed Wranglers, and crisp blue-plaid pearl-snap shirt. Eat your heart out, Cynthia. His eyes, sparkling in the glow of string lights overhead, were only for Eden. He held out his hand.

Up onstage, Wildcat Jack was even more gussied up. He wore a flashy boar suede jacket with long fringe on the yokes and sleeves, with beadwork accenting the shoulders, over his knife-edged jeans and lapis-colored shirt. He wore knee-high boots with long fringe to match the jacket. A beige Stetson with a silver-and-turquoise hatband topped off his outfit.

As she stepped up on the bandstand, Jack pointed at the drummer, who gave a loud drumroll.

"Here's our kick-up-her-heels Eden Rafferty who's gone viral and put our very own Wildcat Bluff County on the map of the world." Jack pointed dramatically at Eden as she stopped beside him.

He was rewarded by cheers from the crowd, but he settled them down again with a few gestures of his hands.

"There's only one catch, folks. We've got to figure out how to keep our hero in her hometown. To do that, we've got to keep that no-good rattlesnake named Graham Tanner from stealing KWCB, our very own ranch radio station!"

Louder and longer cheers followed that call to arms.

"You saw the trash video he put online. All it did was show the fine mettle of our hero. She takes no guff and she don't back down. Give her a big hand for standing up for our county!"

Thundering applause followed those words until Jack quieted the audience again.

"I'm not saying it's gonna be easy. Nothing worth doing ever is. What I am saying is she can have the shirt off my back to help fight that rattlesnake and his fork-tongued mouthpiece. He already took her to the cleaners, and now he's come to Wildcat Bluff to try and take what little she has left. Are we gonna let him get it?"

"No! No! No!" the crowd roared, chanting over and over.

"Then let me hear you say 'Jones'!"

"Jones! Jones! Jones!" the audience chanted this time.

"Jones, where are you?" Jack motioned toward the bandstand. "Come up here!"

Eden watched and listened in stunned surprise as Jack plied their guests with every trick in the book to get them involved in wherever he was taking them. She just didn't know where he was going with all this airing of her dirty laundry. She'd thought she'd just say a few words of gratitude, then hurry back inside. Instead, Nathan was recording every last bit of it. She was through with having her life splattered everywhere in public, but here it came again—even if with good intentions this time.

As she stood there with her back straight, she saw a diminutive woman with straight, black hair and bronze skin, wearing a rancher's fancy crimson jacket with jeans, white shirt, and beaded necklace, thread her way through the crowd, then leap up onto the bandstand.

"Name's Jones." She thrust out her hand to Eden for a shake. "Nocona Jones."

"Good to meet you." She found her hand in a strong grip as she met the intense brown-eyed gaze of a woman who couldn't have been over thirty-five but might as well have been seventy-five for all her projected personal power, confidence, and experience.

"Jones. Jones. Jones," the crowd chanted again.

"That's right," Jack hollered over their words. "Listen up. We're gonna dump those rattlesnakes off their sunny rocks, and then we're gonna send in Jones to tickle their noses."

Jack's words were met by more whoops and hollers.

Eden felt uneasy with the way Jack kept stirring up the crowd, but maybe she was just too tired to appreciate what he was building for her. Shane must have sensed her unease because he moved up closer to her. She was glad for his strong presence, particularly now, when she felt at low ebb.

Suddenly, Jack took off his cowboy hat and tossed it into the audience. Slade grabbed it out of the air, grinning big, and handed it to Morning Glory.

"Y'all go ahead and fill up that hat 'cause Jones here don't come cheap." Jack glanced over at the attorney. "She's still doing her best to replace those horses lost at Palo Duro Canyon."

Eden gave Jones a second glance at the mention of Palo Duro. *Comanche*. She shivered, remembering the tragedy that, even 150 years later, lived on in bleached bones. The U.S. cavalry cornered Quahada Comanche, Southern Cheyenne, Arapaho, and Kiowa in the canyon, where soldiers slaughtered two thousand horses, destroyed lodges, and burned supplies. Nothing was left that might sustain survivors through the winter.

Jones accepted the microphone. "Don't fill that hat on my account. I'm on the job and eager to do it. As most of you know, I come from a long line of eagles that eat rattlesnakes, so I like to tickle noses. And I'm good at it. If folks come into the Cross Timbers with mischief and mayhem on their minds, they'll meet the same resistance they've met for over two hundred years."

"Jones. Jones. Jones," the crowd chanted again.

Eden clasped Shane's hand, feeling more amazed by the moment at the overwhelming support for her.

Jack took back the mic. "Folks, let's still fill up that hat. Eden here is beset from all directions. She can use all the goodwill, good wishes, and good bucks she can get."

Eden felt embarrassed that Jack was asking for donations for her. She wasn't up against a wall—at least, not yet. She motioned for Jack to give her the microphone, then she stepped forward. "Friends and neighbors, you truly honor me by your presence here tonight. I'm not so hard up that I need to take your hard-earned dollars. Keep that for your own families. I can make do."

Shane moved up beside her and leaned down to the mic. "We're doing our best here on the Rocky T to keep her safe—and to keep her on the air."

The crowd roared their approval of Shane's words.

Eden clutched the mic close, feeling her throat tighten again. "I can't promise you that I'll be able to save KWCB, but I'll do my best. And Wildcat Jack, Nathan Halford, and Ken Kendrick are helping me, along with Hedy and Morning Glory and Wildcat Bluff Fire-Rescue and…well, the list is endless. And you're all part of that long list. Just know that I appreciate your support more than I'll ever be able to say." She felt her eyes sting with tears. She quickly handed the microphone back to Jack, out of words and out of voice.

"You heard Eden Rafferty. She's as big of heart as our great State of Texas. Give what you can give. We'll use it to help defray Jones's expenses and whatever else gets thrown at us. But one thing for sure, we're gonna fight to save our ranch radio!" He gave a hand signal to the band. "Now, folks, get back to eating, drinking, dancing, and having the time of your lives. Nothing whets an appetite like getting your blood up."

And with those words, Jack let the band take over and turned to Eden.

She gave him a big hug. "Thanks."

"We didn't come this far to lose out." Jack gave Jones a swift glance. "Did we?"

"I never lose." Jones nodded at Eden with a serious expression in her brown eyes. "I understand there's a deed at the station."

"Yes."

"Would you mind if I had a look at it?"

"You can have it with my blessing." Eden felt a great sense of relief knowing she had such a strong attorney, as well as an entire county, in her corner. "I wish I'd had you in LA."

Jones gave a little shrug. "Past is past. You've got me now."

"I'll get the deed to you tomorrow," Shane said. "Is that soon enough?"

Jones nodded, flicking back long hair as if preparing for battle. "Let's keep the legal end close. If possible, I'd keep your ex and his attorney distracted with online wars. He'll be trying to trash you, while you'll be showing what a great person you are with wide support in your community."

"If we do it right, it ought to work like a charm," Jack said with utter conviction.

"'Underdog overcoming great odds to retrain her voice and save her family ranch radio' is definitely a winner," Jones said. "But he'll be nipping at your heels all the way, so you've got to keep him hopping."

Eden nodded in agreement as she stroked her throat, feeling tired yet buoyed, too.

Jones reached out and squeezed her hand. "You look dead on your feet." She glanced up at Shane. "See she gets some rest. We'll need her strong and focused as we go forward with this battle."

When Shane put an arm around her shoulders, Eden leaned into him as she smiled at Jones and Jack. "Thank you both."

Jones gave a brisk nod, glanced down at the ground in front of the bandstand, then back at Jack with a sly smile. "Looks like your groupies are waiting for a word or maybe even a kiss."

Eden saw a cluster of women of all ages gazing up at Wildcat Jack with adoration in their eyes.

Jack puffed out his chest, winked at Eden, then sauntered, long fringe swaying, over to the edge of the bandstand and knelt down to chat a moment with his fans.

"Well, that's that." Jones straightened her multicolored beaded necklace in the shape of an eagle in flight before she stepped back. "I'm going to hunt down a dance partner. One of those calendar cowboy firefighters ought to do the trick."

Eden couldn't help but grin, thinking how Cynthia would like to be here for just that very reason.

Jones pointed at Morning Glory. "Looks like Jack's hat is about to get filled to the brim. Want me to take charge of the money?"

"Please do," Eden said, feeling amazed—although maybe she shouldn't have anymore—at all the generosity. "But let's use those funds strictly to—"

"No concern," Jones interrupted. "I'll hold the donations in reserve. If we don't end up needing them, we can throw a party for the whole county once we save KWCB."

"Sounds good," Shane replied.

"Now I'm off to find a dance partner." Jones gave them an amused smile before she turned away.

Eden watched her energetic attorney leap off the bandstand and make her way into the audience. Life was definitely looking up.

Shane leaned in close. "Want to dance?"

She tucked her hand through the crook of his arm, wanting nothing so much as to be alone with him. "How about we go upstairs? I've got a horizontal dance in mind."

"You don't have to ask twice." He motioned Jack over to them. "I'm putting Eden to bed, then I'll be down to help you say good night to our guests and close up the place."

"Don't hurry on my account." Jack winked at them. "I promised these beautiful ladies some dances. And I always keep my promises."

Eden leaned over and kissed Jack's cheek. "You're the best."

"Naw." He shook his head as he gave her a mischievous smile. "But I do my best."

"See you tomorrow." Eden stepped down from the bandstand, with Shane right behind her, and about ran into Nathan and Ken. They were dressed almost exactly alike in vintage Wildcat Den T-shirts that they must have dug out of some back corner of the station, faded jeans, ratty sneakers, and zip-up navy hoodies.

"Got good stuff." Nathan tapped the camcorder. "Ken's coming back with me to Thingamajigs to help edit the video. When we're done, we'll post online. It'll knock their socks off."

"What about sleep and school and work?" She suddenly realized how much they were putting their lives on hold to help her.

"It's Friday night. I've got all weekend," Ken said. "Morning Glory says get it done quick. I say stream live from our phones."

"We can't edit that way." Nathan adjusted his eyeglasses. "For this first video, I want a more professional product."

"Okay by me," Ken shrugged. "But if we need to get something out fast, we go to live streaming."

"That's for later," Nathan said. "For now, let's get back to the store and see what I've got in inventory. We may need to order some stuff."

"I don't want you to be out expenses," Eden said. "Please send me a bill."

"No," Shane interrupted. "Send me the bill."

"I don't know about any bills yet." Nathan patted his camcorder. "This could be good for business."

"Right," Ken said. "We're going to get KWCB online, then go from there."

"I'm glad you two are putting this all together so I can focus on the Wildcat Den." She knew she'd never be able to do all the tech stuff on her own, so she was particularly grateful. "Thanks again."

"We're on it." Nathan executed a sloppy salute. "And now we're out of here."

Ken gave them a quick wave before he turned and trotted after Nathan.

"Good guys," Shane said.

She agreed. "The best—just like our entire county."

She glanced around the party, watching folks dance

and eat and mingle again. She knew if she stayed much longer, their guests would feel like they should talk with her, support her, and discuss future plans. She just wanted them to have fun for the rest of the evening, so it was time for her to go.

She squeezed Shane's hand. "Did you say something about putting me to bed?"

Chapter 27

As the wheel of the year turned and settled into April, Eden kept her head down and her focus on the Wildcat Den, doing her best not to think about Graham, Fontaine, and their shenanigans. Nathan, Ken, and Jack conducted online video wars with dignity and finesse. Jones dealt with legal matters. And Shane kept her happy.

She'd been at it all day, talking up the upcoming May Day Rodeo on KWCB. As long as her voice held out, she'd keep reminding folks that their Wildcat Bluff Fire-Rescue needed support. Just as Morning Glory and Hedy had predicted, interest was building, so tickets and entries were swiftly gaining ground. She couldn't take complete credit for the sudden enthusiasm. Shane's Rocky T Ranch welcome-home party had turned into a Wildcat Bluff support party, meaning Graham had inadvertently put their county on the map. Folks near and far were suddenly paying attention to the Wildcat Den as well as the May Day Rodeo.

She tossed back a swallow of Morning Glory's voice concoction, knowing it was helping her keep going, so she could free up Wildcat Jack. For now, she needed a break, so she keyed up Billy Bob, let him take over, and leaned back in her chair. She glanced up at her good mojo. The Highwaymen poster still clung to the wall, so she gave a nod of appreciation to the handsome image of Willie Nelson, Johnny Cash, Waylon Jennings, and Kris Kristofferson. How she would've loved to have been in this studio when they'd passed through North Texas on a tour.

She glanced around, shaking her head. No artists would stop by the Den these days. KWCB was so far behind the times it was laughable—but not funny. She'd made plans with Jack and Ken to sort through the tangle of dusty and dirty wires, cables, and cords that'd been added over decades to keep the equipment running and the lights on. She'd even promised Shane that she would take care of that particular fire hazard, but the best she'd had time to do was buy a couple of big fire extinguishers and stick them in a corner.

So much to do, so little time. And still, she really did need a brief break from the endless stream of backlogged work. She'd thought the fast-paced life in LA had kept her busy, but she'd had professional backup there. Here and now, she was winging it all the way, and she fortunately had terrific help and support by folks who loved KWCB. She chuckled as she stood up, knowing she wouldn't trade what she had in Wildcat Bluff for anywhere or anything else. She particularly wouldn't trade a cowboy named Shane Taggart for anybody in LA.

As she stepped into reception, closing the studio door behind her, the front door popped open. Jack, Ken, and Nathan burst inside, bringing sunlight and raucous energy with them.

"Eden!" Jack collapsed onto the faded and worn blue-plaid sofa that'd been donated first to the fire station but then, after sitting unused, re-donated by Hedy to the radio station. Ken and Nathan crashed down beside him.

She smiled at the sight, wondering what they needed now, because it was always something or other. "How're things going?"

"It has come to our attention that Wildcat Bluff County needs its own narrative to combat the negative creations of somebody who will go nameless," Jack said. "Frankly, I don't know why we didn't think of it sooner."

"Maybe we didn't need it." She sat down behind the desk, leaned back in the creaking chair, and crossed her feet on top of the scarred wooden top.

Nathan hunched forward, putting his hands on his knees. "Yeah. But I bet you've got a voice recording of something somewhere with information."

"I wrote you a brief summary of the county's history," she said, feeling confused about what they needed.

"Right." Ken leaned forward and put his hands on his knees, mimicking Nathan. "But who'll read a bunch of words? We need photos. Videos are even better."

"It's a new world." Jack gave Eden a shrug, as if apologizing for this bit of unwanted news. "As you well know, we are sorely behind the times. Voices alone are good for radio, but it's all about voices *with* action on the internet."

"And that doesn't even get us started on a KWCB platform," Nathan said, sounding impatient.

Eden simply sighed at what they were dropping in her lap. She wasn't completely naive. She knew about a company's need for a platform comprised of social media, website, blogs, and what have you, but platform was so far down her priority list that it hadn't even hit her to-do list.

"Old photos, family photos," Nathan said with

enthusiasm. "It'd be great if they had old cars in them. Maybe folks dressed in 1950s fashion coming in and out of the radio station. Country stars would be best of all."

"We had a Kodak eight-millimeter camera around here back then," Jack said, appearing thoughtful. "We had a screen and projector to go with it. Only way to see what you shot."

"Great!" Ken clapped his hands in excitement. "Let's dig out those films and see them."

"I don't know where they are," Jack said. "Clem threw out a bunch of stuff he didn't use anymore when he remodeled his Quonset hut."

"That's a bummer." Nathan leaned back, sort of collapsing on the sofa. "I wanted to create a KWCB retrospective. I got online access to photos of old radio stations from 1927 on up to show the important historical value, but I wanted originals of the Wildcat Den, too. I'm trying to get permission to use clips from the movies of Gene Autry and Roy Rogers—talk about singing cowboys on radio, television, and big screen! Dale Evans and Gail Davis as Annie Oakley are on our preferred cowgirl list, too."

"I think Clem stuffed most of our history in the storage hut," Jack said, scratching his head. "But it's locked tighter than a tick."

"And we can't find the key." Eden figured she'd eventually run across the key, but at the moment, she didn't have the time to conduct an all-out hunt. "For now, do what you can without it."

"I've got a couple of old photograph albums at home," Jack said. "Morning Glory and Hedy might have some pictures, too."

"Sounds good." She glanced around the group. "The key is bound to turn up, probably in the most unlikely of places."

"It's always the last place you look," Jack said.

"Right," Ken said with a grin. "That's because it is the last place you look."

"So true." She laughed, knowing he was exactly correct. "For today, y'all go ahead with what you've got. I think I'll go over to Uncle Clem's and take a quick nap."

Jack stood up and the other two followed him. "One of these days, you need to start calling that place your home, don't you think?"

She dropped her feet to the floor. "You're right. It's just hard to think of my uncle's home as my own now."

"You might start taking over this very minute," Jack said. "And that includes everything here. It's all yours now, and maybe your family would want it that way."

She felt emotion well up. "It's just difficult to let go of the past."

Jack walked over, leaned down, and kissed the top of her head. "You're carrying the past into the future. Your family will live on in you and the Wildcat Den."

"Thanks. You always know just what to say." She smiled up at him.

"That's my job. I'm a mighty fine DJ."

"You're the best. And Wildcat Jack will always be part of my family and part of KWCB."

Misty-eyed, he gave a little nod before he glanced at his partners. "Come on. Let's go see what we can find in town."

Ken started toward the door, then stopped in his tracks and looked back. "I just thought of something.

Those photos are gonna be black and white." He sounded hugely disappointed at the idea. "Maybe we can find a few color ones."

"If we do, hopefully they won't be too faded, but those can be scanned and restored—if there's time," Nathan said.

"Well, it's been over seventy years now since this all got put on the map." Jack winked at Eden. "Not everything's made to last forever."

"Speak for yourself." Ken pointed at Jack, laughing. "Digital will be here forever."

"Till something better comes along," Nathan called over his shoulder as he stepped outside.

"Maybe I'll invent it!" Ken ran out the door.

"It's good to have some young blood around here," Jack said. "Keeps us from tottering off into our memories and going stale."

"I'm thinking your blood is young forever."

"You never know." He chuckled, adjusting his two long, silver plaits. "Stranger things have happened." He walked over to the front door, paused, and looked back. "I'll take over later. For now, you better get that nap before you're accused of having old blood."

"Hah!" She wadded up a piece of paper and threw it at him.

He batted it aside, laughing, then shut the door behind him.

She took a deep breath, feeling very grateful. How had she gotten so lucky to have so many true friends? Maybe it wasn't her. Maybe it was Wildcat Bluff County. And her family's legacy.

Still, Jack was right. Now wasn't the time to dwell on

the past. She had too much to do and too many depending on her. When she'd thought about returning to Wildcat Bluff, the last thing on her mind had been helping others, planning with others, creating a community. She'd expected to hole up in her uncle's home while she led a solitary heal-my-wounds kind of life until she was strong enough to get back on her feet.

She stood up, smiling at her innocence. From the first moment she'd set foot back in the county, she'd been thrust into a raging river. She wasn't nearly out of the rapids yet, and maybe she never would land on a quiet shore. For the moment, she couldn't even imagine such a life. Wildcat Bluff had become the welcome center of her universe.

She picked up her purse, stepped outside, and closed the door behind her. She started toward Uncle Clem's home—no, her home now—and stopped, turning toward the gazebo.

With spring in the air, she wanted to be outside a moment, so she took the path that wound between wildflowers and flowers gone wild. Rich colors filled her sight. The willow was clothed in bright green, with silky fronds undulating gently in a soft breeze.

She stepped into the cool interior of the gazebo, inhaled the sharp scent of medicinal water, and walked over to the basin. She ran her fingers under the stream of water, wondering how she could let this special place go now that she'd reconnected with it. Yet, in her time back in Wildcat Bluff, she'd learned that the present was more important than the past. She'd wanted to keep this place in stasis, never changing, never evolving, never moving, just like her uncle's home. Maybe she was wrong. Maybe she should let go. Maybe it was time to get on with life.

She closed her fingers as if to hold the water in her hand, but it kept slipping through her fingers and rejoining the constantly moving flow that slid outside and back into the earth. She relaxed her hand, letting go, and felt freed herself to move forward, taking the best of the past with her into the unknown future. Now she could give Shane the gift of water, just as he had so freely given her the gift of love. And she would still find a way to save KWCB's legacy.

With a soft stroke on the side of the basin and a look around at the beautifully designed interior built by artistic hands, she said goodbye and walked outside. Jack was definitely right—she wasn't leaving the past as much as taking it with her. She'd always have the memories of the wonderful times.

She didn't look back as she quickly walked to what had been her uncle's house but was now her very own home. She stepped inside and glanced around the interior. Every single piece of furniture, every single book, every single plate had been picked by him and used by him. She felt comforted here. At peace here. At home here.

Yet she realized that this feeling of being at home wasn't just in her uncle's refurbished Quonset hut. She was at home in Wildcat Bluff County, with people she loved who loved her in return.

She set her purse down on her uncle's table, walked across her uncle's living room, and sat down on her uncle's bed.

And then she smiled, lying down on the bedspread of *her* bed in *her* home.

Chapter 28

EDEN JERKED AWAKE, FEELING DISORIENTED AND CONFUSED for a moment as she glanced around. Everything appeared the same, except the shadows outside were longer. She remembered a sound—something loud and discordant enough to penetrate her deep sleep. She ought to be up and alert anyway, so she could take over the late shift from Rae Dell.

She tossed back the warm throw and put her feet on the floor, still completely dressed in jeans, shirt, and boots. She felt messy and groggy, but also uneasy. Had she left all the doors unlocked again? She just couldn't get used to locking up here, although she should practice better safety with Graham on the prowl.

Maybe Jack, Ken, and Nathan had returned to the station and slammed the doors after Nathan parked his truck in front. If so, she'd better go see what they'd found in town. She hoped they'd located great material.

She opened the front door. No, she hadn't locked it, but it didn't seem to matter now. No vehicles were parked outside the Den, so maybe they'd already come and gone. She'd probably heard doors slamming shut before they left. If they hadn't wanted to disturb her, they would've left photos on the desk in reception. She was anxious to see if they'd uncovered something helpful.

As she started to step outside, she remembered her phone. She wasn't used to being without it, particularly since her LA contacts had only her cell number to reach her. She went back to her purse, pulled out her cell, and slipped it into a front pocket. All set to go, she shut the door behind her.

Feeling good after her nap and earlier decisions, she playfully set the swing to gyrating before she stepped off the deck and headed toward the Wildcat Den. She delighted in the fresh spring air, a mockingbird's elaborate song, and the sheer pleasure of knowing she was in the right place at the right time in her life.

As she neared the station's front door, she caught a whiff of smoke, but it was so faint she figured ranchers might be enjoying an early evening blaze in their fireplaces or maybe the smell came from the residue of their recent brush fire. In any case, she really didn't want to think about fires, controlled or uncontrolled, so she thrust aside even the idea of an acrid scent.

She took the few steps up to the entry, opened the door, walked inside, and checked the desk. No photographs. She glanced around the room. Everything appeared as she'd left it. What had awakened her? Not Jack, Ken, and Nathan. She shrugged, deciding it didn't really matter. She'd just go back, fix something for dinner, and invite Shane to her home—now that it seemed like home—before she went to work.

She'd turned to go outside when she caught a whiff of smoke again. She froze in place, feeling her blood run cold as she sniffed the air. Yes, she definitely smelled smoke. And it was *inside*, not outside.

She glanced back around reception but saw nothing suspicious. She focused on the closed door to the sound studio. Shane had warned her about a possible fire hazard in there. Maybe he'd been right. Maybe not. But she was taking no chances. She leaned across the desk, grabbed the black phone's handset, and dialed 911. Nothing. She tried again. Still nothing. She listened for a dial tone. Nothing. Maybe there was a fire and it had already destroyed the phone line. She dropped the useless receiver on the desk.

As she paced back to the open door, she pulled her phone out of her pocket and hit speed dial.

"Miss me already?" Shane answered in a deep voice.

"I think there's a fire in the Den."

"What!"

"I smell smoke. If there's a fire, it must be in the studio because I'm in reception and it's not here."

"Get out of there!"

"No. I'm not about to lose KWCB."

"That place is a tinderbox. If it goes up, it'll go fast and furious."

"I remember enough from our classes to know I don't want extra oxygen in here." She slammed the front door tightly shut.

"You're not going to leave, are you?"

"Right now, I'm the only one here to stop the fire."

"I'm on my way. Please don't—"

"There's a good chance I can control the blaze in time."

"Okay, Eden, I know you're going in there," he said in a resigned voice. "I want you to be safe, so listen to me."

"I'm listening."

"First, feel the doorknob. If it's hot, wait for the fire-fighters. If it's not, then you can cautiously enter."

She walked across the floor and clasped the knob. "It's not hot."

"Do you have gloves?"

"No."

"I've got some in my truck," he said. "Do you have canisters?"

"Yes. I bought two class C fire extinguishers. I thought dry chemicals would be best in the studio."

"Good. I've got a couple of cans in the truck," he said to the sound of a pickup door shutting. "I'll call Hedy on my way down."

"Thanks."

"Are you still determined to go in there?"

"Yes. If I can save KWCB, I must try."

"Will you go in the bathroom and wet a towel to cover your nose, so you don't breathe the fumes?"

"I'm going there now." She ran into the bath, grabbed a hand towel, held it under the faucet until it was dripping wet, and ran back to the studio door.

"I wish you'd wait for me. I'll be there in a moment."

"Can't do it, but I'll be careful."

"You better be."

Now or never. She slipped her phone into her pocket, placed the wet towel over her nose, and slowly opened the door a crack. She caught the acrid scent of an electrical fire, but she didn't see a roaring blaze bearing down on her. She cautiously opened the door wider and flipped on the inside lights.

She couldn't see flames, but the room was rapidly filling with smoke. She had to do something fast. Fortunately, she had the chemical fire extinguishers. She didn't want water anywhere near her equipment—she didn't intend to forfeit anything to a fire.

She edged into the room, searching for the source of

the blaze. She quickly decided that her best bet was to get the cans and go straight to the tangle of wires behind the board, since that was the most likely origin.

But she couldn't locate the extinguishers. They weren't where she'd left them. Somebody must have moved them out of the way, because she'd kept them near the board. She glanced around but still didn't see them. She looked up and gasped in shock. A line of fire was licking up the wall toward The Highwaymen poster—talk about bad mojo if it got charred to a cinder.

Now she was having trouble seeing, so she dropped to her knees for clearer air and bumped into the two cans under the board. She couldn't imagine who'd put the canisters in such an inaccessible place, on top of them being in the way of sitting down. But she'd found them. Now to remember how she'd been trained to use them. PASS came to mind, as in Pull the pin, Aim the hose, Squeeze the lever, and Sweep the hose.

First things first. She dragged a canister out from under the board with one hand while holding the towel over her nose with the other. She pulled the pin, aimed, squeezed, and caught the blaze full blast before it could reach The Highwaymen. Good mojo.

She got down on her knees again, dropped the towel because she needed both hands, and squeezed under the board. She coughed, trying to clear her throat as she felt the heat, heard the sizzle, smelled burning electrical wires, and inhaled toxic smoke. She dropped flat on her stomach and swept the hose back and forth, coating everything in sight, slowing the fire but not putting it out. She thrust the empty can out from under the board and grabbed for the other one. She missed it, but she felt something sharp and metal under her fingers. A key. What was it doing here? Didn't matter. She thrust it into her pocket, then grabbed the other canister.

She pulled the pin and started another sweep, sweating from the heat, coughing from the fumes and smoke that were irritating her throat. Still, she kept coating the wires until she began to feel light-headed and black spots swam before her eyes. But she wouldn't stop, not until she'd used up every bit of chemical in the extinguisher.

"Eden!" Shane called as he set down two canisters, grabbed her legs, and tugged her out from under the board. "Let me take over. I've got fresh cans."

She tried to respond, but nothing could get past her swollen throat. She started to stand up, but she felt woozy and couldn't quite make it.

"You're scaring me." Shane picked her up, carried her through reception, and eased her down on the top step outside. "Slade and Craig are on their way."

She already felt better in the fresh air, so she glanced up, noting he'd pulled on his firefighter gear for safety. She squeezed his hand, then pointed back into the station.

"Are you okay? I won't leave you if—"

"Go," she whispered, wishing she could put more emphasis on the word, but she could tell he got her meaning clearly enough.

"Okay. Stay here." He ran back inside.

She sat on the top step, taking deep breaths to purify her lungs while wanting to be with him, finishing off the blaze. Fortunately, she'd bought the fire extinguishers and had them handy, or the outcome would have been vastly different. She coughed, trying to clear her lungs as she kept inhaling clean air.

She heard the booster's siren wailing out on Wildcat Road before the rig barreled between the white fences and came to an abrupt stop in front of her. Slade leaped down, grabbed a canister, and ran past her into the station. Craig hurried over carrying an EMT field kit.

She shook her head, indicating she didn't need it, and pointed at the station. "I'm okay. Help inside."

"Slade's got the fire covered. You're my priority." He checked her pulse and blood pressure while looking into her eyes. "Your numbers are okay. Any chest pain? Difficulty breathing or swallowing?"

"Water, please."

He pulled a bottle of water out of his kit, cracked the top, and handed it to her.

She took a long swallow, letting it slide down her throat to wash away the chemical taste and ease the constriction.

"Better now?" He knelt, watching her closely.

"Much better." She took a deep breath and another swallow of water.

"Oxygen?"

"I don't think so. My throat—"

"It'll probably be scratchy for a bit, but it should heal with no problem. You might want to stop by the clinic for a second opinion."

"I'm fine." And she did feel much better as she sipped water.

"I can take her to the clinic," Shane said as he came out the front door followed by Slade.

"Really, I'm okay. Hoarse is all." She smiled up at them. "Thank you all so much."

"You had the blaze well under control by the time I got here, so we just finished it off." Shane squeezed her shoulder.

"Did we save everything?"

"You've got a big wiring problem, but I imagine it's fixable," Shane said, getting a nod from Slade in agreement.

"That's wonderful news. Well, not about the wiring, but about everything else." She felt a vast sense of relief that they could still broadcast, at least once repairs were made in the studio.

Slade walked back to the rig and set his extinguisher inside before he came back. "Odd fire."

"Yeah," Shane replied. "I hate to say it, but…"

"Right." Slade looked down at Eden. "We'll want to do some tests before you clean up, but I suspect arson."

"Arson!" She jumped to her feet, felt dizzy, and leaned into Shane.

"Careful." He put an arm around her waist to steady her.

"But that's impossible," she insisted. "Somebody is there most of the time and we lock up at night."

"Was it locked this afternoon?" Shane asked.

"No. I intended to return after my nap." She thought back. "A loud sound woke me. Do you suppose…"

"I doubt we can prove a thing," Slade said. "But Sheriff Calhoun ought to have a look."

"Why would Graham try to destroy something he wants?" she asked, feeling more puzzled than ever.

"More publicity?" Craig asked as he closed his EMT kit with a *snap*.

As Eden thought about the scope of that idea, Nathan drove up and parked beside the booster.

"Are you okay?" Jack hollered as he got out of the pickup. "Hedy let us know about the fire."

"Just fine," Eden called out to relieve his mind, feeling the strain in her throat but knowing it was a small price to pay for saving KWCB.

"I'm recording this incident." Nathan got out from behind the wheel with camcorder at the ready.

Ken followed them, eyes downcast. "If Morning Glory hears about this, she might not let me come back—danger and all."

"We'll put in a good word for you," Shane said, smiling at him. "I bet she'll understand."

"Looks like y'all got stuff sorted out here." Jack glanced around the area, then refocused on Eden.

"Might not have been an accident," Slade said.

"No-name's doing?" Jack asked.

"Can't know. At least not yet." Shane glanced up at the Den as if he could find something that would explain the problem.

"I suppose this fire will be in the news." Eden wondered if she'd ever get a quiet moment in Wildcat Bluff.

"If not, we'll make it news," Nathan said, insisting. "Suspicious fire at the Wildcat Den. Eden Rafferty saves KWCB, her family's legacy."

"Sounds good." Jack grinned. "Once more, she's Wildcat Bluff's hero."

Ken laughed. "Eat your heart out, Graham Tanner."

"We win again," Nathan said, then looked around the group with a worried expression on his face. "How bad is the damage?"

"Can we go on the air?" Jack asked.

"Maybe it's time for an upgrade." Ken sounded excited at the prospect.

"Wiring's shot," Shane said. "Once the sheriff takes a look and we get samples, it's all yours to fix."

"Okay." Nathan snapped his fingers. "Let's get this story and footage up online. We'll explain that the Wildcat Den is undergoing repairs but will be back on the air soon."

"Too slow," Ken said. "Let's set up social media sites and announce it there."

"Let's do it all." Jack gave Eden a sly wink. "You sure you're okay?"

"I'm getting there."

"In that case, we're out of here. We've got to get ahead of the nameless one on this hot news." Jack headed for the truck with Nathan and Ken right behind him.

Craig rubbed his jaw. "Does Wildcat Jack ever slow down?"

"Not so you'd notice," Shane said, chuckling. "If y'all will finish up here and lock up the place, I'll drive Eden to the house and babysit her."

"Good idea," Craig replied. "Aftereffects of the trauma might set in any moment."

Eden pushed away from Shane to stand up straight, even though she was feeling a little queasy as she came down from her harrowing experience. She didn't want any of them to think she wasn't strong enough to take care of KWCB. "I'll have you know I'm fine. Fighting a fire is all in a day's work."

"Better take advantage of being pampered while you can," Slade said with a sly smile. "We'll call the sheriff and do the dirty work here."

She nodded in agreement, suddenly wanting nothing more than to catch her breath where she felt safe. "You could be onto something there."

"Eden, after Shane takes you to his place, one of us will drive your Bug up there so it's not vulnerable here," Craig said.

"Thanks," she replied. "The key is in the center desk drawer in the office."

"When you leave the VW, just toss the key under the planter beside the back door." Shane tugged her closer.

"Come on," she said, smiling up at him. "Hedy highly recommends your hot tub for smoke inhalation. I'm feeling like it would do wonders for me."

Chapter 29

SHANE SAT NAKED AS A JAYBIRD IN HIS HOT TUB, WATER hissing and bubbling around him, but he was steaming hotter than the water. He reached past his cutoffs where he'd tossed them on the wood rim and picked up an old, chipped KWCB promotional coffee mug. He wasn't risking anything more fragile in his current mood. And that mood was mad as hell.

He tossed back a slug of Slade's wine, feeling it stoke his innards even hotter as he relived that terrifying time back at the Wildcat Den. Once he'd heard Eden's words, he hadn't been able to get to her fast enough, knowing she'd open that door, knowing she'd rush in there no matter how high the flames or dense the smoke. He'd lost years off his life not knowing what he'd find when he got there.

Fortunately, she'd been smart, courageous, and okay. But it could have gone the other way, and that's what made his hands tremble as he gripped the mug with both palms. He swallowed another slug, hoping it'd help ease him down from his ready-to-rock-and-roll emotions.

After they'd put out the fire, they'd stood in front of the Wildcat Den, stinking of smoke and sweat and chemicals. Yet not one of the men had said what was uppermost on his mind. He hadn't said it. Slade and Craig hadn't. And neither had Jack, Nathan, or Ken. And they hadn't said it because they hadn't wanted to spook Eden, so they'd opted to use business and humor to push past the moment. Yet every last one of them had exchanged a worried look that said it all: *Eden Rafferty had been in great danger*.

He rubbed the kink in his shoulder, created by his muscles tensing up in anticipation of cracking Graham Tanner's arrogant nose. He'd use his elbow—no point messing up a hand for a lowlife scumbag like Tanner. Unfortunately, they no longer lived in the Wild West, where justice was swift and certain. They had to play by a few rules, but those could be bent, particularly when it concerned their womenfolk.

Tanner had gone too far. And not one of them today doubted he'd been behind the radio station fire. Time would prove their point, but for now, they moved forward on that assumption. Endanger the ladies of Wildcat Bluff County? Expect to reap the consequences. Maybe it was an old-fashioned attitude, but cowboys had been raised by women and men to respect, honor, and protect their families and friends. And nothing would keep them from it.

He heard his phone chirp, so he quickly set down his mug and slipped his cell out of his cutoffs. He was relieved to see Sheriff Calhoun was returning his call.

"Shane, we got what we needed at KWCB. If Eden's feeling up to it, she can start the cleanup and repair."

"Thanks. I'll let her know or you can call her."

"I already texted her, since she didn't pick up."

"She's probably in the shower." He glanced up at the house, wishing she'd hurry up and come out, so he'd be reassured that she was still doing okay.

"I know you're anxious to hear what we found at the station."

"It's on my ranch, so I'm doubly involved with what's going on."

"I doubt we can prove anything, but we smelled accelerant, so something as simple as gasoline was probably used to start it. No surprise there. What's interesting is the phone line was cut outside. And I mean cut clean. It wasn't frayed with age or chewed by a varmint."

Shane felt his heart rate speed up. "What if she'd been trapped inside without her cell phone?"

"Yeah."

"Maybe that was the original plan, but I got there too fast."

"Could be that or it was meant to scare her." Sheriff Calhoun clicked his teeth in annoyance. "If this is Graham Tanner, he's escalated from verbal attacks to psychological attacks to physical attacks."

"We can't let him anywhere near her."

"Right. For now, let's go on the assumption this is Tanner's work, but I'll keep an open mind if another lead turns up."

"We won't leave her alone." Shane glanced up at the house again. She'd probably complain that she didn't need bodyguards, but he was going to override any of her objections.

"I'll have patrols swing by your place more often."

"We'll up the alert for everybody."

"That'll do it," Sheriff Calhoun said. "By the way, I checked records. Tanner is staying at a motel in Sherman, so he's out of our county but still in the area. Fontaine did his job and flew back to LA."

"Tanner gets anywhere near her or my ranch again and he's going to wish he'd never left LA."

"If he's smart, he'll be satisfied with what he's done today."

"We can't count on him being smart."

"But we can't count on him being dumb," Sheriff Calhoun said. "What we can count on is knowing our county and depending on our people."

"Right."

"Call me if you run into any more trouble."

"Got you on speed dial."

"Good." And Sheriff Calhoun clicked off.

Shane sat there a moment, looking at his phone and thinking about what needed to be done next. He could basically turn his ranch over to Max and the cowboys till Eden was completely safe. He needed to help her and Jack get KWCB back on the air, although Nathan and Ken might be more help with that tech endeavor.

He snorted at a sudden thought. Not too many weeks ago, he'd have thought this was the answer to his prayers. The Wildcat Den was finally off the air after all these years. It'd be the perfect time to step in and convince Eden there was no need to spend all the time, effort, and money on repairs. He'd buy out the rest of her lease, so she'd have funds to get on with her life, and he'd have the spring water, as well as extra acreage. She could sell or move everything, so she'd be more financially solvent.

He picked up his mug and tossed back the last of the wine. What an absolute loss that would've been for him, for her, for their family legacies, and for the county. And he would've been the one to shoulder the complete blame. Worst of all, he'd never have known the depth of love and happiness that he'd experienced since she'd come back to the Rocky T Ranch.

He glanced up at the house again. And smiled. She was waiting for him. He could feel it in his bones. His heart rate kicked into overdrive. He wondered what she was wearing, if anything. He wondered where she was waiting. He wondered how he'd ever thought life could be complete without her.

Galvanized by his thoughts, he splashed water over the edge as he got out and yanked on his cutoffs. He ran up the path, flipped off the lights, slipped inside through the sliding doors, locking them behind him, and listened for her.

Suddenly, he knew exactly where she would be, as if she'd whispered in his ear, drawing him closer and closer to the place he'd wanted to be invited all those years ago. He quickly walked down the hall, feeling his entire body tingle in anticipation, and stopped outside the room she'd slept in when she was younger. Finally, he was free to visit her inner sanctum.

The door was ajar, so he pushed it all the way open. Moonlight poured through the bank of windows to cast soft light across her bed, where she sat with her back propped against pillows. She wore a large, faded KWCB promotional T-shirt that matched the mug he'd left by the hot tub. Tonight, their minds were totally in sync.

He smiled.

She smiled.

And no words were needed between them as she held out her arms to welcome him into her bed.

He slipped off his cutoffs and dropped them to the floor as she pulled the T-shirt over her head and tossed it on top of his shorts.

And then he was in her bed, and she was in his arms as he'd craved for so many long lonely years.

He pressed soft kisses across her face, worshipping her in the only way he knew to show the depth of his feelings without using the one word he feared would drive her away.

And yet, worship could only last so long with her in his arms, returning his kisses and caresses with fevered frenzy. He turned marauder, staking out his claim as he plundered every sweet valley and every tantalizing mound of her soft flesh in his quest to fuse their bodies, so she would never let him go.

She made a soft mewling sound as he kissed up the long column of her throat to nibble on the sensitive flesh of her ear before he returned to her mouth, now hot and swollen from his kisses. He teased her lower lip with his tongue, toying with her until she trembled in his arms and he plunged deep inside to share a kiss that left them both breathless.

He couldn't get enough of her, even though he lay with his entire body pressed down the length of her, so that there was absolutely nothing between them — nothing that could ever come between them. He felt her curves, her muscles, her heat, but it still wasn't enough for him. He wasn't sure anything could ever be enough until he heard that one precious word from her lips that would give him what he craved the most. But until that day came, he would give her what she craved the most.

He rose up on his elbows and looked down at her beauty turned silvery in the moonlight. He pressed a hot kiss to each pink tip of her breasts and watched as they budded with passion. He trailed kisses down to her navel, teasing with his tongue as he stroked her full breasts, feeling her turn restless and needy under his touch. She wasn't the only one who was needy. He was so hard and hot that he could hardly restrain his desire to instantly give her everything she deserved in a man. But he'd been patient a long time.

He stroked downward, using both hands to glide over her silky skin until he reached the apex of her thighs. She spread her legs, watching him watch her with eyes gone dark. He took his time, stroking her soft folds with long fingers, savoring every tantalizing detail of her hidden depths. Hot, she was blazing hot. Wet, she was soaking wet. He couldn't restrain himself a moment longer, so he curled his fingers deep inside and stroked in a way he knew would set her on fire. And it did. She cried out, clenching around him, arching up toward him, moaning in satisfaction.

As she slowly relaxed, she smiled up at him with a mischievous glint in her eyes and pointed toward her nightstand.

He glanced over, grinned, and picked up a condom. He tore open the packet and suited up. He'd been patient long enough. Nothing could hold him back now. He knelt between her thighs and placed her legs over his shoulders. She was completely open to him now—and not just her body. She gazed at him with such soft warmth and tenderness in her blue eyes that it could only be the look of love.

And that was his undoing. He thrust into her, heard her cry out in pleasure, and then he was lost in the throes of a passion he'd never experienced before this very moment. He pounded into her, harder and longer and stronger, until she was clawing at his back, riding him, moaning, crying, clinging, and they were swept together as one into a powerful wave of ecstasy that rolled and hissed and slammed them into an all-consuming crest. Afterward, he lay still and pulled her against his chest. They were both breathing fast, hearts pounding together.

He wanted to tell her he loved her, but he didn't think the timing was good. Instead, he pushed damp hair away from her face, kissed her lips, and gave her the next best thing. "I'll renew your lease."

"What?" She sat up, frowning down at him. "I'm giving you back Wildcat Spring."

"What?" He rose up on an elbow, looking at her in confusion. "But I thought—"

"Now you want to renew the lease? Do you just feel sorry for me after that fire?"

"I could never feel sorry for you."

"Hah!" She jumped out of bed and pulled on her T-shirt. "I've got my own perfectly good home. And I'll tell you something else—I don't have to keep KWCB on the Rocky T. Those buildings were moved here, and they can be moved out of here."

"What are you talking about?" He got up and pulled on his cutoffs, feeling his confusion turn to anger. "KWCB has always been here. How can you even think about moving it?"

"It'd solve all your problems, wouldn't it?" She stalked over to the bench, picked up her jeans, and jerked them on with a huff. "The Rocky T isn't the only ranch in Wildcat Bluff County."

"I give you what you want and you're mad at me?"

He didn't know what to do. He didn't even know what had happened. Maybe she'd inhaled too much smoke or gotten too tired. He had no idea.

She turned toward him, blinking back tears, clenching her fists. "From the first moment I got back here, you've had me on a yo-yo. No lease. Maybe lease. Yes lease. And let's just throw in a little great sex to keep me coming back for more."

"You think the sex is great?" At least he had something going for him in this argument.

"You *know* it's great. That's beside the point."

"Not from where I'm standing."

"Sit down then." She pushed her hair back from her face. "I can't take it anymore. Today, on top of everything else, just about did me in."

"I understand."

"No, you don't. You've got everything in life. It's all zipped up nice and neat. You aren't vulnerable to the whims of a rancher with a hard-on."

He couldn't keep from grinning at the image she'd conjured with her words. One thing about it, she'd sure gotten her voice back.

"It's not funny. What I'm saying is that I'm vulnerable. When the lease runs out, somehow or other, I'm taking KWCB and leaving the Rocky T."

In a world turned upside down, one thing made sense to him. "You're not vulnerable. You've got the entire county behind you. You've got your voice back. You've got talent and a future. You've always had the guts to go out and get what you want in life."

"Thanks for reminding me that I'm a big fat failure." She sat down on the bench and put her head in her hands.

He didn't dare touch her. He hardly dared speak. Everything that meant anything to him hung on his next few words. He was better with animals than he was with people. Still, he'd do his best. He knelt in front of her and drew her hands away from her face. "Look at me, Eden."

"No." She shook her head, causing her hair to fly out then back down. "I want to go home."

"You are home. The Rocky T has always been your home."

"No. It's *your* home."

"You're wrong."

She finally glanced up at him, but only to give him a baleful glare.

"It's *our* home."

"The lease—"

"I told you I'd renew it." He abruptly stood up. "But that won't do now, will it?"

"You can't imagine how badly I wanted to get home, where nobody could take away what was mine and where I could feel secure again."

"So you wouldn't be vulnerable to the likes of Tanner."

"I guess I've been running so hard since I got here, trying so hard to get back what I'd lost, that I didn't stop to think about the reality of my situation. Maybe I should thank Graham for making me see the light of day."

Shane felt sick at heart. He was losing her before his very eyes. And he didn't know how to stop his loss or her pain.

She glanced around the room. "I adore this room, this

house. It's been a wonderful visit to happier days. Thank you."

If he didn't do something drastic, she was going to leave and she wouldn't be coming back. She'd talk herself not only out of his life but out of Wildcat Bluff, too. He couldn't let her do it. He knew her heart. He'd always known it. He'd just grown up too much to remember—or maybe, when she'd left, it'd been too painful to hang on to all the details of that night up on Lovers Leap.

"It's not just a visit. You've come to stay."

"I told you—"

"Do you remember the last thing you promised me on Lovers Leap?"

She abruptly stood up, eyes wide in wonder.

"Do you remember your promise?"

She turned away, paced across the room, and stood with her back to him.

"I waited." He walked closer to her.

"We were young. We didn't mean—"

"I promised I'd wait."

"That's why you didn't marry?" She whirled around, searching every feature of his face with her wide blue eyes.

"I've had your ring for years."

"My ring?"

"You showed me one you liked in a magazine."

She put a hand over her mouth, blinking back tears.

He didn't let her emotions stop or slow him. He had to be ruthless—for both of them. "We could go to Vegas, but I bet Wildcat Bluff would like to see a big, fancy wedding. Summer ought to be about right."

"Wedding?" She stepped back, keeping her hand over her mouth as if to retain words or emotions.

"That's what you promised me."

"When I got back?"

"You told me you loved me and you'd be back to marry me."

"I'm not comfortable with the L word or marriage anymore."

"I love you. I've always loved you. I will always love you." He reached up and gently brushed a tear from her cheek. "I know you love me, too."

She closed her eyes, bowed her head, and then looked back at him. "I tried not to love you. It hurt too much being separated from you. I figured you'd moved on with life. I've tried not to love you since I got back."

"Didn't work, did it?" He felt a small frisson of hope, but he knew he wasn't out of the woods yet.

"No." She straightened her shoulders and stood taller. "But it doesn't matter."

"How can it not matter?" He felt his hope plummet again.

"If I married you, we'd both always wonder if I did it just so I'd have a home on the Rocky T, someplace where I'd feel safe and secure, someplace where I could build KWCB without worrying about losing it."

"Stop right there. We've always loved each other. Marriage has nothing to do with what happened to you in LA. Once you get back on your feet, you won't feel vulnerable anymore."

She reached up and stroked his face with tears streaming down her cheeks. "I love you, but I'm leaving you."

He simply pulled her against his chest, cradling her like he'd done when they were young and she'd stubbed her toe or fallen out of a tree. If she was hurting, he was hurting. Right now, they were both hurting.

She eased back from him and brushed her tears away. "I need to go home."

"You can't go back to Clem's place. It's not safe."

"But I want—"

"You know it's not safe." He put his arm around her shoulders and tugged her against him. "You'll stay here and get a good night's sleep. Everything will look better after you're rested in the morning."

"I guess you're right. It's not safe. But I'll sleep here in my room."

"That bed's too small for me."

"I'll sleep alone."

"We'll sleep in my room." He guided her in that direction. "If I can't watch over you to make sure you're safe, I won't sleep a wink."

She gave a little huff, frowning. "But I'm not sure—"

"And if we both can't get to sleep, we can make wedding plans," he said with a chuckle to ease the tension, but he meant every word of it.

Chapter 30

EDEN KNEW SHE WAS ALL ABOUT SOUND. MAYBE SHE'D BEEN born with that instinct or maybe she'd been bred that way. Maybe both. In any case, when she needed answers or comfort or understanding, she reached for sound to help enlighten her. Now, she needed monumental help.

She listened to the sound of Shane sleeping next to her—soft exhales that marked deep sleep. She listened to the sound of the house—cracks and pops from the heater and hums of the refrigerator. She listened to the sounds outside—birdsong announcing the arrival of dawn, the rustle of leaves responding to a slight breeze, a truck's engine rumbling out on Wildcat Road.

What did she learn? Everything sounded perfectly normal for an everyday work week in the county. Folks would soon be up and about, feeling happy with their lives as they went about their daily routine. She turned her head to look at Shane. He appeared totally relaxed and content after their confrontation.

She was not content or relaxed or at peace. She was embarrassed by her overreaction last night. She had excuses. She'd been stressed and exhausted from the fire. She was in protective mode after her disaster of a marriage and Graham's harassment. She'd been desperately trying to save KWCB. And maybe she was just flat-out exhausted and felt terribly vulnerable.

And then Shane came along, knowing her trigger

buttons and pushing every one of them. He'd made her cry when she'd dried all her tears long ago. He'd made her love when she'd stopping loving long ago. He'd made her remember their promises when she'd forgotten long ago.

All those realizations made her want to cry again because he'd also made her realize the truth about herself. She understood now that she'd thought if she ran long enough, fast enough, far enough, she could outrun all the heartache, all the loss, all the pain. But she hadn't counted on running straight into a man's arms—a down-to-earth cowboy who wouldn't let her turn away from the truth any more than he would turn away from it.

And the truth was she loved him. She'd always loved him. And this morning, she even remembered that she had proof of what he'd always meant to her. She wanted to give it to him to show that he wasn't the only one who'd treasured what they'd always meant to each other. But she needed to go to her place to get it.

She slipped out of bed, picked up her T-shirt and jeans, and walked quietly out of his suite. She carried her clothes to her old bedroom, put them on, and slipped into her boots. She hurried down to the kitchen, where there'd always been a magnetic notepad with attached pen on the refrigerator. She scrawled a quick note to Shane, telling him that she was going down to her home to pick up something and she'd be back soon. She placed the note on the dining table, so he would see it when he got up and came looking for coffee.

Outside, she found Betty's key under the planter. She sat down in the Bug, started the engine, and heard it backfire several times before settling down. She took off down the lane, watching the white fences zip past in a blur until she turned onto KWCB property. She popped out of Betty, started to walk away, then remembered to lock up. She fitted the VW key into the driver's side door lock and turned it. If some cowboy or other walking muscle mass didn't simply pick up Betty and stroll away with her, the bug was safe.

She paced around the area, taking inventory. If she owned land, the station building and Quonset huts could be moved to a new location. If she had money, the buildings could be set up with new wiring and new everything. If she did all that, maybe she should start with new buildings anyway. She walked toward the lane, saw a long shadow, and glanced up. She'd forgotten the transmission tower. It was like a silver-colored metal sculpture reaching high into the sky. How could she ever move it? Maybe there was new technology that made a tower unnecessary. Anyway, this was KWCB. If she moved the Den's home, would it still be her family's radio station?

Yet she wasn't here to think about the Den. She walked back, knocking loose rocks aside, scuffing an errant yellow dandelion. She felt a deep peace and relaxation here that comforted her. She unlocked the front door, slipped inside, and locked the door behind her.

Home sweet home. She tossed her keys on top of the bar as she glanced around her cozy, little place that made her feel as if she were wrapped in the comforting safety of her uncle's arms. If not for Graham, she could be happy here. She could slowly heal her wounds. She could rebuild her life. *With Shane*.

She walked over to the bookshelf, reached to the

top, and selected a rock from the assortment of keep-
sakes there. It wasn't big. It didn't look special. But it
meant the world to her. She'd found it on her last ride
with Shane to the large sandstone rock where they'd
frequently climbed to the top, so they could look out
over the pastures. She'd saved the rock to remind her of
that special time. Uncle Clem had understood and kept
it for her. After all these years, she wanted to share the
memory it represented with Shane.

She felt so much at peace that she wanted to savor
the moment. She set the rock on the bar, then went
into the kitchen and washed her hands at the sink. She
pulled out the coffeemaker, put in a filter, added coffee,
and poured in water. It was such a comfortable-routine
type of activity that she couldn't keep from smiling in
pleasure. She was in her own home. Truly.

She stopped in her tracks. That's what she'd been
missing in her life. Generosity from Wildcat Bluff
County or Shane or Morning Glory or Hedy or any
number of local folks was wonderful and helpful. Love
and friendship were icing on the cake of life, but somebody had to bake the cake first. And that had to be her. If
she was going to take back her self-esteem, self-respect,
and self-confidence, she had to salvage her own life
first. She didn't just owe it to herself. She owed it to
Shane, too.

Now was the time to start fresh, with the dawning of
a new day. Most of her clothes were here, so she'd just
get cleaned up before going back to the ranch house. She
took a quick shower and changed into clean jeans and a
long-sleeve T-shirt. She tossed her old T-shirt and jeans
that smelled of smoke into the washer for later attention.

She poured a cup of coffee, unlocked the front door, walked barefoot onto the outside deck, and sat down in a chair. She set her cup on the small table and simply enjoyed the warm blush of color on the horizon that heralded a new day. She had more blessings than she could count on two hands.

In a moment, she'd call Shane and see if he wanted to join her here, but for now, she simply savored the moment. As she sipped her coffee, she heard his pickup head down from the ranch house. When he parked beside Betty, she gave a little wave and beckoned him over.

He stepped down from his truck, wearing boots, jeans, shirt, and jean jacket and looking every bit the strong cowboy. He reached back inside and came out with a huge crystal vase containing two dozen yellow roses. He turned toward her with a mischievous smile.

She stood up, feeling happiness race through her at the sight of him.

He stepped up on the deck and held out the flowers. "These are for you."

"They're gorgeous." She clasped the heavy vase with both hands, stuck her nose in the bright blooms, and inhaled rose fragrance. "But where did you get them this early in the morning?"

"I bought them last night and planned to surprise you with them this morning, while I served you breakfast at the ranch house, but this is a good place, too."

"Thank you."

"I missed waking up with you beside me." He studied her face as if she might have changed in a couple of hours. "Are you okay?"

"I just decided to get a jump on the day." She opened the front door. "Want coffee?"

"Thanks. That'd be good."

She led the way inside and set the roses in the center of the table. "They're perfect. I'll enjoy them."

"Good. They suit you."

She poured him a mug of coffee. "I have something for you, too." She pointed toward the rock on the bar.

"What's this?" He picked up the rock and turned it over and over in his hands.

"Remember our last ride up to the big rock?"

"How could I forget it? That's when we carved our initials inside a heart deep in the soft sandstone."

"I picked up this rock that day as a memento."

"And you kept it all this time?" He glanced at her with a warm smile that crinkled the corners of his eyes.

"Uncle Clem kept it for me." She reached out and closed her palms around his hands holding the rock. "If you want, I'd like you to have it now."

"Thanks. I'd like nothing better." He leaned down and placed a warm kiss on her lips. "You were thinking about me."

"Always."

"Good." He glanced around as he slipped the rock into a pocket and picked up his mug of coffee. "I can see why you like it here. It's cozy and perfect for one."

"Thank you. I think so, too." She'd left her cup outside, so she quickly grabbed a new mug and poured coffee.

"But it won't do for more than one."

"No, I suspect not. But I'm only one."

"I thought we settled that last night."

"Settled what?" She didn't think they'd settled anything.

"You're not one anymore. You're two. And later, hopefully more."

"Shane, not now." She set down her mug, feeling her stomach churn with restrained emotion.

"I know you think you're not ready. You made that clear last night." He sighed as he cradled his mug in both hands. "I want to give you something. Maybe it'll make a difference. You can throw it out if you don't want it. That's okay. It's yours. It's always been yours."

She backed up a step, feeling uneasy about his gift.

He set down his mug, reached into the inside pocket of his jacket, pulled out a small white box, and set it down on the bar between them.

She took another step back. It looked suspiciously like a ring box.

He flipped up the lid. "Star sapphire. Diamond accents. Platinum."

"You found the exact one?"

"Yes." He gave her a warm smile. "I like it because when the light's just right, your eyes look like star sapphires."

She trembled with emotion as she repressed her sudden desire to cry with happiness. He'd chosen a ring that he knew she liked. He'd chosen a ring that revealed the depth of his emotions for her. He'd chosen a ring that reminded him of her. She wanted nothing so much as to throw her arms around his neck and give him anything he wanted—especially marriage. And yet, until she could come to him with her life in order and everything to offer, she couldn't accept his ring. Otherwise, it wouldn't be fair to him.

"Say something." He tapped the top of the box. "You love it? You hate it? I can get any ring you want. Just tell me."

"It's gorgeous. It's perfect."

"That's a relief." He smiled, eyes twinkling with pleasure.

"But still—"

He picked up the box, fumbled with it because his hands were so large, and finally removed the ring, which looked tiny between his fingers. "Will you let me slip this on your finger? I think it'll fit."

She put her hands behind her back and gripped them together.

"Eden, what is it?" He stopped mid-motion as he held out the ring.

"I can't wear it." She almost choked on the words.

"Why not?" He looked hurt and confused and angry. "I love you. You love me. It's not rocket science."

"Maybe it is."

"What's that supposed to mean?" He dropped the ring on top of the bar.

"It's me. I just can't commit to marriage now."

"You already promised me years ago."

"That was then. This is now."

He rolled his broad shoulders as if trying to release tension. "Are you saying you don't want me? If you are, I'm not getting that message."

She felt terrible. She was hurting him, and it was the last thing she wanted to do. "I do want you. I want every little bit of you." She threw her arms around his neck and hugged him hard.

He gently set her back from him. "Tell me what's going on before this gets completely out of hand."

"My life is a mess."

"You're putting it back together."

"It's not there yet."

"Takes time."

"I want to be standing firmly on my own two feet before I wear your ring."

"Why? You're already a strong woman."

"If I accept now, neither of us will ever know for sure if I'm just marrying you as a port in a storm or if—"

"Stop right there." He pushed the ring toward her. "I can see that living in LA got your mind twisted around, so you're not thinking straight about us. We were a team before you left, and we're a team now that you're back. Like a team of horses, sometimes one pulls a little more weight and sometimes the other one does. That's where we are right now. But in the end, it all evens out."

She smiled, nodding. He did have a way of simplifying things.

"Okay. I got it. You're not ready for that final step of joining us for the rest of our lives. I can wait. I'm a patient man for something I want as badly as I want you."

"But—"

"We go on like we've been going, I can live with it." He pushed the ring toward her again. "That's your ring. When I see you wear it, I'll know you're ready to marry me."

"But—"

"Let's get to work. I'll talk to Max about running the ranch, then I'll be back here to help you get KWCB on its feet."

And then he was gone, out the door, back to his truck.

She was left wondering how she'd gotten so lucky.

Chapter 31

HOURS LATER, EDEN CLOSED HER LAPTOP ON KWCB's reception desk and leaned back in her chair, hearing its usual squeak of protest. Like most everything else in the Den, the chair needed a little work if not outright replacement.

Shane, Jack, Nathan, and Ken were all clustered in the studio, putting the finishing touches on the new radio system. Nathan kept running in and out, picking up supplies in town, and bringing them back. She sincerely hoped they could be on the air by late afternoon.

She wasn't needed in there, so she'd been filling her time with researching what-if dreams and what-if possibilities. She particularly admired The Warrior radio station in Bonham, Texas. The country station had been established in 1948 but updated and upgraded to give its audience access to all the latest tech advantages.

Everything she'd discovered online simply confirmed the knowledge she'd brought back from LA. Long gone were the days when there wasn't competition in local areas such as Wildcat Bluff County. Not physical competition now, of course, but a wide variety of radio content was readily available to listeners across many delivery formats.

In addition to AM and FM broadcasting, KWCB now competed with newer technology like satellite radio, HD radio, and internet radio. Microwave receivers and relays as well as satellite dishes had joined traditional towers to broadcast signals. There were public, community, and commercial radio stations.

And then there was radio content—live, canned, syndicated, podcasts, which all came in several formats. Lots of content could be bought if you had the bucks or pay-to-play if you had the audience. She didn't have the resources for either. What she did have was Wildcat Jack. And now Eden Rafferty. She could create a new show for each to go along with the regular music, news, weather, and infomercials. But what would be the focus of their programs?

She picked up a pen and doodled on a piece of blank paper. Country music was their bread and butter. And she loved it, along with other listeners in the big audiences of the United States, Canada, and Australia. When she thought about it, maybe KWCB was more Americana, a type of country station that played classic era, alt-country, and cult musicians. Americana usually developed strong cult followings, and that fit with the Wildcat Den's listeners. But how did she capitalize on this audience segment, as well as enlarge it?

She shifted in her chair, glancing past the open door of the studio. She hoped all was going well. The place reeked to high heaven. It'd be a long time before the stench was gone, but if everything actually worked, they could live with the smell.

She glanced at her doodles and added a few more circles. Even if they wanted it, they couldn't afford to pay for current pop country—disdainfully called "Nash Vegas" by country purists—like the mainstream country stations played for their listeners. KWCB used playlists created over time with songs that were in the public domain because they were free to play, no matter performer or performance date. They'd picked up wonderful music way back to the 1920s. They also played unlisted, locally produced music that avoided music-licensing fees.

Fortunately, the Wildcat Den had advertisers that appreciated all demographics, so she could appeal to a wide age range. Another plus, the station did manage to turn a slight profit every month. All good, but it wasn't good enough to get back in the bigger game that would give her what she needed to revamp the station.

She sighed and ran a hand through her hair. KWCB needed a hook—a great big one—to break out of the pack. Graham had put them on the national, as well as global, map with all his shenanigans, but how did they capitalize on the priceless publicity? It'd take more than a snazzy platform and clever jingle. It'd take something she didn't have right now, something she couldn't even imagine, and something she didn't know how to get.

She dropped her feet to the floor. She could only take so much pie-in-the-sky when she didn't even have a viable radio station at the moment. Still, she needed to think positively about the Wildcat Den. The station hadn't come together overnight. It had taken faith, hope, and lots of hard work. Now was the time for her to do the same thing as her ancestors. *Believe*.

As she glanced at the stark utilitarianism of reception again, she wished she'd brought the yellow roses with her. They'd have brightened up the area and sweetened the air at the same time. But they'd looked perfect on her dining table, so she'd left them there to enjoy when she returned home. She also wished she could wear Shane's star sapphire ring, but she'd tucked it away in the bookshelf for safety, even though it tugged at her heart just knowing the precious ring was there and not on her finger.

"How're you doing?" Shane stuck his head out of the studio, looking at her in concern. "Feeling okay?"

"I'm fine. Any big news for me yet?"

"I don't know if we'll get it done today, but we're making progress."

"Anything I can do to help?"

"Chuckwagon takeout later would be mighty appreciated."

"You got it." She tapped her pen on her doodles, wanting to share with him what was bothering her most. "I just don't see a way out of where KWCB is stuck. We need so much more here. Maybe it really is time to let the station go."

He walked over, planted both hands flat on the table, and stared her in the eyes. "I don't want to hear it. And you know why."

"The ring?"

"Right. You can find a way to pull KWCB out of its doldrums. You just need to up your game. Besides, the Wildcat Den and the Rocky T are a team. How can we have one without the other?"

She rolled her eyes. "You know good and well the ranch can stand on its own two feet."

"So can the Wildcat Den."

"If so, I need something to make it happen. I need a hook, an idea, anything that'll make KWCB stand out in the marketplace and draw new listeners."

"What do you mean?"

"We need a bigger base. I'm talking about a size-able cult audience that'll help bring in more ad revenue. To do that, we need a larger presence. Website. Email. Podcasts. Mobile apps. We could even sign up with a system that's already in place on the internet, so we're not just sitting out there on our lonesome."

"Is that what Nathan and Ken have been talking about?"

"Somewhat. We need an entire platform and package."

"What's stopping you from getting it?"

She sighed as she motioned around the radio station. "Time. Energy. Money. You name it. I don't want KWCB to be just another country station. I want us to be extra special, so we'll draw a loyal audience."

"The Wildcat Den has always been special."

"Not anymore." She abruptly stood up, frustration setting her on edge. She paced across the room and back again. "After we get the Den back on the air, I'll talk with Wildcat Jack. He may have ideas that wouldn't occur to me."

"You probably know as much about this station's history as he does."

"But he's got more experience."

"True." Shane glanced back at the sound studio. "You'll come up with something. Right now, I better get back and help them."

"Thanks. Repair absolutely does come first."

After he walked away, she picked up the black phone's receiver, thought about how long it'd been in use, then set it back in place. At least it worked again. She drew another series of doodles. She didn't have much she could accomplish while she waited to get back on the air. She'd already written a few more catchy phrases to promote the May Day Rodeo.

She listened to construction in the studio, noticed the smoke stench again, and suddenly remembered the key in her jeans pocket. With all the excitement of the fire, she'd forgotten she'd picked it up while putting out the blaze. Could it be the lost key to the Quonset hut storage? Maybe. Probably not. But what if it was? She leaped to her feet. Now was the time to find out.

She hurried outside, ran into her home, opened the washer, and pulled out her jeans. She hoped the key was still there and hadn't been lost again. She felt in a front pocket. Nothing. She tried the other, felt a hard shape, reached inside, and emerged with the key, triumphant.

She felt her heart pick up speed as she quickly walked over to the storage hut. It'd obviously seen its fair share of rough weather over the years, as evidenced by metal dents and flaky paint, but it still looked sound outside. As far as she could tell her uncle had kept it tightly closed to keep out bugs, dust, and moisture, but she wouldn't know for sure if that had worked until she looked inside.

Now or never. She inserted the key in the lock and tried to turn it. Nothing happened. She jerked out the key, feeling disappointed that it might not be right for this lock. She inserted it again and gently jiggled as she turned the key. Finally, the lock popped open. She tucked the key safely back in her pocket, feeling excitement race through her.

She slowly opened the door, hearing the hinges creak as if she'd suddenly stepped into a horror movie. She couldn't see much because sunlight only slightly penetrated the gloom inside. She looked for a light switch and finally saw a cord hanging down near the door. She pulled it, and an overhead light bulb coated in dust came on to cast a dull glow over the front of the hut.

She hesitated before she took a step onto the concrete floor, concerned about disturbing wasps or spiders or scorpions. She couldn't see far into the semidarkness, but she caught the strong plastic scent—sort of acidic—that came from disintegrating old reel-to-reel tapes. She could also smell musty, aging paper. She assumed there must be other overhead lights with strings she could pull deeper in the hut. A path wound between rows of cardboard boxes. They were stacked haphazardly down the long room with tan-colored dust as thick as flour coating the top of everything. Some boxes had collapsed from the weight of those on top. Overall, it looked fairly neat but not touched in a long time. Her uncle had obviously not gotten around to going through the contents.

She felt a vast sense of relief because everything here felt peaceful, calm, and as if it were waiting for a new beginning. She could understand the feeling because she was in that very same place herself. It was time to build on the old to create the new. Whatever little nuggets of gold were here, she wanted to find them.

And yet, it'd take a minor miracle to locate anything, but maybe over the years, the boxes had been labeled in some way. She'd probably find handwriting by Mom, Dad, Uncle Clem, Jack, and maybe others. She very much wanted to embrace her past and carry it forward with her into the future.

She walked down the center aisle to the end of the circle of light. On her left was a stack of dusty boxes with the word *taxes* written on them in Uncle Clem's handwriting. Those she could definitely leave for another day. On the right side, a box had been crushed between two stronger ones and the side had crunched out. Several items had fallen, so she leaned down and picked up a flat, square box with writing in red grease pencil on its side. She looked in the box and saw a reel-to-reel tape. She couldn't imagine what it had on it or how old it was, but it probably wasn't important. Still, she looked to see what was written on the box.

She felt a chill run up her spine and her hands trembled with excitement as she read aloud, her words filling the hut. "The Highwaymen interview by Wildcat Jack for KWCB."

She hugged the box over her heart, then carefully set it aside before she picked up another box. Hank Williams. He was still considered one of the ultimate leaders in country music and that made his music and everything about him completely collectible. She could just imagine him being driven up to the station in a gleaming new 1950 Cadillac, maybe after hosting one of his popular "Garden Spot" radio shows in Waxahachie, Texas.

She set that tape beside other one before she moved farther into the hut, feeling her heart beat fast in anticipation. She opened another crumbling cardboard box, sneezing from the dust, and found more valuable tapes. George Jones back when he had a flat-top haircut. Conway Twitty when he thought he was the next Elvis. Loretta Lynn as a hopeful teenager. Buck Owens before he invented the Bakersfield sound. Patsy Cline when she was country's sophisticated songstress.

Excitement building, Eden reached up and pulled on another light. She walked down the aisle, stopped beside other crumbling boxes, and found more collectibles. Pristine recordings of local bands. Rock and roll that had been sent to the station but never played because it didn't fit country music—plenty of *Rock It*, *Shake It*, *Bop* in the titles on obscure labels that she'd never heard of before. She discovered boxes of perfect records, although she knew the real money was in the programming.

She took a deep breath of dust-laden air and turned back. She didn't need to look any deeper—she'd found her miracle.

She picked up The Highwaymen and Hank Williams tapes, clasped them to her chest, and hurried outside, leaving the door wide open. She dashed up the steps into the radio station, through reception, and over to the studio. She paused on the threshold, not wanting to interrupt Shane, Jack, Nathan, and Ken as they huddled in deep discussion over the new setup.

She'd come to see the Den fire as a blessing in disguise because she'd been forced to update, and so far, it'd been less expensive than she'd anticipated. Gearheads Nathan and Ken had done a good job of shopping online to find electronic bargains. Empty boxes of all shapes and sizes from several delivery services were piled in one corner.

They'd figured out they could run an updated version of the station off a laptop and shareware. They'd installed a laptop specifically for scheduling and automation, integrated a used compressor limiter, and hooked up the internet to the studio. For now, the old hardware and equipment had been shoved against a wall to make room for the new leaner and cleaner setup with high-tech equipment that took up less space and required less wiring. They'd saved the 1940s microphone that gave KWCB its rich sound and was far superior to anything modern.

Jack glanced her way, dark eyes shining with the thrill of the new. "What's up?"

She held out the tapes. "The Highwaymen! You interviewed them?"

"Sure. Think they sang a little for me, too."

"Sang a song?"

"Absolutely."

"I found these two tapes in the Quonset storage."

Ken's head snapped around as he glanced at her with wide eyes. "You opened the hut?"

"I found the key. Place is full of boxes."

"Yeah," Jack said. "When we got too full in here, we'd box up stuff and stick it out there. Your folks and Clem never liked to throw much away."

"I'm holding a Hank Williams tape."

"Nice guy. Great singer."

"The historical value alone is tremendous." She felt light-headed as she clutched the tape to her heart. She glanced up at the The Highwaymen poster. Not just good mojo—astounding mojo.

"Are you calling me old?" Jack asked with a chuckle.

"I meant—"

"If you are, you're right. And if I'm real lucky, I'll get a whole lot older."

She leaned forward and kissed his cheek. "You better."

"I'm working on it." Jack gave everybody a big grin.

"If you want old stuff, I guess those interviews and live recordings are still out there. We've got forty or fifty years of football games, too. Local folks might want to revisit their youth."

"Great idea for special programming. Lots of small stations monetize running football games." Eden glanced around the group. "We could start Friday afternoons and run till midnight."

Jack nodded in agreement. "Call it something like 'Wildcat Football Lives On.'"

"Sounds good to me," Shane said. "Friday nights were fun on and off the field."

"The tapes may not be in very good shape," Jack said thoughtfully.

"Lots of great tech to fix stuff like that nowadays. Right, Ken?" Nathan looked up from where he was fiddling with the computer.

"Right," Ken said.

"Eden, where are you going with this?" Shane cocked his head to one side as he gave her a puzzled look.

"Don't you see?" She glanced around the group in happiness. "We're sitting on a gold mine and didn't know it."

"Do you mean to say," Jack asked, "folks would pay good money to hear my old interviews?"

"Oh my, yes, I do think so." She grinned at him, clutching the tapes tighter. "Think about it. We're old and new. Male and female. Beloved, experienced, old-style delivery and new, fresh LA approach. Old microphone and classic country with new equipment that allows us to reach a broader audience and internet exposure. We launch to an audience hungry for both."

Jack nodded with a sly smile. "I'm all in."

"We're all in," Shane added, looking happy.

"No doubt about it." She held out the tapes. "KWCB just got its hook."

Chapter 32

A WEEK AFTER EDEN HAD DISCOVERED KWCB'S TREASURE trove and they had the Wildcat Den back on the air, Shane sat on a bench in Wildcat Spring. *Alone*. He could hear water trickling into the basin, smell wildflowers, and hear birds chirping in nearby trees. Spring had sprung, but he felt like he was living in winter. Even worse, he felt as if he were living in the midst of a country song, lamenting lost love.

He'd figured Eden would be sporting his ring on her finger by now, since she had the means to total independence and financial security. Instead, he wasn't even sure she remembered it. She'd plowed into that storage Quonset hut like a banshee, a woman on a do-or-die mission, dragging boxes into reception and her home till there was no more room except a narrow path to get through both places. She'd pushed everybody to their limit trying to find out what was in the hut, catalog it, and make it ready by May Day, so she could present a new and improved KWCB to the world.

A worthy dream, but it wasn't possible. Too much stuff. Too little time. Too few workers. Everybody was flagging, no matter how hard she cracked the whip. And she was carrying the brunt of it, hardly eating, hardly sleeping, hardly speaking. He'd had about enough of it, as well as everybody else in her vicinity. But she had the bit between her teeth and her focus was strictly on that goal way down the road.

To top it off, Tanner was still nosing around the area. If he got wind of the discovery, he'd try to take it, one way or another, and if that didn't work, he might try to burn it for sheer spite, if nothing else. Cowboys, deputies, and firefighters had been trading off watching the place, but they couldn't keep it up forever. For now, they were keeping knowledge of the contents limited to as few folks as possible, making security all about keeping Eden safe.

He walked over to the basin and cupped his hand under the spout, cool water hitting his palm and trickling out to join the deep pool. Good, dependable water, but wasted water. It was worth its weight in gold, just like the hut's contents. As long as he hadn't known what was in storage, it hadn't concerned him. Now he felt uneasy about it all the time. All those priceless recordings and whatever else had been squirreled away was on his land and under his protection. If something happened to it, she'd never forgive him and he'd never forgive himself. Kind of like the water. If he didn't do something with it, he'd never forgive himself, either.

Hedy and Morning Glory had come to him that morning, asking him to talk reason to Eden. The May Day Rodeo was coming up fast. Ken wasn't out of school yet. Jack was pushed to his limits. And Nathan had a business to run. They were helping out when and where they could, but they had businesses, too. And Shane was getting way behind on ranch chores and figuring out a permanent way to get water to his herds.

It was a mess, pure and simple. His life had been

turned upside down since Eden got back to town. The highs with her were heaven, but the lows with her were hell. If she'd put his ring on her finger, they'd… He snorted before even finishing his thought. He might as well be writing country music lyrics. Except it wasn't funny. He was worried about her, just like everybody else was.

He flicked water from his fingertips, stepped under one of the arches, and walked over to his fence. He continued down it, looking right and left across the pasture, thinking, figuring, calculating. The stock tanks were working out well, but he kept damning Lander and the new owners of the Lazy Q Ranch. Still, that was water under the bridge. He didn't suspect them of trying to take over his ranch now, so that was a plus. He simply had to find his own way to a permanent water solution.

He put his hands on his hips as he surveyed the area, noting as he did the beauty of the Rocky T. He looked back at the WPA spring gazebo built in 1927, noting its beauty, too. He couldn't let that unique heritage get torn down or destroyed any more than he could let his herds go without water.

Bottom line, he couldn't assume Eden would want to keep KWCB on the ranch. Universities would probably vie to house some of the hut's contents. She had the funds to build a new, state-of-the-art, climate-controlled building in Wildcat Bluff to be closer to resources and security. It wouldn't be ranch radio anymore, but who even remembered or cared that many of the early stations were on ranches? She could shut it down and sell it all. She'd eventually get Tanner off her back, so she could return to LA if that truly suited her heart of hearts.

As much as he hated to admit it, everything was on the table—especially the star sapphire ring. He'd had enough of running after Eden. If she couldn't see the good in what he offered, then what good was it to offer?

He enjoyed a fine life on the Rocky T, and he'd enjoyed it all his life. Yeah, Eden could make it better. She'd made him see that he was ready for family and all the trimmings. He wanted what his parents had created in their relationship. He wanted it now. And he wanted it with Eden. But it might not ever be enough for her. If he wasn't enough, if his ranch wasn't enough, if Wildcat Bluff wasn't enough, then now was the time to find out, so he didn't go holding out hope till the end of his days and wind up a lonely, disillusioned man.

With a heavy heart, he turned back to the spring. He was at the end of his rope in so many ways, but he wouldn't give up hope just yet. At the same time, he wasn't going to stand by and let Eden hurt herself and others. Lots of folks loved and depended on KWCB. How could he let them lose their radio station? If it came to it, he could buy the Den. Wildcat Jack would still be on the air. He wouldn't have Eden, but he'd still have the Wildcat Den. It wasn't an even trade-off, by any means, but it might end up being the best he could do. And the Rocky T Ranch would still host a ranch radio.

Good. He was starting to think out of the box. He'd gotten so focused on helping Eden with her issues that he'd almost forgotten that he was in control of the ranch and his own life. He'd still help her over this rough spot, because that's what friends did in Wildcat Bluff, but he'd now do it with a firm hand.

He glanced back at the fence, then at the gazebo

again. There had to be a way to satisfy all their needs. It'd come to him. As he walked back toward the station, he heard a pickup pull up and park. He rounded the corner of the building and smelled food about the time he saw Jones, wearing jeans, shirt, and jacket, step down from her truck with a sack in one hand.

She saw him and shook the sack. "Hungry?"

"Starved." He walked over to her.

"Eden around?"

"She'll be in one of the buildings."

"I've got news."

"If you're planning to eat around here, you'd better go to the gazebo. It's the only place still left that's usable."

"That bad, huh?"

"Gets worse every day. She needs a separate building to sort the stuff. Right now, she's using the station and her home." He shook his head. "And there wasn't ever enough room in them to swing a cat to start with."

"If you'll go get her, I'll meet y'all at the spring."

"Okay. I think she was recording some stuff for the May Day Rodeo, so she ought to be in the Den."

"Good. I'll wait, but not too long. I'm mighty hungry." She grinned, tossing long, dark hair over one shoulder before sauntering away.

He bounded up the stairs to the radio station. He opened the door and took a cautious step inside so he wouldn't put a big boot onto some priceless object. The place smelled like dust, mildew, and burnt wire, so he left the door open to try and air it out a bit. The door to the studio was closed, and he figured she was in there.

He glanced around, hoping to see some improvement, but now even the sofa was stacked with boxes in various stages of being opened and unpacked. If anything, the place looked like a disaster zone. He didn't know how she could run KWCB with this big of a mess. Somebody had to get through to her that she couldn't keep on this way. He guessed that job fell to him.

About the time he'd settled on a path to navigate to the studio, the door opened and she stepped out. He felt his heart sink at the sight. She'd lost more weight, so her jeans hung on her like they belonged to somebody else, and the long-sleeve T-shirt appeared as if he ought to be wearing it. She'd pulled her hair back into a tight ponytail and hadn't bothered with makeup, not even to cover up the dark circles under her eyes. She'd smeared dust across her forehead and appeared unsteady on her feet.

She looked like hell, but he'd never say it to her face. Instead, he plastered on a smile. "Jones is here. She brought news and eats."

"Jones?" Eden glanced around as if expecting to see her attorney pop out of one of the boxes.

"I sent her to the gazebo. More room there."

"Good." She glanced around again. "I'm not very hungry, but I've got some bottles of water around here somewhere."

"I set them in a cooler outside."

"Is that where they went?"

"Yeah. And you need to eat."

She swiped a hand across her forehead, smearing the dust even more. "I don't know if I can eat anything. My stomach is—"

"You're going to eat." He'd had enough of her starving her body.

She cocked her head to one side. "That sounds like an order."

"It is." He motioned toward the open door. "Come on."

"I don't take orders well."

"I'm worried about you." He took a step toward her, trying not to crash into anything. "If you don't go to the gazebo by yourself, I'll carry you."

She shrugged as she rolled her eyes. "You needn't get pushy. I'm going because I want to talk with Jones. I hope she has good news."

"Okay." He carefully backed up till he was on the top step, watching as she walked right around the boxes and scattered contents as if she were easily making her way through a big pasture.

He leaped to the ground, pulled three waters out of the cooler, and turned around to make sure she was with him.

"I don't know what's gotten into you," she said as she joined him. "Just because I'm not eating at your house, you act like I'm not eating at all."

"About that—"

"Come on!" Jones hollered from under an arch. "Food's getting cold."

"Chuckwagon?" Eden asked as she drew near the gazebo.

"Bluebonnet Café. I was in Sure-Shot, so I ordered there."

"Great." He hurried forward, feeling his stomach growl. The Bluebonnet was his second favorite place to eat in the county.

When he got inside, he smiled to see that Jones had

set up the same dining configuration as Eden had done when they'd met there the first time after she returned to town—food in the center, three cushions positioned in a circle on the floor. He quickly sat down. Jones and Eden joined him. He handed a bottle of water to each of them.

Jones picked up a covered container and a prepackaged spork with a napkin. She handed them to Eden. "I brought you mac and cheese. I thought maybe comfort food was in order."

Eden gave her an appreciative smile. "Sounds wonderful. My tummy's been a little touchy about rich food."

"No wonder," Jones said. "Shane, we get the cheeseburgers and fries."

"Great." He grabbed a burger and took a big bite. It was just as good as always, so he bit into it again. "Next time, I'll treat us all to chicken-fried steaks."

"That's a winner," Jones replied, then dunked a fry in ketchup.

Eden ate several bites. "This is really good. I guess I'm hungrier than I realized."

He started to comment on that statement, but Jones caught his eye and shook her head, so he stayed quiet and continued to eat. She was right. There was no point in ruining good food by talking too much. And he'd remember that Eden needed mild meals, not barbecue or anything too spicy. He could fix macaroni and cheese if that's what would get her to eat.

Jones finished her food, then focused on Eden. "I've got good news and bad news."

"Don't even ask," Eden said. "Good news first."

"Okay." She grinned, showing her pearly whites like

a dog bent on destruction. "Fontaine agreed to withdraw Graham's request for your property."

"Really?" Eden grinned just as big. "That's wonderful news!"

"It sure is." But Shane wasn't too surprised because Jones was that good at riding horses and roping opposing counsel.

"But how did you get him to agree?" Eden set down her empty container.

"He came to understand that we do things a little differently in Wildcat Bluff County. An attack on one of us is an attack on all of us, meaning we have unlimited resources, patience, and persistence to counter anything he might throw at us."

"But that's not entirely true, is it?" Eden asked.

Jones shrugged as she cracked the top of a bottle. "He's been here, or he might not have believed me." She took a sip of water. "Maybe he's watched too many Old West movies, but I got the impression he might have been imagining that shoot-out at the OK Corral in Tombstone, Arizona—with him on the losing end."

Shane couldn't keep from laughing at that image. "Wonder how he could have gotten that impression?"

"No idea," Jones said in a matter-of-fact tone. "In addition, I believe he saw the writing on the wall. He wasn't going to come out ahead, either promotion-wise, or finance-wise."

"We're definitely winning the online wars," Eden said, "but we haven't been able to spend as much time on it lately, so Graham could still pull ahead."

"That brings me to the bad news," Jones said. "As far as Fontaine knows, his former client is going to stay in our county and continue his plea, as in harassment, so his ex-wife will eventually see reason and share her radio station."

"What's the point?" Shane just wanted it to all be over.

"What else has Tanner got?" Jones asked. "He gets notoriety this way, so maybe he gets his foot back in some door. He won't care just so long as he doesn't look like a loser…or a fool."

"We can't let him know about what we found in storage." Eden put her hand over her mouth as if she might hold back the information that way.

"But I thought you were going to announce it to the world," Shane said.

"I was," Eden said, "but now, I'm not so sure."

"You can't let Tanner ride you into the ground," Jones said.

Eden nodded thoughtfully. "You know what I'd like to do? I'd like to make him look like the loser he is, so he'll slink back to LA with his tail tucked between his legs. And stay there."

"I'll second that." Shane thought this might be Eden's turning point.

Eden looked from one to the other, then gazed thoughtfully out an archway toward the radio station. She gave a big sigh. "What I've been doing—it's not going to work, is it?"

Shane held his breath, hoping she was coming to see reality, no matter how difficult or unwanted right now.

"In time, yes, it'll work," Jones said in a gentle tone. "But by May Day, I don't see how."

Shane quickly agreed. "You've got a lot of delicate material to deal with, and that takes time."

"Vinyl." Eden looked back at them with excitement shining in her blue eyes. "I found boxes of records yesterday. Who knows their value? It'll take an expert to figure it out. I heard there's a great one in Dallas."

"That's wonderful news." Jones gave her a big smile. "Want my opinion?"

"If my current plan isn't going to work, I better get a new one." Eden picked up her bottle of water, slapping it into her palm.

"You already said it." Jones leaned toward Eden. "Overwhelm Tanner. Embarrass him. Make him want to play nice and get the hell out of Wildcat Bluff."

"But how?"

Jones stood up. "You've got the means. Now use it."

Chapter 33

EDEN SAT ACROSS FROM SHANE, FEELING STUNNED BY Jones's news and Shane's revelations. What had she been thinking for the past week? She felt as if she'd woken up from a dream, maybe a nightmare. She wiped fingertips across her forehead and came away with soot or dust, wondering where and when she'd gotten it.

With Jones gone, she felt the emotional cushion go with her. She was face-to-face with Shane. And she didn't know what to say or how to act. She glanced down at her hands. *No ring.* She'd hardly thought about his proposal in a week. What must he think of her? Had he given up? Had he moved on? Had he washed his hands of her?

She almost wished Jones was back or that Jack or Ken or Nathan would show up. They'd all been working so closely together that there'd been no private moments with Shane. Had she neglected him? And herself? Yet nothing had seemed more important than rolling out the new KWCB platform once she'd found the storage hut filled with invaluable history that could be shared with listeners. And it was an unexpected way to rebuild her self-confidence and self-esteem, secure her future, and help her feel worthy of Shane's love and commitment. But had she lost him in the process?

She sipped water, stalling so maybe he'd be the first to speak and let her know how he truly felt now. But he

was waiting her out or being sensitive or something that
she couldn't fathom.

"I guess I've been obsessed," she finally said, not
looking at him because she didn't want to see disap-
pointment in his eyes.

"Do you want to take a little time off today?" He
spoke in a slow, gentle tone, as if he couldn't be sure
she would hear or understand him.

She cocked her head to one side, considering his
meaning as well his words. He didn't expect her to
agree. He no longer expected her to want to spend time
with him. And yet he still gave her a chance to go away
with him. "What did you have in mind?"

"Max is up at the barn. I could text him, so he'd have
a couple of horses saddled and ready to ride when we
got there." He hesitated, not looking at her as he tore
off strips of his bottle's label. "We wouldn't waste any
time that way."

"You want to go for a ride?" she asked, wondering
why he'd want to take a leisurely ride when there was
so much to do.

"Yeah. It's about the water." He gave her a sly smile.
"I've had an idea I think will work."

"Really? That sounds great. Do you want to show
me?"

"Yes."

She quickly stuffed empty containers in the paper
sack. "Let's go."

"You're sure you can take the time?"

"It's important so I'll take the time." She clutched the
sack in one hand and stood up.

"Good." He got to his feet as he pulled out his phone.

She quickly walked out of the gazebo, heart beating fast. She hadn't handled that well and knew it. She just couldn't get past her worries about losing him for no better reason than a radio station. She really had lived too long in her LA world, where nothing took precedence over that next step up the ladder or the next Botox injection to make sure you stayed on your current rung and viable for the next one up.

"Let's take the truck," he said as he caught up to her.

She stopped by the station, lifted the lid to the plastic garbage bin she'd placed near the door, and tossed in the food sack. She quickly walked over to his pickup, opened the door, and sat down in the shotgun seat.

"You in a hurry?" he asked as he sat down beside her and turned on the engine.

"Guess I've been running so long I don't know how to stop." She sounded stilted and knew it, but she was having trouble turning her mind from the storage hut to what he wanted to show her.

"Yeah." He huffed before he headed up to the barn, not looking at her, not saying anything else.

If she didn't know better, she'd think he was feeling the same thing she was feeling about not wanting to break anything that wasn't broken and wanting to repair anything that was cracked. But she was the one who'd dug into the storage hut like a wild woman, pushing everything and everyone away in her manic quest to save KWCB. He'd been steady as a rock.

When they reached the outbuildings, two saddled horses were waiting for them. Max tipped his hat and then retreated into the barn. Shane parked in the shade, and she quickly jumped out before he had a chance to walk around and open her door. She was afraid if he accidentally touched her, she just might break down for all she thought she'd lost in her zealous quest. Wasn't there some type of old adage about not knowing what you valued or wanted till you'd lost it? She felt as if she were living too much of that wisdom right now.

She settled into the saddle of a roan, while Shane put a boot in the stirrup and straddled his buckskin. He didn't know it, of course, but he looked deliciously wanton performing the little mundane chore of getting into a saddle. She turned her eyes away, realizing that her body was coming alive again—at a very inconvenient time.

He led the way out of the double gates and into the pasture. She caught up and rode beside him as she had so many times when they were young. Everything felt the same, except everything was different. She didn't know how long she could keep up this little game of indifference they were both playing. It wasn't natural, and it wasn't their style. But she rode on beside him, still quiet, still not looking at him. And he rode the same way.

Finally, he came to the line of stock tanks he'd installed so the boosters could fill them. He stopped his buckskin and sat there a moment, looking at them, before he glanced back toward Wildcat Spring.

She followed his line of sight, wondering what he was thinking, what he was revealing, what he was imagining. Unfortunately, she didn't have a clue. But if he wasn't going to bridge the gap between them, she had to try.

"Nice day for a ride." As soon as the words were out of her mouth, she realized how mundane they sounded after not that many words for a week. "I mean—"

"I know." He pushed back his cowboy hat as he looked around the pasture. "Reminds me of the old days."

"Me, too."

"Eden," he said, not looking at her, "I'd hate to lose what we've always had here."

She felt hope spring up fast and strong. *He meant her, yes!*

"The Rocky T and KWCB have always been a team. Ranch and radio."

She felt the bottom drop out of her hope. *Not her.*

"I don't want to put you in a bind about the buildings."

"I've got time."

"I mean *ever*." He settled his hat back into place. "But I need the water."

"It's okay. I understand. I want your herds to have the water."

"Appreciate it." He adjusted his body in the saddle, as if pulling up strength from deep in the earth. "I want to preserve Wildcat Spring—at least the gazebo."

"I don't—"

"Wait a minute." He drew a line in the air over the ground from the gazebo to the stock tanks. "What if I installed a pipeline from the spring to the tanks and used a pump to get the water here?"

She looked back and forth a moment, seeing it all in her mind's eye in one blaze of excitement. "I can't think why it wouldn't work."

"Me either."

"Would there be any water left in the basin and for the weeping willow?"

"If you want," he said, thoughtfully rubbing his chin, "I don't see why we couldn't leave a trickle there."

She couldn't hold back a smile. "That'd be perfect."

"You think?" And he finally gave her a fleeting look before he glanced away again.

But it'd been enough to give her hope because she'd seen uncertainty but also speculation in his hazel eyes. "Oh, yes."

"That way, everything stays the same. I mean, as much as you want stuff to stay the same."

And now, finally, she began to understand his cautious steps around her. She could do anything she wanted to do now that she'd found KWCB's treasures of the past, which could completely change her future. He'd known it from the first moment she'd revealed The Highwaymen tape. But he hadn't tried to stop or change or alter her drive, even realizing he might lose her in the process.

It was a heady moment, as if they were caught in a wild current that propelled them downstream in a river fraught with rocks and eddies and rapids that might toss them into a raging waterfall or land them on a soft, sandy shore. No way to know. No way to figure out. No way to stay safe. It didn't matter. Wherever they ended up, she was willing to take a chance with Shane.

"I've been thinking about our rocks—your little chip and our big one." She was almost overcome with a sudden surge of emotion as she relived the memory of their first kiss. It'd been just an innocent peck, but commitment nonetheless. They'd always sort of thought of it as *their* place.

"Want to go see if our initials are still there?" He hesitated, looking up ahead. "Might be a wasted trip. Sandstone's soft, so weather could've eroded them away by now."

And then she knew he was thinking what she was thinking about *their* place—initials gone or not didn't matter. If there was ever a place to bring them together again, no matter ranch or radio, it'd be the place where, once upon a time, they'd had an idyllic setting where they could retreat to be alone and puzzle out the vagaries of life.

"Think you can find it again?" She was teasing, knowing he knew his acreage like the back of his hand.

"Yeah, with enough incentive." He gave her a quick glance and a sexy, little smile before he urged his buckskin forward.

She rode by his side, feeling as if they'd settled everything without words—or at least direct words. Maybe there was no need to talk about what had been between them for the past week on a pretty spring day with no work ahead of them for now.

She leaned her head back and felt the sun warm her face. She inhaled the scent of grass, wildflowers, and tree leaves. In the distance, she saw cattle contentedly grazing on new growth. Birds flitted overhead, busy as they searched for food to take back to hungry babies. Only now did she realize how much she'd missed being close to nature. Bright lights and cityscapes were good, but the Rocky T Ranch was better.

"Still like it here?"

She glanced toward the sound of Shane's deep voice. He'd moved closer. They were riding side by side now, just like the old days. She gave him a tender smile, knowing it was sweet and soft because that's how she felt looking at him.

He smiled back at her, nodding as if knew just how she felt.

"I guess," she finally said, "you can take the cowgirl out of the country, but you can't take the country out of the cowgirl."

"That's what I wanted to hear." He reached over and squeezed her hand before he urged his horse forward into a lope.

She followed, feeling a powerful surge beneath her as she again matched her pace with his mount. They pounded across the prairie together, flushing cottontail rabbits from hidey-holes as well as buff-breasted barn swallows with swept-back wings into the air. Monarchs hovered over Indian paintbrush, primrose buttercups, and crimson clover. Mockingbirds wheeled overhead, as if sharing the exciting adventure.

When Shane finally pulled up, she was breathing fast with excitement and exhilaration. She stopped beside him, looking beyond to see if their rock still rose into the sky as if lifted by a giant's hand.

And there it was, all big and beige and streaked with black stains. It appeared as if hadn't changed in eons, but would their initials still be carved together on the windswept surface?

Chapter 34

AFTER EDEN SAW THEIR ROCK, SHE DIDN'T HESITATE. SHE jumped down, hurried over to it, and bent down, running her fingers across the rough surface near the base until she felt the indentations. She pushed aside tall weeds and knelt in the grass. And yes, there were their initials still carved inside a heart. She heard Shane walk up behind her, but he didn't bend down to look.

She glanced up at his face. "You knew, didn't you?"

"I figured as much." He nodded with a slight smile. "They were here the last time I checked, but weather could've erased them."

She rubbed her fingers across the indentations, almost able to feel the urgency, the excitement, the determination of that time when they'd used his pocket knife to cement their feelings for each other into rock. "Did you ever think we'd be back here together?"

"I hoped so, but life—"

"Can get in the way of the best of intentions."

"Sometimes."

"But not always."

"Right." He motioned with his head toward the top of the rock. "You want to sit up there like we used to do when we looked out over the ranch?"

She nodded, feeling her throat tighten with emotion. How had she let so much slip away from her? Yet, she knew. And he knew. Now, it felt as if they were each other's destinies. Ranch. Radio. Maybe this moment in time, when they came back together here, at their special rock, had been preplanned as well because it felt so very right.

She walked around to the other side with him behind her. She looked for the old toe- and handholds and was surprised to see them easily. She glanced back at him.

He smiled with a twinkle in his eyes. "Yeah, I enlarged them when I was last here."

"And when was that?"

"Not so long ago."

She couldn't keep from chuckling. "Like yesterday?" She didn't say how touched she was that he'd been here over the years, thinking about them, checking on their initials. It was one more thing that proved his love.

He joined her laughter. "You've had me too busy to get away."

She easily climbed up the rock and stood on top, looking into the distance as she turned around in a circle. She could see the radio station, the spring, the ranch house, barns, and outbuildings. She could see cattle, buffalo, and horses. She could see birds, trees, and acres of prairie. And she could feel the air, the earth, and, finally, Shane's arms embracing her, tugging her back to his chest, so there was no longer any distance between them.

"You belong here, you know," he said in a deep, rough voice, breath stirring up tendrils of her hair.

She relaxed against him, feeling his strength, his endurance, his determination matching the ancient land around them. This earth had been here long before them, nurturing plants, animals, insects, and people. It would be here long after they were gone, nurturing all that came after them just as it had all that came before them. Maybe others sometime in the distant future would carve their initials onto this rock, too. Maybe even their children would leave their marks.

And then she knew—knew it with every beat of her heart that he was right. She did belong here. *With him.*

"I hope you'll leave KWCB on the ranch."

She turned around in his arms, put her hands on either side of his face, lifted up on her toes, and pressed a soft kiss to his mouth. "Make love to me."

He blinked, looking surprised and pleased, then not so sure.

"No one can see us." She popped open the snaps of his shirt, and she rubbed her palms over the hard muscles of his chest before jerking out his shirttail so she could follow the line of hair that led down to the indentation of his navel and the bulge below.

"The rock's hard," he said in a strained voice.

"We'll leave on our clothes."

"Still hard. And rough."

"I'll put you on bottom."

He grinned as he reached into his back pocket, pulled out a condom, dangled it before her, then slipped it into his front shirt pocket.

She couldn't keep from laughing at the sight. "Always prepared?"

"Around you, I always live in hope."

"Hope no longer."

And then he was kissing her as if there were no tomorrow with arms wrapped like steel bands around her. Soon, she was kissing him back, twining their tongues together, nibbling his lips until he groaned and grabbed her butt, so he could pull her against his hardness.

She caught her breath, looking up at him and feeling so much love in her heart that she was surprised it still had room to beat. "Did you ever think of doing this when we were here that last time?"

"Yes." He kissed her lips. "Other times." He kissed the tip of her nose. "Teenage angst." He returned to her lips, licking, sucking, nipping until she moaned and pressed harder against him.

"Let's make up for all those times right now."

"No." He dropped his hands and stepped back, looking her over from her head to her toes and back to her eyes.

"No?" She suddenly felt cold and alone and bereft.

"Once is not enough." He sucked in a deep breath. "A lifetime is not enough. If you can't ever love me like I love you...if this is just a lark for you, then—"

She went down on her knees in front of him and clasped both his hands, rough and rugged and hot, just like all of him. "Shane Taggart, will you marry me?"

He appeared shocked for just a moment before he dropped to his knees and put a hand on each of her shoulders and held her still in front of him. "Do you really mean it?"

"I've never meant anything more."

"Do you love me?"

"I've always loved you."

"Yes, I'll marry you." And his eyes lit up like sparklers.

She pressed a soft kiss to his lips, feeling happy and thankful and oh so content.

He answered her with a hot, hungry kiss that made her melt down to her very own hot, hungry core.

"Love me. *Now*."

And those were her last words before he slid her T-shirt up and over her head, tossing it aside. He quickly sent her bra flying, and then he was feasting on her breasts, teasing and tormenting with his lips, his teeth, his tongue, as he drove her higher and higher. She was flying—light as a feather that had burst into flames from the heat of his mouth, his hands, his body—with only the strength of him to keep her tethered to the earth. She dug her fingers into his thick hair, clasping his shoulders, drawing him closer while she felt as if she were melting from the inside out—so hot, so wet, so needy.

He raised his head, gazing at her through eyes dark with desire. "I can't wait."

She quickly unbuckled his belt, pulled it free, tossed it aside, then unbuttoned his jeans to expose the heart of him. Hard. Heavy. Handsome. She stroked his big length up and down, glorying in the feel of him. And then she kissed the tip, made a little swirl with her tongue, grabbed the condom, and slipped it on him.

"I can't wait," she said with a growl as she unzipped her jeans, pulled them down, and straddled him.

As she pushed him onto his back, he grabbed her hips, held her for a moment as they locked eyes, and then he slipped inch-by-inch deeper and deeper into her. She moaned in frustration, digging her fingers into his shoulders, until she felt him fill her utterly and completely, and then she kissed him with all her pent-up passion. He thrust hard and fast as she gyrated against him, spiraling higher and higher as they held each other, rocked each other, loved each other until they burst into a kaleidoscope of color that brought them to the height of ecstasy.

She held onto him for a long moment, catching her breath as waves of pure pleasure slowly wound down until she was left with the soft, warm connectedness that nothing could ever destroy. She lay back on the hot rock beside him, feeling the hardness, the roughness, but also the warmth from the sun shining down on them.

He sat up, gently pushed damp hair back from her face, and kissed her. "Do you realize how happy you've made me?"

She smiled, suddenly feeling lighthearted and carefree, after trudging so long uphill with the weight of the world on her shoulders. "If that made you happy, wait till you experience what we do next."

He gave her a longer, hotter, almost savage kiss. "That was good, but you know what I mean. *Marriage*."

"I know." She pushed back memories of her disastrous union with Graham. That was in the past and no longer even felt real.

"I won't wait long." He pushed back tendrils of her hair as he lovingly gazed at her face. "I mean, I've already waited a lifetime."

"But there's so much to do. Music. Water. May Day."

"I don't mean tomorrow, although that sounds good." He chuckled as he stood up, removed the condom, tied it off, and chucked it over the side of the rock. "Now I really feel like a teenager."

She smiled in contentment as she sat up, thinking every move he made was like the melody of a song just waiting to burst into life. And now she was writing country lyrics in her head, but that was how much he inspired her.

"I'll pick it up later. I'm not about to litter my own ranch." He started putting his clothes back together.

"Do we have to go back so soon?"

"It's your call." He knelt beside her, reached out, and stroked her hair. "But you reminded me how much we have to do before we can get married, so I'm raring to get going."

She pressed a kiss to the palm of his hand. "You're right. I'm just not sure where to start."

"We start here." He picked up her bra and let it dangle from his outstretched hand.

She chuckled as he helped her dress, lingering over straps, hooks, cups, until she felt like she was wearing him instead of the bra. When he got to her jeans, he wasn't the least bit of help because he acted as if he'd just discovered the hot and wet folds between her thighs that required immediately investigation from his long strong fingers. Soon, she was writhing up against him, moaning as she clutched him harder, tighter with every stroke that sent her spiraling upward and outward, until she broke free into pure ecstasy, toes curling, back arching, breath catching, and called his name over and over with wild abandon.

By the time he finally tugged the T-shirt over her head, she was panting and trembling and ready to take it all off again.

"How long did you say you wanted to wait for our wedding?" he asked with a deep chuckle.

She gave him a mock glare. "That's not fair. You make me weak and willing."

He grinned at her with a predatory gaze. "Glad to know my intentions are working just right."

"Too much right." She tried to throw off the remains of her lust-filled lethargy to think straight, but she wasn't sure if that was even possible with him looking at her with hungry eyes.

"If it helps, you're not alone." He suddenly sounded serious. "I could eat you up right now and come back for more."

She covered her eyes and turned away from him. "If you keep looking at me like that, telling me things like that, I might never leave this rock."

"We could honeymoon here. I'd go out for food and bedding."

She chuckled, glancing at him before she looked toward the Wildcat Den. "I'm ready for a honeymoon with you, but I want it to be someplace with a soft bed and warm breezes."

"Desert island?"

"Perfect." She gave a big sigh and straightened her spine, forcing them to get down to business. "But before we get to that—"

"The wedding."

"Wildcat Spring. Wildcat Den. And Graham Tanner."

Shane groaned loud and long. "Will Tanner ever be out of our lives?"

"Not unless we make him."

"What do you mean?"

"If he learns about the KWCB treasure trove through some misplaced word here or there before I have time to announce it, he'll come after me hard and the Den harder."

"True. We need to nail him before he learns about it." Shane leaned toward her. "For that matter, you'd best not leave all those boxes scattered about three buildings. Anything could happen to them—fire, water, tornado, theft. I'm worried about them all the time."

"I am, too, but I don't know what else to do."

He grasped her fingers and squeezed. "We need to make plans. We need to secure our future. We need to get rid of Tanner once and for all."

"Agreed. I've got some ideas."

"I do, too." He pointed back toward his ranch house. "Let's go back. We'll get some food, get comfortable, and—"

"Get busy."

Chapter 35

TODAY WAS THE DAY EDEN PUT HER SAVE-THE-RADIO-station plan into action. She couldn't wait any longer, since the first of May was only a few days away. Interest for their May Day Rodeo benefit had peaked, slots had filled, and seats had sold. Nobody could say promotion on KWCB didn't work, particularly because the Den was bringing in more advertising revenue than ever, since she and Jack had started the May Day spots.

To get to this point, it'd been a lot of hard work before hours, during hours, and after hours by everyone, including Morning Glory and Hedy. Somehow or other, Jack, Ken, and Nathan had managed to get a basic platform for KWCB pulled together and online in time for her announcement. She'd always be grateful to them for their enormous help. Now, it was time to win all or go bust. She intended to win in a big Texas way.

They hadn't let the cat out of the bag about the Quonset hut storage good-as-gold items, but that was about to change. Graham Tanner was going to learn a sharp lesson that folks in Wildcat Bluff County didn't roll over just because a big dog went woof. When she revealed the ace she had up her sleeve, she figured he'd turn tail and run back to LA.

For now, she had already worked with Nathan to create the narrative they wanted to share with the world. She'd recorded voice-overs, taking advantage of the

Texas angle of their story. He'd be shooting close-ups of the horses, the boots and spurs of riders, the leather fringe on Jack's jacket, and other shots unique to KWCB. They'd also positioned stacks of old reel-to-reel boxes with crates of records in the Quonset hut's entry, so they could let the enormity of their find speak for itself.

On the KWCB website and ready to be included in the video they'd be producing from today's live stream, she had picturesque shots of the Quonset hut with its open doors and treasure trove inside and old photos of her grandparents, parents, and uncle standing in front of the Den with a younger Wildcat Jack. She also included glossy black-and-white photos of big-name acts that had come through the station. And last but not least, she showcased beautiful photographs of the Rocky T Ranch through the ages.

She took a deep, satisfied breath as she stood in front of the Wildcat Den "all dolled up," as the old saying went, in the turquoise dress and boots that MG had loaned her. Nathan waited in front of her for the go-ahead, holding a camera for live streaming and wearing his usual jeans, T-shirt, and hoodie. With his black eye-glasses, he appeared smart, savvy, and sharp.

Wildcat Jack was dressed up in his suede fringe jacket, jeans, and cowboy boots and was waiting inside the station for her signal. Shane was at the barn with Ken, and both were "cowboyed up," as Ken liked to say. Serena had driven over from Sure-Shot to make certain hair and makeup for everyone was in peak condition, despite protests from the guys. Cynthia was even standing by in LA to give a report on how it looked to her.

Now that the sun was at the correct angle in the sky, sending beautiful sunbeams down on her and KWCB, it was time to put everything on the line. She nodded at Nathan. He gave her a big grin before he used his fingers to count down five to one.

And then she was broadcasting live.

"Eden Rafferty here…coming to you from the heart of Wildcat Bluff County, Texas"—she turned and gestured toward the radio station—"and KWCB, the Wildcat Den, serving North Texas and Southern Oklahoma with ranch radio since 1946."

She gave Nathan time to pan the buildings that they'd spruced up as best they could while keeping intact their historic and authentic character. She swallowed to moisten her throat, grateful for Morning Glory's tonic.

"We've been having quite a time around here since I returned to my hometown and cowgirl roots. Some of you may have kept up with our news, while some of you are joining us for the first time today." She remembered to smile as she swallowed to moisten her throat again.

"I'd like to give a shout-out to DJ Graham Tanner for bringing attention to our little corner of the world. And I'd like to thank all of you for coming to visit us here on the Rocky T Ranch…where we always have a hootin' hollerin' heck of a good time." She finished those last words while Nathan panned to a long shot of the ranch's three-slat, white fence and a dozen sleek chestnut horses grazing behind it.

"Ranch radio has a proud history in the United States, dating back to the 1920s. Nowadays, you know it primarily as a music format, but here at KWCB, we've got it all…a ranch radio station on a working ranch."

She wished she could see the comments coming in to know if she was putting everyone to sleep with an info dump or if they were actually interested in what she had to say. No way to know without input, so she plowed ahead with her memorized script.

"Gene Autry, a wonderful singing cowboy, makes me think of ranch radio. He was born in Texas and grew up just north of the Red River, roping, riding, and singing. He starred in many popular movies, but he also hosted *Melody Ranch*, a half-hour variety show based on his 1929 act that featured music and tall tales. He always told his listeners that his radio broadcasts were coming to them from his home at Melody Ranch in the San Fernando Mountains."

She swallowed again to wet her dry throat, still smiling at Nathan as she moved further into her story.

"And so today, I'd like to say I'm broadcasting to you from my home at the Rocky T Ranch in beautiful North Texas, just south of the Red River." She glanced at KWCB while Nathan panned to the radio station's front door.

Jack stood in the open doorway, then he stepped down, swaggering a bit as he walked toward her looking a lot like Willie Nelson.

"Please join me in welcoming DJ Wildcat Jack, who has been spinning tall tales as well as western swing for well over fifty years now."

Jack stopped beside her and doffed his cowboy hat to Nathan. "I'm here to tell all you cowgirls and cowboys, whether you can tame a horse, shoe a horse, or ride a horse don't make me no never mind…you're all welcome at the Wildcat Den to sit and rest a spell from your cruising and perusing the airwaves."

"Thank you, Wildcat Jack." She smiled at him, glad as always that he was such a professional that nothing bothered him—or at least, if it did, he never showed it. "I couldn't have said that better myself."

"Well, look who's here to help us welcome our guests today." Jack took off his hat with a flourish and held it out toward the lane.

She felt a jolt of surprise when she realized he was going off script, but that was pretty much a Wildcat Jack trademark. He did whatever he wanted, whenever he wanted, however he wanted. And it always came out great. She trusted him enough to go along with his new scenario, so she kept a smile in place and waited for the kicker coming as she turned to look where he'd focused his attention.

Shane and Ken she'd expected to see at some point, but not Hedy, Morning Glory, Serena, and Craig all riding horses alongside Shane and Ken. They looked great, as in totally authentic, wearing colorful cowgirl and cowboy clothes and riding superior horses with silver-studded tack. And then she noticed Ken was on a horse, too. When had he learned ride? She had to wonder how many things they'd been keeping secret to surprise her. She was thrilled for Ken and even more thrilled with their terrific visual for the camera.

"Oh, yes," she quickly ad-libbed, upping her enthusiasm to share with their viewers. "Here comes our ranch radio team to join us. I'm sure they've been out working cattle before coming to work at KWCB." She almost couldn't keep from chuckling at the unusual sight of six horse riders bearing down on them, appearing as if they were ready for a rodeo, not a day at the ranch, but it worked perfectly for the camera.

As the riders came closer, their mounts pulled at reins, swished tails, and eyed Nathan with his camera. The horses looked magnificent, drawing even more attention to the uniqueness of a working ranch radio with actual cowgirls and cowboys.

Wildcat Jack gave a big, white grin as he donned his hat with a flourish and pointed at each rider as he named them. "I'd like y'all to meet our Ranch Radio Rowdies—Kid Ken, Smilin' Shane, Cactus Craig, Hussy Hedy, Magic MG, and Sure-Shot Serena."

Eden felt her eyes widen in surprised delight as she watched each one of them lift a hat, give a big smile, and nod at the camera upon introduction. Wildcat Jack— showman that he was and always would be—had obviously thrown out her carefully scripted history of ranch radio in favor of a WWE show. And now that she saw what he'd created, she realized he was absolutely right to do it.

"And of course," Wildcat Jack added, tipping his hat to her, "we're all led by the royalty of ranch radio— Queen Eden."

She couldn't keep from chuckling and giving a quick curtsy to the camera at Jack's clever moniker. He was leaving no stone unturned in putting a colorful spin on KWCB for the world stage.

"But around here," Wildcat Jack continued as if she was well aware of all he was presenting live, "we like to call her Queenie."

She gave Jack an exaggerated wink for the camera, to let their audience know they were getting a behind-the-scenes glimpse into their Wildcat Den Wild West World of ranch radio.

Finally, Wildcat Jack motioned toward the Quonset hut storage. "We all wanted to be here today to help share the big news Queen Eden is about to impart to you. Hang on to your hats because we're talking about a time that dates all the way back to when KWCB turned on its transmitter and let its signal fly."

She nodded in agreement, recognizing that Jack was getting back to their original script.

"Queenie, are you ready to share with the world what we discovered in your family's KWCB storage unit?" Jack prompted her.

"Yes indeed, Wildcat Jack. I'm thrilled to share our surprise." She turned toward the Quonset hut. "Please follow me over there."

As if on cue, all the riders, except Hedy, leaped from their horses, ground tied them, and bunched up behind her.

She felt as if she were leading a parade as they followed her to the hut, then spread out around her with Hedy as sentinel on her horse. She had to admit Jack had come up with a colorful visual to offset the plainness of the storage building. Now she was ready to get the truth on record before Graham found out and tried to take her heritage from her again. She'd already contacted an auction house in Dallas to help establish provenance of all the items. She took a deep breath, swallowed again, and smiled at Nathan.

"My grandparents established KWCB in 1946. My parents and uncle inherited it from them. And finally, the radio station came to me. As you might know, I hosted *Sugar Talk*, a nationally syndicated radio program for many years before I moved back home."

"And we're mighty glad she's back." Jack moved so he was centered in the lens beside her.

"Wildcat Jack has been an integral part of the Wildcat Den for over fifty years. I'd be lost without him." She gave him a quick kiss on his cheek.

He gave a slightly embarrassed look at the camera. "Queenie knows just how to leave a man speechless."

She chuckled as she gazed fondly at him before refocusing on the camera. "If you know Wildcat Jack at all, you know he's never at a loss for words."

He joined her laughter, as did the group around them.

"For many years, Wildcat Jack interviewed some of the greatest and most beloved country stars of our day," Eden continued. "They answered his questions. They sang and played popular songs. And he recorded it all right over there in the KWCB studio." She grabbed a drink from a bottle of water while Nathan panned back to the radio station.

"It was my pleasure," Wildcat Jack said, sounding humble and sincere.

"And now it's our pleasure to share the Wildcat Den Vault with listeners around the world." She opened the hut's door and gestured inside, where bright light illuminated the boxes and crates that stretched into the back of the building. "This is not only *my* heritage, but it's *your* heritage, too. It's *our* heritage."

She firmly shut the door and turned back toward Nathan. "Trucks are waiting right now to be loaded with the contents of this Quonset hut. We will move all the items into a climate-controlled storage unit before we start the process of unboxing and cataloging all the items. We've already found an interview with Hank Williams that we'll be playing for you as soon as we get it digitized. We'll share with you what we discover on an ongoing basis."

"That's right," Wildcat Jack said, gesturing around the group. "Ranch Radio Rowdies will be on the job, never fear."

"And I want to assure each and every one of you," Eden added, "that I'll be staying at KWCB to bring you the high level of radio programming you've come to expect from me over the years. I'll be sharing music and interviews from the Wildcat Den Vault utilizing all media sources. And I'll be bringing it to you from right here on the Rocky T Ranch."

"Sounds to me like I'm gonna get updated and upgraded," Wildcat Jack said, grinning at Nathan. "Better stick around to watch the show."

"I'm so glad you could join us today," Eden added, ready to wrap up the segment. "Please join us live for our May Day Rodeo in Wildcat Bluff." She smiled at the camera as she signed off. "And come back to visit us real soon here at KWCB, the Wildcat Den…where we always have a hootin' hollerin' heck of a good time."

She gave Nathan the signal to stop shooting and gave a big sigh of relief that her voice had held out and all had gone well. She glanced around the group, grinning at their success. "Thanks. Y'all are really colorful and look just perfect."

Jack laughed out loud in delight. "Glad you like our antics. I thought we ought to liven up the show a bit, like the old days."

"You thought right." She started to lock the storage

hut when she heard a loud motor as a vehicle raced up the lane toward the radio station.

A small gray sedan came to a stop almost on top of the group, spraying them with dust and debris. Graham Tanner jumped out. He stalked over to Eden, hair mussed, suit smudged, shoes scuffed. He looked as if he hadn't been having an easy time in Wildcat Bluff County.

"I saw your show." Graham gave a dismissive glance at the group around her. "What are you assembling here, a rodeo team? Real cute."

She used just her fingers in a subtle signal for Nathan to start live streaming again while Graham was totally focused on her.

Shane stepped up beside her. "Didn't you hear? We're the Ranch Radio Rowdies and we like to pound heads into cow patties."

"Is he for real?" Graham leaned in close to her. "If I'd known you had all that stuff squirreled away in this trash of a building, I'd have burned it to the ground before I let you make a dime off it."

She stood up straighter and leaned right back in his face. "Wise up. You lost. And you lost big time. You got *Sugar Talk*, and you trashed it. You got my home and savings, and you blew it." She gestured behind her. "I have to wonder if you might have been a little bit nicer to me if you'd known I was sitting on a treasure worth more than all you took from me."

He appeared offended at her words. "I was plenty nice to you."

"In the beginning, yes. After you got the big head, no." She noticed from the corner of her eye the cowgirls and cowboys protectively sidling in closer to her.

Graham glanced at them, then up at Hedy on her horse. For the first time, he appeared concerned about his safety, but he still focused back on Eden. "Tell me one thing. Did you always know about your personal, little gold mine crouching here looking like nothing?"

She smiled as she reached behind her back and patted the door to the hut. "You'll never know, will you?"

"I damn well will know, and you'll tell me right now." He grabbed her wrist and jerked her toward him, snarling in fury.

Shane stepped into the fray, shoving Graham away from Eden and twisting both of his hands behind his back. "Hedy, throw me a rope. Tanner needs to learn some manners."

Graham tried to break free, but pretty quick, he had his hands tied behind his back. He glared at Eden.

"We don't cotton to strangers coming into our county thinking they can take whatever they want," Shane said. "Your next interview will be with Sheriff Calhoun."

"I'll be happy to load him in my truck and take him to the sheriff," Craig said, rubbing his hands together with gusto.

"Eden, do you want to press charges?" Shane asked, keeping a firm grip on Tanner.

She looked Graham over, wondering what she'd ever seen in him and shaking her head at all the trouble he'd caused so many people. "If the sheriff wants to escort him to the county line and if he goes quietly and never comes back to Wildcat Bluff County, I won't press charges. But I'm going to put this attempted assault into the record, so if he ever dares come back, I'll have a restraining order on him in a heartbeat."

"You heard her," Shane said, jerking the rope binding Tanner's hands. "You're getting off easy, so keep it in mind if you ever think you'd like to tangle with Eden or Wildcat Bluff again."

"Don't worry." Graham gave the group around him a look of pure disgust. "You're a bunch of Wild West throwbacks. I can't wait to leave here and go back to the real world."

"Craig, get him out of here." Shane pushed Tanner forward. "He's stinking up the place."

"My pleasure." Craig led Tanner to a nearby pickup, hoisted him into the shotgun seat, then leaped inside and quickly drove away.

"I can hardly believe Graham's harassment is over." Eden watched the truck disappear in a cloud of dust onto Wildcat Road.

"Believe it," Shane said, putting an arm around her shoulders. "Tanner is done."

"I'm so relieved and thankful to you all." Eden smiled at her loyal group of friends as she felt her phone vibrate in her pocket. She'd almost forgotten in all the excitement that Cynthia was supposed to call with a report about their live streaming. She slipped out her cell and set it on speakerphone.

"Eden!" Cynthia screamed loud enough for everyone to hear. "That was fabulous! I couldn't have scripted it better myself. KWCB has gone viral! Everybody's talking about your show. Groupies are setting up social sites for each of the Rowdies. They're speculating on personalities, likes and dislikes, clothes, homes, the works. You better get prepared for a media onslaught. How did you come up with such terrific monikers? Queenie? I love it! And the Vault! You didn't just dig out a gold mine. You're swimming in diamonds."

"Thanks, Cynthia." Eden glanced around at the shocked looks on the newly minted Rowdies. "We're just glad to be rid of Graham, so we can go forward with KWCB."

"Forget him. He was always a loser. Listen," Cynthia said, lowering her voice, "if you're ever in need of my kind of help, don't hesitate to call. Cowboys, firefighters, rowdies—Wildcat Bluff County has just become a major port of call for hungry women everywhere."

Eden laughed at the thought. "I'll keep your offer in mind, but we're really a kind of quiet, laid-back place."

"I get it. Nobody'd blame you for downplaying your hot county to keep it all to yourself, but trust me, the cat's out of the bag."

"Thanks for the heads-up."

"Anytime. Later, girlfriend."

As Eden clicked off and tucked her phone away, she glanced around at the Rowdies. As one, they burst into laughter at the absurdity of her friend's words—except for Wildcat Jack.

"Queenie," he said thoughtfully, "I think we better start work on a new show for the Ranch Radio Rowdies."

Chapter 36

"I'M SO GLAD YOU COULD JOIN US HERE TONIGHT FOR OUR May Day Rodeo in Wildcat Bluff, Texas." Eden smiled warmly at Nathan, who was live streaming from his camera while Ken trailed behind, using his cell phone to monitor viewers' comments.

"As I mentioned earlier this evening, seventy-five percent of firefighters in Texas are volunteers. That's why the success of our benefit for Wildcat Bluff Fire-Rescue is so vital to the safety of our county."

She gestured toward the arena full of spectators. "As you can see, folks really came out in support of our fire-fighters. Our rodeo may not be big like those in Fort Worth and Mesquite, but we've got just as big a heart and drive to win—particularly for our community.

"I want to take this opportunity to thank each and every one of our friends out there who couldn't be with us at the rodeo but who have donated online to help Wildcat Bluff Fire-Rescue. We appreciate your generosity. No amount is too small. Thank you so much for all your help."

She took a deep breath and swallowed to moisten her throat, while Nathan scanned and zoomed across all the activity. Like KWCB, Wildcat Bluff's rodeo arena hadn't been updated or upgraded in ages, so it was basically unpainted wooden bleachers for seating and you had to be careful not to get a splinter. She glanced up at

Wildcat Jack and Slade Steele, who looked particularly handsome in their fancy western wear. They sat in folding chairs on a raised platform, where they were making official announcements and colorful commentary over an antiquated PA system. They were obviously having a great time making jokes, telling tall tales, and reliving past rodeo wins and losses for the audience.

Ken stepped up and bumped her elbow, pointing at his phone. Hearts blossomed across the screen, indicating that folks were watching and loving KWCB's content, as well as making donations. He was keeping up with the responses, answering questions, and letting her know what viewers were asking to see at the rodeo. She could still hardly believe how quickly and how well they'd put together KWCB global communication.

She gave him a warm smile, feeling relieved they weren't falling short in this new-to-KWCB medium. She was quickly realizing that live streaming wasn't all that different from talk radio. She just needed to remember that folks were watching her in person, as well as listening to her voice. With that in mind, she'd worn her crimson pearl-snap shirt, blue western jacket, jeans, boots, and hat. At this rate, she was going to need to visit a western wear store soon, so she'd have an assortment of clothes to put on for standing in front of a camera.

When Nathan panned back to her, she smiled and glanced behind the stands. "A viewer has asked if we could go backstage, so to speak, and get a glimpse of what's going on there. Why don't we do that right now, while we're waiting for the next event to start?"

She walked easily and casually, smiling as she passed folks she knew and didn't know, and she received friendly responses from everyone. She moved into the staging area, where pickups with attached horse trailers and fancier horse trailers with living quarters were parked one after another under overhead lights. Here and there, cowgirls walked their horses to keep them warmed up, while cowboys held the reins of several mounts and talked with other riders.

"As you can see, animals—and that includes rough stock—are of supreme importance in a rodeo and receive the best of care." She chuckled, smiling warmly at the camera. "I can tell you right now that, like your cat or dog companion, these animals quickly learn how much they're loved and needed, as well as the importance of their jobs, so they are in it to win just as much as the people."

As she looked around, she saw Jones strutting her stuff in a rhinestone-crusted lapis-colored shirt, a wide leather belt laden with sparkling crystals, and a hand-painted cowgirl hat emblazoned with her name. She was definitely dressed to wow under the arena lights.

Jones saw her, waved, and walked over, leading a magnificent horse with flashy tack. She tossed the reins to Eden. "Hold him a minute, will you?" She quickly turned and disappeared into the crowd.

"Good boy." Eden held the reins with one hand as she looked into the horse's big brown eyes and the horse looked back, sizing her up as if to decide if she was friend or foe. They quickly came to a mutual understanding, and she stroked down his long nose in friendship.

She glanced back at Nathan, realizing this was the perfect opportunity to fill some time and entertain with a few fun facts. "I guess this just goes to show that nobody stands around empty-handed at a rodeo. If you're here, you're going to be part of the action, one way or another. In this case, I'm delighted to help out."

From the corner of her eye, she saw Ken hold up his phone, with hearts zinging across the screen again. Okay, they appeared to be on a roll. "If you don't already know it, I'm holding the reins of a palomino. His pure golden coat with ivory mane and tail make him perfect for showing or riding in a rodeo.

"All these horses around us are American quarter horses. You'll notice they're primarily a reddish-brown color. That's because they stem from the base colors of black, bay, brown, and chestnut or the result of modifying those colors."

She was glancing around for something else to discuss to keep her audience interested when she saw Jones headed her way with a tall cowboy wearing an emerald-colored shirt and pressed Wranglers with russet hat and boots. He also sported a big grin on his handsome face. She felt her heart accelerate at the sight of her one and only.

When they drew close, she tossed the reins back to Jones, and then she gestured toward Nathan and his camera. "If you two have a moment, would you say a few words to our KWCB friends out there?"

When they both nodded in agreement, Eden smiled at the camera. "This is Nocona Jones and Shane Taggart. They're both volunteer firefighters. Wildcat Bluff County is grateful for all their help."

She turned to Jones. "I understand you're competing tonight."

"Yes, I am. Barrel racing." Jones looked up at the

palomino, smiling, and stroked his wide jaw. "Tosahwi runs like the wind, and he likes to win. I hope not to disappoint him."

Eden glanced back at the camera. "I'm sure Nocona Jones and Tosahwi will appreciate each and every one of you rooting for them tonight."

"Thanks," Jones said. "And, Eden, thank you and thanks to KWCB for supporting our firefighter benefit with your many contributions."

"We're happy to help out." She watched as Jones walked away, then turned her attention to Shane. "I understand you're also competing tonight."

"That's right. Team roping," he said in his deep, rich voice. "Craig Thorne and I will be on horseback, heading and heeling steers."

"Is it dangerous?" She knew the answer, but she thought her viewers might like to know more about the event.

He shook his head. "What we need are good horses, strong arms, stout ropes, and exceptional speed. If it all comes together just right, we win. If it doesn't, the other guys win."

"You sound like a good sport."

"I'm here for the enjoyment of rodeo and to support our Wildcat Bluff Fire-Rescue."

"Thank you," she said, winding up the segment until she saw Ken motioning to her and pointing at his screen. While the camera was still focused on Shane, she looked at the viewer requests and quickly readjusted her interview.

"My pleasure." Shane tipped his cowboy hat.

She gave him a warm smile, knowing she had a twinkle

in her eyes as she prepared to surprise him. "Would you please give us a moment more of your time?"

He nodded in agreement, even as he stepped back as if ready to return to the rodeo.

"Visitors to KWCB recognize you as one of the Ranch Radio Rowdies from your appearance the other day when we were live streaming at the Rocky T Ranch."

"That's right. Smilin' Shane at your service."

"Uh, Smilin' Shane, our friends out there want to know when the Ranch Radio Rowdies show will be up and running." She couldn't help but notice that now he had a twinkle in his eyes, too, as if he was still enjoying how they'd surprised her with the Rowdies.

He gave the camera a big grin. "Queenie here is in control of programming, while I'm out herding cattle. As far as the Rowdies go, you'll hear from us when you hear from us. For now, I've got a little roping and riding to do."

"Thank you for your time. And good luck," she said in a straight voice, even though she was laughing inside at their new monikers.

He glanced down at her left hand where she wasn't yet wearing his engagement ring, gave a slight shake of his head, and sauntered away.

She hoped he didn't get upset that she still had a bare ring finger, because she had something special in mind about it. Still, if she waited too long—no, she wouldn't go there, particularly not with a camera trained on her. She put a smile on her face as she looked at Nathan.

"And there you have a behind-the-scenes look at our May Day Rodeo," she said. "Why don't we go back to the arena, so you don't miss out on any of the fun headed your way tonight?"

She continued to smile at the camera, knowing she needed to give her voice a rest. She was holding up, but she needed a few swigs of MG's miracle throat tonic to get through the rest of the evening.

"While I take a break to round up even more excitement for y'all, go ahead and enjoy our May Day Rodeo. And remember, any donations you care to send our way will be greatly appreciated and judiciously used by our Wildcat Bluff Fire-Rescue. And don't forget, you're always welcome to visit us at KWCB, the Wildcat Den, in Wildcat Bluff, Texas."

She adjusted the left lapel of her jacket, a signal she'd set up with Nathan, so he'd know when to turn off the directional mic yet keep recording interesting sights.

When he gave her the nod, she sighed in relief. After everything she'd been through of late, she was about ready to drop, not to mention the fact that her throat was getting scratchier the longer she broadcast. She kept going because of the importance of their firefighter benefit and because she knew that, in just a couple more hours, she could finally take the break she'd needed since she'd set foot back in Wildcat Bluff.

"We're doing great." Ken moved in close, holding up his cell so she could see the screen. "People like us. They're donating. And they want more of the Rowdies."

"Ranch Radio Rowdies." She sighed. "I guess I'll have to come up some kind of a show. Maybe on the order of Gene Autry's *Melody Ranch*."

"Count me in!"

"We can talk about it later." She read a few positive comments and saw more hearts. "For now, I can't thank you and Nathan enough for getting us here."

"As soon as I'm out of school for the summer, I've got a part-time job at Thingamajigs. Nathan says it's the best way to learn."

"It is. And congratulations."

"What I mean is—thanks for getting me here. If not for you and the Den, I'd be bored out of my skull and maybe headed back to Dallas."

"Think you're putting down roots in Wildcat Bluff?"

"I've got too much to do to go. Anyhow, I can't leave Morning Glory or you or Jack or Nathan or the Rowdies in the lurch. We've still got to build out KWCB's platform and dive into the storage boxes. I mean, if you still want my help."

She smiled at his enthusiastic expression. "I think it's about time we put you on salary at KWCB."

"You mean it?" He gave a pump in the air with his fist. "I'll make a DJ yet."

"It won't pay much, at least not yet. And school always comes first."

"Once I'm out for the summer, I belong to KWCB and Thingamajigs."

She couldn't keep from chuckling at his positive and happy attitude. He'd brightened up her life every step of the way. "I'll count on it. For now, why don't you catch up with Nathan? I think it's about time we did some live streaming of Jack and Slade sharing their tall Texas tales with the world."

"Right!" Ken pumped his fist in the air again. "Can't wait to see what folks say about those two firefighting cowboys."

She watched as he ran to catch up with Nathan, feeling like she should be going with them and pushing longer, harder, faster, but maybe it was time to step back and let others take over the limelight for a while.

As she slowly walked along behind the bleachers, she caught the mingled scents of dust, animals, food, and folks. It was the smell of rodeo. It was the smell of Wildcat Bluff. It was the smell of her new life. Sheriff Calhoun had confirmed Graham Tanner's flight out of DFW airport, so she was rid of her ex-husband. And that meant she was finally free to step forward into the future with confidence.

She glanced down at her ring finger that now felt naked without Shane's star sapphire ring.

But that was about to change.

Chapter 37

AFTER THE RODEO WAS OVER, AFTER THE LIGHTS WERE OUT, after everybody was headed home or to Wildcat Hall, Eden clasped Shane's hand, leaned into his strong body, and whispered in his ear.

She didn't have to ask twice. He simply put an arm around her shoulders and walked with her to his pickup. Once inside, she set her purse on the floorboard and leaned back against the seat. He gave her a lingering kiss before he started the engine and headed north toward the Red River.

She closed her eyes as she listened to the drone of the motor, inhaled his tantalizing scent of sage and leather, and felt the tension melt out of her body as he turned onto No-Name Road leading to Lovers Leap.

When he reached the top of the bluff, he parked under the spreading limbs of an ancient oak now clothed with the green leaves of early spring. Moonlight turned the ribbon of river below into a mysterious silver trail that led into the distance while stars twinkled overhead in the endless sky.

"I'm proud of you," Shane said in his deep, melodic voice. "You handled the entire event just like the pro you are, like you've always been."

She glanced over at his profile, so strong, so reassuring, so dear to her heart. "Thank you."

"The rodeo was a big success, wasn't it?"

"Oh yes." She exhaled on the words, feeling so happy that all had gone well. "I bet between the rodeo admissions and online donations, we made enough to keep Wildcat Bluff Fire-Rescue in operation till Christmas."

"That's the truth. And we couldn't have done it without you and KWCB."

"I was only a small part of making the rodeo a success."

"You were an essential part. And you really did well tonight."

"Thanks. I wasn't sure my voice would hold out. I'm so much better, but—"

"Never doubt the power of Morning Glory. She's healed half the county with her tonics, lotions, or kind words at one time or another."

"She's special, isn't she? Then again, all of Wildcat Bluff County is so very special."

He reached over and squeezed her hand. "Is anybody in the county particularly special to you?"

She returned his squeeze, reveling in the powerful connection that zinged between them with just a single touch. "Let's see. Could it be a big, strong, handsome cowboy firefighter?"

He slanted a teasing glance her way. "There are plenty of guys in this county who fit that description. I'm starting to get jealous."

"No need." She raised his hand and placed a soft kiss on each fingertip. "There's only one cowboy firefighter in the county who holds my heart in the palm of his hand."

"You'd better be more specific before I—"

"Give me what I'm waiting for?"

"I'm happy to give you anything your heart desires, but first I want to hear the name of that cowboy fire-fighter on your lips."

She smiled, enjoying their banter. "You've heard his name on my lips plenty of times—at very particular times."

He chuckled as he leaned toward her, hemming her in with his broad shoulders. "And what's his name?"

"His name?" She teased him as she pulled her hand away and put a fingertip to her chin, as if trying to remember.

"That's it!" He opened his door, leaped out, and started around the front of his truck.

Now she had him exactly where she wanted him. Outside. She quickly reached into her purse, pulled out the beautiful star sapphire ring, and slipped it—almost reverently—onto the fourth finger of her left hand. It felt just right. She opened the door and stepped out as he reached up for her. She slid into his arms, all done with teasing banter now.

"Do you remember that night?" She tugged him out from under the oak's thick foliage and toward the river's edge.

"How could I forget?" He put an arm around her shoulders and snuggled her close. "You were all dolled up, looking like a princess and smelling like heaven."

"You took me to heaven." She glanced up at the sky, where stars sparkled like jewels across the dark canopy. "Remember how we saw the shooting star?"

"I'll always remember."

"I knew in that moment we were meant to be together at least once before I left town."

"I knew it, too, but I never wanted to let you go."

She raised her hand, revealing that she finally wore his ring, and traced a line across the heavens with the star sapphire shining in the moonlight. "Now you need never let me go."

"Never." He clasped her hand and placed her palm over his heart as he rubbed his thumb back and forth across her engagement ring. "Our shooting star is another reason I chose the star sapphire. It's a symbol of our magical midnight."

She turned to look up at his face. "Shane Taggart, I love you and I desperately want to marry you."

"I've loved you forever and I'll love you till the end of time."

She felt tears fill her eyes as happiness cascaded through every little bit of her.

"Let's get married soon," he said. "I can't wait for you to permanently move into the Rocky T ranch house."

"I feel as if I never left."

"You didn't—not all of you."

"Do you think we could elope?"

"I wish, but we'd never hear the end of it." He looked out across the river, then back at her. "I suppose we'd better throw a big wedding party on the ranch. I wouldn't be surprised if Wildcat Jack turned up live streaming for KWCB."

She smiled at the thought, knowing it was absolutely true. "If all of Wildcat Bluff County is going to be at our wedding, then why not invite the whole world?"

"I guess this is what comes from marrying a star—a shooting star. But no cameras get past our front door."

"You don't want to share your ranch house?"

"*Our* home." He lifted her hand, so the star sapphire sparkled against the black velvet of the night. "Once we lock the door and go into our bedroom, the world can party on its lonesome."

"While the two of us party together forever." And she pressed a hot kiss to his lips…just at midnight.

Read on for a look at the next
Smokin' Hot Cowboys novel,

COWBOY
FIREFIGHTER
Christmas Feast

Available October 2019

from Sourcebooks Casablanca

Chapter 1

"THERE'S NEVER A DULL MOMENT IN LIFE, NOT WITH SISTER Fern stirring it up," Ivy Bryant said to the silent walls of one of the oldest dance halls in Texas. She did a little twirl on the scuffed, slat-wood floor as if she had a dance partner. Wildcat Hall might not be as famous as Gruene Hall in the Hill Country, but her honky-tonk had a sterling reputation in Wildcat Bluff County.

"And Fern promised she'd stay put this time." Ivy thrust out her arms to both sides and twirled harder in the center of the large room that had rows of long, narrow, hand-made wooden tables with matching benches placed on each side of the dance floor. "Famous last words of a rolling stone. Did I really believe her, or did I just want to believe her?"

She stopped, let her arms fall to her sides, and looked with a kind of wonder toward a recessed, raised stage and hand-painted backdrop. "In Houston, I'd be designing websites by day and enjoying my friends at night. Here I'm still designing websites by day but running a honky-tonk at night."

She chuckled, still feeling surprised at the turn her life had taken. She was here to manage the place, but she hardly believed it, because what did she know about running a dance hall? It was now all hers—or at least the half her sister didn't own, but Fern was gone on a gig for who knew how long, dropping the Wildcat Hall ball into Ivy's hands.

She put her fists on her hips as she glanced from the stage to the other end of the dance floor at the long bar that served munchies, beer, and wine. Two open windows allowed bartenders to service customers on the dance hall side and on the front bar side at the same time. It seemed to her that it was a practical setup, although she was certainly no expert.

She walked into the front bar through an open doorway. For her, this room was the heart and soul of Wildcat Hall, and she relished the cozy, old-fashioned ambience that had nurtured folks for well over a hundred years.

Decor was minimal. Rusty metal beer advertisement signs had been tacked around the walls along with sepia-toned photographs of cowboys on horseback and country music legends. A framed Lone Star State flag hung in back of the bar, and a rack of deer antlers loomed above the double front doors.

Ivy glanced at the tattered cardboard box of Christmas decorations that she'd found in a storeroom. Businesses were already putting up holiday decor, and she didn't want the Hall to be left behind. She pulled out a long string of red tinsel, walked over to the antlers, and tossed the strand upward. It fell back. She needed a ladder, but she hadn't found one yet. She picked up the tinsel and tossed again. No luck.

As she gazed at the antlers with a skeptical eye, she heard a truck pull up outside. By now, folks should've heard the honky-tonk was closed for a week while she figured out how to manage it. Even if the front door was unlocked, since she'd been running in and out, there was a big sign with bright red letters on the door that read *CLOSED*. No need for folks even to get out of their pickups.

She looped the tinsel around her neck, picked up a straight-back chair from under a table, and set the chair under the antlers. Now she was getting somewhere. She stood on the seat, adjusting her stance to keep her balance while the chair wobbled on uneven legs. She lifted the strand as high as she could manage, but she still couldn't drape it around the antlers. The Hall's high ceilings made for good airflow, along with an impressive historical statement.

Not as big a statement as fancy honky-tonks like Billy Bob's Texas in the Fort Worth stockyards, with 127,000 square feet of boot-scooting space, or the famous Longhorn Ballroom in Dallas, with 20,000 square feet. But Wildcat Hall was plenty spacious, with 4,000 square feet inside and room for more in a large beer garden with picnic tables outside. She just wished the Hall had the tourist draw of those two famous places, but a major destination attraction and music venue could be built with the right promotion and entertainment. Still, she was getting ahead of herself. For the moment, she just needed to put up a few decorations to add Christmas cheer to the place.

As she stood on her tiptoes with arms raised again, she heard the side door that led to the beer garden open and boots hit the floor with determined stride.

"We're closed!" she hollered, not bothering to look over her shoulder. "Come back next week."

"You look like you could use a little help."

She froze with her hands in the air as she felt the

deep male voice, with that melodic slow cadence of a born and bred Texan, strike her body and go deep, as if she'd been pierced by a flaming arrow. Talk about red hot. She tried to shrug off the heat, but the chair shifted under her, making her sway.

"Easy does it," he said. "Chairs have a way of pretending they're bulls sometimes."

"Bulls?" She didn't know whether to laugh at a joke or appreciate he'd tried to make her feel better about almost toppling to the floor. Still and all, if she'd known she was going to have company, she'd have put on something besides formfitting yoga pants and top in hot pink with black trim. He was getting an eyeful.

"In my case, I always tried to pretend bulls were chairs."

"How'd that work out?" She eyed the antlers, mind half on her next throw and half on the amusing man behind her.

"About like you can imagine." He sighed, as if life had been unfair. "I finally had to give up bulls for chairs."

"I bet the bulls were grateful." She definitely wanted to see the face that went with the voice, but she wanted more to finish her task.

"Yeah…but I've broken a few chairs."

"Maybe even my chair."

"Looks like it's keeping an uneasy peace with the floor."

"That's one way of putting it." She rose to her tiptoes again, trying one last time to get the tinsel to disobey the laws of gravity.

"Let me help." He spanned her waist with large hands and lifted her so she could easily reach the antlers.

She caught her breath in surprise at his strength—and his boldness. But she wasn't looking a gift horse in the mouth. She quickly twined the antlers with red tinsel until they looked festive for the holidays.

"Pretty," he said.

She felt his breath caress the bare skin on the back of her neck because she wore her auburn hair in a ponytail. She shivered in response. What had gotten into her? She should be struggling to get away. Instead he was revving her up with his hot breath and hotter hands.

"Got any more tinsel to put up?" he asked in a deep voice gone husky. "I could hold you all day and into next week."

"I suggest you put me down before you get into trouble."

"If you're the one handing out trouble, I'd wait in line to get it."

She couldn't help but chuckle, because he was laying it on thick in that teasing way Texas men would do to get them out of problems with women. "Better put me down before your arms give out."

"Not a chance. You're light as a feather."

She laughed harder. "Guess some women would fall for that one. What are you selling?"

"As a matter of fact, I'm here to help you, but you might consider it selling to you, too." He gently set her down so her feet were steady on the floor, and then he stepped back.

She turned to face him—and felt her breath catch in her throat at the tall hunk of a cowboy.

He wore pressed Wranglers that accentuated his long legs and narrow hips, with a wide leather belt sporting a huge rodeo belt buckle. His blue-and-white-stripe, pearl-snap shirt, tucked neatly into the waistband of his jeans, emphasized the width of his shoulders and breadth of his chest. Blond-haired. Blue-eyed. Square-jawed. Full-lipped. He looked as if he'd been made to dazzle—and she was suddenly and breathtakingly susceptible to every single one of his charms.

"Whatever you're selling, I think I'm buying." She spoke the words with a teasing lilt in her voice and a mischievous smile on her face. Still, she meant it. And he probably knew it, because he was definitely heart-breaker material. How many women had already fallen to his charms and been left in the dust? She didn't intend to be a notch on his belt, but if she'd known leaving the city for the country paid off so well in eye candy, she might've followed her sister sooner.

He chuckled at her words and held out his hand with the thick muscular wrist that came from control-ling thousand-pound-plus beasts. "Slade Steele. If you haven't heard of me, maybe you're aware of the Chuckwagon Café and Steele Trap Ranch. Family busi-nesses. I'm not just any guy off the street."

"You're definitely not just any guy." She slipped her hand into his big one and felt him gently enclose her fingers.

"And you're definitely good for my ego," he said with a smile as he let his gaze drop all the way down the length of her and back up to her face. "I thought your sister was lovely and bright and talented, but you leave her in the shade."

"Smart guy to throw a few compliments my way. Guess you're more than a pretty face." She tried to keep the teasing going so their interaction stayed on a light note, but he was still holding her hand and she wasn't pulling away, and his eyes were heating up to a blazing, blue fire.

"Nothing but the truth."

"Fern is the star." She tried to tug her hand away, but he held on another long moment, nodding as if deciding something or conveying something or accepting something before finally letting go.

He grinned with a gleam in his eyes, revealing teeth white against the tan of his skin. "Yeah, she is that...but you make the earth move."

"Oh my." She returned his grin while fanning her face with one hand in that old Southern way as if he was too hot to handle. "You really do want to sell me something, don't you?"

"How am I doing?"

"Not bad." She pivoted and walked away from him, intentionally putting the heat they were generating behind her. She wasn't in Wildcat Bluff for a guy. She was here to salvage her financial investment. She had to keep that fact firmly in mind because she was city, not country, and she was here only so long as it took to take care of business. A good-looking, fast-talking cowboy wasn't anywhere on her agenda, particularly one who might slow down her getaway.

"How is Fern?"

"My sister is always okay." She leaned her elbows on top of the bar and resisted a long sigh because she'd been here before one too many times. She heard Slade approach, noticing the unevenness of his step for the first time as if he limped from an injury. She wondered how he'd been hurt, thinking how he'd mentioned bulls, but knew it'd be rude to ask. She glanced over at him, deciding to get the explaining over as quickly as possible.

"She left without a word," he said quietly but intently—almost accusingly.

"That's Fern." She turned around and leaned back against the edge of the bar and propped a heel on the long runner. "I suppose she left broken hearts and broken dreams behind her."

"Something like that."

"If it helps, it's not personal. She's a singer, so she's a rolling stone." Ivy took a closer look at him, feeling a sudden tightness in her chest. "I hope you aren't one of the—"

"Not me. But there is a guy. Craig Thorne. Singing cowboy. They performed together on the Hall's stage. He thought they had something special."

"Guys always do, bless their hearts." She glanced over as Slade leaned his elbows on the bar. "She must've liked this Craig more than a little if she picked up and ran that hard that fast."

"I doubt he'd agree, but she did leave things in a muddle."

"That's where I come in." Ivy turned toward him. "My parents named us well. I'm the ivy that holds everything together while she's the fern that spreads up and out."

He nodded, glanced around at the room, then back. "So, what do you plan to do here?"

"I'm considering my options."

"Folks are wondering about Fern…about the sister who showed up to take her place…and about Wildcat Hall."

"Fern ought to be back at some point."

"Will she?"

"That's the plan, but you never know about the timing. Right now she's entertaining on a cruise ship."

"We all thought she was dedicated to preserving and expanding Wildcat Hall."

"Y'all aren't the only ones. It's always been her dream to own a venue where she could nurture country musicians."

"Heard that. Plus, Bill and Ida Murphy hooked up with her on a genealogy website and discovered they were long lost cousins. The Hall always belonged to somebody in their family. Otherwise, they'd never have sold to an outsider. Lots of folks in our county would've stepped up for Wildcat Hall to preserve it because it's been the center of community life here from the get-go."

"Guess y'all were surprised when strangers took over. I'm half-owner since I helped finance her dream, but I'd intended to be a silent partner. Now—"

"I got it. But if you're anything like your sister—"

"Not so much."

He nodded again, considering her with watchful blue eyes.

"I'd appreciate it if you'd let folks know I'm here to take care of Wildcat Hall."

"Will do." He cleared his throat. "I came over because…well, it'd be good to generate more interest in the Hall."

"I agree." She smiled, cocking her head to let him know she was listening even as she decided he took up way too much physical space and created way too much heat for her to be easy in his presence. She didn't need a too-hot cowboy disturbing her already disturbed thoughts. She needed to think straight so she could get a handle on what she was going to do with the honky-tonk.

"Good." He rapped the top of the bar with his knuckles, glanced around, and refocused on her. "Place is still good but stale. Christmas is coming up. It'll take more than a few prayers to put Wildcat Hall on the map again."

"Maybe a sound marketing strategy?"

"That too." He smiled with a teasing glint in his blue eyes. "If you'll let me, I'll be glad to help out. I have a few ideas."

She returned his smile, feeling his magnetism tug at her, stoking fires she'd thought long gone. She could see how he'd be the perfect answer to a lonely lady's prayers, but she needed something else from him. "Do tell."

Acknowledgments

Once more I'd like to thank all the folks who generously shared their time, expertise, and encouragement.

George Gimarc, music and comedy radio programing guru, as well as founder of the Texas Musician's Museum, contributed wonderful advice and knowledge about the intricacies of radio.

Darmond Gee deserves great credit for describing his own personal firefighter experience in the dozer scene as well as taking me on a research trip to Medicine Springs, the real-life basis for my Wildcat Spring.

C. Dean Andersson, horror and fantasy writer, gave great pacing feedback throughout this book.

Elisabeth Fairchild is a beloved historical fiction author who brought important details to my attention with her fine editorial eye.

John Wooley kept me toe-tapping with Swing on This (Public Radio Tulsa 89.5), where he has been celebrating western swing and cowboy jazz for more than fifteen years. He is the prolific author and editor of over forty books, and he was the first writer to be inducted into the Oklahoma Music Hall of Fame.

Ramona Reed Blair continues to inspire me with her wonderful singing and yodeling. She debuted on radio at KTMC, McAlester, Oklahoma, in 1949 when she was fifteen. She went on to star in the Grand Ole

Opry, where she stood out in a line of all male per-
formers. She was inducted into the Oklahoma Music
Hall of Fame for her many contributions to western
swing.

About the Author

Kim Redford is the bestselling author of western romance novels. She grew up in Texas with cowboys, cowgirls, horses, cattle, and rodeos. She divides her time between homes in Texas and Oklahoma, where she's a rescue cat wrangler and horseback rider—when she takes a break from her keyboard. Visit her at kimredford.com.

Also by Kim Redford